WASHOE COUNTY LIBRARY

3 1235 0   P9-DTC-197

"Yona Zeldis McDonough is at her best with *Two of a Kind*, a sumptuous romantic feast of missed opportunities on the road to true love. Whether you take this to the beach or curl up with it on a rainy day, this hilarious and heartwarming story will give you hours of reading pleasure."

—Adriana Trigiani, *New York Times* bestselling author of
The Shoemaker's Wife

"A beautiful and heartfelt novel, *Two of a Kind* tells of the unexpected love that blossoms between a most unlikely duo. With an exquisite eye for detail, McDonough pulls you into her characters' world and keeps you rooting for them until the final page. If you've ever longed for a second—or third—chance, this book's for you." —Camille Noe Pagán, author of *The Art of Forgetting*

"Tightly and beautifully plotted, with such winning characters. A compelling and moving novel."

—Gregory Murphy, author of *Incognito*

"A deeply touching and romantic exploration of the joys and complications of falling in love the second time around. Christina and Andy's journey to navigate the waters of new love and blended families always rings true; you'll root for McDonough's winning characters from the very start."

—Erika Marks, author of *The Guest House*

continued . . .

Written by today's freshest new talents and selected by New American Library, NAL Accent novels touch on subjects close to a woman's heart, from friendship to family to finding our place in the world. The Conversation Guides included in each book are intended to enrich the individual reading experience, as well as encourage us to explore these topics together—because books, and life, are meant for sharing.

Visit us online at www.penguin.com.

"With grace, sensitivity, and humor, but pulling no punches, *Two of a Kind* explores the trickiest of relationships—both romantic and parental—immersing readers in the lives of four people over the course of a year. In deft and captivating prose, these characters quickly become as real as your neighbors, your friends, your family, as they finally face losses they've tried to forget, learn to live in the present, and ultimately face their futures together with the greatest healer of all: love."

—Sharon Short, author of *My One Square Inch of Alaska*

"McDonough takes readers on an intriguing ride throughout the New York area—Manhattan, Brooklyn, and Long Island—as she deftly brews a novel like a perfect cappuccino, with the ideal balance of substance and lip-smacking froth."

—Sally Koslow, author of *The Widow Waltz*

Praise for
A Wedding in Great Neck

"A touching, airy novel that manages to meld the concerns of family members spanning four generations into a delightfully well-written story. Readers who enjoy Mary Kay Andrews and Nora Roberts will relate to the Silverstein family as it embraces the deep wells of emotion that seem to surface only at major family events. With an authorial voice that switches deftly between impulsive teen-speak and a stately matriarch's flashbacks, McDonough's skill is to be commended. A tender, clever story with emotional heft."

—*Booklist*

"In prose as sparkling as a champagne toast, McDonough's delicious new novel gathers together one extraordinary wedding, two complicated families, and then shows how a single day can change everything. A funny, moving look at the bonds of love, the ties of family, and the yearning for happily ever after."

—Caroline Leavitt, *New York Times* bestselling
author of *Pictures of You*

"In this delightful tale, Yona Zeldis McDonough limns the ups and downs of family life with a grace that brings to mind Cathleen Schine at her best. McDonough does not shirk the dark side, but her characters, as flawed as they may be, retain their humanity in the face of life's slings and arrows. A wise and witty novel from an author at the top of her form."

—Megan McAndrew, author of *Dreaming in French*

"Spirited, entertaining, and a delight to read, *A Wedding in Great Neck* offers a penetrating glimpse into the lives of one particular family, with its myriad shifting alliances, disappointments, and secrets."
                                —Lucy Jackson, author of *Posh*

"Emotional and evocative, hilarious and harrowing, *A Wedding in Great Neck* is a must read for every mother and daughter who've ever dreamed of, fought over, and loved each other through a wedding day."
                —Pamela Redmond Satran, *New York Times* bestselling
                                author of *The Possibility of You*

"Deftly handling a well-drawn ensemble cast of characters, *A Wedding in Great Neck* is a playful yet touching parsing of the tugs and tangles of familial bonds. This breezy novel offers the reader graceful writing while exploring contemporary suburban turf with an anthropologist's sharp eye."
                —Sally Koslow, author of *Slouching Toward Adulthood:
                Observations from the Not-So-Empty Nest*

"Yona Zeldis McDonough is a born storyteller and her powers of perception are at full tilt in *A Wedding in Great Neck*. Beautifully structured around the secret longings and high emotions visited upon that special day, the book explores the fraught love between siblings, the rich wisdom of their elders, and shifting class values in one family. McDonough's *Wedding* is a page-turner—you'll feel as if you were there."   —Laura Jacobs, author of *Women About Town*

"With her trademark wit and keen eye, Yona Zeldis McDonough has created a confection that is not only a page-turner but a poignant view of family life. This elegant novel is a must read for long-married wives and any woman who longs to be married. Book clubs will swoon."   —Adriana Trigiani

"An interesting take on the wedding novel that doesn't place the bride and groom at the center. Fans of women's fiction about weddings and family drama are sure to enjoy."   —*Library Journal*

ALSO BY YONA ZELDIS McDONOUGH

A Wedding in Great Neck

TWO
of a
KIND

Yona Zeldis McDonough

NAL Accent
Published by the Penguin Group
Penguin Group (USA), 375 Hudson Street,
New York, New York 10014, USA

USA | Canada | UK | Ireland | Australia | New Zealand | India | South Africa | China

Penguin Books Ltd., Registered Offices: 80 Strand, London WC2R 0RL, England
For more information about the Penguin Group visit penguin.com.

First published by NAL Accent, an imprint of New American Library,
a division of Penguin Group (USA)

First Printing, September 2013

Copyright © Yona Zeldis McDonough, 2013
Conversation Guide copyright © Penguin Group (USA), 2013
Cover photos: chairs by Todd Pearson/Digital Vision/
Getty Images; woman © Olena Zaskochenko/Shutterstock Images;
man © Vladimir Gjorgiev/Shutterstock Images.

All rights reserved. No part of this book may be reproduced, scanned, or
distributed in any printed or electronic form without permission. Please do not
participate in or encourage piracy of copyrighted materials in violation of the
author's rights. Purchase only authorized editions.

ACCENT NAL REGISTERED TRADEMARK—MARCA REGISTRADA

LIBRARY OF CONGRESS CATALOGING-IN-PUBLICATION DATA:

McDonough, Yona Zeldis.
  Two of a kind/Yona Zeldis McDonough.
    pages cm
  ISBN 978-0-451-23953-2
  1. Widows—Fiction.   2. Interior decorators—Fiction.   I. Title.
  PS3613.C39T96   2013
  813'.6—dc23   2013015546

Printed in the United States of America
10 9 8 7 6 5 4 3 2 1

Set in Palatino
Designed by Spring Hoteling

PUBLISHER'S NOTE
This is a work of fiction. Names, characters, places, and incidents either are the
product of the author's imagination or are used fictitiously, and any resemblance
to actual persons, living or dead, business establishments, events, or locales is
entirely coincidental.
    The publisher does not have any control over and does not assume any
responsibility for author or third-party Web sites or their content.

for Paul, one of a kind

ACKNOWLEDGMENTS

With thanks and gratitude to Linda Bernstein, Deborah Flomen-haft, and Cathy Tharin for background information on the School of American Ballet, to Sally Schloss and Jennie Fields for showing me where to begin, to Tracy Bernstein for keeping me on track, and to Judith Ehrlich, my guiding light the whole way through.

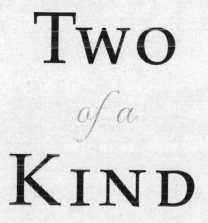

Two *of a* Kind

ONE

Christina Connelly sat in the tent, waiting for the wedding ceremony to begin. Her fourteen-year-old daughter sat beside her; Jordan had never attended such a lavish event and was fairly popping with excitement. Her sleeveless dress with its scoop-necked bodice revealed her slender arms and accentuated her long neck; in it, she looked every bit the budding ballerina that she was.

Looking down at her own silk tweed sheath—an interweaving of tiny black and white flecks—and the single silver bangle on her wrist, Christina felt the familiar pinch of insecurity; this Great Neck crowd was a moneyed one, and around her sat thousands of dollars' worth of clothes, shoes, and jewelry. Her work as an interior designer often put her in contact with people like this, and most of the time she was able to tamp down the old feeling of being insufficient, a beggar at the banquet, but sometimes it pushed through to the surface. Still, her own dress was Italian and couture, scored secondhand at one of her favorite charity haunts in the city—she was a brilliant secondhand shopper—and the Elsa Peretti bangle had come from Tiffany, a gift from her late husband, Will. She knew she didn't look opulent, but she liked to think she was elegant in an understated sort of way. She sat up straighter, determined to focus on the service that was about to start.

The rest of the wedding party had already gathered—bridesmaids, immediate family members—and the dark, ruggedly handsome groom stood under the white, flower-covered canopy. *Chuppah,* Christina corrected herself. She had been to enough Jewish weddings to know the term. Then a slight current seemed to circulate among the guests, an energy like the moment the curtain went up at the theater, and yes, here was the bride, Angelica Silverstein, floating down the aisle on her father's arm, her head, neck, and shoulders swathed in a froth of white netting.

"That dress!" breathed Jordan.

That dress, or at least what was visible of it, was a sumptuous gleam of heavy white satin; to Christina's trained eye, it looked like upholstery fabric. When the pair reached the chuppah, Angelica's father—who was not, she knew, the owner of this god-awful house and its surrounding property—gently moved the veil back to reveal the bride. A collective gasp rose; Christina's small intake of breath was part of it. She had known, of course, that her client was a beauty; the months spent in her company, working on the redecoration of Angelica's Riverside Drive apartment, had made that abundantly clear. But the radiant young woman who stood before the assembled guests still surprised her.

Christina blinked back the tears that gathered—sudden, stinging—in her eyes. It wasn't just that Angelica was beautiful. It was also that she was so clearly, incandescently in love—

with the groom, of course, but with everyone else too: her parents and grandmother, whom she looked upon with such sweetness, her nieces, siblings, bridesmaids, friends, the musicians, the guests—everyone seemed to be bathed in the transformative power of that emotion.

Christina had once been in love like that. She and Will had not had a posh affair like this—it had been just the two of them down at City Hall on Centre Street. She was a Catholic girl from Brooklyn and Will a Protestant from North Carolina. Instead of arguing over the ceremony—her father and the aunt who raised her would have campaigned, vigorously, for a wedding at St. Augustine's on Sixth Avenue, where the family had gone for decades—Christina and Will had impulsively decided to just take care of it themselves. He'd worn a slightly rumpled summer suit and straw hat he'd bought on Chambers Street that morning; she wore a thrift shop dress—even then she was doing the secondhand thing—of white eyelet. But when they were pronounced man and wife, she had been every bit as rapturous as the woman now under the chuppah. Christina sniffed, and dabbed at her eyes with the white linen square that she kept tucked in her bag.

"Mom, are you all right?" Jordan asked.

"I'm fine," said Christina, and when it looked like Jordan did not believe her, she added, "Really I am." She gave Jordan's shoulder a little squeeze before turning her attention back to the ceremony, which had just started.

First the rabbi spoke and then the bridal couple began reading passages from the Song of Songs, first in English and then in Hebrew. As Christina listened, she discreetly looked around. No expense had been spared at this wedding, from the elaborate tents to the lush garlands of white flowers with

which they had been decorated. The wine served at the cocktail hour had been exquisite, the hors d'oeuvres sumptuous. And there was still a three-course dinner to follow. What
a luxury it would be to have so much money to burn; Christina's own habit of thrift had been ingrained for so long that
she could not even imagine how that would feel.

Her attention settled on Angelica again. Just as the groom
was about to place the ring on her finger, Christina heard the
small but insistent noise of someone's phone. An irritating little buzz, like a wasp or a bee, but still, it was a *wedding*—how
rude! Her own phone had been switched off the minute she
arrived. Christina turned, ready to impale the boor with a furious look. But the perpetrator—a man in his forties wearing
an expensive, putty-colored suit—had already risen from his
seat. As he hurried away, she distinctly heard him say, "*How
many centimeters?*" The guests nearby looked annoyed too,
though the man seemed oblivious; the phone remained glued
to his ear. Christina stared at his receding form, wanting him
to feel her wrath, even from a distance.

Fortunately, no one up at the chuppah seemed to have noticed and the exchange of rings, the kiss, the napkin-muffled
crunch of glass—Christina was told it was a lightbulb, not
a goblet—went smoothly. When the service was over, she
steered Jordan toward the receiving line. Jordan had been as
taken by the entire spectacle as her mother was. "When I get
married, I'm going to have a reception *exactly* like this," she
said, gesturing at the plush green expanse of lawn and, beyond that, the magnificent rose garden where the cocktail
reception had been held.

Christina knew that day was still far off in the future.
Right now, almost all of Jordan's attention was focused on the

classes she took at the School of American Ballet on West Sixty-fifth Street. Boys, other than as possible dance partners, were not on her radar.

When they reached the bride and groom, hugs and kisses were exchanged. Angelica exclaimed over Jordan—*How she's grown! What gorgeous posture!*—and the two women made noises about getting together. Although Angelica's apartment was technically finished, their relationship had shifted from one that was purely professional to one bordering on friendship.

After the receiving line, it was time for dinner. Jordan went off to sit at the teens' table, along with Angelica's twin nieces and several of the groom's relatives. Christina stood watching; she did have such perfect posture, and such a perfect dancer's body too. Only maybe that body was just a *little* too thin these days; from the back, she seemed positively gaunt. Christina considered this as she made her way to her assigned table. Urging Jordan to eat never worked; the more she pressed, the greater her daughter's resistance. And Christina understood the pressures Jordan faced. The world of classical ballet was ferociously competitive, and maintaining a lean, attenuated line was essential to success. Jordan didn't have an eating disorder; she was just responding to the harsh demands of her chosen field.

As other people were finding their seats, exchanging greetings, hugs, and kisses, Christina reached her table, where she admired the etched glass water pitchers and crystal goblets that sparkled against the heavy white tablecloths. Each bone china place setting was adorned with a place card of heavy white vellum that was encircled by a few smooth white stones. She picked one up and held it in her hand: a nice touch.

Although her business dealt strictly in interiors and the antiques with which she often filled them, she could still appreciate and admire the work of another talented professional. The flowers in the centerpiece—a cluster of white roses, freesia, lilies, and gardenias—spilled up and over the sides of the glass vase, giving it a natural, unstudied elegance.

"Too much white; it's like being lost in a snowdrift."

"Excuse me?" Christina turned.

"The decorations. They could have used a little color *somewhere* in here." The man who delivered this uninspired assessment was the same man whose phone had buzzed during the service. What bad luck to be stuck at his table.

"Actually, I find the decorations in exquisite taste," Christina said coldly. No manners and no taste either. She turned to the woman seated next to her in the hope of discouraging any further conversation.

"I'm Andy Stern," he said, extending his hand.

He had not read what she thought were her very clear signals. "Christina Connelly." She took his hand reluctantly and let her eyes shift again to the woman sitting on her other side. The woman reached for her glass and Christina pounced. "What a beautiful ring!" she exclaimed. "Is that a fire opal?"

"Yes," said the woman, clearly flattered.

"The color is exceptional." Christina and the ring's owner launched into a discussion about opals in general and fire opals in particular. Andy Stern, thankfully, was forced to turn his attention elsewhere. Throughout the elaborate meal that followed, Christina tried to ignore him. But Andy Stern was not easily ignored.

"How's your fish?" he asked.

"Excellent," she said.

"Really? I think mine's been cooked a little too long, but the wine they paired it with—exceptional."

Christina did not look up. Unfortunately, Ms. Fire Opal was talking to someone else, so there was no possibility of a rescue from her. Andy Stern kept on as if he believed he were the most fascinating man on earth. Finally, after the lime mousse, petits fours, and sugar cookies had been served, Christina excused herself, saying she wanted to find her daughter.

"Is she at the teen table?" Andy asked, and when Christina admitted that, yes, she was, he added, "That's where my son is sitting too; I'll walk over there with you." Christina was sorry she had told him; now her escape plan was thwarted. And they could not get through; several silver-tray-carrying waiters had blocked their way. So Christina was forced to endure still more of Andy's self-absorbed patter. He was an ob-gyn with a high-risk Park Avenue practice; it had been one of his high-risk patients who buzzed him during the service, so maybe it was a forgivable offense; he lived in the Trump Palace on East Sixty-ninth Street, the tallest, and ugliest, building in the neighborhood, and rented a place in the Hamptons—where else?

"It's a great house: four bedrooms, five baths, and a stunning pool." He contemplated the wineglass he held. "My wife would have flipped for that house." There was something wistful in that last statement. "There's a view of the water from the second floor that seems to go on forever. She always loved to be near the water." His tone had changed: no longer boastful, but muted, even sad. She was tempted to ask about his wife—there was no ring on his left hand—but that was not the sort of thing you asked someone you had just met and didn't like besides. "She died," he added bluntly. "Ovarian cancer, which was kind of ironic given my profession. It'll be two years in July."

"Oh," said Christina. She too had lost a spouse, more than a decade ago, and remembered the savage, grief-crazed year following Will's death. "I'm so sorry." The sky had darkened and against the jewellike blue, the white tablecloth and napkins seemed to glow. "That must have been hard."

"Was and is," he said. His close-set eyes, she noted, were an intriguing color, light brown, the pupils ringed with gold. He had the eager, attentive look of an Irish setter or a Lab, she decided. Not so bad after all, but definitely in need of being kept on a leash.

"My husband died too," she said. "So I know."

"How?" he asked.

"In a fire."

"Horrible," said Andy.

"Yes," she said quietly. "It was." She was not going to tell him how Will, a lawyer turned high school history teacher, had been on an overnight class trip when the small inn where they were staying caught fire. He had sacrificed himself to save a girl who had been overlooked in the frenzy. A thousand people had been at the funeral held in his hometown; everyone from his kindergarten teacher to the girls and boys—now women and men—from his high school swim team had come to say good-bye. As she stood there with Andy Stern, it came flooding back, but then just as quickly receded. It would always hurt, but the worst was over. "It gets better," she said. "You can't believe it now, but it does. Children help. You just have the one?"

"Just the one," he said, and his mouth turned up in a smile. "Come on; you can meet him."

The waiters had dispersed and Christina was able to follow him to the teen table, where Andy introduced his son, a blond, curly-haired boy of about sixteen who had been talking to Jordan. Oliver offered a perfunctory hello before turning his attention back to Jordan, who sat with her hands in her lap, dessert untouched in front of her. Christina was not surprised; Jordan would no more have eaten a petit four than she would one of her pink satin point shoes.

"How are you doing over here?" she asked.

"Oh fine, Mom. Just great." Jordan seemed to eye the petit four with longing.

"They'll be cutting the cake in a little while. Do you want to see?" The cutting of the cake was another of those iconic wedding moments and she thought Jordan would enjoy it. Jordan, however, was not interested. She seemed to want her mother to leave, which Christina found interesting. Did she like this boy who sat pulling on his springy blond curls? Or was she just embarrassed by Christina's presence? Christina turned to go, and when she did, Andy Stern was right there beside her.

"Pretty girl," he said.

"Thank you," she replied stiffly. She was not sure she liked him offering his judgment—even though it was positive—about her daughter. Was he going to corner her at the table again? She hoped not and was trying to devise some other means of escape when she came face-to-face with Angelica. The veil had been removed, leaving her lustrous black hair uncovered.

"So how have you two been getting along?" she said, looking from Christina to Andy. "I seated you together because I wanted you to meet."

Christina felt her cheeks heating. So this had been a setup?

Widow and widower meet and find love at a wedding? How predictable—and how odious. She hated being set up with men as if she were a lone sock or glove, useless without a mate. She'd had a mate. A mate she adored. And in the ten years since he'd died, none of the men she had dated had come even remotely close to him. Being alone was better than settling. Besides, she wasn't alone—she had Jordan.

Christina was so uncomfortable she could not even look at Andy Stern, and kept her eyes focused on Angelica, who added, "Andy needs some work done on his apartment." She seemed unaware of Christina's discomfort. "And I thought you'd be the perfect person for the job."

"You're a decorator?" Andy asked. He sounded skeptical.

"Yes, I am," said Christina. His tone riled her, but it was because he'd touched a nerve. She had no formal training for her job; she'd found her way to it through a serendipitous offer, postcollege, to intern at an interior design firm where a college roommate's mother held a key position. The roommate had been all set to take the position but at the last minute had decided to go backpacking through the Yucatán and so Christina stepped in. She loved it and saw that, with her own desire to rummage and collect, she could make a life's work of it.

"She's a superlative decorator," Angelica was saying. "She did my place and I just adore it. You've got to see her work, Andy; Christina, you can send Andy pictures, right? And of course he can come to my apartment."

"Do you have an office in the city?" asked Andy.

"No, in Brooklyn," Christina said. And though she did not say it, until the recent downturn in the economy, it had been a very lively, even thriving business. People in the neighborhood knew—and loved—her work; she had been much in de-

mand for a certain kind of warm, idiosyncratic, old-plus-new
interior.

"Brooklyn!" said Andy. It was practically a sneer.

"Yes, Brooklyn. Park Slope, actually. It's a beautiful, historic neighborhood and I love it." Relief that this was not a
misguided attempt at matchmaking turned to bristling self-
defense.

"She's right, Andy," Angelica said, putting a hand on his
wrist. "Park Slope *is* a beautiful neighborhood and if you saw
what Christina has done with her house, you would be totally
awed. You just have to get over your Brooklyn phobia, that's all."

"Well, I am looking for someone to do work on my place,"
he said. "And Angelica's recommendation means a lot. Maybe
I could show it to you and you could let me know how you
might handle the job."

"We could set up a time later this month," said Christina.
She hoped her voice masked her complete lack of enthusiasm.
Whatever fragile thread of connection she'd felt with him had
been snapped; he had reverted to the arrogant, self-satisfied
man she'd endured at the dinner table. But a couple of key
clients had lost their jobs, another was moving to Chicago, and
yet another had been very slow in paying her bills. Work was
work.

"Perfect," Angelica said. "Do you have a business card or
should I just give Andy your coordinates?"

"I think I have one." Christina popped the clasp on her
black satin clutch and rooted around inside. Yes, here it was;
she handed it to Andy.

"*Christina's World,*" he read off the card. "*Antiques, Interiors,
Gardens.*" He looked at her. "Gardens? In the city?"

"Park Slope has a lot of gardens," she said. "Lovely gardens, in fact. I've designed many of them." Why did she feel this was another slight?

"Here's my card," he said. She looked down at the fat, block lettering, and the string of degrees that followed the name. She put it in her purse, wishing she did not need, so badly, to use it.

"Get in touch with her," Angelica was saying to Andy. Then someone called her name and she turned. Before she moved off in the direction of the voice, she added, "You won't be sorry." Fortunately, Andy was waylaid by someone else and Christina was finally able to escape.

She didn't want to go back to her table, but it seemed too early to leave; the cake hadn't even been cut. Maybe she could go back to the rose garden. But her fingers were sticky from the cookies; what she wanted to do first was wash up. There were luxury portable restrooms set up at the far end of the lawn; Jordan had used one and told her it was even air-conditioned. But Christina wanted to find a bathroom indoors—mostly because she wanted a peek inside.

She went around to the front and slipped in. The foyer was as big as most New York living rooms and it was done in a gargantuan black-and-white marble tile and a ghastly, glittering chandelier. This was exactly the sort of decorating she hated: overdone, overwrought, mindless. Christina tried a couple of doors before finding the right one. Inside, she washed her hands and splashed cool water on her cheeks. The gilt-framed mirror was parked between a pair of ornate brass sconces. So *crass*, she thought as she smoothed her hair—done in a simple French twist—and dusted her nose with pressed powder. A swipe of lip gloss and a few dabs from the tiny flacon of Diorissimo she kept in her purse and her toilette was complete.

As she looked in the mirror, she saw her own still-attractive face with its delicate features and gray-blue eyes, but she thought of Andy Stern. Arrogant, self-important, opinionated—was there anything she'd left out? But although she neither liked nor respected him, she was going to go after the job anyway. Business was slow. Private school, even with a generous financial aid package, cost money. And her nineteenth-century row house always demanded something; this time it was the front stoop, whose crumbling steps needed resurfacing. She had inherited the narrow, four-story brick structure with its glass-paneled double doors and Japanese maple out front, and though she loved it dearly, it was certainly a money pit.

Lately, she'd been feeling so strapped that she actually applied for a full-time job at a design firm based in Greenwich. Giving up her own business to work for someone else would be, in her view, a comedown. But the Greenwich job offered a steady salary and good benefits. Anyway, it was a long shot; she'd sent the résumé in weeks ago, gone up for an interview, and heard nothing since. All the more reason to call Andy Stern.

By the time Christina made her way back to the table, the cake cutting was in progress. Angelica and Ohad, her Israeli groom, fed the first slices to each other, amid enthusiastic clapping and cheering. Then the servers took over, expertly slicing and distributing pieces to everyone else. Before Christina took her first bite, something caused her to look across the tent. There at the other end stood Andy Stern. On one side stood his son, Oliver, and on the other, Jordan. Oliver had a slice of cake in his fingers and was devouring it without the assistance of fork or plate. Jordan's hands were empty, and she watched Oliver as though he were crazy, dangerous, or both.

Why did it trouble her to see the three of them standing

there together, like they were posing for a family picture? Something about Andy, that was it. It was his body language— so commanding and assertive—and the way he seemed to take up so much space, to *own* everything around him.

As if he were aware of her unflattering assessment, Andy Stern looked straight at her, pinning her with his bright, focused gaze. As his fork impaled a morsel of cake, he grinned. Now, why did that grin unsettle her so much? Christina didn't wait to find out. Setting down the plate with its untouched cake, she sped off to the rose garden to escape.

TWO

ordan slammed the locker door shut. Finally. School was over and now came the best, the most real part of the day: the ballet class that unfolded at the soaring white studio on West Sixty-fifth Street. She needed to hurry. The subway was a short walk, and even though Jordan was loaded down—backpack with all her school stuff, canvas tote crammed with practice clothes, ballet slippers, a towel, and hair gear—she made good time. But once in the station she had to wait for the train. Anxiously, she paced the platform. She *hated* being late to class. Finally, the train arrived.

The ride into Manhattan took more than forty minutes, time Jordan had learned to use well. First, she permitted herself something to eat—she'd had no breakfast and lunch had been only a salad—because her stomach was rumbling too loudly to ignore. After she consumed the protein bar and three almonds she'd found nestled in a Baggie beneath her tights, she was good. She pulled the heavy history textbook out of her backpack and opened it. Her father had been a history teacher, though he'd gone to law school. "He decided he liked kids more than he liked law," her mother said. Would he have liked *her*? Dumb question. Parents loved their kids. Though Jordan knew of parents who didn't think their kids were smart or pretty or driven enough. Jordan found history boring, but then, she found pretty much everything apart from her ballet classes boring; that she excelled in school in no way reflected her interest level. How would her father have reacted to that? He had died when she was only four and what she had, mostly, were sense memories: the scratchy feel of his tweed jacket when he picked her up and pressed her to him, the warmth of his big palm when it enveloped her tiny one.

When the train emerged from the tunnel and went over the Manhattan Bridge, she looked up from her textbook. That wide view across the water, framed by the surrounding city, filled her with a sense of widening possibility. She loved being at SAB, despite all the rushing. And in September, she'd be moving up to the next level, B2. She'd be taking character, point, variations, adagio, and even a weekly class in piano. If *only* her mother would let her transfer to the Professional Children's School on Sixtieth Street, life would be so much easier. But her mother refused on what she called *educational grounds*. So they had reached a compromise: in September, Jordan would be starting at the Cromley-Blandon School. Her mom liked that they offered Chinese, Arabic, and advanced Latin, but the only thing Jordan cared about was the location—Seventy-fourth and West End Avenue—which was only minutes away from SAB. She'd still have to commute, but at least it would be at the beginning of the day, not when she was on her way to ballet class. At Forty-second Street, Jordan got off the train and caught a local to Sixty-sixth Street and then hurried up to the building, through the reception area, and into the girls' dressing room.

"You're late!"

She turned, and there was her best friend, Alexis, already dressed for class. She and Alexis had started at SAB together when they were both six; they bonded when they both played candy canes in the annual production of *The Nutcracker.*

"Am not." Jordan dropped down to rummage through her bag. But Alexis was right: she *was* late. Yanking out the tights, leotard, and shoes, she stripped off her jeans and oversized T-shirt, stuffed them inside, and put on her practice clothes. The black flats she wore were kicked off and abandoned. There was just enough time to redo her bun before the opening strains of the piano music signaled that class was beginning.

Jordan took a place behind Alexis at the long wooden barre attached to the wall as the strains of Chopin filled the studio. That stuck-up Francesca Karatasos was at the front of the barre—naturally—but Jordan forced herself not to look, and instead focused on melting into a deep, rich *plié.* Down and down she went, and then as soon as she was at the bottom, the rising began again.

The *pliés* were followed by the *tendus,* the *tendus* by the *degagés, degagés* by *ronds de jambes, fondus, frappés, developpés,* and *grands battements.* When the barre was over, there was a break. Francesca stood admiring herself in front of the mirror; she was able to lift her long legs higher than anyone in class and sometimes her point work looked so perfect it made Jordan insane. Alexis tapped her on the shoulder and Jordan followed her out to the water fountain.

"She is *so* conceited," Jordan said, glancing back to where Francesca continued to preen.

"But she's really good," said Alexis. Jordan couldn't argue. "Want to come over later?" Alexis asked. Since Alexis lived in an apartment on West Seventy-eighth Street, they liked to hang out there.

"I can't; we're having company for dinner," said Jordan. Her mother had invited Misha and Stephen, the couple who had started out as their tenants and become their friends, to join them. It was their anniversary or something.

"Tomorrow, then," Alexis said. Jordan nodded as the teacher, Ms. Bonner, strode back into the room and began the center work. Mostly this was a recap of what they had done at the barre, but one of the combinations contained *pirouettes*. She fixed her thoughts exclusively on the small spot where her foot rose on *relevé* and then pivoted, imagining herself stuck there, like with a glue gun, unable to shift her foot at all. The only possible movement was around, around, and—yes!—around again. She finished cleanly, in a small burst of triumph—three neat, complete *pirouettes*. Francesca, who turned like a top, could do three *pirouettes*, but Jordan never had before.

"Nice turns!" said Ms. Bonner as she looked in Jordan's direction.

Jordan stood there, chest heaving. *Three,* she thought, *three perfect turns.* The class seemed charmed after that—during the adagio she was able to lift her leg higher than usual, and she caught on to the *balancé* combination right away. Jordan still marked it dutifully along with everyone else, but when it was time to actually do it, she gave herself over to the music—a waltz—completely.

"Everyone, please stop," Ms. Bonner said with a loud clap of her hands. The room went still and Mr. Strickland, the pianist, took his fingers off the keys. "I'd like you all to watch

Jordan. She's got more than the steps; she's got the *soul*. Jordan," she said, gesturing to a place alone, in the center of the floor. "Please." Ms. Bonner looked at Mr. Strickland.

Jordan was nervous as the first few bars began to play. But once she began to perform the long, sweeping *balancés en tourant*—waltz steps that crossed the floor in a diagonal—the smaller *balancés* that rocked from side to side like waves, the *piqué arabesque*, in which she was required to strike and hold the pose, and the tight spin of the *chaîné* turns at the end, she wanted the combination to go on and on.

"Brava!" said Ms. Bonner when it was over. "Very well done."

Jordan could feel everyone looking at her, especially Francesca, and Alexis gave her a high five as they passed. The glow stayed with her right on through the rest of the class and the final *révérence* where they all curtsied to the teacher. Then class was over; Mr. Strickland stood and gathered up his music; the sweat-slick young dancers filed out of the room.

Jordan was mopping her face with a towel when Ms. Bonner stopped her. "I've been watching you for a while now," she said. "And I like what I see. Keep it up, and things—*good* things—will be coming your way." She put two fingers under Jordan's chin and smiled; Jordan was almost afraid to return that smile. But she smiled all the way back to Brooklyn, on her walk from the subway station and through the front door of the house on Carroll Street.

She got there just in time to see two men, both dark skinned and one wearing a turban, looking at the house. It looked like the one with the gelled-back hair was taking a picture; he held his phone up to the facade. He was speaking very rapidly while the other man just nodded without saying anything back. Jordan was confused. Who were these guys and what were they doing in front of her house? She was about to ask them, but when she approached, they startled like a pair of birds and rushed off down the block. She watched them go with some satisfaction; although she had never seen them before, she felt, instinctively, that they were intruders. Next door, she saw the flick of the lace curtain on the ground floor. That meant their neighbor Miss Kinney had seen them too. She was ancient and spent a lot of time sitting out front or looking out of her window. Maybe she would know what this was about. Or else Jordan's mother would. But once inside, Jordan's need to share her own news crowded out thoughts of the two strangers.

"Mom!" she called as she came through the door. "Mom, where *are* you?"

"In the kitchen," Christina called back. "Misha and Stephen will be down soon." The kitchen was at the back of the house's ground floor; in the front was their living room. On the parlor floor was their formal dining room, along with her mom's office and showroom; on the floor above there were two bedrooms and a bathroom in back. Misha and Stephen rented the top-floor apartment.

When Jordan burst into the kitchen, she found her mother, dressed in a tea-colored linen dress and a strand of carved ivory beads, rinsing lettuce. "You sound so excited," Christina said.

"I am!" Jordan dropped her bags on the floor. "I just had the best ballet class *ever*."

She proceeded to tell her mother about the turns and waltz and what Ms. Bonner had said.

"How wonderful," Christina said softly, stepping back.

She had the misty-eyed look she sometimes got; it could be annoying, but right now, Jordan was drinking in every misty-eyed second. "A red-letter day." Then Jordan ran upstairs to shower and change before Misha and Stephen came down. They had become like uncles to her, making a fuss over her consistently excellent grades, buying her little presents, and taking her on what they liked to call "cultural outings."

Dinner, served in the dining room on the parlor floor of the house, felt like a party. There were tiger lilies in a crystal vase and the table was set with their best china, no two plates the same, and the heavy white linen napkins her mother had been collecting for years; they were so soft and thick, so what if they had someone else's initials embroidered onto them? Along with salad, Christina had made wild rice and poached salmon, topped with a caper-dill sauce and presented on one of her big blue and white platters. Jordan knew her mom was always worried about money, but she managed to turn out these fancy meals anyway.

Jordan ate the salad, ignored the rice, and meticulously scraped all the sauce off the salmon before putting a few bites of it in her mouth. Misha—tall and lanky, with a thick shock of hair that fell across his forehead—went downstairs for the champagne Christina had in the fridge. "You have to let her have a taste, Christina," he said. "It's a special day for her too."

"All right, just a tiny taste," Christina said. The silver bracelet she always wore was bright in the candlelight; she had lit several long white tapers and placed them along the pine sideboard. Misha popped the cork, which shot across the room like a rocket, making them all laugh. Christina made a toast to the two men—they were celebrating their ten-year anniversary together—and then Stephen stood up.

"To a three-pirouette day," he said, lifting his glass in Jordan's direction. "May you have many more." He touched the rim of Jordan's glass with his own. "Drink up, darling." He drained his glass quickly and poured himself another. Then he turned to Christina. "How was the wedding of the century?"

"Beautiful," Christina said. "The decorations, the food, the flowers . . ." She sipped delicately at her champagne. "Though you should have seen her stepfather's house; it was beyond tasteless!"

"Do tell!" Stephen leaned in closer. He was a fashion stylist and Misha was a set designer; they both cared a lot about how things looked. So Christina obliged and pretty soon all three of them were giggling like a bunch of kids.

"Speaking of weddings, are you two going to tie the knot?" Christina asked. Stephen and Misha exchanged a look.

"Well, it's complicated . . . ," Stephen said. As the conversation turned to same-sex marriage, only recently made legal, they all grew more serious. Jordan stopped paying attention. The champagne was like soda, but crisper and less sweet. Good—it probably didn't have so many calories. She took another sip and it was soon gone. When Christina went to the kitchen to get dessert, Stephen poured her a little more. "Sh," he said, "don't tell your mom."

Jordan drank that too, and for the rest of the evening felt blanketed by fog. When Misha and Stephen said good night, Jordan was about to go to bed too; she was tired. But she was stopped by the sight of her mother, seated alone at the table, shoulders slumped and head down. Jordan's champagne-induced haze was pierced by this unsettling image.

"Mom?" she said. "What's wrong?"

"Nothing," Christina said. "Go up to bed now, darling. It's after eleven."

"I don't believe you," Jordan said, and went to join her mother at the table, which was covered with dirty dishes.

"Well, I guess I might as well tell you now; you'll find out soon enough. Do you remember my client Mimi Farnsworth?" Jordan nodded. The Farnsworths had a huge limestone just above Eighth Avenue on Third Street; Christina had recently completed a very big job there. "I just found out today that Mike Farnsworth was caught embezzling money from his firm. There's going to be a trial and he'll probably go to jail. The house will be seized and all their assets frozen. She doesn't know how she'll begin to pay the legal fees. Or me."

"But you have other money, right? Other clients? And there's the rent that Stephen and Misha pay."

"That's a huge help, of course," Christina said. "But it doesn't cover all our expenses. When Daddy died, I had to refinance the house." Jordan must have looked blank, because Christina continued. "That means I went to the bank to get another mortgage on it. I'm still paying that off."

Jordan tried to make sense of this information; her mother had never talked to her so openly about money before. Then she had a terrible thought. "Do you think we would ever have to sell *our* house?"

"No!" Christina said. "I would never do that."

Jordan was relieved. She knew how much her mom loved their house; she'd grown up here, and inherited it from her dad when he died. "When did you find out about Mimi?" she asked.

"This afternoon," said Christina.

"So why did you wait to tell me?"

"I was going to bring it up at dinner; you know I can tell Misha and Stephen anything. But then you came home with your lovely news and I didn't want to spoil the mood."

"Oh, Mom!" Jordan flung her arms around her mother's shoulders, inhaling her familiar lily-of-the-valley scent. Could there be a better mother on the planet? "I don't want you to treat me like a baby anymore. You can tell me stuff."

Christina smiled, but she did not look happy. "There is one more thing," she said as Jordan released her and sat back in her chair. "I got a job offer today."

"You did? Congratulations! You should have brought *that* up at dinner; we could have celebrated."

"When you hear the details, you may not think so. It's in Greenwich."

"You mean like Connecticut?"

"That's exactly what I mean."

"Oh," said Jordan. "Oh."

"I applied weeks and weeks ago and after the initial interview, I hadn't heard anything back. So I just assumed they weren't interested. But then I got a call today; they're offering me a full-time position with some very attractive benefits."

"What about Christina's World?" Jordan asked.

"I'd have to close it down. At least for a while."

"That would make you really sad, wouldn't it?" Christina nodded; to Jordan it looked like she was going to cry. "And where would we live?"

"For the time being, right here. I'd commute; it wouldn't be so bad. Though at some point I might consider relocating."

"But you just said—"

"I know, I know—that I would never give up this house.

But maybe I could rent it out and we could find an apartment in Greenwich."

"Greenwich is a long way from West Sixty-fifth Street," Jordan said quietly.

Christina got up from the table. "Let's not be so gloomy, okay? I haven't taken the job yet." She waved her hand over the cluttered table. "I'll deal with all this tomorrow; we should both go to bed now."

Jordan followed her mother upstairs. She must really be upset; she *never* left dirty dishes overnight. Jordan wanted to comfort her but did not know how. What if they did have to move to Greenwich? That would be *awful*.

Jordan got into bed. What a relief to lie down and close her eyes. In the dark, her worry about her mother receded and in its place came an image of Ms. Bonner. The ballet teacher's words reverberated, not only in her head, but also in the cavity of her chest, her lungs, and her beating, yearning heart. *Just keep it up, and things—*good things*—will be coming your way.* But good things came only to those who worked hard. She would have to work even harder to live up to Ms. Bonner's prediction, harder than she had ever worked in her whole entire life.

THREE

*O*n the Tuesday morning following the wedding, Andy Stern was up sixteen minutes before his alarm went off at five forty-five, sixteen minutes in which he was able to don his workout clothes, stride into the stainless-steel and granite kitchen for a quick infusion of espresso, and march down the hall to his son's bedroom. "Ollie," he said, rapping on the door. "Ollie, you told me to get you up early today." Nothing. "Ollie," he tried again, and when there was still no reply, he turned the knob and peeked in.

There was his son, sound asleep and splayed like a starfish on top of the jumbled bed. He wore a tie-dye T-shirt—had that trend really come back around again?—and faded boxers. Around him, the room erupted in a familiar sort of chaos, with clothes strewn everywhere and the floor a minefield of soda cans, textbooks, crumpled napkins, and dirty plates. On one wall, a built-in desk and shelf unit housed all of Oliver's techno-toys, which included a large flat-screen TV, the latest-model iPhone, iPad, and several laptops. "Ollie, you said you had a paper to finish."

"Paper," Oliver mumbled. His eyes opened and he propped himself up. "Right."

"Are you awake?"

"Yeah, up." He stood and picked his way across the floor to the bathroom. "I'm going to shower."

The bathroom door closed and seconds later, the sound of running water could be heard. Andy stepped into the room, looking for . . . what? Clues to his son's evident unhappiness? He made his way over to the desk, stepping on something disgustingly slimy that turned out to be part of a red pepper and mozzarella sandwich that had probably been here for a week. Jesus. He picked up the offending mess and stuffed it into a plastic bag he plucked from the clutter. He'd have to speak to Oliver about leaving food around; it really wasn't sanitary. On the desk, along with all the gadgets, he saw open boxes of LEGOs, wooden trains, and a very elaborate helicopter he seemed to recall Rachel buying when Oliver was about eight.

Andy stumbled toward the bed—this time his foot had an unfortunate encounter with something molten that turned out to be a chocolate bar, its wrapper haphazardly torn open—to investigate an odd lump he spied behind the pillow. The chocolate joined the remains of the sandwich in the bag. Moving the pillow, Andy found a stuffed elephant that was more than a decade old. Once blue, it was now a soiled gray, and missing an eye besides. Buster, that was the name Oliver had given it. Andy tugged Buster's outsized ear by way of greeting and tucked him back under the pillow.

Then he felt something else odd. Andy pulled out a small plastic bag filled with rolling papers and, damn it, marijuana; even without sniffing the contents, he could tell by the dry, twiggy look of it. The discovery explained a lot of things—the way Oliver seemed to burn through the money Andy gave him, his erratic performance in school, the maddening funks into which he seemed to slip so easily. It was troubling too that his son could be so casual, even brazen, about his recreational drug use. Lucy changed his sheets on a regular basis; didn't he care if she found that bag? Andy checked his watch. The shower was still running and anyway there was no time to deal with this now.

He pocketed the bag. Oliver would not ask him about it; of that he was sure. Then he went back down the hall, to the exercise room on the other side of the apartment. The trainer, Cassie, was now four minutes late and her lateness annoyed the hell out of him. But he tried to subdue his irritation with a few deep squats and a stretch. Then he walked to the window, where he stood forty stories above the city, gazing out at the sparkling ripples and toylike boats of the East River.

When the concierge buzzed—*finally!*—Andy turned away from the view. The fitness room boasted an elliptical trainer in one corner, StairMaster in another. A wall of free weights, each set color coded. A bench press. Mats. He viewed this room as a necessary sanctuary; while he was here, he tried to keep the outside world at bay. As soon as Cassie came in, they began; he knew the basic drill—stretch, warm up, quick cardio blast followed by the core work she favored. Planking, her core technique du jour, was a bitch. He'd worked his way up to just over three minutes and was trying to reach four today. He assumed the position with his arms along either side his body, his toes flexed and sustaining his weight. At 90 seconds he was still in command; at 120, the strain was apparent.

"You're doing great." Cassie's upbeat voice provided the necessary encouragement. Andy had just passed the three-minute mark when Oliver came charging into the room despite having been told, numerous times, not to bother his father while the trainer was here.

"I have to see you," he said in response to Andy's request that he leave, *now,* and save whatever it was until Cassie had gone. "It's, like, urgent," he said, pushing the hair—long, blond, springy, and so like his dead mother's that it made Andy want to weep—out of his face. Andy wavered; he did not want Oliver to think it was okay to come barging in here whenever he felt like it. But he loved the kid and didn't want him to feel ignored. Reluctantly, he got up from his plank, and excused himself to speak to his son.

"All right," he said, "what's the emergency? Does it have to do with your paper?"

Oliver shook his head. "It's Cunningham, Dad. He said that since I missed my third appointment with the school psychologist, I couldn't go on the eleventh-grade retreat. And I *have* to go on that retreat, Dad. I just *have* to."

"When did you find this out?" Andy asked. It was only six thirty in the morning; school would not start for another hour and a half.

"Yesterday," Oliver admitted.

"And you waited until now to tell me?" Andy asked.

"Uh, well, yeah." Oliver had the grace to look abashed.

"All right, Ollie," he said. "As soon as I'm done with my workout, I'll see if I can get Cunningham on the phone to discuss it. When does the retreat start?"

"Today. We're supposed to leave right after school. The bus will be waiting at three fifteen."

"Pack your stuff and go to school now. I'll text you later."

"Thanks, Dad," Oliver said. He fingered the hole in his

faded gray T-shirt, stretching the dime-sized opening to that
of a quarter. All the money Andy spent—and gladly!—on the
kid's clothes and still his son insisted on wearing stuff not
even fit to donate.

Andy returned to his workout, but his concentration was
shot. It wasn't just this thing with Cunningham. The kid
was all over the place. Excelling in some courses, failing
others. Took the PSAT last fall and scored a cool eight hundred
on the math, yet this year he was getting a D in algebra. It was
the loss of his mother, of course. Andy sympathized. Empa-
thized. Hell, he wasn't over Rachel's death and he was a man;
Oliver was still just a kid.

A little more than an hour later, Andy was showered,
dressed in a bespoke suit and crisp white pima cotton shirt
from Brooks Brothers, and walking through the door of his
Park Avenue office. It was still dark when he entered; as usual,
he was the first to arrive. He had two C-sections scheduled
later on, but he reserved these early-morning slots for meeting
new patients. He flipped on the lights and walked through the
reception area with its framed vintage movie posters, sleek
black leather sofa, and wall-sized aquarium before reaching
his sanctum.

Today he was seeing Beth Klein, a woman who had gone
through four first-trimester miscarriages in the last two years.
Her fifth and last pregnancy had lasted six months, only to
end when a raging bacterial infection had necessitated induc-
ing her; she gave birth to a one-pound baby girl who'd lived
for half an hour and died in her arms.

He opened the file and began to read. Beth had an incom-
petent cervix as well as an abnormally shaped uterus—a
cramped almond instead of a roomy triangle. Why the idiot

doctor who'd treated her before had not ordered bed rest and had her surgically stitched was a total mystery to him. Letting her run around, *take Pilates and play tennis even*, with all those miscarriages behind her? But it would do no good to dwell on this. He needed to help Beth bring a healthy baby to full term.

There was a light tap on the door, followed by the appearance of his newish secretary, Joanne. "Here's your breakfast, Dr. Stern." She set the Morning Glory muffin and freshly squeezed carrot-apple-orange elixir from the juice bar on Lexington Avenue in front of him. He took a long swig of juice and unwrapped the muffin. Stone-cold. Joanne *knew* he liked his muffin toasted, damn it. Was that so hard to remember? He was just about to call her back when his eyes settled on the framed photograph of Rachel that had pride of place on his desk.

It was his favorite photo, taken on the beach some years before she'd gotten sick. Her corkscrew blond curls were partially contained by a red bandanna, and her eyes, the clear, light blue of a swimming pool, looked straight at him. *Give it a rest, Andy-boy,* she seemed to be saying. *Joanne's a good egg and you know it. So she forgot about the muffin today. Is that such a big deal?* Rachel had this way of talking him down from himself. He was a better man in her presence and now that she was gone, he missed the person he'd been when he was with her almost as much as he missed her.

Biting into the cold muffin, Andy looked down at the file, though he wasn't really seeing it anymore. He was thinking of his Rachel, and the unbelievable irony that she'd died of ovarian cancer, when he was in fact a gynecologist, trained to diagnose such diseases. Of course he hadn't been her gyn; that was a breach of protocol. But still, he felt haunted by the idea that somehow he should have *known*.

There was a knock on the door. "Dr. Stern, your first appointment is here," said Joanne. "And oh, I realized I forgot to have them toast your muffin; sorry about that. I'll make sure it's done tomorrow."

"Thanks, Joanne," he said, glancing at the photograph. *See*, Rachel seemed to say. *You can have your muffin toasted without being an ogre.* "Send them in."

Beth and her husband, Bob, entered his office. She was thirtyish, with pretty features clouded by an anxious look; the husband held her arm like he thought it might break. Andy took in Beth's expensive-looking slacks and top. On her arm she carried a quilted Chanel bag—he recognized it because many of his patients carried those bags—that cost more than four grand. But all the women he saw had money; he charged a *lot* and took no insurance. Only the very wealthiest women could afford him.

Even though he now made plenty of money, Andy never quite shook off the feeling of inferiority when he met people like the Kleins. He'd been a scrappy kid from the Bronx, dying to claw his way out of the neighborhood where the three of them were crammed into a tiny apartment above a butcher shop; life there had been permeated by the smell of blood. His parents were always fighting and Andy's memories included slammed doors, dishes hurled, and plenty of shouting. It was a relief when his father finally left. He and his mother moved in with her best friend while Ida looked for work. She'd found it too, and she was able to see him through City College, where he'd been in the top one percent of his class. She even helped with his medical school bills, though he'd taken out plenty of loans to pay those. As for his father, there had been sporadic attempts to stay in touch, but eventually those petered out. Andy had moved from grief to anger to apathy; he never thought about his father anymore. The man had been dead for twenty years now.

"Please sit down," he told the Kleins. "I've read through your history," he began. "That last pregnancy must have been excruciating."

"It was," she murmured, looking down.

"I know. Which is why I am going to make sure that nothing like that happens the next time."

"Next time?" This was from Bob. "Will there be a next time?"

"Absolutely," said Andy. "We know that Beth can *get* pregnant. Now we just have to make sure she *stays* pregnant."

"Do you really mean it?" Bob said. His wife was weeping softly and he took her hand.

"Yes, I do." Andy handed Beth a tissue. "Now, let me tell you exactly what we're going to do." For the next fifteen minutes, he outlined a plan. Pending the results of the pelvic exam and the sonogram—he needed to see whether there was any residue from the last pregnancy—he would urge her to begin trying again, using an ovulation predictor to speed the process along. Once she was pregnant, he'd stitch her cervix until it was as tight as a cork in an unopened bottle of wine. Then he'd place her on total bed rest. The only thing she would be allowed to do would be to come—in a taxi—to see him. Would it be an ordeal? You bet, he told her. But at the end of it, she would have her baby.

"You'll take up knitting," he told her as he escorted her to the examination room. "Or read *The Magic Mountain*. In German." This elicited a smile. "Why don't you have a seat in the waiting room?" he told Bob. "We won't be long."

Andy waited the requisite few minutes while Beth undressed and put on the blue paper gown; after Pam, the technician, completed the sonogram, he went in, scrubbed his hands, and donned the latex gloves. The instruments had been warmed and he kept his tone genial, conducting the exam with such delicacy that he actually had her smiling while her feet were in the stirrups.

Beth got off the table, dressed, and came into his office while Joanne got Bob from the waiting room. "Everything looks good," Andy said. "The sonogram was all clear." He could see how their faces began to open, like flowers in the sun. Once they were gone, Andy saw his unfinished muffin and juice still sitting there. He dumped the muffin, drained the juice, and pulled out the next file. By lunchtime, he was ravenous and he had Joanne order him a tofu platter and a cup of gazpacho, both of which were consumed at his desk. Andy scrupulously watched what he ate and was proud that in his mid-forties he still weighed 178 pounds, the same as he had the day he graduated from college.

While he ate, he scanned the messages on his phone. Here was one from Cunningham, whom he'd contacted even before coming to the office. One was from his mother and another from his old buddy Gavin Rothberg; he hadn't talked to Gavin in ages. And look, here was a message from that decorator he'd met at the wedding, Christina Connelly. Now, he had never expected to hear from *her*. His verdict? Classy but cold. Icy, even. Still, he did need some work done on the apartment. He'd call her tomorrow.

The last message was the best of all, a flirtatious text

from Jennifer Baum, the sexy little blonde he'd been dating for the past few months. He smiled when he thought of Jen. Her text was brief. *See u 2nite? Planning what NOT to wear. XOXO.* Obvious, yes. But effective too. He quickly texted her back.

Lunch finished, he launched into the next phase. First he phoned Cunningham and managed to smooth things over at least enough so that Oliver could go on the retreat. Oliver was happy when he got the text letting him know, but Andy understood this was just a Band-Aid. As a condition of allowing Oliver to go on the trip, Cunningham had insisted on a meeting in his office next week: the school psychologist and Andy would be in attendance as well. "We won't exactly call it an intervention," Cunningham had said. "But that's what it is." *Oh great,* thought Andy. Still, an *intervention*—a bullshit term if there ever was one—was better than a *suspension* or an *expulsion.* Then Andy headed over to New York Hospital, on East Sixty-eighth Street. On the way, he called his mother. She answered on the first ring.

"I went shopping today," she announced. "That *gonif* at the Food Emporium charged me the regular price for the cheese; the sharp cheddar was supposed to be on special this week."

"You don't have to worry about money, Ma," he said gently. "You know I'll take care of you."

"Please," she said. "It's not about that. It's the principle of the thing."

"I know."

"And another thing: I gave that fellow downstairs a big tip to fix the leak in my bathroom faucet and it's *still* dripping. The sound is driving me crazy at night."

"Is he a plumber?" Andy asked, glancing at his watch.

"No, but he said he could handle it."

"Ma, I think you need a plumber to take a look. Do you need me to call one?"

"I'd appreciate that," she said.

Again, Andy checked his watch. "Can I call you later?" he asked.

At the hospital, both C-sections went extremely well. Julie Bixby delivered a perfect little boy—seven pounds, five ounces—and Samantha Kane hit the jackpot with triplets, all of them girls. They were preemies of course, whisked off for testing practically the second they came out. All three were more than two pounds each, which was tiny but still viable. And their vital signs looked good. When Andy held the first one in his arms, she screwed up her face and looked at him with such indignation that he wanted to kiss her. *Feisty,* Andy thought. *This one is going to make it.*

So he was in an excellent mood while he made his rounds and then left the hospital. He planned to walk up to Seventy-ninth Street, which was where Jennifer lived. But just as he crossed Seventy-third Street, his phone buzzed again. This time it was his service, calling to inform him that Linda McConnell, one of his patients, was in labor *now*; she'd been monitoring the contractions for the last hour. Which would have been fine except that she was only twenty-six weeks pregnant; the baby in there was not fully cooked. He called her back immediately.

"Tell your husband to take you to the ER; I'll meet you there. And have him call an ambulance."

"All right, Dr. Stern." She was crying of course. They all cried.

"And Linda? I want you to hang on. Tell yourself you are *not* going to have this baby until you get to the hospital." He said good-bye and checked his watch. No way was he going to make that date with Jen. Then he raised his arm and hailed a taxi to take him straight to the hospital.

FOUR

*O*liver sat on an ornately carved wooden bench outside Cunningham's office, which was on the ground floor of the fortresslike building that housed Morningside Grammar and Prep. The seat of the bench was worn in places, evidence of all the kids who'd waited here before him. Oliver wasn't looking forward to this meeting, but his father had made it clear that Cunningham was insisting on it. "And this time you'd better show up," his dad had said. "Otherwise, you'll be spending your senior year somewhere else." Oliver might not have cared about this had it not been for the presence of Delphine, an incredibly hot French girl who had shown up in his grade this year. The thought of being apart from her this summer—she was going back to France—was bad enough; he had to know that he would be seeing her in September.

Oliver looked around the waiting area. There was a frayed rug in front of the bench, and the table in front of him was scratched. Everything about this place was worn-out. But the

lack of attention to appearances was a reverse kind of snob-
bery. *We don't care about any of that statusy stuff,* it said. *We just
care about the life of the mind.* Which was pretty funny when you
considered that Morningside was a third-rate school for kids
who couldn't cut it at Dalton, Spence, Chapin, Brearley, or any
of the other really good private schools. Oliver used to go to
Dalton, but that was before his mom died and everything
went totally to hell.

On the table sat copies of the student paper and yearbook.
Once, he'd thought about becoming involved with both; now,
like most of his classmates, they just seemed stupid to him.
Delphine was the only one who was different; she just seemed
to understand things that other people didn't She was tall—
taller than he was, even—with long, shiny brown hair. Her
clothes were different too: short, pleated skirts, sweaters that
looked like they belonged to her older brother, button-up
blouses with funny old-fashioned collars, black tights, flat
shoes. And that accent of hers: he could come just hearing her
say his name—Ol-lee-*vair* —with the emphasis on the last syl-
lable. She was the reason he'd been so insistent on going on the
retreat; otherwise, he'd have totally blown it off.

Just then, Cunningham opened the door and stuck his big
head out. In a deep, fake-friendly voice he said, "Come in,
young man. Come in, come in." Oliver shuffled into the office
and sat down on the lumpy, blue-flowered sofa that everyone
called *the hot seat.* His dad was already here, sitting in a stiff
chair and trying not to look at his watch; it was like a tic or
something with him. Ms. Warren, the school psychologist,
was here too. Her gray hair had a serious case of bed head,
though he did like the cherry red frames of her glasses; his
mom might have worn them. Rounding out the group was Mr.

Pollock, the grade dean. He had a pathetic comb-over and called the boys *dude*; no one thought he was in the least bit cool.

Cunningham shut the door with a definitive smack. "Thank you all for coming," he said, looking around the room. "And thank *you*, Oliver, for gracing us with your presence." Was the guy sincere or ragging on him? Cunningham droned on for a few minutes. . . . *Bright boy, not living up to his potential, potentially at risk* were some of the phrases that flitted across Oliver's radar, but then they too were gone.

"So, Oliver, what do you think of what Mr. Cunningham just said?" asked Ms. Warren.

Oliver looked at her and blinked. "Uh, I'm not sure."

"Dude, were you even listening?" Mr. Pollock chimed in. Oliver ignored him and focused instead on his dad, who was of course checking his watch.

"You can go," he said to his father. "Really, Dad, it's okay. If you're busy, you can just leave now and I'll tell you about the conversation when you get home tonight." He had a phony smile pasted on his face, but inside he was seething. *Yeah, throw me under the bus, why don't you? Throw me under the bus and let it roll right over me.*

"Leaving? No one's leaving until we're through here," Andy said. He sounded pissed off, but he was finally able to pull his glance away from his wrist.

"Mr. Cunningham was saying that he thought your behavior might have to do with your mother's death; do you think that's true?" Ms. Warren looked at him earnestly.

"I don't know. I don't think about her death too much," said Oliver. Now, that was a major lie. It seemed to him that he thought about little else, except for smoking weed and, lately, Delphine. She had art this period; he'd memorized her schedule.

"You must miss her," Ms. Warren continued as if he had not spoken. "And missing her might make you act out in ways that are not always in your best interest."

Miss her? Of course he missed her. Did Ms. Warren need a wall full of degrees to figure that out? She was his mom, after all. He had loved her and been devastated when she got sick. But what no one seemed to get was that he didn't accept that she was dead, not really. He knew she had *died*; he had seen her at the end, scrawny and terrifying, the remains of her curly hair like wisps of fluff around her poor, nearly naked head. That she *stayed* dead, though, day after day, month after month—that was the part that tripped him up. When he'd once said as much to his best friend, Jake Horowitz, Jake just tapped a hand to his forehead. "You'd better get some help, man," he'd said. "Because you're nuts." Oliver never brought it up again.

Cunningham was still talking; just the sound of his voice made Oliver desperate to be somewhere, anywhere, else. "So what you're saying is that Oliver has to see a school-recommended therapist once a week over the summer and that this person will be providing a full report of his progress in September?" said Andy. Oliver knew his dad liked to sum things up quickly; he got antsy when you took too long to explain something.

"As a condition of his remaining here with us for his senior year, yes." Cunningham pinned Oliver with his gaze; Oliver looked away.

"And in September, he'll resume his sessions with you and you'll be reporting back to me," Andy said to Ms. Warren, who nodded.

"I'll keep you in the loop about grades," Mr. Pollock said. "Right now they're erratic."

"I'm missing physics now," Oliver said. "Maybe I should go."

"All right," Cunningham said. "Back to class with you, young man. And I expect to see some improvement— substantial, even *radical* improvement—very soon. Is that understood?"

"Yes, sir." Oliver decided to toss in the *sir*; it was an easy enough concession to make. It seemed to work, because Cunningham gave him this big, phony grin and clapped a hand on his shoulder; Oliver had to resist the urge to peel it off.

After physics, which by this time would be pretty much over, Oliver had a free; he could use it to hunt down Delphine in art class. The hand remained on his shoulder, though, weighty as a slab of raw meat.

"I'm hoping you'll have a productive summer," Ms. Warren said.

"Dude, we're all rooting for you." That gem was delivered by Mr. Pollock. What an a-hole.

"I'll see you tonight." His father stood up and checked his watch. *It must have been hard to ignore it for so long, Dad,* Oliver wanted to say. *Just think of all those minutes going by and you had to miss them.* But he just nodded and, as soon as Cunningham removed his paw, made for the door.

When he had bounded up to the art room on the top floor, Delphine was not there. Her friend Rebecca volunteered that she was home sick. "What's wrong with her?" Oliver said anxiously.

"I don't know," Rebecca said. She was intent on her acrylic rendering of some turdlike fruit and this hideous vase. He left the art room and clattered down the school's central staircase and into the boys' room on the lower level. There he used his cell phone to call that florist his dad always used and ordered a *mammoth* basket of flowers, some with names he had never even heard of, to be delivered to the Central Park West apartment where Delphine lived.

After his tree, he had lunch, and then English. They were reading *King Lear*, a play Oliver actually liked, though he kind of thought Lear deserved what he got from his daughters Regan and Goneril, what kind of father asked those questions anyway? Though maybe they did take it a little bit too far in the end; that scene of Lear wandering around the storm was, like, too much. He raised his hand.

"Yes, Oliver? You have a question?" The English teacher, Ms. Konkel, looked at him expectantly.

"Where is their mother?" he asked. He knew Ms. Konkel liked him.

"Excuse me?"

"The mother of Cordelia, Regan, and Goneril?"

"Shakespeare doesn't tell us, does he?"

"No, which is weird. The play is all about the king and his daughters. But what about his wife? The mother of his children? Is she dead? Or did she, like, run off with one of the courtiers or something?"

A few kids laughed and Jake lobbed a tiny spitball in his direction; it eluded Ms. Konkel's notice and landed on the floor near his chair. Oliver leaned over to pick it up, and began to massage it gently between his fingertips.

"Do you think her absence is meaningful in some way?" asked Ms. Konkel. "Was it intentional on Shakespeare's part?"

"I don't know if it was, like, intentional. But it *is* meaningful. These are motherless girls, right? Maybe that's why they behave the way they do. Maybe they miss their mother and are . . . acting out." Oliver had heard that phrase used many times to describe *him*. He pressed the spitball hard between his thumb and forefinger; it took some pressure, but he succeeded in flattening it.

"That's an excellent observation, Oliver," Ms. Konkel said. "Does anyone want to elaborate on Oliver's point? Or have anything else to add?" Molly Hahn raised her hand and so did Adam Schwartz; Oliver used the distraction to check his phone, but there was nothing from Delphine. Dejected, he put the phone away.

Even the words of praise from Ms. Konkel did not do anything to lift his spirits and he was glad that he had a joint buried in the pocket of his jeans; he intended to smoke it later, a comforting if not exactly joy-inducing thought. He could have sworn he had a pretty full bag tucked away in his room somewhere. But the last time he checked under the pillow— his usual spot—it was gone.

The afternoon was warm and golden when he got out of school at three o'clock; he decided not to go straight home, but over to Jake's, on West Ninety-seventh Street. Jake lived in a town house where he had a whole floor to himself. Turned out Jake had a joint too, and they could enjoy their weed in peace up there; the smoke didn't seem to register with Jake's mom. He didn't leave until after five o'clock, though the light seemed hardly different than it had been two hours earlier.

Oliver headed south along Central Park West, just because it was where Delphine lived. He texted her to see whether she had gotten the flowers, but she didn't respond. To distract himself, he decided to walk home through the park. Yeah, that was a good idea. The park was, like, beautiful in June. He entered at Eighty-sixth Street; the trees were a hyperlit green and the flowers—he didn't know their names—were so bright they might have been covered in paint. He stopped to watch a pair of sparrows, and became fixated on the subtle distinctions of their feathers—gray, brown, black. When they flew off, he felt a loss so keen he wanted to cry. Being stoned affected him like that sometimes.

Around Seventy-second Street, he got a sudden attack of the munchies, so he bought a Häagen-Dazs ice-cream bar from a vendor and finished it in, like, a minute; then he bought another, and ate it more slowly. When he reached his own apartment building on East Sixty-ninth Street, he was still floating. After riding up in the elevator to the fortieth story, he let himself into the apartment quietly. Nothing brought him down faster than having to engage with his dad.

Oliver said hello to Lucy, who was in the kitchen making dinner. It would be low fat or low carb or both; his dad was on this kick about healthy eating and gave Lucy strict instructions. Not that any of this was new. But when Oliver's mother had been alive, the food thing hadn't seemed so . . . relentless. Good thing he'd had the ice-cream bars.

Then he went down the hall, toward his own room. When he reached his dad's study, he stopped. The door was closed, but he heard voices coming from inside. One was his dad's voice. The door opened. "Ollie," said his father, using the nickname that his mother had given him; Oliver wished he wouldn't. "I'm glad you're home. There's someone I want you to meet."

"Meet?" Now the weed was making him fuzzy. Damn. He really wished his dad had not been here.

"Yes. Could you come in, please?"

Oliver tugged on a coil of hair as he shuffled into the office. It was neater than neat, with nothing on the long desk other than a high-powered lamp and a stainless-steel cup that held several weapon-sharp pencils. The shelf unit opposite the desk held his perfectly lined-up books, and a few framed family photos. His mom was front and center; around her were pictures of Oliver on a tricycle, Oliver in a stroller, Oliver in a wading pool, clutching a rubber shark. It was like his dad wanted to freeze their family in time; nothing on display was even remotely current.

"Ollie, this is Christina Connelly," said his father. "You met at the wedding, remember? You were sitting next to her daughter, Jordan." Oliver swiveled around. He felt like he was moving in slow motion; it seemed to take him a half hour before he was actually facing her.

She stood up, this Christina person, and extended her hand. For a second, Oliver's weed-clouded brain could not make sense of this gesture, but he recovered and took it. Definitely not his dad's type: drab dress, hair pulled up and away from her face, no makeup.

"Oh, right." Jordan was the one who cut her food into teeny, tiny pieces, pushed it around on her plate, and called it eating.

"I'm interviewing Christina about a job," his father explained.

"A job?" What could this woman possibly do that his father would want?

"I'm planning to redecorate the apartment."

"Redecorate?" said Oliver. "Why? Everything looks okay around here. Everything looks *fine*." Oliver's head felt like it had come loose from his body and was floating somewhere up in the vicinity of the ceiling. He needed to sit down, and lowered himself onto his father's beige and cream tweed sofa, where he perched, tensely, at its edge; if you got, like, even one little spot on that sofa, Andy would pitch a fit. Was this one of the things in need of redecoration? Oliver could totally get down with that but not with anything else.

"Oliver, you're being rude," his father said. "What's the matter with you?"

"He doesn't want the home where his mother lived to be changed," said Christina.

"You get that?" Oliver was surprised. He would have guessed she'd say just the opposite.

"Of course. My husband died a number of years ago. For a long time, I wouldn't change anything in our house. I kept thinking that if he came back, he'd want things to be just the way he'd left them."

"Then you thought that too?" Oliver couldn't believe she was saying these words, this was *exactly* the way he felt about his mom.

"Thought what?" his father asked. Oliver ignored him.

"That the person who died is not really dead. That she's coming back, and it's your job to preserve everything so that she'll be able to find her way home," said Christina.

"That's it!" Oliver burst out, not caring how stoned he sounded. Christina Connelly was all right.

"What are you two talking about?" Andy seemed genuinely confused, and at another moment, Oliver might have relished this, but right now he was too busy looking at Christina.

"The dead," she replied. "And the way they won't move

on." She turned to Oliver. "I just want you to know that if your father decides to hire me, it won't be my goal to eradicate your mother's presence from the apartment. It will be to honor it."

Oliver looked at her, seeing, as if for the first time, the way her hair—light brown and very smooth—was swept off her face, the tiny earrings that pierced her lobes, the kind of retro summer dress she wore, which was not drab at all, but instead way cool, with a pattern of little birds all over it. "Sweet," he said, his face splitting into a wide, goofy grin. "Sweet."

Oliver trailed Christina and his dad to the door and waited while they said good-bye. Then he started to go back down the hall to his own room, but before he could make his escape, he heard his father's voice. "Could I see you about something?" *Yeah, whatever,* he was about to reply. But then he turned and went still; no words came out. There, dangling between his father's two tightly pinched fingers, was his missing bag of weed.

FIVE

hristina studied the house—a double-wide brick on Third Street—before mounting the steps. The bricks were pale, almost apricot, and both longer and narrower than the standard issue in the neighborhood. They were beautiful, even historic bricks. But they needed work.

If she got this job—and it was a big if—she would recommend repointing immediately. She would also address the other signs of neglect, like the big urn by the door, empty save for some weeds, that was peeling in long, curling strips, and the ancient metal trash cans—who even had metal cans anymore?—that were painfully battered.

It's a huge job, Mimi Farnsworth had told her. But a huge job was just what Christina needed, and she was grateful that Mimi had recommended her. *I feel like I owe you, Christina,* she said. *Seriously.* But Mimi's recommendation, while helpful, was not a guarantee. Christina still had to meet the owners, a wealthy hedge fund manager and his wife, and convince them to hire her.

Years ago, it was common to see these once-grand houses sink into ruin. Their owners had fled in the frenzy of white flight, and the architectural carcasses left behind had been carved up into apartments or single-room occupancies. Drug deals went down on corners that Christina knew enough to avoid when she was growing up here. There were bands of tough kids, angry, testosterone-juiced boys looking for an excuse to commit some petty crime. The girls who circled them were equally scary, with their thick eyeliner and thicker accents. Some of them went to the parochial school where Christina had been a favorite of the nuns; she knew they resented her exalted position and she kept her distance.

But things in Park Slope had changed. New money from Manhattan poured in, houses were bought, renovated, their prices shooting up along with their restored facades and fresh coats of plaster. If their house on Carroll Street had been worth what it was worth today, Christina's father would have sold it immediately and relocated to "the Island," as he called it; he had never gotten over his longing for the suburban dream of a freestanding dwelling, golf-course green lawn out front and patio with a grill out back.

The front windows of the Third Street house were open and Christina could hear voices coming from inside. "Stop!" said a woman. "I said no jumping on the sofa!" There was the sound of giggling and then a yelp. "Okay, that's it! Time-out for both of you!" Christina waited a minute before she rang the bell. "Coming!" called the same woman's voice. "Coming, coming, coming!" The door was pulled open and there stood Phoebe Haverstick, the woman who had recently inherited this derelict house. "Sorry for making you wait."

"Not a problem," said Christina. There were no signs of the children she'd just heard.

"Anyway, please come in. The place is a mess." Phoebe used a well-muscled forearm to brush the hair from her face. She was a sturdy, athletic-looking sort, with tanned, powerful limbs revealed by her gray shorts and white tank top.

"Yes, you'd said your great-aunt hadn't touched it in what—forty years?"

"Make that fifty," said Phoebe. "Can I get you something?"

"Nothing for now," said Christina. She followed Phoebe past the foyer into the parlor. There, she actually gasped. The entire room—walls, ceiling, furniture, carpeting, even the baby grand piano that stood at the far end—had been painted or upholstered in the same celestial shade of blue. "Please, sit down." Phoebe gestured to a Louis XVI sofa covered in shredding pale blue silk. Christina hesitated but then saw that all the furniture in the room—the matching Louis XVI chairs, blue velvet settee—was in an equally deteriorated condition, and so she perched carefully on the sofa's edge.

"She certainly had a point of view," Christina began.

"Did she ever! Wait until you see the rest of the place." Phoebe had flopped down on the velvet love seat, drawing her strong legs—she'd played field hockey in school, no doubt about it—under her.

"How long did she live here?" Christina let her eyes travel the room. No paintings, but a large mirror in a sky blue frame hung above the sky blue mantelpiece, and several smaller mirrors were dispersed on other walls.

"Her parents bought the house in 1915—she was about five years old. She lived here her whole life. Never married, never moved."

Christina reached into her bag and pulled out a black Moleskine notebook. "I'll want to see the whole thing, of course. But I want to hear more about you first—what your goals for the house are. How you envision it changing and growing along with your family. Then I can tell you about how I might help you." As if the word *family* were the prompt, there was a thud and then a shriek, both emanating from somewhere above.

Phoebe leapt up and sprinted toward the sound. Christina followed more slowly, climbing the center staircase that was covered, of course, in balding sky blue carpeting.

Upstairs, the monochromatic motif continued, but now in a pale, buttery color. In one of the golden rooms, Phoebe introduced Christina to her two daughters; the seven-year-old, Torry, was the namesake of Great-aunt Victoria. Once the girls were safely parked in front of Phoebe's laptop, Phoebe showed Christina the upper two floors, one done in lilac and the top one in pink.

When they were through, they went back down to the blue floor again. Christina had a brief, irrational desire to tell Phoebe to leave all of it, every last stained and shredded scrap, intact. But of course she would not say such a thing, and anyway, how ridiculously impractical would that be? Phoebe needed a more family-friendly kind of space; she had two daughters—*and a third on the way*, she had said confidingly, patting the front of her shirt. Christina had not realized she was pregnant, but now she saw it, the barely perceptible bulge. The woman was so taut and solid it was easy to miss.

Back in the parlor, Christina asked more questions, took notes, and began formulating a plan. She wanted to maintain these light colors, but give them a more relaxed, contemporary spin. The moldings, pocket doors, and the like—those hard-to-replicate details that made these old houses so prized—she would recommend keeping, though she envisioned low-slung, informal furniture, bright rugs, and natural wood.

Phoebe listened intently, and spent a long time looking through the book of photos Christina had brought. Finally, Christina got up to leave.

"I'll be in touch," Phoebe said as they walked to the door. "And I do like your ideas for the nursery. A sweet, safe little space where I can bond with the baby."

"An oasis," said Christina, extending her hand. "A home within a home."

"Exactly!" Phoebe took her hand and shook it vigorously. She had a grip like a python and Christina resisted the impulse to massage her own hand until she was on the street and safely out of her sight. When she turned the corner onto Carroll Street, she noticed a man with a turban standing in front of what she judged to be her house. At his side stood a woman and a child. Both wore scarlet saris; Christina assumed they were mother and daughter. And yes, they were all standing directly in front of her house. Why? But before she could ask, they saw her and, appearing startled, retreated. The man ushered the woman and child into a black Mercedes that had been double-parked by the curb, and the driver took off, driving much too quickly down the street. She did not see the plates on the car, only two heads—hers sleek and dark, his swathed in its nimbus of white—as the car sped away.

The sound of a door opening attracted her attention and she turned to see one of her next-door neighbors, Charlotte Bickford, standing on the stoop with a sour expression on her face. Had she noticed the Indian family too? But Christina would not ask; she thought Charlotte—who never cleaned up after her wretched little dog and whose loud, drunken shouting matches with her husband were often audible—was a detestable person and she kept her distance.

Christina wondered about the Indians as she let herself

inside. Yes, Park Slope had become a much more moneyed enclave in recent years. Still, this block and certainly her house were hardly the most outstanding examples of what the neighborhood had to offer. Why were those people looking at it? And why had they sped off when they saw her? They had seemed almost . . . guilty. But of what?

SIX

*T*he sun was just coming up as Christina drove across the Brooklyn Bridge the following Saturday. There was scarcely any traffic and the white Saab sped merrily along, its windows rolled down to admit the breeze. The illuminated green numbers on the dashboard read 5:26; she'd be at Andy Stern's apartment by 6:15. She slid a CD—*South Pacific*—into the car's player and sang the words to "Happy Talk" right out loud along with the recording. She'd never, *ever* sing if anyone else was in earshot, but the warm June morning, with its pink-gold sky and fleecy clouds, was hers alone and she could indulge. Besides, she was in a good mood. Mimi had called to say Phoebe Haverstick had really liked her vision for the house and, while the job was not yet hers, she was in serious contention. And surprisingly, the job with Andy Stern had not been nearly as bad as she had anticipated.

She was over the bridge in a matter of minutes, and followed the signs for the FDR Drive. Now she could see the East River on her right, its rippling surface turned dull pewter in the morning light. Andy's apartment had views of this river, and he did love them; appalling as Christina found the building, she found they seduced her too.

The FDR was as scantily trafficked as the bridge, and she decided to get off at the Sixty-first Street exit, park the car—an urban miracle—and duck into a café on First Avenue. She bought a latte and a scone; she enjoyed both while sitting in the parked Saab across from Andy's building on East Sixty-ninth Street. She would have bought Andy a latte and a scone too, but she'd already been exposed to his tedious views on eating and didn't think he'd permit himself either.

At exactly six fifteen, he emerged from the building's doorway. He wore pressed khakis and one of those shirts with an alligator appliqué sewn on the front of it. The shirt was more revealing than the usual button-downs and blazers she'd seen him wearing and she had to admit that he was certainly in great shape, very lean and muscled. Slung across a shoulder was a backpack with the linked initials *RL* stitched all over its surface. Did he wear *anything* that didn't double as an advertising platform? Well, yes—the logoless baseball cap that was on his head.

"You're right on time," Andy said as he opened the door and slid into the passenger seat. The backpack came off and was stowed by his feet.

"There wasn't any traffic," she said.

"You'd have been on time even if there had been traffic." His approval was evident.

Christina just smiled. They were on their way to an estate sale in Dutchess County that had sounded promising; she'd mentioned to Andy that she was planning to go and he'd surprised her by asking if he could tag along. She was looking for a mirror, a coffee table, and the small chest of drawers she'd envisioned to replace his current nightstand. His apartment had been decorated by a notable downtown firm and was quite austere, with lots of sharp angles and sleek surfaces; the color scheme was confined to a muted palette of gray, ivory, taupe, and black. Christina could recognize the intelligence of the design and appreciate the care with which it had been executed, but it left her cold. Andy said he had loved the decor at first, less so now. "When Rachel was alive, she seemed to give the place personality," he said. "But now that she's not . . ." He said he wanted more of everything: more color, more pattern, more texture.

"So you think we can get there by nine?" he was saying now, strapping the seat belt across his chest. He consulted his watch—he did this constantly—a bulbous, complicated thing crammed with tiny dials that indicated the time not only all over the world but most likely on several nearby planets as well.

"Depends on the traffic," Christina said.

He nodded, still looking at the watch. Then he looked up. "Have you eaten?"

She nodded. "But if you're hungry, we could stop along the way."

"No, I come prepared," he said, and reached into the backpack to produce a power bar that was identical to the ones Jordan seemed to think were an essential food group. "We can split it if you like."

"No, thanks," Christina said. She'd tried one of those bars—never again.

"Twenty grams of protein in here," Andy said, opening the foil wrapper. "And seven grams of fiber."

Christina tried to keep her face a blank; why would anyone eat something that tasted so awful, protein and fiber
notwithstanding? She concentrated on getting back onto the
FDR, and then onto Harlem River Drive. Traffic slowed for a
while; an accident up ahead turned the stream of cars into a
trickle. But things opened up again and soon they were on
I-95, heading north. She glanced over at Andy. His eyes were
closed and he appeared to be dozing; the empty power bar
wrapper was in his lap. She was relieved, actually, not to have
to make small talk with him. He could be bossy and brusque
and she'd had to contend with his pen-tapping-wristwatch-
checking brand of impatience. But he was also willing to consider her suggestions with an open mind, and was refreshingly
decisive, a rarity among clients. In the three or so weeks since
she'd been working for him, he had selected all the paint
colors, decided on a very expensive new rug for the living
room, and approved her purchase of a new lamp, as well as a
cunning little movable bar that was designed to look like an
old steamer trunk.

She glanced out the side window. I-95 was so boring—the
occasional rest stop, endless signs for McDonald's, Wendy's,
and their kin—and she wished she could have turned on
South Pacific again. But it seemed rude to wake Andy, and
though she had headphones buried somewhere in the car,
there was no way she could dig them out now. So she drove in
silence, plotting her course at the sale. Caryn Braider needed
a sofa and an armoire; she was also looking for a wrought iron
chandelier and a folding screen—if she could find such a
thing. Then there was the Haverstick house, but Christina
wasn't going to buy a thing for that; it might jinx her chances
of getting the job. She was able to keep these running lists in

her mind, though in the backseat, alongside her ample tote bag, was a three-ring binder with all this information and more—dimension requirements, color and material preferences, price ranges, fabric swatches, and paint chips. Inside the tote itself were a flashlight, rope, rubber gloves, sunblock, a baseball cap, a plastic rain poncho, and a bottle of water—she came prepared. Even her outfit—worn chinos, white T-shirt, Keds—was utilitarian rather than fashionable. Her only nod to self-adornment today was the handwoven belt she'd bought on a trip to Mexico some years ago and her silver bangle.

Andy woke up just as they were pulling up to the house. He pressed his hands to his face. "I must have conked out."

"You slept almost all the way up here," Christina said. The dashboard clock said eight fifty; the sale started at nine. There were already cars parked and waiting; a couple of them had New York plates.

"I performed an emergency C-section last night," Andy explained. "I didn't get to bed until three o'clock."

"Three o'clock!" said Christina. "You should have told me—I would have understood if you needed to cancel."

"That's all right," Andy said. "I was looking forward to driving up here with you. It's a nice change of pace."

Christina grabbed her bag and binder and got out of the car. Then she and Andy walked across the lawn toward the house, which was set back behind a low and serpentine stone wall. She loved walls like this, each stone selected and set in by hand, the whole thing kept together by the dynamic tension of the parts. A house with a wall like this had promise, and her heart started its eager, anticipatory thrumming as they got closer.

This was the best part of her work—the hunt, and the

sifting through the accumulated possessions of the dead, their precious lives both revealed and defined by what they had chosen to keep. In a way, she hated to carve it all up, the books and bibelots, the rugs, the furniture, the collections of candlesticks and teacups, thimbles and botanical prints. But she couldn't buy it all, much as she sometimes wanted to. No, the accretion of these particular objects was over now; their story had ended. It was time for these things to return to the stream again, ready to be scooped up and made part of someone else's life.

"Hey, wait for me," Andy said as he came up behind her.

"Sorry," she said. "I didn't mean to get ahead."

"You were practically jogging," he said.

"I just get excited, that's all." She was at the house now, taking her place beside the other people waiting there. Just then the door opened and a frosted blonde with pale pink lipstick greeted them.

"Welcome, folks," she said. "Most everything is marked; if it's not, just come and see me. There's stuff in all the downstairs rooms. Second floor too, though not the rooms with the red tape Xs on the doors; the stuff in there has been claimed by the family or sold already." She had the eager air of a den mother about to release her charges into the wild. "Happy hunting!"

She stepped aside; the small group entered and quickly dispersed. Christina immediately went upstairs; if there was an armoire, it was likely to be up there. Andy trailed behind, but she barely noticed him; she had caught the scent and was not easily distracted. She made a quick tour of the rooms on the second floor. No armoire, but a big mirror shaped like a sunburst sat on the floor, propped against a wall. It was a gaudy thing, probably from the 1960s, but was also kind of wonderful in its way. And it might work very well in Andy's place.

"What do you think?" she asked.

"It's a little over the top," he said, kneeling down for a better look. "But I kind of like it."

"So do I." She checked the price: two hundred dollars.

"Seems reasonable," Andy said.

"It is. But I can get it for less."

His eyebrows moved up. "Really?"

"Really." Christina left Andy standing watch while she went to find the woman with the frosted hair. After a few minutes of polite but firm negotiation, Christina had gotten the price down to one hundred and seventy dollars. A red SOLD sign was taped to the mirror.

"Hey, you're good," Andy said as he followed her into the next room. "*Very* good, in fact."

"Thanks," she said. "I have plenty of experience."

There was nothing else of interest upstairs, but downstairs, in the sunroom, Christina found an ottoman in mahogany leather that Andy loved and a box stuffed with vintage tablecloths, napkins, runners, dresser scarves, and doilies. Many were yellowed or stained, but she could bleach and restore them. She didn't have an immediate use for these linens; still, they were of too high a quality to pass up. Some of the runners had handmade lace trim and the jacquard weave of the napkins was exceptionally fine. She bought the whole batch for twenty-eight dollars. The dining room yielded an assortment of crystal glasses and goblets for any drink imaginable: champagne, wine, port, sherry, sidecar, and old-fashioned. And because they were odd pieces, they were only a dollar each.

"You have to get these," Christina said to Andy, guarding the table where the glasses were grouped. "We can use some of them up in the bar we bought."

"I have plenty of glasses," he said.

She lowered her voice. "These are Baccarat. And they're *old*. They'll be perfect in that bar."

"How do you know that they're Baccarat?"

"Trust me," she said. "I know." Counting thirty-three pieces, she offered the woman with the frosted hair twenty-five dollars for the whole lot and then stood wrapping each one in a sheet of newspaper—some dating from the 1970s—because she did not trust anyone else to do it. When she was done, there were smears of newsprint on her white T-shirt and her hands were grimy.

Once the glasses were safely packed, Christina continued her hunt. Yes, there was a sofa, with pretty curving legs and down cushions, but Caryn wanted something more modern and she herself had nowhere to put it—her showroom was packed—so she reluctantly let it go. She did buy several un-framed needlepoints that she would turn into pillows, as well as another small oval mirror in a simple cherry frame, a bat-tered watering can, and a star-shaped nail cup—used, she told Andy, by cobblers to hold their various-sized fasteners. "How do you *know* this stuff?" Andy said as she picked it up to test the heft of it. Sometimes weight alone decided her; she hated anything that felt too flimsy or cheap.

"On-the-job training," she said. The nail cup felt agreeably heavy in her hands; she would buy it.

"What are you going to do with it anyway? You can't have too many clients who are cobblers."

"Once it's been cleaned up, it will make an excellent serving piece—see all these little compartments? They're perfect for setting out different foods. You can put olives in one, roasted peppers in another, nuts in another." Christina loved this kind of repurposing; it involved a certain slant of mind to take something intended for one use and put that thing to an entirely different one.

It was close to noon by the time they emerged from the house; by this time, the sky had grayed a bit and in the distance, a bank of clouds lay low on the horizon. It had gotten warmer too; Christina felt a fine sheen of sweat coating her face and arms. Andy helped her put all their purchases into the car. "I'm starved," he said. "Do you have time to stop for something to eat?"

"I know a diner not too far from here," she said. "They serve the best coconut custard pie; they make it right there." As soon as she said it, she realized that Andy wasn't about to eat a piece of pie. It was like being with Jordan. Still, she was hungry and needed some food before getting on the road again. Andy Stern could order what he wanted; *she* was having pie for dessert.

Christina located a box of baby wipes in the car and used several to clean her hands and face; she offered the box to Andy, but he shook his head. He seemed as fresh as he had this morning. Christina drove in the direction of the diner. "It's coming right up," she said. That red barn was familiar, and also that white church with the graceful steeple. Now there was a fork in the road and she needed to bear right—

"Whoa!" Andy said. "What's *that*?"

The car gave a convulsive shudder and sputtered for a few seconds, seconds in which Christina was able to get over to the side of the road, and out of the line of traffic—not that there was any traffic; they seemed to be on their own here. Once the car was at the shoulder, the shuddering—and everything else—stopped.

Christina turned off the ignition and got out to inspect. She gamely popped the hood and peered inside, hoping she might somehow identify the problem. "I don't see anything," she said. Not that she knew what she was looking for; her ability to tend to her car was confined to empty gas tanks, flat tires, and overheating.

"Do you think it's the battery?" Andy said. "Or the fuel pump?"

"I'm not sure," she said. "But whatever it is, we're going to need help." She tried not to let her alarm show. What was wrong? How expensive would it be to fix? What if it couldn't be fixed? She *had* to have a car; it was imperative for her work.

Andy seemed oblivious to her rising panic. "Help," he said. "Right." He pulled out his phone and began to punch some numbers in. His face settled into a scowl as his tapping on the keys grew more agitated. "I can't get a signal," he said. "We must be in some dead zone."

"Really?" She reached into the backseat to get her phone. The result was the same. "I can't believe it," she said. They looked at each other for a long, uncomfortable moment. Was Andy going to blame her for this? Would she end up losing this job? And the day had been going so well too. "Maybe we can flag someone down," she said, trying to sound hopeful.

"*If* there's someone to flag down," he said. He was right. In the several minutes they had been stranded here, not a single car had passed. It was a strange, even eerie feeling. Christina thought of the church and the barn they had passed; how far back were they? And how far ahead was the diner? Surely someone would be on this road in search of it; that pie was so good it was a destination experience.

They positioned themselves by the stalled car, looking anxiously down the road. The sound of an engine in the distance was promising; maybe this would be their salvation. But the car tore past them it must have been doing fifty—without its driver giving them so much as a glance. "Speed demon," Christina said. "And on a winding road like this too."

Andy coughed a bit from the road dust the car had left in its wake but didn't reply. She saw him consult his watch, and tried to see things from his point of view. Hadn't he said that he'd performed an emergency C-section last night? He was probably thinking of his patient.

They waited a few more minutes. The day had grown progressively more humid, and Christina was sticky in her pants and dirty shirt. She was also ravenous; that coffee and scone had been hours ago. She glanced at Andy. His eyes were still fixed on the road. Again, they both brightened at the sound of an engine; this time, it was a leather-clad guy on a motorcycle who zoomed by. If that car had been doing fifty, the motorcycle was doing seventy.

"Damn!" Andy said. He stood staring at the quickly vanishing sight of the cyclist.

"Maybe we should start walking," she said.

"Where?"

"Up ahead. Toward the diner. There has to be a phone there we can use."

"How far is it?" asked Andy.

"A mile," she said, though it could have been two. "We can do it."

"I guess we'll have to," said Andy. Eyeing her sneakers, he added, "Good thing you're not in heels."

Christina felt stung. As if she would be so stupid. He *did* blame her in some way for what had happened; his comment made it clear. Of course he wasn't even thinking of what this might mean to her financially; he was too dense and self-involved to think of that. She retrieved her money, phone, keys, and sunglasses from the car. The bulky tote and the binder, both covered by the blanket she kept in the trunk, were left behind. Then they set off.

As they walked, the air was hot and still. Mosquitoes buzzed and Christina angrily swatted them away. The road was lined on either side with trees, trees, and more trees. She saw no sign of a building anywhere. A mosquito landed smack in the center of her forehead; even though she slapped it, the welt it raised began to itch almost immediately. After about fifteen minutes, the sky began to turn perceptibly darker and the clouds overhead had thickened, forming an ominous gray blanket above.

"How far did you say it was?" Andy asked finally.

"A mile or so."

"Or so," he repeated.

"I never measured it exactly." She tried not to claw at her forehead; she would only make herself bleed.

"Uh-huh." They continued walking, the silence as heavy as the clouds.

"Look, I'm sorry."

"I'm sure you are." It sounded like a reproach.

Christina was willing herself to compose a tactful reply when he stopped, pulled out his cell phone, and again tried making a call. Something seemed to be happening on the other end because she heard him say "Hello? Can you hear me? *Hello?*" He held the phone to his ear but after a few seconds took it away. "Dropped call."

"Let me try," she said, reaching for her own phone.

"What for? Why do you think your phone will work when mine didn't?"

How rude. Still, she needed this job. She could control herself; she *had* to control herself—she would start with her hair, pulled up and off her face in its usual twist, which had started to come undone. Vainly she tried to pat it back into place without the aid of a mirror, brush, or comb. "Andy, I know you're upset. And I've said I'm sorry. But it's hardly my fault that—"

"Upset!" he interrupted. "Upset! You bet I'm upset! I'm stuck out here in the middle of nowhere, I'm hungry enough to eat my belt, I can't reach my service, I don't know *how* my patient is, and I have no idea when I'll be able to find out." He was fairly panting with indignation.

Christina had had enough. Job or no job, she wasn't going to be talked to this way. Andy wasn't the only one feeling the stress. She was mosquito bitten, sweaty, dirty, and just as starved as he was. And she would no doubt have to contend with a ruinous bill for the car when she finally got it towed. But before she could open her mouth to tell him off, there was a loud clap of thunder in the dark sky above and then a virtual torrent of water began to pour down all around them.

"And now it's raining!" said Andy. "That's great. Just *great*."

"So are you going to stand here and complain?" she shot back. "Or are you going to try to come up with a constructive solution?" She was gratified to see a look of surprise cross his arrogant face. Good. If he was going to dish it out, he'd better learn to take it too. Christina started walking again, this time even more quickly than before. There had to be some form of help along this road—a store, a service station, a house, something—there just *had* to. After a few seconds, Andy started walking too. His stride was longer and he caught up right away. Christina did not look at him, though; she didn't want to. Instead, she concentrated on putting one foot in front of the other, though in a matter of minutes, both feet were thoroughly drenched. So was her hair—a limp, bedraggled mess, she was sure—and the rest of her. She thought miserably of the rain poncho back in the car. Why, oh *why* hadn't she thought to bring it along? And she was so hungry! If Andy had had another one of those protein bars, she would have eaten it in two bites, leathery texture and all. As it was, she trudged on in grim silence.

Rain was trickling down into her ears now, and rain was sloshing around in her sneakers; with every step she took, there was a soft, squelching sound. She didn't even mind. The water was soothing to her multiple insect bites and it was rinsing away the sweat and the newsprint too. It might even wash her shirt. She looked down, almost as a reflex. Oh no! The torrential rain had plastered the soft white material to her body and the sheer bra she wore was no protection at all. Her nipples were totally visible through the thin cloth; she could have entered a wet T-shirt contest—and won.

Instinctively, she crossed her arms over her chest. Had Andy noticed? She hoped not. She realized that she might be calling even more attention to her predicament, but she didn't care. Once more, her face felt hot, though this time it was from shame. Once a Catholic girl, always a Catholic girl. She remembered how Sister Bernadette would advise them to wear a second layer underneath anything light, white, or sheer. Good advice if she'd bothered to take it. Christina risked looking over at Andy; his face, in profile, betrayed nothing. But then he did an astonishing thing: he peeled the bright red shirt—also sopping—from his body and handed it to her. "Here," he said. "You can put this on."

"Excuse me?" She took the shirt.

"Go ahead," he instructed. "I know it's soaked, but it's the only thing I have." When she continued to stand there— unsettled by both the gesture and the sight of his bare, muscular chest, slick with rainwater— he added, "You'll be more comfortable if you put it on." She nodded and quickly yanked the thing over her head.

"Thank you," she said. "Thank you very much." What a relief to be covered.

"You're welcome," he replied with great courtesy.

What a contradictory man. Before she could say anything else, he began, to her surprise, to sing. *"I'm gonna wash that man right outta my hair,"* he sang in a respectable baritone. When Christina said nothing, he stopped. "Come on," he said. "You have to sing too."

"Me?" she asked, surprised.

"Yes, you. I know you know the words."

"What makes you say that?"

"I saw the CD case in your car. You were listening to it. Maybe even today."

"I was," she admitted. "I love that musical."

"So do I," he said. "So come on, sing. Sing with me."

"Oh Andy, I don't know. . . . I feel so silly."

"Any sillier than me?" He gestured to his naked torso and wet pants. When she didn't answer, he took up the song again, and this time, she joined in, tentatively at first. *"I'm gonna wave that man right outta my arms."* The blending of their voices, hers higher and lighter, his deeper and richer, actually sounded all right together. No, they sounded *good*.

Surprised at herself, Christina sang louder, and with greater enthusiasm. Andy kept time with his hand, drops of water flying from his moving fingers. They sang the song again, from the beginning, and then moved on—easily, naturally—to some of the other songs too—"I'm in Love with a Wonderful Guy," "Younger Than Springtime," "Some Enchanted Evening"—from the same musical. Christina was so engrossed that when Andy stopped singing, she was actually disappointed. "What's the matter?" she asked. "Am I out of tune?"

"Look," he said, pointing straight ahead. There was the diner they'd been headed toward, its pink and green neon sign a welcome beacon in the rain. "Let's go in. You can order a piece of that coconut custard pie you've been telling me about while we're waiting for the tow truck—it's my treat." And he pushed open the door, allowing her to enter.

SEVEN

*A*fter the brutal heat of the sidewalk, Andy was grateful to step into the florist's at the corner of Sixty-ninth and Lexington. An air conditioner was humming and the cooled shop was heady with scent. "Hello, Dr. Stern. What can I do for you this evening?"

Andy looked over to see Gus Hendelman, the owner. Under a recessed light in the ceiling, Gus's bald spot shone brightly. He had patronized Gus's shop for years; whenever he needed to send flowers to a patient, colleague, or friend, this was where he came. He'd had a standing order of two dozen yellow roses for Rachel's birthday, their wedding anniversary, Mother's and Valentine's Day; he'd ordered a massive spray of those same yellow roses to adorn her plain, pine casket, for which Gus had refused payment.

"Hi, Gus. I'll need a small bouquet and I'll be taking it with me."

"Then I'll wrap them carefully so they won't wilt," Gus said.

Andy picked out a few asters, sweet William, and roses in pink and red; Gus added some greens and put the whole thing in some kind of rustic, rough-hewn basket. "The ladies just love these things," he said.

Back outside, the blazing disk of the sun was still visible in the sky. Andy walked east, toward Third Avenue and the Atlantic Grill, another place where he'd been a regular for years. He was meeting Jen and he was eager to see her. The date he'd broken to deliver Linda McConnell's baby had not been successfully rescheduled until tonight. Jen had been out of town on business, and he'd had what seemed, even for a practice like his, an unusual number of emergencies. But tonight they would finally be able to get together.

Andy was already planning the evening. He'd bring the flowers to the table, where they could remain while they ate; Jen would like that sort of romantic gesture and he enjoyed pleasing her. Then it would be a short walk back to her apartment on Seventy-ninth Street, where he would tenderly and ceremoniously remove each of her garments and fuck her silly on the queen-sized bed in her room. Just thinking about it got him stiff. He could admit to himself that while he liked Jen, he didn't love her. But he was profoundly grateful for the pleasure he derived from her lithe, pretty body. That body did not make him forget Rachel, but still.

Just as Andy reached the restaurant, his phone buzzed. Jen! "Slight change in plans, darling," she said. "David just canceled at the last minute and I can't get a sitter for Drew on such short notice."

"Do you want to make it another night?" He hoped she'd say no.

"Why don't you come here? I'll order takeout and we can watch a movie. Or something."

"Or something." He was relieved she wasn't canceling. "I'm in the neighborhood; I'll be right over."

Andy walked the few blocks quickly and announced himself to the doorman. Jen was waiting at the door. Her wavy blond hair tumbled appealingly around her shoulders and she was dressed in a short black skirt and high-heeled gold sandals that made her tanned legs look a mile long. Above the skirt she wore a silky green top and a chain with a medallion that nestled between her small, pert breasts. He handed her the flowers, an offering that elicited small coos of delight. "You look terrific," he said, his gaze traveling slowly up her body and back down again.

"Thanks," she said. "And for these—they're gorgeous."

"You're welcome." He took her in his arms then, inhaled her fragrance. She did feel good, all silky hair and golden skin. He wanted to lead her into the bedroom *now*—dinner could definitely wait. But then, over her shoulder, he saw a little blond girl looking up at him, eyes opaque, mouth a straight, unsmiling line. Drew. Jen must have sensed the change; she turned in the direction of his gaze.

"Drew, this is Mommy's friend Andy. Come and say hello." Drew said nothing but continued to stare at Andy. Andy was discomfited by her stare, and stepped back. It seemed wrong to be embracing Jen in front of this disapproving child. "Drew," Jen repeated, a touch more sharply than Andy thought necessary, "I told you to say hello." Drew said nothing and instead popped her thumb into her mouth.

"Would you stop that?" said Jen, and when Drew did not remove her thumb from her mouth, she reached over and tugged gently on her wrist. Drew dropped her hand; her thumb, still glistening, grazed the edge of her dress.

"It's the divorce," Jen said to Andy. "Makes her regress.

And of course it doesn't help that David canceled at the last minute." She smoothed a blond wave from her face. "He's such a prick." Andy flinched at the word, tossed off so casually. Not that he was a prude. Still, her daughter was right there and David *was* her father. He looked at Drew: no reaction. But when Jen looked away, the small thumb went right back into her mouth.

Dinner was strained. Andy ate his sushi because he was hungry, but it was merely fuel, not enjoyment. Drew picked at her *gyoza*; Jen was impatient and scolded her several times. When the meal was over, Jen excused herself to put Drew to bed. Andy waited in the living room, channel surfing on the large, flat-screen television. He watched a few minutes of a *Law & Order* rerun he'd seen before, then switched to a cooking show, and finally settled into *Casablanca* on TCM. Jen returned just as Ingrid Bergman's lovely face—an unusual combination of refinement and sensuality—filled the screen. "Finally!" she said, settling down beside him. "I thought she'd never go to sleep." She began to nuzzle his neck, planting tiny kisses behind his ear. Usually this turned him on, but he couldn't shake the memory of that small, grave face. "Hey," Jen said, sitting up. "What's the matter?"

"Nothing," he said. Now Humphrey Bogart had come into the frame.

"Liar," she said. "You're like ice."

"I'm not," he said, turning his eyes reluctantly from the television screen to look at her. She *was* pretty, with full lips and big brown eyes; she had accentuated them with some kind of bronze, sparkly powder. He kissed her then, sending his tongue deeply into her open mouth. Maybe the evening could be saved. Caressing her throat, he let his hand graze the skin exposed by the opening in her blouse. He felt himself getting hard. "Let's go into the bedroom—" Andy stopped, sensing someone behind him. He didn't need to turn around to know who it was.

"Drew!" Jen pulled away, flushed and annoyed. "Why aren't you asleep?"

"I *couldn't* sleep, Mommy." She put her thumb in her mouth and began to suck vigorously. Andy realized this was the first time he had heard her speak.

"Well, it's back to bed for you," Jen said. She got up and tried to pull the hand away from Drew's face, only this time, Drew would not budge. Jen tried again, a little harder, and Drew uttered a tiny sound, somewhere between a grunt and a mew: clearly Jen had hurt her. But Drew won this round: the thumb remained planted firmly in her mouth. "I'll just be a few minutes," she said to Andy.

"That's all right." Andy stood up. "I'm really tired. Wiped out, in fact. Why don't I phone you tomorrow?"

"But I won't be long," she said.

"It's okay." Andy moved toward the door. Jen looked disappointed. God, he hated to disappoint a woman. But the mood had been broken. If he waited and let Jen tempt him back to bed, his heart would not be in it and he really, truly didn't want that. It had taken him nearly two years to get to the point of feeling something, anything, for a woman again; that feeling was too new and too precious to taint.

"I'll call you," he said. He walked to the door and said good night with only a chaste peck on her cheek.

Outside, it was darker but not appreciably cooler. Andy walked slowly downtown, toward his apartment. He was in no hurry to go home. He'd been looking forward to seeing—and,

okay, screwing—Jen, but the evening had been ruined.
Couldn't she see how her kid was hurting? It was so clear. But
then he thought of Oliver; was he any more clued in? After the
discovery of the Baggie filled with pot under Oliver's pillow,
there had been the obligatory *just-say-no-to-drugs* talk. Oliver
had made a show of listening, said he was sorry, and promised
to stay on the straight and narrow. Andy believed not a word
of it, but what could he do? The kid had started seeing the
school-vetted shrink a couple of weeks ago. Maybe it would
help; Andy certainly hoped so. If Oliver got himself kicked out
of Morningside, there weren't too many options left.

He stood at the corner of Seventy-second Street, waiting
for the light to change. He wasn't on call tonight: a rare evening of freedom. So what could he do with it? He'd already
eaten dinner and he wasn't the sort to sit in a bar by himself.
It was too late for the theater or a concert and somehow a
movie didn't seem appealing. What he really wanted to do, he
realized, was see Christina Connelly. Ever since her little
wardrobe malfunction, he found himself thinking about her
in an altogether new way. Before, she'd struck him as prim
and sexless, but that brief glimpse of her breasts—perfectly
outlined by the wet shirt, their pinkish nipples erect—had
been wildly erotic. Or would have had she not been so utterly
mortified; he had seen the embarrassment register on her face
with the force of a slap. So instead of enjoying a sexy or even
humorous moment—he imagined another woman might have
just laughed it off—he found himself behaving in a chival-
rous, old-fashioned way. Offering his shirt had been such a
throwback it was almost comic, except that her profound gratitude made it anything but. He decided not to mention it
then—or ever—and once they had started singing and found
the diner, the equilibrium between them had been restored.

Except now, here he was, alone on a steamy night in late June, feeling like things had been totally upended again. Was it too late to phone her? He checked his watch; it wasn't even nine. Still, he'd never called her outside of business hours. And even if he did call, what would he say? *Hi, I've been thinking about how great you looked in that wet shirt.*

Andy realized he was standing in front of the florist again. The gate was partially down, but the lights were still on and he could see Gus moving around inside. When Gus looked up and saw Andy, he waved and motioned for him to come in. Andy bent down to slip under the gate as Gus unlocked the door. "I didn't expect to see you again tonight, Dr. Stern. How did she like the flowers?"

"She loved them," Andy said. God, he sounded glum.

"Good," said Gus. "We aim to please." He swept a large pile of leaves and stems into a green garbage bag, and then wiped down the work space with a sponge.

"You're here late," Andy observed.

"Last-minute request from an old customer," Gus said. "And I never like to say no to an old customer." He straightened a pile of green aprons—they reminded Andy of scrubs—on a shelf above the sink. "Remember, anytime you need another bouquet for the lady, you let me know," said Gus. Reaching up, he started switching off the lights.

"Probably not for *that* lady," Andy said. As soon as the words were out, he knew it was true. Something had changed in his perception of Jen tonight; everything about her felt suddenly wrong.

"Oh," said Gus. "I see."

"I thought she might be the right one, but now I'm not so sure." Gus nodded sympathetically and walked to the door, Andy following. When they had both gone under the gate,

Andy stood there while Gus finished pulling it down and locking up.

"How long have you been married?" Andy surprised himself with the question. He'd never talked to Gus in this way before.

"Thirty-seven years," Gus said. "Thirty-seven years, three kids, five grandkids." He fished in his pocket to retrieve his phone and scrolled down. Then he held out the phone so Andy could see the attractive woman with ash-blond hair and a wide, easy smile. Tiny wrinkles fanned out from her eyes, and her arms were extended around a bevy of children.

"Nice family," Andy said. They were standing on the corner of Sixty-ninth Street and he had no desire to go home. "I was just going to stop in somewhere for a glass of wine." Not exactly true, but as soon as he said it, he thought, *Why not?* "Maybe you'd like to join me."

"You know, that would be great. The wife's out in Jersey this weekend; she's helping our daughter throw a birthday party for the three-year-old. The place seems kind of lonely without her."

Tell me about it, Andy thought as he and Gus headed uptown and east, to a wine bar just below Seventy-second Street.

"So this lady—what's she like?" Gus asked when they were seated. While Andy told him, their order arrived.

"Give it another chance," Gus said, reaching for a slice of his mini-pizza.

"You think?" Andy sipped his white wine. If he hadn't already eaten, he would have ordered one of those pizzas—it was topped with golden peppers and roast duck breast and looked delicious. But no way was he eating dinner twice.

"I do. You said she's the first woman to make you feel anything since your wife's death. That's big, Dr. Stern. Really big."

"Please—call me Andy."

Gus took a long sip of his red wine. "Andy." He put down the glass. "Maybe she was just having an off night with her kid; everyone loses it once in a while."

"I'll drink to that," Andy said, raising his glass. Gus raised his too and for the first time all evening, Andy actually felt okay. When he saw that Gus's wineglass was empty, he added, "How about another round?"

By the time they left, it was almost midnight. Andy walked into his building, nodding to the night doorman. When he opened the door to his apartment, he found it still and dark; Oliver had texted him to say he was spending the night with a friend. What else was new? Andy went into the kitchen and poured himself a glass of filtered water; whenever he drank wine, he always made sure to take this precaution against a hangover the next day.

He walked into the living room. There was the bar-shaped-like-a-trunk that Christina had found for him; lined up on its shelves were the crystal glasses she'd urged him to buy. On the far wall hung that crazy mirror she'd found at the estate sale; they had thought it would work in the bedroom, but they both thought it looked better in here.

Andy drained the water from the glass. He'd decided to give it another chance with Jen, and that was what he would do. But he was now pricked by the desire to ask Gus to create a small yet stunning arrangement, of white—and only white—flowers, and when it was complete in its snowy perfection, send it to Brooklyn, to the home of Christina Connelly.

EIGHT

*O*liver walked into the Dakota, a ginormous structure on the corner of Seventy-second Street and Central Park West that looked like a cross between a wedding cake and a castle; Delphine had just texted him that it was okay to come over and so here he was. He gave his name to a guy in a fancy uniform with gold buttons and gold braiding everywhere. He waited while Gold Buttons called upstairs and waited some more before he was directed to the elevator.

Delphine was at the door. "Hello," she said. Except it sounded like *Allo* and it gave him an instant boner. She'd said her parents would be out; could that mean she was interested? On Sunday, she was leaving for the summer, so this would be his last chance for a while. "Hey," he said, and leaned over for the kiss-kiss thing on either cheek that she'd taught him. But since she was taller, he ended up kissing her chin. As she led him through the apartment, he noticed a lot of paintings, statues of naked girls, and a bronze fountain filled with tiny, glittering stones instead of water.

"Your parents have some interesting stuff," he commented.

"My dad's an art dealer," Delphine said with a shrug of her perfect shoulders.

Finally, they reached her room and she invited him to sit down. He did not dare to join her on the bed—big, brass, and covered in a velvet spread the color of an eggplant—so he took the only chair there was, a carved, thronelike thing.

"You're headed back to France on Sunday, right?" he said.

Delphine nodded, her head bent in concentration over the joint she was rolling. Her clothes were the usual Delphine-ish jumble of things: a lacy white top under a shrunken T-shirt, a short polka-dot skirt revealing her pale, sculpted legs, and battered cowboy boots.

"I'll bet Paris is a way cool city," he said. "I'd love to go to Paris."

"We're not going to be in Paris," she said. *Par-ee* was the way she pronounced it. "In the summer, we go to Provence."

"Provence, right," he said. "Provence is cool too." Though how would he know? He'd never been to either place.

But Delphine just smiled and offered him the joint. As they smoked, Oliver cautiously permitted himself to relax. He wondered whether he could make his way—casually, of course—over to the bed. Not that he would dream of doing anything that she would in any way consider gross. Oliver, like all the guys he knew, was on good terms with Internet porn; he and Jake routinely sent each other links to new sites they found; SexyBabe and FuckBunnies were two of his current favorites, while Jake liked TitsOnParade and CumNow. But though the images of naked bodies doing, like, *everything* were certainly hot, they had nothing to do with how he felt about Delphine. Delphine was not a sexy babe or a fuck bunny. And she would never put any part of herself on parade. No, she was a goddess, *his* goddess, and he wanted to worship her body, not just get off on it. Her body was just a portal to her soul.

When she handed him back the joint, their fingers touched for a brief and, to Oliver, electrifying second, but if she felt it too, she gave no sign. She waited for him to take his toke, and then when it was her turn, she inhaled deeply, closing her eyes. Then she opened them again, and her smile reappeared, this time even wider and more welcoming.

"Come," she said, patting the place beside her on the bed, "sit with me."

Oliver actually tripped in his eagerness to comply. He could smell her now: crushed rose petals, rock candy, and maybe a little vanilla thrown in there too. He was high, and he was having yummy olfactory hallucinations. He laughed.

"What's funny?" she said. The joint was barely more than a glowing ember; she put it out in a water-filled wine goblet.

"Nothing," he said, easing his way a little closer to her. "Or everything."

She looked at him carefully, as if trying to decide something. "Oliver"—*Ah-lee-Vair*—she began. "Do you know why I invited you over?"

"To say good-bye before you went to Paris? I mean Provence," he ventured.

"Well, yes and no." She had reached for the embroidered silk pouch where she kept her weed. "I wanted to say good-bye. But not just because I'm going to Provence."

"Huh?" He was not following her.

"I'm saying good-bye, Oliver. Good-bye to you. Good-bye to us."

"Oh," he said. She might as well have dropped a refrigerator on his head; that was how flattened he felt.

"I do like you," she went on. "I like you *so* much. But I don't want to go out with you. You're like my brother." As she spoke, her fingers delved into the little pouch and began rolling another joint. When it was done, she lit it and handed it to him. "You first."

Oliver accepted the joint and took a deep hit. He wanted to . . . what? Start sobbing and beating his fists on the floor? But he just sat rigidly on her bed, smoking her dope and saying stupid shit like, *Yeah, I understand,* and *It's cool,* and stupidest, shittiest of all, *Sure, we can be friends. I'll always be your friend.* They listened to some music—all in French; he couldn't tell what the words meant—and she told him some more about Provence. He kept nodding his head, all the while thinking, *When can I go—please, can I go now?*

When the second joint had fizzled out next to the first one in the goblet, Oliver finally saw a moment to make his escape. He got up, stretched, and let Delphine escort him back through the series of rooms that led to the front door. This time he noticed that one of those mammoth paintings had a big gash—shaped like an evil grin—at the bottom left corner and the statues were headless. Inside the fountain, the stones looked vicious, like broken glass.

He had a brief, fleeting impulse to walk over to one of the large windows, open it, and calmly step out. But the moment passed. He miserably endured the kiss-kiss on either cheek again, the light brushing of her lips against his skin a small agony, and then went down in the same elevator that had brought him up.

When Oliver reached the street again, he had no idea of

what to do or where to go. He started walking uptown, just to be moving. Jake. Yeah, Jake would talk him down. Jake was a friend, a *real* friend. Would Jake be home, though? He could have texted him, but he didn't want to give Jake a chance to say no—that is, if he was in fact home. So Oliver continued up Central Park West, passing the San Remo, the Beresford, and the Eldorado. Had he not been so upset, he would have stopped to check them out. He liked old buildings, liked them a lot better than the tacky tower his dad had chosen as their home. His mom hadn't liked it either, but because it was so near the hospital, his dad won that round. Now his mom wasn't even here anymore and Oliver supposed he'd be stuck in that sterile box until he left for college. *If* he even got into college.

When he reached Jake's house on West Ninety-seventh Street, Oliver texted: *U there? Got to c u. Urgent.* He waited for a few seconds and then the reply came. *Yeah. No weed tho. My mom is getting nosy.* Oliver was so relieved he started trembling a little. Weed or no weed, Jake would know what to say. Jake let him in and they went up to his big bedroom on the top floor. It was as messy as Oliver's. Funny how his mess didn't bother him but Jake's grossed him out. Books, papers, empty cups from Starbucks—Jake was an iced cappuccino hound; he practically mainlined the stuff—greasy food wrappers, balled-up napkins. How about that pile of laundry? It was pretty rank. Still, he flopped down in Jake's beanbag chair and stretched out his legs; he had a feeling he would be here for a while.

"Delphine dumped me," he began.

"No shit," Jake said. "When?" He was sprawled on the couch that opened into a futon; Oliver had spent plenty of nights on that thing, getting high, talking, watching movies.

"Like, an hour ago."

"Dude, that sucks."

"You can say that again."

"Here," Jake said, springing up. His nickname at school was "Jake-in-the-box." He opened the small fridge that was on the far wall, producing two bottles of beer. "Good for what ails you. And my mom won't ever have to know." Popping the tops, he handed one to Oliver. Oliver took a serious swig and then burped.

"Gross," said Jake, but he was grinning.

"Like you're not," Oliver said. "Look at this place. It's a fucking sty."

"And your room is any better?"

"A sty," Oliver chanted. "A piggy, piggy sty."

"Oink," said Jake, "oink, oink."

Jake made a very convincing pig and despite his massive heartbreak, Oliver let out a little snort that might have been construed as laughter.

"Good to hear you laugh, dude," said Jake, swigging his own beer. "You're getting too upset. It's not like you were fucking her or anything."

Oliver's smile calcified and he had to restrain himself from flinging what was left of his beer in Jake's face. "What does that have to do with anything?"

"Well, that would be, like, different." Jake seemed oblivious to the change in Oliver's mood.

"Says who? You? And who are *you* anyway? Some dumbass douche bag? Some clueless dickwad?" And he had thought Jake was a *friend*.

"Whoa, dude, settle down." Jake set his beer on the floor and reached over to touch Oliver's arm.

"Keep your hands to yourself," Oliver said, flinching like he'd been burned.

"All right." Jake pulled back. "Whatever." He ambled over to the fridge and pulled out another couple of beers. "Why don't you have another beer and chill?"

"Why don't you fuck off?" Oliver stood up. That was when he saw it, the book, splayed and facedown on the wreck of Jake's floor. He picked it up by the dog-eared corner, as if it were contaminated. *"Toujours Provence,"* he read.

"Give me that," Jake said.

Oliver ignored him and started leafing through it. Whole sections were underlined in neon green highlighter, and there were scrawled notes—all illegible; Jake had the penmanship of a chimp—in the margins. "Since when do you read anything when you're not in school? Excuse me—like, when do you read anything at all?"

"I told you—give it back!" Jake lunged, but Oliver swiveled and held the book high above his own head, where Jake could not reach.

"Why can't I see it?" Oliver said. "What's the big deal?"

"You just can't," Jake said. He stared at the floor.

Suddenly, Oliver understood. Delphine. "She invited you to visit, didn't she?" he said. "Her parents have a place. She told me they weren't going to *Par-ee*; they were going to Provence." He dropped the book on the floor.

"I didn't want to tell you, dude." Jake looked at him then; there was pity in his eyes.

"I'll bet you didn't," said Oliver. Jake's expression made him seethe; not only had Oliver been dumped, but he had officially been rendered pathetic in the eyes of his former friend, and now rival. "So, like, are *you* fucking her?" Jake's slow pink flush, from his neck up to his forehead, told Oliver all he needed to know. "Traitor," he spit. "Scumbag, cocksucker, ass wipe." Jake did not attempt to defend himself; he just stood there while Oliver fumed and swore. This made Oliver even angrier. "I thought I could trust you," he said. "My buddy, my pal, my homey."

"Sorry, Ollie," was all Jake said. Now, when had Jake ever called him that? Only his father used that nickname. And his mother, but she was dead. She was dead last year and she'd be dead next year. She'd be dead forever. His heart was ready to combust with sorrow. And although he no longer felt the least bit drunk or high, the next few seconds, seconds in which he drew back his arm and clenched his fist, seemed suspended in that slow-motion-high-as-a-kite kind of way. But the punch, when it landed, happened in real time and the impact was so startling that he felt that he, not Jake, was the one who'd been hit.

There was an awful sound, flesh and bone hitting flesh and bone. Jake crumpled instantly to the floor, hands flying up to cradle his face. His nose was bleeding, thin, bright trails from each nostril; blood dripped down his chin and onto his pale green shirt. One dot, two, and then a third. Soon the shirt would be covered in them. "Son of a bitch," he murmured. "Son of a fucking bitch."

"Shit, are you okay?" Oliver had never hit anyone in the face in his entire life; his fist and his whole body were shaking. It was horrible. *Horrible.* His hand was like this foreign thing. This *weapon.* He thought he might puke and he pressed his splayed fingers over his mouth just in case.

"Go," Jake croaked. "Go now, before I hit you back."

Oliver took a last look at his best friend, maybe his *only* friend, curled up on the floor like a shrimp. Then he clattered down the stairs, flung open the front door, and got the hell out of there.

NINE

The intercom in Andy's apartment sounded with an insistent buzz. "Maybe that's Jordan," Christina called out as Andy went to answer it. "I told her to come up if I wasn't down by six thirty." She was crouched on the floor of Andy's study, straightening the new rug. It had just arrived today and its sophisticated colors—grays and black enlivened by unexpected bursts of citron and teal—really warmed this austere room. Andy did not reply, but when he walked back into the room, he said. "No, it's not Jordan."

Christina did not ask anything else; it wasn't her business. She got up and began to experiment with the placement of the lamp. The buzzer sounded again. "Now, *that* must be Jordan." It was getting late and she needed to be going. She and Jordan were going to have a quick dinner—never mind that all Jordan's dinners were quick—before they headed downtown to see an off-off-Broadway production for which Misha had gotten tickets. Once more, Andy went to answer the intercom. When he returned, he said, "Jordan's on her way up."

"Good." Christina straightened up. Now the door to the apartment buzzed and Lucy, Andy's housekeeper, went to answer it. Christina heard Jordan's voice saying hello, but there was another voice too. Had Jordan brought a friend? She hoped not; Misha had only given them two tickets.

Then Jordan herself came into the room, bun crowning her head, long skirt swishing around her delicate ankles. But who was with her? The woman was blond, and looked to be in her thirties. She was attractive in a predictable sort of way. She wore a low-cut magenta dress and high-heeled black pumps. Glitzy jewelry exploded from her wrists and throat. "Jennifer Baum, Christina Connelly," Andy said. "And this"—he turned—"is Christina's daughter, Jordan." Jennifer walked over to Andy, letting her fingers, with their shiny pink nails, rest lightly on Andy's wrist. *Mine,* the gesture seemed to say. *Don't touch.*

"I'm wrapping things up here," Andy said to Jennifer.

"We were just leaving now anyway," Christina added. She did not want it to seem like she was intruding on their date—because it clearly *was* a date.

"Nice to have met you both," said Jennifer without any enthusiasm whatsoever.

"Nice to meet you too," Christina lied.

When they were in the elevator going down, Jordan shifted her bag—it looked so heavy, Christina fretted she'd hurt her back from lugging it around all the time—from one shoulder to the other and said, "I don't like her."

"Why not?" Christina asked.

"You don't like her either," said Jordan.

"I didn't say that. You did."

"I can tell, though, Mom. You didn't like her and I want to know why."

"I don't dislike her," she said when they reached the lobby. "I just thought she seemed a bit cold. Also—overdone, if you know what I mean. All that . . . pink." Even though she had no claim to Andy herself—nor did she want one, she told herself—Jennifer's possessive gesture had riled her.

"She's perfect for him, though."

"What makes you say that?" Christina asked. They had walked through the lobby and left the building, heading toward the subway station on Lexington Avenue.

"Isn't it obvious? He's obnoxious; they deserve each other."

"Oh, he's not so bad . . . ," Christina said.

"Mom! He's *awful*."

"Well, right now, Mr. Awful is helping to pay the bills." She still had not heard back from the Haversticks and was now feeling like she was not going to get the job after all. The knowledge gnawed at her late at night and early in the morning, when she should have been sleeping.

Throughout dinner—a macrobiotic place of Jordan's choosing that offered five kinds of seaweed—and during the performance, Christina's thoughts kept wandering back to Jennifer. How old was she anyway? She had that well-tended Upper East Side look: expensive highlights, bleached teeth, an even, applied-by-spray-bottle tan. Added to that were the nails, the clothes, the whole glossy package. Christina discreetly looked down at her well-cut dark linen skirt and silk shell; she'd thought the outfit looked understated and tasteful when she'd put it on this morning. But right now she felt rumpled and drab. Then she chided herself for devoting this much time to a subject so superfluous. Misha had gone out of his way to get these seats; the play, a new work by an up-and-coming Irish playwright, was interesting and provocative. Christina willed herself to pay attention. Still, the image of

Jennifer's arm on Andy's was stubbornly etched somewhere in her consciousness and it would not be easily erased.

First thing the next morning, Christina was at the Sarnells' to oversee the delivery of eight dining room chairs. "Just put them over there, please," she instructed the men carrying them into the house. She tore the protective paper away from the first chair. The fabric was pulled taut across the seat and finished nicely underneath. She had never worked with this particular upholsterer before, but Tara Sarnell had insisted on using him. Well, so far, so good. She continued unwrapping all eight chairs, lining them up on the far side of the dining room as she went. Then she saw it. The pattern—gold fleurs-de-lis on a maroon background—was not consistent; on six of the chairs the fleurs-de-lis faced up, but on the remaining two, it faced down. "The fabric hasn't been put on right," she said, trying to control her annoyance, and, yes, panic.

"What are you talking about?" said the man; he was young with heavily tattooed arms and a bushy black beard.

"Can't you see?" She pointed. "Here the design element faces one way, but on these chairs, it faces the other."

"I don't know anything about that. I'm just delivering them." He crossed his arms over his chest.

"Just a minute," said Christina, and she pulled out her phone to call the upholsterer. She was just leaving him a message when Tara Sarnell came home.

"I don't understand," she said. "He came so well recommended." Christina said nothing but prayed the upholsterer would call her back—and soon. "There must be a reason," Tara was saying. "Maybe you didn't tell him that all the flowers needed to be going in the same direction."

"Any decent upholsterer would know that," Christina said. "It's so obvious it doesn't require an explanation."

"Evidently it *does*." Tara's voice was frosty.

Christina fumed all the way home. The upholsterer called when she was halfway there, and said he would send someone to pick up the chairs the next day. Fortunately there was enough fabric left, but he couldn't guarantee that he would have them done in time for the big party the Sarnells were hosting at the end of the month. Given how long he had taken to get these done, Christina highly doubted it. And Tara Sarnell was blaming *her*, as if this whole mess were her fault. Just as she was putting the key in the lock, she got a call from yet *another* client, who said she would have to delay an upcoming job. And there was still that client who was behind on her payments.

She dropped her bag, and went straight to her desk where a pile of bills seemed to reproach her mutely. How was she going to pay them? Without telling anyone, she had begun pulling things from her own collection—her stash, as she liked to think of it—and selling them. There were a few pieces of sterling silver hollowware, quite ornate, she'd stumbled on during a buying trip to Canada, a small but beautifully rendered Art Nouveau bronze figurine, a Wedgwood vase in a haunting shade of blue. One by one, she brought these treasures to a dealer she knew in Manhattan; he always gave her fair prices. It hurt her to pillage her own rich storehouse, cannily and patiently accumulated in the nearly two decades she'd been reclaiming the artifacts of other lives and weaving them into her own. There was no choice, though; she needed the money.

In her flush of enthusiasm about Andy Stern's job and the

one she'd hoped to get from the Haversticks, she'd turned down the offer in Greenwich. Now, staring at the pile of bills, she wondered whether she'd made a mistake. "We're sorry you won't be joining us," Alice McEvoy, the head of the firm, had said. "Let me know if you change your mind." If nothing new came through by the end of the month, she just might do that.

She got up, too anxious to sit. Rubbing the knot of tension at the base of her neck, she began the familiar ritual, the one she thought of as *taking inventory*. This consisted of a walk through her house to both check its present condition and see what needed repairing or freshening. Her office, with its one pink lacquer wall, zebra-print armchair, and tightly packed shelves with hundreds of books—art, design, fashion—from which she sought inspiration, was looking a bit overstuffed. She would set aside a couple of hours to edit and prune. In the kitchen, she saw a loose tile near the stove; in the dining room, she decided she could use a new centerpiece for her table. As she walked, her tension slowly dissipated; she liked to reacquaint herself with these rooms on a regular basis; she had lived in them all her life.

When she was a little girl, she lived on the lower floors with her parents; her maternal grandmother had lived above them. Christina remembered nothing of this time. Her mother had died when she was barely a year old and her grandmother shortly after. Then her aunt Barb had moved into the upstairs apartment; that was where her memories began. Barb had never married, but she had rarely been alone either. She'd cycled through a series of roommates, and the occasional boyfriend had moved in too; Christina remembered a policeman named Frank who had a bristling, black crew cut and a barking laugh. Her father hadn't liked the idea of Frank's living there—*You're not married; it's not setting a good example*—but he hadn't liked much about the way Barb lived. Her collection of teapots—all of which Christina now owned—her bed covered in its explosion of frilly pillows, the dozens of framed photographs that hung on the walls or clustered on the surfaces. *It's like a goddamn gift shop up there*, her father would fume. But he needed Barb and so he had put up with all of it. Eventually the policeman moved on and her father's irritation simmered down.

Christina had bathed in Barb's excess—of spirit, of things. She knew she had developed her own love of objects at Barb's side. They had spent weekends at flea markets and yard sales on Long Island, in New Jersey and Connecticut. Barb taught Christina how to collect: furniture for her dollhouse (also found at a sale), old perfume bottles, printed handkerchiefs, compacts, and evening purses.

After Christina's father died and Christina went off to Vassar on scholarship, Aunt Barb moved downstairs and rented out the apartment above to an ever-changing cast of friends. Sometimes the friends were behind on the rent; Barb always let it go, though Christina knew this would have driven her father not so quietly mad. Good thing he did not live to see it, or to see Barb's indifferent approach to home maintenance and repair. The roof developed a leak; she simply placed pots strategically around the top-floor rooms to catch the drips; the backyard had gone wild, lush with crazy, sprouting weeds she considered flowers. Neighborhood cats strolled by, drawn by the dishes of food she regularly set out.

When Christina married Will, they both thought that the move into her family home was a temporary one; Christina

was anxious to escape so much about her working-class up-
bringing, including the house where it had taken place. But
when Jordan was born, she had a change of heart. If they
stayed on Carroll Street, Barb, now retired but still brimming
with energy, could take care of the baby. Christina began to
put her own stamp on the house, redoing the kitchen, recon-
figuring the space. Then Barb had died and Will too, and how
glad she was that she had hung on to the house. It was her
anchor, her shelter, her past, and her future. She would never
leave it. Never.

Christina left the bills in a neat pile and went outside to
bring the trash barrels to the curb. The sun was setting and
there were wild streaks of pink and gold when she looked
west. When she turned back, she was startled by the elegant,
dark-skinned man standing by the stoop to her house. Where
had he come from?

"Ms. Harris?" he asked in a British-inflected accent. He
wore an expensive-looking suit and his black hair, shining
with gel, was combed back from his face.

"Actually, it's Connelly." To her father's unending irritation, she had never taken Will's last name.

"My apologies." The man inclined his head. "I hope I'm
not intruding."

"That depends," she said cautiously. He did not look like
he would ask her for money, but his appearance, like his cultivated manner, could just be part of whatever scam he was
running.

"I'm here about your house." He made a sweeping gesture
with his hand. "It's a lovely house, a fine house. The finest on
the block."

"Thank you," she said, softening a little. The steps still

needed work, but the house *did* look good, with the carefully tended planters, now filled with zinnias and marigolds, and the fresh coat of shiny bottle green paint she'd applied to the doors. The brass mail slot and doorknobs, both flea market finds, were polished to a hectic gleam; the glass in the windows sparkled.

"I'm actually interested in purchasing it," he said. "Or rather, not me, but my clients. You may have seen them—the Sharmas? I know they've been by a couple of times."

"I think I have," she said. "He wears a turban and they have a little girl?"

The man nodded. "They said they had seen you and were afraid that they might have offended you. That's why they didn't introduce themselves."

Christina remembered the way they hustled into the waiting car. "The house is not for sale."

"I know," said the man. "I checked to see if it was on the market before I approached you."

"Then why are you here?" She was beginning to get annoyed.

"Because I have a very good offer." If he was aware of her annoyance, he gave no indication. "My clients are prepared to offer you a very good sum for this house. And they would pay in cash—no banks, no brokers, no commission. Just an easy exchange—their money, for this house."

"It's still not for sale," she said.

"But I haven't told you the price."

"That doesn't matter."

He looked at her almost pityingly. "You might want to at least consider it," he said. "You won't get an offer like this again."

"Why this house?" Christina asked abruptly. "There are better houses in the neighborhood, even on the block. Bigger, more valuable . . . If your clients can pay cash, why would they choose this house?"

"It's Mira." He smiled. "Mrs. Sharma. It's a whim of hers. And Raghubeer likes to indulge her whims."

Christina did not smile back. "Well, you can thank them for their interest, but the answer is still no."

"For now," said the man easily. Nothing seemed to ruffle his smooth feathers. He reached into his breast pocket, pulled out a card. First he wrote something on the back and then handed it to her. Christina's hands remained by her side. "It can't hurt to take it," he said, his voice soft and coaxing. She accepted the card only because it seemed rude not to. The name *Pratyush Singh* was engraved in elegant black script on the heavy vellum stock. Below it was a telephone number and an e-mail address, but nothing else.

"Thank you for your time, Ms. Connelly," he said. "I hope I'll be talking to you again." Then he turned and began to walk at a leisurely pace down the block.

She waited until he had gone before she turned the card over. The number he'd written on the back—three million— was nothing short of astonishing. The house was not worth that much, even in this inflated market. Christina sank down to the stoop—the bottom step was the most deteriorated—and considered for the briefest of moments just what such an amount would mean to her. Then, tucking the card into her back pocket, she mounted the stairs.

When she reached the top step, she spotted Charlotte, who had come outside to look down the street. Seeing Charlotte was never a pleasant experience and today Christina didn't think she could rise to the challenge of being civil. Fortunately Charlotte's antipathy made it unnecessary. She glared at Christina before stepping back inside, and seconds later, her door closed—a little more forcefully than necessary—and the sound of the lock turning in the tumbler could be heard. Opening her own door, Christina was so relieved not to have to talk to her that she didn't even register the insult.

TEN

*A*ndy met Christina at the door and immediately offered her a glass of wine. Although she didn't usually drink on the job, she bent her own rule and said yes. She
was actually a little nervous; they were meeting to discuss
how to handle what had been his late wife's home office. A
small room off the kitchen, it held a desk, a chair, a computer,
and a couple of shelves of books. Christina had seen it only
once, but she knew Andy had left everything exactly as it had
been when Rachel died. She also knew that any discussion
about it would require sensitivity and tact.

"White would be lovely," she said, putting down her bag
and following him into the living room. The ebbing light on
the river had turned the water a dark, metallic blue; she stood,
rapt for a moment, until she sensed him behind her and accepted the glass he held out.

"Cheers," she said, tapping the rim to his; at the same
moment he said, *"L'chaim."*

"I know that anything we do in this room is going to be

difficult," she began. "So why don't you tell me what you had in mind?"

"I thought I could turn it into a guest room," he said. "Not that we have all that many guests. Still, my mother stays over sometimes and it would be nice for her." He took a sip of his wine. "I want it to reflect Rachel somehow. But I don't want a shrine."

"Of course not." Christina also took a sip; the wine was excellent. "I was thinking we could involve Oliver in some way too."

"That would be good," Andy said eagerly. "Great, in fact. How?"

"Well, if you want to order some new furniture for the room, I could show him the options, get his input. Same with any window or floor treatments. Maybe even let him choose some of the colors." The wine was crisp and refreshing; it went down so easily.

"Do you think, I mean, I know it's unorthodox, but do you think he could come to a showroom or two with you?" asked Andy. "He's been moping around here all summer, not seeing any of his friends."

"I don't see any reason why not," Christina said. She twirled her goblet between her fingers as she spoke; this was one of the glasses she and Andy had bought at the estate sale. Just thinking about their trek in the rain, and how she'd been for a brief moment so exposed, was unsettling. It took her a few seconds to realize that the memory was actually exciting to her; she was aroused. She looked over at Andy, so earnest in his desire to help his son, so clueless as to how. She had an urge to lay her hand on his cheek. *Bad* idea. What was wrong with her anyway? It was the wine. The wine and a long, dry spell in her romantic life.

She set down the glass. "I'll look at my book and see what kind of time I have next week. And do you want to go take a look at the room together?"

"Good idea." He stood and finished his wine. If he noticed that her glass was still partially full, he didn't mention it. Christina followed him through the kitchen and waited while he stood in front of the door. "I keep it closed," he said. "Lucy goes in to dust and vacuum, but that's all."

The room was white, with a simple white shade at the window. Over the desk was a bulletin board filled with photographs, torn magazine pages, business cards, ticket stubs, and a menu. Against one wall was a sewing machine. Some of the books contained quilt patterns, or photographs of antique patchwork quilts. "She liked to sew?" Christina asked. Andy nodded. "She used to make all of Ollie's Halloween costumes. Then she got into the blanket thing."

"You mean quilts?" Christina asked.

"Right. Quilts."

"Did she ever finish one?" Christina took a book from the shelf and began leafing through it. Two small squares of fabric fluttered out and to the floor.

"She got sick. . . ." He trailed off.

Christina knelt to retrieve the squares. "Do these look familiar?" Andy just shook his head. Someone—presumably Rachel—had circled one of the patterns in the book using red marker. *Wedding Anniversary Quilt.* There was a diagram on the facing page and beneath the title, a description. *This charming design utilizes some of the traditional motifs of eighteenth- and nineteenth-century quilts. The two interlocking circles represent the two wedding bands, locked together in an eternal embrace. . . .*

"It looks like she was planning to make this." Christina looked more closely at the squares of fabric. One was a tight plaid of dark red, cream, and taupe; the other used similar colors but was a tiny and bustling floral print. "Maybe these were two that she liked." What if she found them, these two patterns, or ones very much like them? The fabric could be used for shades or curtains and, because there would need to be a bed in here, for a bed skirt, or a fabric headboard. On the walls, she saw wallpaper, no, not wallpaper, but fabric—maybe a raw linen or a muslin of some kind—something that would give the room some warmth and texture, as well as refer to Rachel's interest in textiles. And of course there ought to be an actual antique quilt—or two; one for the bed itself, and another she could hang from the wall, suspended on a dowel. When she looked again at the bulletin board, another idea came to her. She would get a blank scrapbook and arrange everything from the bulletin board in it. It would be a nice way to gather the last bits of ephemera from Rachel's life and give those fragile pieces a meaning, an order. And she could enlist Oliver's help in that too.

"You're not saying anything," Andy pointed out.

She looked over at him. "Sorry. The wheels were turning. Let me tell you what I was thinking."

"Sure," he said. "Would you like another glass of wine? Or even better, what if I ordered us some takeout? Lucy's got the night off and I was going to do that for myself anyway."

"All right," Christina said. Was it a good idea to have dinner here? She decided that as long as they remained focused on the job, it would be fine. Jordan was going to be at Alexis's tonight, so there was no one at home anyway. Andy ordered up Japanese food, which they ate in the kitchen as Christina outlined her plans for the new guest room. Oliver came shuffling in, and though at first his responses were merely monosyllabic, he did show some interest in the quilts, and especially in the scrapbook.

"I remember some of this stuff," he said. "The movie ticket. That menu. The pictures." He nodded, and Christina was sure she could smell pot emanating from him; did Andy smell it too?

"And what about the quilts?" Christina asked. "Could I show you some of the ones I'm considering?"

"She once took me to some quilt exhibition," Oliver said. "At first I thought it was going to be stupid and, like, too girly, but it was actually pretty cool. Those things took years to make. Decades even."

"What exhibit?" Andy asked. "I don't remember it."

"You weren't there. It was that summer I went to camp in Vermont. She came up for visiting day, but you didn't."

"Right . . . I was at a medical convention that year. Geneva, I think."

"They were having this show at some, like, art center in town and Mom wanted to go." Oliver continued as if his father had not spoken.

"So you saw the kinds of quilts she liked," Christina prompted.

"Yeah. All these different patterns. And colors. She loved the colors."

Christina looked over at Andy, who was nodding. "I know you're going to be a big help in this, Oliver."

"You think?" He looked at her, eyes bright beneath the fringe of blond curls.

"I know." To Christina, he didn't seem high; his pupils were not dilated and he seemed alert. Maybe he'd only been with some kids who had been smoking?

After he'd gone to his room, Christina wanted to help clean up, but Andy told her not to bother. "There's nothing to clean," he said. "Just some recycling and some trash." Without asking, he refreshed her glass of wine—Christina had sipped a bit during the meal—and they took their drinks into the living room.

"Thank you for being so gentle with Ollie," he said.

"I have a teenager too," she said.

"Nothing I say seems to penetrate," Andy went on. "Or else it does—in the wrong way. I make him angry. Upset."

"That's because you're his father. He knows you love him, so it's safe to act out with you."

"You're a good mother," Andy said, sitting up very straight. "I can tell."

"Thank you," she said, not sure how to interpret this sudden declaration.

"Being a good mother is a very important quality in a person. A woman. I mean, in a woman."

Christina smiled down at her glass. They had switched to red now and the wine looked almost black. "Yes, I guess it is." It sounded to her like alpha, always-in-control Andy was a wee bit tipsy. Yes, Dr. Stern, Dr. *Stern*, was drunk. Why she found this amusing, she was not sure, but she did.

"That's the trouble with Jen," Andy was saying. "I like her, but when I see her with her daughter . . ."

"Jen?" asked Christina. She knew who Jen was. But why was he talking about her now? And to her of all people?

"Jen Baum," Andy said. "You met her, didn't you?"

"Yes," Christina said, and nothing more.

"I told Gus I'd give it another try. So we went out last Friday. Her daughter wasn't even there; she was staying with her dad. And everything was great, but then—" He stopped.

"And then?" asked Christina. Who was Gus? And what did he have to do with anything? Oh, Andy was drunk all right. Drunk and rambling.

"I got to thinking that if I were going to get serious with this woman, I'd have to spend time with both of them. Because her daughter would be a big part of our lives. So I suggested we spend a day together—the zoo, a playground, gelato. . . ." He trailed off. "But Jen doesn't have any empathy!" he said. "And I can forgive or explain away a lot of things. But not that."

"What do you mean?" She knew, though; that woman looked brittle, like she'd been shellacked.

"The entire day, she acted like she wanted her daughter to go away so we could be alone together. Like her daughter— her five-year-old *daughter*—was some major annoyance. A bother. And of course the kid feels this and tries even harder to get her attention. Which her mother just will not give her."

"She does sound a bit obtuse," Christina ventured.

"The kid looked miserable, so I suggested we stop into FAO Schwarz—we were right nearby—and I would get her a little toy. But she says, 'No, Mommy. I want *Daddy* to buy me a present.' And Jen says, 'Well, Daddy's not here, but Andy wants to buy you a present.' Kid digs her heels in; she wants Daddy's present and *only* Daddy's present. I'm ready to let it go; it doesn't matter."

"But her mother was not as understanding?"

"Not a bit. Told her she was a spoiled brat. So of course the kid has a meltdown."

"What did you do?" Christina asked.

"I told Jen to wait there. I raced into the store, grabbed the first thing I saw, which happened to be this big stuffed kangaroo, and I bought it. When I got back out, Drew—that's her name—Drew was crying and Jen was standing there not even looking at her. I gave Drew the kangaroo, hustled them both into a taxi, and went home." Andy drained the last of his wine. "What a *day*."

"Exhausting," said Christina.

"You see what I mean? No empathy. But you—you would have handled it differently, wouldn't you? I know you would have. Because *you*, Christina Connelly, are an empathetic woman." And before Christina could respond, Andy had leaned over and planted a kiss on her most astonished but quickly parting lips.

ELEVEN

The ocean, just down the path from Andy's East Hampton rental on Further Lane, glittered in the morning sun. As he walked, the water lapped at his bare feet and ankles. He maintained a steady pace, occasionally breaking into a light run; then he lapsed back into his power walk once again. It felt good to be out here in the sun, using his legs, his arms, his breath, to propel himself forward. The scene from the other night kept looping through his mind: the wine, the talk, and the kiss. The kiss. He'd kissed Christina Connelly. And she kissed him back—or he *thought* she had; he was lit and not entirely sure—before stepping away and excusing herself to use the bathroom. When she emerged, she thanked him for the wine and took off; clearly she had not wanted things to go any further. They had not spoken since.

After about a mile, Andy turned and started heading back to the house. The sun was higher in the sky, and the beach, formerly deserted, was now dotted with a few early risers. He wondered whether his mother would be up by the time he got back. He'd sent a car to bring her down to Manhattan on Friday afternoon, and then along with Oliver, they'd driven out here together. As Andy made his way up to the house, he saw that not only was Ida up; she was dressed and had made herself a cup of coffee, which she had taken out onto the deck. She wore enormous black sunglasses and, above them, a black straw hat. Her small frame was covered by a long dress in a bold black-and-white pattern.

"Morning!" she called. "Did you have a good walk?"

"Great walk," he answered. "Tomorrow we'll do it together." He joined her on the deck.

"I'd love to," she said. "Maybe Oliver will come too."

"Is he up yet?" Andy asked.

"I haven't seen him," Ida said.

"He's been sleeping late all summer," Andy said. The coffee smelled good; he could go for a cup right about now.

"He's still growing; growing tires a boy out."

"I guess it does." He turned to go into the kitchen. "Have you had breakfast?" Ida shook her head. "Me neither. Let's go out."

While she was getting her purse, Andy knocked on Oliver's door, once, twice, and then a third time. When there was still no answer, he cracked it open. The room was cool and dark. Oliver's blond curls peeked out from one end of the blanket; a bare foot poked out from the other. "Ollie," he said, and then louder, "Ollie."

"Yeah?" Oliver emerged from the cocoon of the blanket.

"Grandma and I are going out to breakfast. Would you like to come?"

"Sleep," Oliver said, sliding back down under the quilt. "Need to sleep."

"Right," Andy said. Why did his son's voice sound so plaintive, and so small?

They drove into town in Andy's Lexus, and found a parking spot easily enough. But when they got to Babette's on Newtown Lane, there was already a sizable line. "Do you want to wait?" he asked her.

"Of course," she said.

Andy watched how she looked around, checking out the clothes and jewelry of the women milling around as well as every woman who walked by. She might be past eighty, but she was still in the game, he thought. He loved her for it. Then someone sang out his name.

He turned in the direction of the voice just as the woman with bangs and a pageboy came striding toward him. She was pushing a stroller that held three babies. He remembered them as much smaller, but that was not unusual; he'd last seen them as newborns, when he'd delivered them.

"Melanie, it's good to see you," Andy said. "Let me introduce my mother, Ida Stern."

"Your son is a miracle worker," Melanie said. "We just about worship him, don't we, honey?" She turned to her husband. His name was Henry or Harry; Andy wasn't sure.

"We sure do," said Henry-or-Harry as he pumped Andy's hand.

"He was always a good boy," Ida said serenely.

"Let me look at them," Andy said, bending down closer to the stroller.

"This one is Tyler," said Melanie, indicating a chubby baby who was waving his fists in the air. "And that's Aidan." Aidan was asleep; a tiny bubble of spit rose and fell on his parted lips. "And here's Mommy's little princess, Emma." Emma's wispy brown hair was kept out of her face by a purple head-band topped by a large purple bow. It had been a harrowing birth and Andy thought he might lose her. But she had pulled through, and now look at her: rocking that headband here in East Hampton. "Hey there, Emma," Andy said softly. Emma looked at him, and began to bawl. What had he done?

Melanie scooped up the screaming baby. "Don't you like Dr. Stern? He only saved your life, love muffin." Emma kicked her legs and pressed her face into her mother.

"I'm so sorry!" said Emma's dad, whose name still would not coalesce in Andy's mind. "She's been really fussy today."

Andy stepped back. People were looking at them; he fervently hoped that they did not blame him for the baby's sudden eruption.

"Don't cry, baby girl," soothed Melanie, jostling Emma in her arms. "Dr. Stern is a nice man. The *nicest* man."

Excited little whispers started to eddy through the crowd. *That's Andrew Stern, the best ob-gyn in the city. Everyone says that he's brilliant. If you've ever lost a baby, go see Stern. He's your man.* Andy smiled, flattered and a little embarrassed too. Ida, however, was eating it up: *My son the famous doctor,* said her expression. *He's a prince, a god, and a wizard rolled into one.* Her only regret, he knew, was that her Riverdale coffee klatch was not on hand to witness his triumph.

"Dr. Stern?" A Babette's employee stepped up to him. "The people at the head of the line want to give you their table and take your place instead."

"That's not necessary," Andy said.

"Please, Dr. Stern. They were quite insistent."

So Andy gave his arm to Ida and escorted her into the restaurant; she was fairly levitating with pride. When they had ordered, Ida took off her glasses and placed them on the table.

"So how are you?" Andy sipped his coffee. "Everything okay up in Riverdale?"

"A-OK," she said. "What about you?"

"Getting along. Did I tell you about my latest celeb patient?"

"Scarlett Johansson?" she asked, leaning forward in anticipation. "Or Anne Hathaway?"

He grinned. "Not this time. But what would you say to Xiomara?" Andy named a recent Grammy-winning singer with a worldwide following.

"Xiomara?" Ida looked excited. "Can I tell the girls?"

"I'd rather you didn't," he said. "At least not until the baby is born. There's going to be enough of a media circus when she delivers anyway."

Their omelets arrived and they began to eat. "How about your personal life?" she asked. "Is there a special lady friend you want to tell me about?"

"No, Ma, there isn't." He took a bite of his seven-grain toast.

"I thought you mentioned someone. . . . Jen or Jenny something."

"Jennifer Baum, but I'm not seeing her anymore."

Ida put down her utensils. "Why not?"

"It just wasn't working out," he said.

"Andy, sweetheart, I know it's not my business—"

"You're right—it's not."

"Maybe you're being too picky. I know Rachel, may she rest in peace, was a paragon among women, but Rachel's gone and you're still a young man—"

"With so much to live for," Andy finished for her. "Look, Ma, I know you mean well, but when a woman is not right, she's not right. Better to just move on."

"Move on to what?" Ida said. "Another blind date, another woman who may or may not be right? And this Jennifer, she's Jewish, right? That's so important; you don't want to go falling for some *shiksa*. At some point you just have to settle, Andy."

"When Dad left, did you settle? Was *good enough* good enough for you?"

"I didn't have your . . . opportunities," she said with quiet dignity.

Andy reached out to cover her small hand with his. "I'm sorry," he said. "That wasn't nice."

"No," she said. "It wasn't." She looked around for the waitress. "I'd love another cup of coffee."

"I'll get her attention," said Andy, sorry he'd taken the bait. He signaled to the waitress; the conversation shifted to other, less volatile subjects. "Oliver seemed very . . . quiet . . . when we were driving out last night," Ida said.

"He's been quiet for months," Andy said.

"Does he have any friends out here?"

Andy shook his head. "I asked if he wanted to bring along his friend Jake from the city. He looked at me like I had suggested inviting the headmaster from his school."

"He must be lonely," Ida said. "Maybe he'll play cards with me. We used to play all the time when he was little. Go Fish, gin rummy . . ."

Andy said nothing. He wasn't sure that Ollie would want to play gin rummy with his grandmother. But what did he know? Jake had been his blood brother; what could have driven a wedge between those two?

He ordered cinnamon-swirl French toast to go for his son and paid the bill. Ida went to the ladies' room and he stepped outside. He was looking down at the fender of his Lexus—was that a *scratch?*—when he heard his name again. There was Christina, dressed all in flowing, summery white, a jaunty straw hat obscuring the top of her face.

"What are you doing here?" He was unable to hide his delight.

"Oh, we're just day-trippers—Stephen has a place in Sag Harbor and we go out there a lot, but this morning we thought we'd drive over to East Hampton for a walk through town."

It was only then that Andy registered Christina's escort, an exceedingly handsome black man who wore madras shorts and a very well-fitting shirt that emphasized his trim build. The man nodded, and Andy willed himself to be polite when they were introduced. Ida walked over and Andy introduced her as well; while they were chatting, he tried to decipher the body language between Christina and Stephen. The guy was certainly attentive, and stood closer to her than Andy would have liked. Was she *dating* him? Christ, he hoped not. It was only when he saw the tiny gold hoop in the guy's ear that his jealousy dialed down a notch. Although the hoop wasn't a guarantee, he had a hunch the guy was gay. But a hunch was only a hunch; he had to find out for sure.

"What are you two doing for dinner?" he said, abruptly interrupting the conversation.

"We didn't have any special plans—," Christina was saying while Stephen said, "Actually, there are three of us; my partner, Misha, is back in Sag Harbor."

Partner! Bingo! Andy grinned like an idiot. "Well, why don't you all come over to my place? I'll just boil up some lobsters and grill some corn and we can sit on the deck and enjoy it while watching the sun go down."

"That's very gracious of you," said Stephen.

"You don't have to go to all that trouble." Christina looked straight at Andy.

"Lobster?" said Ida, clearly puzzled by the turn the conversation had taken.

"Great! Done! Settled!" Andy said. *Partner.* He liked the sound of that word, yes he did. "How's seven? Is seven good?"

"Who is Christina Connelly?" Ida asked when they were on their way back to the house.

"Oh, she's that decorator I told you about." He had to stop himself from humming.

"I remember," said Ida. "You like her."

"Who, Christina?" He feigned nonchalance, all the while reveling in the serendipitous meeting. So Stephen had a place in Sag Harbor. So she came out here often. Who knew?

"Yes. You like her a lot."

"Well, yes, I do. She's been doing a very good job." When Ida said nothing, he nattered on, "Ollie really likes her too; she's really sweet with him."

"Sounds like you're thinking of her as more than a decorator."

"And if I am?" He pulled into the driveway of the house and turned to look at her. "Is that a crime?"

Andy left Ida in the house with Oliver, who had finally gotten up, while he returned to town to buy groceries. Gliding the car into a vacant spot and putting it into park, Andy reviewed the list he'd hastily scrawled back in the kitchen. *Lobster, corn, salad, sherbet, fruit, cookies.* Stephen had insisted on bringing the wine for the evening, so he wouldn't have to think about that.

Andy had to admit that at this moment the plan seemed a little daunting—he'd never made dinner for six people before, especially not when there was one in particular he wanted to impress. But he broke the job down into its constituent parts: boil the lobster, grill the corn, chop and dice the salad vegetables, scoop the ice cream, slice the fruit, and arrange it on a platter. Hell, he brought babies into the world, didn't he? How hard could it be to assemble a meal?

Several hours later, racing around in the rental house's kitchen, he found out. Even after pressing Oliver into service shucking corn, things were not going smoothly: long strands of corn silk were everywhere, tomato pulp and seeds covered his freshly pressed shirt, and the peaches were mealy. Fortunately he had the sherbet and a lemon chiffon cake, purchased on impulse from one of the nicer bakeries in town.

"How are you doing?" asked Ida. She had changed, again, and was wearing a coral dress, gold sandals, and big gold earrings.

"Okay. I think."

"I can help, you know."

"That's all right, Ma. I've got it covered."

Ida looked pained. "You really want to impress her, don't you?"

"Yes," he said. "I do."

"But, Andy, I don't think she's Jewish. Is she?"

"What difference does it make?" Though he had given this some thought too—not that he would tell her that.

"What difference? To start with, *you're* Jewish. *I'm* Jewish. Your *son* is Jewish. *Rachel*"—she let the name hang in the air— "*was* Jewish."

"Rachel is dead," he said. "Rachel is dead and for the first time since she died, I feel a spark for someone, I'm really *excited* about someone, and *you're* worried because she isn't Jewish."

"You know about me," Ida said, breaking the angry silence. "My past. What I went through back then. And all because I was Jewish."

"Yes, I know," he said quietly. He did know about her past: the deportation, the camp, the small blue number that was still on her forearm.

"So if you know, why would you do this to me? Why?"

"I'm not doing it *to you*," he said. "I'm doing it *for me*." There was a pause during which he thought she might break down weeping. The moment passed.

"I overstepped," she said. "You'll do what you want. You're a grown man. I can't help the way I feel, that's all." She looked down at her gnarled hands with their shiny, painted nails.

"Look, they'll be here any minute," he said. "Can you please, please, *please* just drop it?"

Ida huffed off to set the table and Andy turned back to the meal. He opened the bakery box. The cake had shifted radically during the ride home; it was now totally squashed on one side. Andy checked his watch: too late to drive back to town to find a substitute. Damn.

"Hey, when's Christina getting here?" Ollie ambled out of his room in torn jeans, neon green sneakers, and a faded, stretched-out T-shirt that said, *Coke: Good for Sipping, Spurting & Snorting*. Jesus, did he have to meet company looking like that? Before Andy could say anything, the bell rang. Show-time.

"Great to see you!" Andy gushed, shaking first Stephen's hand and then Misha's. "Come on in." He ushered them inside and accepted the wine Stephen had brought without even looking in the bag. He was too interested in greeting Christina, who wore some diaphanous dress of a silvery gray, her silver bracelet, and a pair of simple but sexy black shoes. Her hair was swept up and back from her face in its usual style and two pearl drops quivered from her ears. "I'm glad you could make it," he managed to say when she wandered into the kitchen.

"Me too," she said, but did not linger. He watched her retreating back with a slump of disappointment, but then he rallied: he had a dinner to serve. He pulled the salad from the fridge; he'd dress it when it got to the table. Right now he wanted to start the corn and light some candles. He hurried to follow Christina into the other room and caught the tail end of Misha's comment about some off-Broadway play whose name he recognized. He had been dragged to it by Jen of all people; she had read the very positive reviews. "Oh, that was the play about those three sisters all in love with the same guy? What a melodramatic piece of crap," Andy said.

There was an awkward pause before Misha said, "The director is a very good friend of mine. We've worked together for years and I did the lighting for that production." Andy said nothing; he wanted to stuff the words right back into his mouth. "The lighting was good!" he croaked. "The lighting was great!" The stupid candles would wait; he turned and fled to the deck, where the massive stainless-steel grill—ready to roast a bison should he have happened to spear one—gleamed in the setting sun. But when he went to turn it on, it wouldn't light, and after several frantic minutes, he realized he was out of propane; he'd neglected to check the tank earlier in the day. Shit. Well, he'd have to boil the corn; he just hoped there was another pot in there big enough. He rummaged frantically through the cupboards. Too small, wrong shape—ah, here was something. He pulled it out and sent several others clattering to the floor. The conversation in the other room stopped and Ida called out, "Need any help?"

"No, I'm fine. Fine!" He scuttled back outside, scooped the ears into the pot, sending several of them spiraling onto the deck below. Luckily, no one saw and he gathered up what he could, figuring that the boiling water would kill any germs. Then he placed the remaining ears of corn on the counter, filled two pots with water, and brought the salad out to the table.

"Voilà!" he said, setting it down right in front of Christina.

"This looks so nice," she said. He reached for the vinaigrette he'd prepared earlier and poured it over the greens. But he was a little too enthusiastic and the dressing splashed up from the salad bowl, right onto Christina's face and dress.

"Jesus, I am so sorry!" he said.

Christina said nothing and only reached for her napkin.

"Seltzer," said Stephen, rising from his seat. "Right away. Want me to get it?"

"No, no, I'll go," said Andy.

"Don't worry. I'm sure it will be all right," Christina said, dabbing at her chin.

"Don't do anything to the dress until he brings you the seltzer," Stephen instructed as he sat back down. "You don't want to set the stain."

Andy rushed into the kitchen, grabbed the unopened bottle of seltzer that he had fortunately picked up at the market. A quick twist of the cap and—whoosh! The seltzer erupted like a geyser, sending a spray all over the floor. Now it was slippery—great. All he needed was for his mother or one of the guests to fall. He grabbed a wad of paper towels and dove for the wet spot; his outstretched arm knocked the cake clean off the plate and onto the floor, where it landed in the puddle of seltzer. *Jesus fucking Christ.* The cake, now wet as well as lopsided, fell apart when he tried to rescue it. He dumped it into the trash, washed his hands, and returned to the table with the seltzer. "If it doesn't work, I'll pay to have your dress cleaned," he said to Christina. "Or I'll buy you a new dress."

"I'm sure that won't be necessary," Christina said. Stephen wet the napkin with the seltzer and began dabbing.

"Please," Andy begged. "Let's start." He began by passing the salad bowl to Misha, whose eyes he still could not meet.

"There," said Stephen. "That should do it." He sat down and they all began to eat. For a few minutes, it seemed like everything might actually be all right. The salad was good, and so was the dressing. When everyone had finished, Andy collected the plates and went back to the kitchen.

The water was boiling in both pots; Andy set the timer and slid the corn in. When he went to retrieve the lobsters, he noticed a tin of chocolate-dipped biscotti perched on top of the fridge; he could serve that with the sherbet and no one would even miss the fruit or the cake. He pulled the tin down from its spot and set it next to the bags. See? He could do this, he could.

Now it was time to cook those crustaceans. Even though the claws had been secured with rubber bands at the fish market, Andy did not want to put his hand inside the bags and instead used a pair of scissors to snip the paper away. There, black and gleaming, waited the lobsters. He looked at the one closest to him, noting the flecked pattern on its black shell, which, upon closer inspection, was not really black at all, but a medley of deep, aquatic blues, colors created by and uniquely suited to the ocean's rayless floor. The creature's antennae waved listlessly; he could swear the lobster was looking him straight in the eyes. The famous scene in *Annie Hall* was played as comedy: Woody Allen and Diane Keaton giggling as they tried to capture the escaping lobsters. Here, in this pristine East Hampton kitchen, the scene was more tragedy than farce. The lobster, and the five others sitting alongside it like a row of condemned prisoners, were going to meet their end, and he was the one who had to deliver them to it.

The timer pinged, giving him a start, and he rummaged around looking for tongs so he could remove the corn from the water. It would cool quickly; he needed to get those lobsters into the pot. Andy turned away. He couldn't. Could. Not. The lobsters, the pot, the dancing flame, the first moment they hit the water with an all-too-brief exhilaration before they began to feel the inevitable heat. "Andy?" He turned, and there she was, silvery dress a cloud of sparkles as she moved. "Is everything all right? You seem so . . . stressed."

Everything's fine, he wanted to say. Instead he pointed to the row of lobsters and said, "It's them."

She followed his mournful gaze. "I see."

"I'm embarrassed to admit it, but I can't boil these guys."

"All right, then," she said. "You don't have to." She walked over to the stove, turned off the flame, and poured the water down the sink. "Can you find me a bag? To carry them?"

Grateful that she was taking charge, he looked under the cupboard again and came up with a roll of heavy-duty garbage bags. Christina divided up the lobsters, three to a bag, and handed him one. "We'd better hurry," she said. "They won't last long." Astonished, he watched as she picked up a bag and carried it toward the door and then out onto the deck. "Well," she said, stopping for a moment. "What are you waiting for?"

Andy picked up his bag and followed her. They both kicked off their shoes and hauled the garbage bags down along the beach. The sand was cool and powdery under his feet until they reached the water's edge, where it turned gritty and damp. Christina set her bag down so that the opening faced the lapping waves. The first lobster tottered out, claws still secured. He reached for his Swiss Army knife and slit the rubber bands on each of the lobsters as they came out of the bags and scuttled toward the water. He saw the first one propel its body down and disappear into an oncoming wave, and then the next. Within minutes, there were only empty bags, the lapping waves, and the two of them. Andy was electrified, drained, and totally in awe of the woman standing by his side.

"You," he breathed, "are *amazing*." And then he kissed her, a lingering, heat-infused kiss. He could have remained there all night, but he had a houseful of people to feed, so he reluctantly pulled away. "Now what the hell am I going to serve for dinner?"

"Do you have eggs and milk?" she asked. He nodded. "And how about cheese?" He nodded again. "I hope you like corn frittata." This time she was the one who kissed him— lightly, tantalizingly—before stepping back. "Because I do make a mean one."

When they got back up to the house, everyone was there to greet them on the deck. The story of the lobsters' liberation was met first with disbelief, and then with great amusement and fanfare. Christina's frittata was delicious. So were the biscotti and the pomegranate sherbet. The guests stayed late

and polished off all the wine. Even Ida had a glass and de-
clared it delicious. Then she sat down next to Christina; Andy
immediately went into alert mode.

"Where did you say your family was from?"

"I didn't, but they're from Brooklyn. Park Slope actually,"
said Christina.

"And that's where you live now?"

Christina nodded. "In the same house where I grew up."

"But you're not married anymore? You're a divorcée?" Ida
asked.

"Ma!" Andy could not help himself. "Christina's husband
died. I *told* you that."

"You did not!" Ida said. "I hope I haven't offended you."

There was a pause before Christina murmured, "No, that's
all right." But a moment later she excused herself and got up.

Andy had to wait a few minutes before he was able to get
Ida in the kitchen alone. "What did you go and say *that* for?
Are you trying to get rid of her?"

"It was an accident," Ida said, sulking. "Like what happened with the cake."

"How did you even know about that? Anyway, there were
cookies!"

"Yes, there were cookies, Mr. Big Shot. Cookies that were
so hard I nearly broke a tooth!" And with that, she swept
regally—or as regally as was possible for someone of her di-
minutive stature—from the room.

The next day it rained and they decided to drive back to the
city early; they reached Andy's apartment by five. He called
a car service and stood under an umbrella in front of the
building with Ida while they waited for it to arrive. She hugged

him good-bye without mentioning Christina again and he was relieved to be spared. Upstairs, Oliver, who had slept the entire ride back, was now wide-awake. "I'm going out," he said.

"Oh?" Andy said. "Anywhere in particular?"

"I'm . . . going over to Jake's."

"Jake." Andy smiled. He hadn't heard that name in a while and was glad to hear it now. "Bring him out to the beach with us next time we go."

A stricken look seemed to cross Oliver's face. "Yeah, sure, whatever," he said.

After eating the leftovers of a dinner Lucy had prepared, Andy checked his phone. Nothing. He turned to his e-mail. There were messages, including a thank-you from Stephen, but none from Christina. It was as if the other night had not happened.

Then it hit him: he should contact her. She was obviously a holdover from the days when the girl—or woman—was supposed to wait for a signal from the man. Immediately, he began tapping out a message and then stopped. What should he suggest? Dinner? Movie? Theater? Then he realized it didn't matter. He just wanted to see her again.

TWELVE

*A*venue C had been busy enough on this Sunday night, with lots of people strolling along in the summer dark. But once Oliver turned the corner, he saw that East Seventh Street was deserted. He walked quickly until he came to the battered metal door and knocked. Nothing happened, so he tried again. When there was no answer, he pressed his ear to the scarred surface. The guy he'd met in the head shop on St. Marks Place had given him specific instructions: north side of East Seventh Street, between Avenues C and D, two steps down, a gray metal door with no number on it. This had to be the door, and behind it, the place. He knocked again, pounding his fist.

This time the door was yanked open and a guy with rust-colored dreads under a top hat stared at him. "Yeah?" He wore suspenders but no shirt, and a pair of denim cutoffs so bleached they were white.

"Jojo sent me," Oliver said nervously. Jojo was the kid Oliver had met in the head shop. "He told me to ask for Raven."

"Raven's in there," said the dread guy with a sharp jerk of his chin. "You can come in, but you better be quick. He's kinda busy."

Oliver followed him inside. The door slammed shut behind him with an awful, wheezing clang; he had an urge to push it open and run. But Jojo said Raven could get weed, so Oliver wasn't going anywhere until he'd scored. Since he was no longer speaking to Jake, his supply had dried up. In desperation, he'd started hanging out at the head shop; that was where he'd met Jojo, and Jojo had directed him here.

The room was dimly lit, with exposed pipes running along the low ceiling and up some of the walls. There was carpeting so filthy it was hard to tell what color it had been, and the place was filled with a weird assortment of furniture: an imitation-suede couch with collapsed springs and stuffing oozing from its various slits, a claw-footed bathtub covered by a thick wooden board, a row of seats that looked like they had been yanked from a movie theater.

On one side of the room there was a pool table; the guy he assumed was Raven was holding court next to it. His hair was the shiniest, blackest hair Oliver had ever seen on a person, and it framed his face in graceful waves. It was actually pretty, like a girl's, except Raven's mean, glittering eyes and thin slash of mouth were neither pretty nor girlish. He held a pool cue in his hands, but he did not actually seem to be playing. Instead, he was telling a story to the bunch of guys ringed around him. The story ended and the guys laughed. Oliver took the opportunity to edge closer.

Raven was on him in a nanosecond. "Do I know you?" he said. The laughter stopped.

"Jojo sent me—," Oliver began.

"Like I care," snarled Raven.

"Yeah, well, he said that you had . . . I mean, I've got money," said Oliver.

"I don't want *your* money," Raven said. He used the pool cue to poke Oliver in the chest. "Now get out. Go back to your mama."

Mortified, Oliver turned and went for the door. As he pulled it open, he heard Raven's falsetto: *"Jojo sent me,"* which made all the guys burst out laughing again. The tip of the cue had caught the soft space between his ribs; it hurt.

Out in the street again, he didn't know what the fuck to do. Why had Jojo sent him to Raven? Did he get off on humiliating people? The door squealed open and Oliver jumped away, expecting another poke from Raven's cue. But it was Dread Guy "You looking for weed?" he asked.

"Why are you asking?" Oliver was not about to walk into another trap.

"I heard what happened in there and I felt sorry for you, man. I'd sell you something if you wanted."

"Like what?"

"Like this." Dread Guy reached into his pocket and pulled out a small, rumpled paper bag. He unfurled the top and invited Oliver to sniff.

"How much?" he said warily.

"Fifty," said Dread Guy.

"Are you fucking crazy?" That was, like, a total rip-off. So much for Dread Guy feeling sorry for him.

"It's really choice stuff."

"So you smoke it." Oliver turned to go. He wanted the weed, but no way would he pay fifty for what was at most thirty dollars' worth.

"I'll throw these in too." Dread Guy opened his hand. In his palm were four oval tablets.

"Vicodin?" asked Oliver.

"Mystery pill," said Dread Guy. "But it will make you feel good."

Oliver didn't usually like pills; he preferred weed, which was in his mind a natural high, as opposed to a chemical one. Still, he wanted the weed, and the pills might be all right, especially if he used the two together. "I'll give you forty," said Oliver.

"Fifty's my price," said Dread Guy. "And you'll be back for more—you'll see."

"All right." Oliver handed him two twenties and a ten. He took the tablets and put them in the bag; then he shoved the bag way down into the pocket of his jeans, where it made a little bulge. He'd have to find a new hiding place; he didn't want his dad finding *this* stash.

Later, at home, Oliver rattled around the apartment. His dad's door was closed, which meant he was asleep—good. Although he was itching to try some of the weed he'd just scored, he knew the smell would linger. Better to try one of the pills instead. He crushed it with the back of a spoon and snorted the resulting powder.

Then he went back to his room and flipped open his laptop. He was about to do something he knew he shouldn't do, but what the fuck, he was going to do it anyway. He logged onto Facebook, where, amazingly enough, neither Delphine nor Jake had unfriended him; he could follow—and had been following—their time together in Provence. *Toujours Provence*, he remembered bitterly. The open book on the floor of Jake's room was like a taunt, a fucking punch in the gut. Only he was the one who'd punched Jake, and then, like the wuss that he was, regretted it.

So there they were: against various backdrops of palm trees and blue sky, Jake feeding *pommes frites* to Delphine; Delphine offering Jake a lick of *glace au chocolat* to Jake. They both looked tan, happy, and totally into each other. And look, here was Jake showing off the tattoo he'd gotten: a map of France on his left forearm. What a total suck up. What if she dumped him? He'd be stuck with that stupid-ass map on his skin forever.

Oliver suddenly felt thirsty. Maybe it was the pill. He got up, taking the laptop along, and went into the kitchen, where he downed a tall glass of water and immediately poured another, which he drank more slowly. The door to his mom's office was open. The room was different now; the desk was gone, and there was now a bed in its place. There were several bolts of fabric propped in a corner and a new chair he did not recognize. The mattress was still covered in plastic and on top of that was a shallow cardboard box. He left the empty glass on the granite counter and went over to investigate.

There was all the stuff that had been on his mom's bulletin board. He picked up a pair of ticket stubs from *Rent*, which she had taken him to see. Some of his friends' parents had been a little shocked; *too much adult content*, they said. But he'd loved the play and loved his mom for understanding that he was old enough to appreciate it. She never talked down to him; that was only one of the things he missed about her.

Usually, seeing all this stuff would have bummed him out. But the pill must have been, like, blunting his perceptions or something, softening them so that the raw, jagged edge of pain was gone. *She touched this,* he thought, his fingers rifling through the contents of the box. *And this, and this.*

As he stood there, the room started to melt, the walls becoming elastic, the window, liquid. He lurched toward the door. Maybe he'd feel better somewhere else. Laptop tucked under his arm, he made it into the living room. Yeah, that was better. It was dark in here, dark and quiet; the only light came from outside, the water sparkling insanely, like all the stars had dropped from the sky and were floating on its surface.

Oliver sat on the couch and opened the laptop again. What had he been looking at? Oh yeah. Jake and Delphine. He started to read some of Jake's posts: *Loving la vie en rose,* posted Jake. *Vive la France.* That was the best he could do? *Vive la France?* He'd never thought Jake was some kind of brain, but really, this stuff he was posting was a new low, even for him. He was, like, a retard, not that you were supposed to say that anymore. A fucking moron.

Then he came to another photo: Jake and Delphine on the beach, arms wrapped around each other's waists, squinting slightly from the sun and smiling. Jake wore bright red baggy trunks and a blue bandanna tied around his head, channeling some hippie dude from the sixties. Delphine wore a black bikini bottom . . . and nothing else. Her tits—smallish, perfectly shaped, and capped with delicate little nipples—were out there for anyone and *everyone* to see. And there were no visible tan lines either. He knew about those beaches where the girls went topless; it was, like, very European. But to think that Delphine would be one of those girls—it just did not compute. Oliver stared at the picture. He knew that it would be gone very quickly; Facebook didn't allow any nudity on the site. But until it was taken down, he could look as long as he liked. He kept thinking it was a mistake of some kind, that he was not seeing what he was seeing.

And then he got it: the mistake had been *his*. He'd been

wrong about Delphine, completely and totally wrong. It wasn't that she was, like, a slut or something. It was just that she was not different, not special. She did not have a rare soul. She was just a girl, prettier than some, cooler than most, with a great accent, and great tits. But his longing for her ended that minute. Game over. Done. He looked long and hard at the picture, as if to memorize it.

Then he navigated away from the page. He would never look at it again. In fact, he never even wanted to look at this laptop again; it was, like, *tainted*. He closed it, a practically brand-new MacBook Air, and held it in his hands. Now the living room had started to sway too. He could swear the floor was trembling and the furniture was humming, a low, soft murmur. It was actually kind of a nice sensation. The laptop, though, seemed dangerous, like it was leaking poison gas. He had to get rid of it, make sure he could not see it or touch it again.

With some effort, he stood and went into his dad's study. On the desk sat a digital clock whose green numbers glowed with eerie precision: 12:32. There seemed to be some significance in that—it was a new day. Still clutching the laptop, Oliver went to a door that led to a balcony. When his mom was alive, she liked to sit out here early in the morning and "feel the city waking up." He had not been on that balcony since she died and he didn't think his dad had either. The lock in the door stuck a little, but he pushed and was able to get it open.

Outside, there was a breeze, and the fuzzy gray clouds tumbled along like a bunch of wasted kittens. The balcony did not face the street, but the back of the building. This was good. He did not want to hurt anyone. He just wanted to be free of it, free from that picture. The ledge of the balcony was high, but Oliver was tall enough to reach over without straining. He looked down first. As he expected, no one was there. Then he raised the laptop up, like an offering, up and over the ledge. He released his grip and let the thing drop. There was no sound, at least not any he could hear. And it was too dark to see anything. But the act of letting go was a release and his face bloomed in a peaceful smile. The laptop was gone. He felt rinsed with an enormous sense of relief, and calmly, he walked back into the kitchen for yet another tall, cool glass of water.

THIRTEEN

Although it was not even eleven o'clock, the August morning was steamy and the streets smelled like ripe garbage. But Jordan didn't care. Hot, smelly, whatever, she could deal with it. She was here, in her city, in her element, where she truly belonged. In another month, the summer would be over, and she'd have moved up to the next level at SAB; she was so ready she could taste it. She had just finished the advanced ballet class at Dance West and was ambling down Broadway toward the subway. Usually, Alexis would have been with her, but Alexis's grandmother had gone and died and her parents had made her attend the funeral. So Jordan was alone, and in serious need of a Diet Coke.

The streets up here were thinning out. People were away—the Hamptons, the Jersey Shore, Cape Cod. Her mom had asked whether she wanted to spend a weekend out in Sag Harbor with Stephen and Misha; they pretty much had an open invitation. But even though Jordan loved her adopted godfathers and had had wonderful weekends with them, she did not want to take time off. Dance West offered classes on Sunday, so she didn't have to miss even a single day.

Across the street, she spied a deli and sprinted across Broadway just before the light changed; in her rush, she collided with a boy standing on the corner. "Oh, I'm so sorry!" she said. "I hope I didn't hurt you."

"That's okay," said the boy, who had a head full of blond curls. "Hey, I know you."

"You do?" Jordan thought he looked familiar too, but she couldn't place him.

"Your mom is Christina, right?"

"Right," said Jordan.

"She's redecorating our apartment. I met you at that wedding. I'm Oliver."

"And I'm Jordan. Your dad—he's that doctor." Now, that didn't sound very nice. "He delivers babies, doesn't he?" There, that was better.

"Yeah, and he thinks he walks on water too."

Jordan's hand flew to her mouth and then she realized he was kidding. But it was true—his dad *did* act like he walked on water.

"So, like, what are you doing up here? Don't you live in Brooklyn?" asked Oliver.

"Dance class," she said.

"Do you, like, go every day?"

"Every day," she said.

"Wow," he said. "You sure are serious."

"You have to be serious if you want to succeed," she said.

"And you want to. Succeed." He looked at her intently.

"More than anything," she said. "I was just going in to get a soda," she added. "Do you want one?"

"Me? A soda? Nah. But I'll come in with you. If it's okay."

"Why wouldn't it be?"

They went into the deli, where Jordan chose a Diet Coke and Oliver went for some kind of organic juice blend that probably had more than a hundred calories a serving. He insisted on paying for both.

"So where are you going?" she asked once they were back outside.

"Home," he said. "I'm going to walk through the park."

"Sweet."

"You can come if you want," he said.

"I guess I could. Cross the park and take the train on Lexington." She popped open her soda and took a long drink.

They entered Central Park at Seventy-second Street. "I love Bethesda Fountain," Oliver said as they approached it. "I used to come here all the time with my mom."

"You miss her," Jordan said.

"Yeah," he said. "How about your dad? Do you miss him?"

"I hardly remember him," Jordan said. "You don't miss what you don't remember."

"My dad's father disappeared when he was pretty little. He didn't miss him either."

"Disappeared?" Jordan asked. The water rippled out from the center of the fountain in ever-widening circles.

"He left and my dad hardly ever saw him after that."

"Oh," Jordan said. "Too bad."

"Yeah, I sometimes think that's why he's such a lousy dad. He didn't have, like, any role model."

"Is he really that bad? I mean, as a dad?"

"He's not the worst guy. And he's a really good doctor. But he forgets that not everyone is his patient, and that he's not always in charge."

Jordan finished her soda and looked for a place to toss the

can. When she looked back at Oliver, she saw that he had lit a cigarette. No, not a cigarette. A *joint*.

"You're going to smoke that here? There are people all around," she said nervously.

"It's cool," he said. "No one cares." He inhaled deeply and offered it to her. "Want a hit?"

"No!" she said, backing away. "And I'll bet the police would care. I'll bet they would care a *lot*."

"Hey, don't freak out," he said. "I'm sorry." He took another deep drag before dropping it on the ground, where he carefully extinguished the burning tip with his heel, and then picked it up again.

"Why do you get high?" she said. They were almost across the park now; she would be able to get away from him.

"Why don't you?" he asked, his blue gaze level and frank.

"What are you talking about?" she said. "Why would I?"

"You've never tried it." It was a statement, not a question.

"No, and I don't want to."

"You don't know what you're missing," Oliver said, regarding the half-smoked joint as if it could tell him something. "But that's cool too." They had come to Fifth Avenue. "So you get the train at Lexington and Sixty-eighth Street?"

"Uh-huh."

"That's right by where I live; I can walk you to the train." Jordan's face must have revealed how badly she wanted to get away from him because he added, "Or not. I guess that joint kind of killed it for you."

"Drugs just scare me, that's all," she said, relieved to be able to tell the truth.

"Weed is not a drug," he said. "It's a plant with a long and proud history."

"Whatever. It just weirds me out."

"How about if I promise never to do it again around you?" he asked.

"Deal," she said. He stuck out his hand. She took it and they shook. She liked him, she decided, weed and all.

At the entrance to the subway, they said good-bye. "Friends?" Oliver asked.

"Friends." She watched as he gave her a wave and then loped off.

When Jordan let herself into the house, she found Christina out in the garden fussing over a wire mesh cage that contained, of all things, a rabbit. She decided not to mention running into Oliver. "Where did this come from?" She knelt to get a better view of the animal; it looked positively petrified.

"Mimi Farnsworth." Christina sighed.

"I don't get it," said Jordan, still watching the rabbit, which was white, with diamond-shaped gray markings.

"I told you about Mimi's husband, right?"

"Oh, yeah. I remember," Jordan said. The rabbit's nostrils twitched continually.

"Well, she hasn't sold the house yet. But she's been in a frenzy of purging; if you go into my showroom upstairs, you'll see all the things I bought from her today. Some of them I even bought *back*—they were things I had found for the house when I first started the job. It's all very sad."

"And the rabbit? Did you find the rabbit too, Mom?"

Christina smiled. "No, it belonged to her sons, but now Mimi is moving them all in with her mother, who is horribly allergic to anything with fur. Even the word 'rabbit' will make her break out in hives. I said I would try to find a home for it."

"Can I pet it?" Her mother nodded and Jordan opened the cage. Instantly, the rabbit retreated to the farthest corner, where it huddled, trembling. "Is it a boy rabbit or a girl rabbit?"

"It's a male."

Jordan put her hand inside the cage. She did not attempt to touch the rabbit; she just let her hand remain there, and after a minute or two, the rabbit's eyes seemed a little less wild and its trembling less pronounced. Only then did she actually pet the fur, which was very soft. She slipped her other hand in, so she could coax the creature out of the cage. In her arms, the rabbit felt shockingly animate and alert. The small body vibrated; the nostrils continued to twitch. So did the ears. Under her fingers, Jordan felt the rabbit's heart, a steady, rhythmic beating. "Can I keep him?" she asked.

"You want a rabbit?" her mother asked.

"No," Jordan said. "I want *this* rabbit. You said he needs a home."

"Are you sure? Because you're the one who'll have to take care of him." Jordan nodded. "Well, Mimi will certainly be relieved. And her boys could come over and visit him from time to time, right?"

"Sure," said Jordan. "Whatever." She didn't care about Mimi's boys but only about the rabbit, which she had already decided to call Harlequin—Quin for short—after the character in the ballet *Petrouchka*; the rabbit's markings reminded her of the Harlequin's diamond-patterned costume.

"All right, then," her mother said. "I'm going to let Mimi know." She went inside to start dinner.

When she had gone, Jordan remained standing in the garden with the rabbit in her arms. She'd never wanted an animal before and she had no idea why she wanted this one now. But she did want him. No, that wasn't it. She *needed* him. And when she felt the gentle weight of his warm, furred body pressed against her, she was sure that he needed her too.

FOURTEEN

ndy had just finished an examination when he heard the deep, gravelly voice of Sonny, one of the doormen. He told Joanne to have the patient wait in his office while he stepped out to the building lobby to investigate. There was Sonny with one of those god-awful reporter types—he could spot them a mile off. This one wore a short, black skirt, a white blouse, and heels; at first glance, he might mistake her for a waitress. But she had that determined look in her eye and the pit bull set to her mouth. Also a mammoth bag slung over her shoulder, phone welded to her ear, and iPad clutched under her arm. "I don't see why I can't wait outside—"

"Miss, I told you before: you can't wait in the lobby, by the door, or anywhere in front of this building. If you want to wait somewhere, you'll have to go across the street."

"The street is public property; you can't tell me I can't stand here."

"I can't?" Sonny towered over her. "Just try me."

Reporter girl glared back at him as she walked away. She didn't bother to look at the light, which was red; an oncoming car had to stop short to avoid hitting her. As the driver stuck his head out the window to yell at her, Andy turned to Sonny. "Thanks," he said. "Nice work."

"Is that singer coming here today?" Sonny asked. When Andy nodded, he sighed. "That means there'll be more of them."

"Sorry, Sonny. Goes with the territory." Andy went back inside. There were now three patients waiting, which was not his style at all. But he'd crammed them all in this morning because Xiomara, his celebrity patient, was scheduled for the early afternoon and he'd promised to make sure the waiting room was cleared before she showed up. Even so, the paparazzi sniffed her out. Sonny was right: there would be more of them later. Andy was half expecting someone to try to bribe him for confidential information or, when that did not work, go ahead and steal what could not readily be bought.

All this was a hassle, and made Andy's day even more complicated than it might have been. But he'd agreed to take her on—and not because she was famous, rich, talented, or heart-stoppingly beautiful, though she was certainly all these things. No, he agreed because the first time she had come to see him, she told him about the three miscarriages and the ectopic pregnancy she had had—none of which, amazingly, had been leaked to the press—and her terror that she'd lose this baby too. "You're my last hope, Dr. Stern." Of course he'd said yes.

It was nearly seven that evening when he began the walk back toward his apartment. When he arrived, he found a package waiting for him: a padded envelope from Christina that he tore open eagerly. Inside were some fabric samples for Rachel's office; he was glad to get them, then disappointed that there was nothing personal in her note. But the package galvanized him. "Could you hold this for me?" he asked, handing the package back to the doorman. "I'll be right back."

Outside, Andy headed west, toward Lexington Avenue. If he hurried, he might just make it. And look, the lights were still on in the florist's window, and Gus was still inside, getting ready to close. Opening the door, he felt the familiar burst of cool air, the subdued but still heady scent of the flowers in the shop rising up to greet him.

"Evening, Dr. Stern. I mean Andy," said Gus. "You need something tonight?"

"I do. But it needs to be delivered to Brooklyn. Can you do that?"

Gus thought it over. "We don't usually go to Brooklyn," Gus said. "But if it's very important . . ."

"It is," Andy said. "Very important. Remember what you told me? About giving it another chance?" Gus nodded. "Well, it was good advice. Great advice, in fact."

"Oh, so it worked out with your friend?" Gus looked pleased.

"Well, no. It didn't. But there's someone else. . . ." Andy told Gus what he was after: a bouquet of white, and only white, flowers.

"I'll use freesia," Gus said. "Roses, of course. White lilies. And I'd like to put some gardenias in the mix. Also an orchid or even two."

"That all sounds great," he said. "Do you have a card, so I could write a note?" Gus provided a folded sheet of paper and Andy began to write.

Dear Christina,

I don't know if I ever mentioned that Rachel
was a big fan of the NYCB and because of her
interest, we donated money to the company.
After she died, I continued to donate; it was a
way of remembering and honoring her. We
used to go to the gala performances, and this
year is no different. I've got two tickets to the
upcoming gala on September 20th and I would
like it very much if you would be my date.

                              Yours in hope,
                              Andy

He'd been thinking about her nonstop, but although he'd
asked her out twice since that night at the beach, they had not
managed to get together. Once he'd had to cancel and the next
time she had. Maybe the third time would be the charm. He
slipped the note into the envelope and wrote her name across
the front. Then he licked the gummed edge and handed it
to Gus.

"Let me know if she likes them," Gus said.

"You bet," said Andy.

Today was the day that Christina had decided she was going
to call Alice McEvoy. Maybe the position was still available.
She doubted it, but she had to try. Once she'd made the decision, though, she did everything she could to procrastinate.
She invoiced clients, cleaned out her dresser, swept and
mopped a floor that didn't need either, and, in a last desperate

attempt to forestall the inevitable, went to Jordan's room to offer the rabbit, a nervous, shifting creature she'd never entirely grown used to, a handful of shredded lettuce leaves. Only then did she go into her office to look for Alice McEvoy's telephone number. To her vast relief, Alice wasn't in, so she left a message and then made another call to Alan, her dealer friend. He said he'd be glad to look at anything she had.

All month, she'd limped along, moving the pile of bills from one corner of the desk to another, until they had made a full circuit and were right back where they started. So now here she was, en route to selling yet another of her beloved possessions, this time a nineteenth-century bisque doll she had owned—and cherished—since she was twenty. She remembered borrowing the car from her roommate to go to the estate sale near Millbrook, and the musty barn where she had uncovered it, shrouded in straw and disintegrating newspaper, at the bottom of a steamer trunk she'd bought for five dollars.

Alan's shop was on Seventy-ninth and Lexington. Many of his well-heeled customers were away in August, but here he was, dressed in a sport coat and tie and seated at his desk—an elaborate eighteenth-century piece that was crowded with papers, a crystal decanter, several crystal ashtrays, and a clock under a bell jar. As always, he seemed glad to see her.

"Got anything interesting for me today?" he asked. Alan's roots, like hers, were in Brooklyn; he'd never lost the accent.

Christina peeled back the layers of tissue and bubble paper and set the doll on the counter. Alan examined her carefully, taking note of her exquisitely sewn white kid body, lace-trimmed, peach satin dress, fraying only the slightest bit at the back. Her wig was made of human hair done in tight ringlets and was topped by a straw hat with a black velvet ribbon. Apart from the minor damage to the dress, she was in excellent, and all-original, condition.

"She's very nice," he said. "French or German?"

"French. Jumeau." Christina showed him the identifying mark.

"Are you sure you want to sell her?"

Christina did not answer. The doll had survived intact for all these years. Where was the little girl who had played with—so decorously, so tenderly—and loved her? Long dead now. She had been instantly drawn to the doll's deep blue glass eyes—Emile Jumeau had a patent on their production— the rosy fullness of her painted cheeks, the pearly and vaguely feral little teeth. She had a couple of other bisque dolls she'd acquired, but this one was her favorite, and had been given pride of place on the mantel in her bedroom. She was also the most valuable.

Alan reached for the wad of cash he kept in his pocket and began peeling off the hundreds—one, two, three, four, five, six. When he finished, there were ten in all. The doll might have fetched more at auction, but Christina did not want to wait—she needed the money now. "Thank you," she had said, reaching for the bills. She was putting them in her wallet when she realized that Alan had pushed something across the counter in her direction—the doll.

"I just sold her to you," she said.

He shook his head. "No, you didn't."

"The money you just gave me—"

"Will be for something else. You always bring me good pieces, Christina. I can afford to extend you credit."

"That's so . . . nice of you," she said. She felt tears rising. He was so kind. Was it because he pitied her? And if so, did it matter? She needed the money; she wanted the doll. He made it possible for her to have both. On the way back to Brooklyn, the doll, nestled in her wrappings, sat in a shopping bag placed securely between Christina's ankles. She had just finished placing her back in her spot when she heard her phone. Maybe it was Alice.

"Christina, it's Phoebe Haverstick. I know we've taken *forever* getting back to you, but Ian insisted that we do our homework before making a decision."

"Of course," Christina said. "It's a big commitment." She tried to sound calm. Was this the call she'd been hoping for? The one she stopped believing would come?

"It sure is! But we've decided we want you to do the job," said Phoebe. "If you're still available, that is."

Was she available? But she checked herself and said coolly, "Let me look in my book," and then waited a couple of beats before saying, "Yes, I can fit you in."

"You can? Terrific! So when do you think you could get up here again?"

As they were settling on a date, the doorbell rang. Christina went to answer it while still on the phone. Flowers! Who was sending her flowers? She waited until she'd finished her call before opening the card. She read it once, twice, and then a third time. Andy Stern was inviting her to a gala. And he'd written *Yours in hope*. So he was still thinking about her that way. Well, ever since their crazy stunt at the beach, she had been thinking about him too. She had been moved by his tenderness. Excited by his ardor. But she was confused too. He seemed so wrong for her. His brash manner, for one. His wealth, or more precisely his way of flaunting it, for another. His being, in effect, her boss. She'd agreed to go out with him a couple of times before, but when their plans fell through, her disappointment had been laced with relief. He unsettled her and she'd been glad to let her worries—money (or lack of it), Phoebe—chase him from her mind. Now he was back again, and more insistent than ever.

Christina pressed her nose into the bouquet and inhaled deeply. She had not a clue as to how she wanted to reply. But Stephen would help her figure it out. She brought a bottle of wine, a loaf of bread, and a wedge of cheese to the glass-topped table in the garden and waited for him to get home. When he did, she ambushed him.

"You like him, right?" he asked. He was sitting across from her, carving the bread. Christina nodded and he added, "Then go for it."

"Well, it is a little awkward; I'm still working for him."

"And doing a fine job too, right? Isn't he happy? And the pothead son too?"

"Stephen! He's not a pothead. Not exactly." She had confided in him about her suspicions, but right now that was all they were—suspicions.

"Whatever." He took a sip of his wine. "But there's no reason to feel awkward. A gala is a very public event. It doesn't mean he's going to make a move on you. "Unless"—he paused to study her—"you *do* want him to make a move. Or maybe he's made one already."

"He did kiss me," Christina said, looking down. "Twice."

"And you didn't tell Uncle Stephen? Shame on you, girl!"

"Well, the first time he was a little bit drunk. And I was too."

"And the second?"

"On the beach. After we let the lobsters go free."

"I knew it!" said Stephen. "I told Misha I could almost see the sparks."

"Misha probably thinks he's just awful."

"Well, he is," Stephen said matter-of-factly.

"What do you mean?" Even though she agreed, she rallied to Andy's defense.

"And at the same time, he isn't," he went on. "He's oafish. But endearingly oafish. That thing he said to Misha about the play—his foot was so far in his mouth he could have bitten his ankle. And then he spent the rest of the night making it up to him. Plus he sent a hefty contribution to the theater company responsible for the play; Misha just found out today."

"That does sound like Andy," Christina said.

"So okay, you've gotten drunk with boss man, you've canoodled with him, and now you're worried about sitting across from him at a table along with ten other strangers? I'd say you were worrying about the wrong thing."

"What should I be worrying about?"

"What you're going to wear, of course!"

"That's true. I don't have anything to wear," she said. "Not anything that's suitable anyway." She took a sip of her wine.

"Well, you can come up with something affordable, can't you? You—you're the thrift shop queen."

"But the other women are going to be so over-the-top."

"Which just means you have to go all out. You want to take his breath away."

"Is that really what I want to do?"

"From where I sit: yes."

"But, Stephen, he's all wrong for me."

"Christina, you haven't had a guy in your life in what, four years?"

"Five," she said in a small voice.

"Five. Right. And here comes a guy who is ringing all your chimes—"

"I never said that," she interrupted.

"You didn't have to. I could see it written all over you. Now, forget about who's right for you and who's not and just let your fairy godmother Stephen dress you for the ball."

FIFTEEN

A week later, Christina and Stephen were walking up Third Avenue, intent on making the rounds at the cluster of high-end thrift stores—CancerCare, Sloan-Kettering, Arthritis Foundation, Spence-Chapin—that lined the street. Here was where New York's richest women—and men—donated last year's Chanels, Célines, and Chloés. Christina had been shopping these stores for decades, but never with such a sense of well-honed purpose. Yet when they walked into the Arthritis Foundation's store on the corner of Eighty-first Street, everything looked awful to her, a veritable sea of polyester, elastic-waisted pants, freakish power suits robbed of their power, stretched-out T-shirts, and pilled sweaters.

"Let's go," she said. "There's nothing here."

"Are you nuts?" he said. "You haven't even looked."

"I can just tell," she said.

"Christina, what is with you?"

"I don't have the touch today," she said.

"Come on," he said, taking her elbow and guiding her to the back of the store, where the gowns and long dresses were hanging. "Uncle Stephen will lead the way." But when they examined the offerings—a taxicab yellow number with rick-rack along the triple-flounced skirt, a floor-length hooded dress made of what could have been a horse blanket, and several droopy, jersey things—Stephen had to admit that she was right.

"Now can we go?" she said.

"Not so fast. I've still got work to do." In much the same way Christina bought things to stock her showroom, Stephen was always on the lookout to augment his stylist's closet; today he found several silk scarves, a few pieces of costume jewelry, and an honest-to-God tiara, albeit made of rhinestones, not diamonds.

"Now, who is going to wear *that*?" Christina asked.

"Oh, I don't know," he said. "Maybe you?"

"In your dreams!" she said. But she was smiling. And although they had not found The Dress yet, she felt the familiar thrill of the hunt kicking in. Of course Stephen was right: they would find a dress. Would it take Andy's breath away? Did she even want it to?

But Christina did want to be well attired when she appeared by his side at the gala, so she plunged into the task at hand. After hitting all the stores on the strip, they finally narrowed it down to two choices: one black lace and the other blue and covered in sequins. Christina was more partial to the black dress, though Stephen preferred the blue. "Black is a bit predictable, don't you think? Whereas the other . . ."

They decided to mull it over while searching for accessories. A pair of strappy, black suede sandals from Yves Saint

Laurent was only forty-five dollars, and as Stephen pointed out, they would work with any of the dresses. "The heels are kind of high," said Christina.

"The better to go teetering into Prince Charming's arms," said Stephen.

"He's not exactly charming," Christina said. Still, she bought the sandals. By this time it was after three, and Christina was ready to make a decision. But when she found out the two dresses had been radically marked down, Christina bought them both. Stephen would take the one Christina did not end up wearing for his own inventory. Back at home, Christina hung the two gowns side by side in her closet. The black lace was bold and dramatic, while the shimmery blue was dreamy and ethereal. Each represented a choice, a persona she could assume; which of these two women would she decide to be when she joined Andy at the gala?

SIXTEEN

When Christina arrived at the Haversticks', the construction crew was deep in the plastering of the downstairs rooms; the sanding and painting would begin when they had completed the job. The wall colors had been selected and the paint order placed, so they were in good shape. The grand old house buzzed with new life: the workers talking in Spanish, the lilting rhythm of the music coming from their portable radio, the excited voices of Phoebe's girls and two of their friends as they tore through the mess.

"I've got to get them out of here," Phoebe said. She wore black athletic shorts and a white spandex top under which the protrusion of her pregnancy was now quite visible. "Ian will be home early and is taking everyone to a movie; you and I will have some peace!"

Christina was relieved. The husband would be coming home but then immediately leaving. Perfect. Ian had been the only sour note in this whole production; he seemed to view Christina's job either with lofty disdain or faint alarm whenever he thought they were spending too much.

"Can I go upstairs until you're free? I've got a couple of things I need to measure."

"Sure; I'll meet you when the coast is clear." Across the room, she spied one of the girls attempting to dip a spoon into an open bucket of plaster. "Torry! Out of there!" Christina took the opportunity to head upstairs. The work here was not as far along, but that was all right; Phoebe wanted easily washable wallpaper, and not paint, for these rooms. Christina was envisioning a series of conjoined spaces—bedroom for an au pair or a nanny, playroom, and nursery. She was also thinking of installing a small, second laundry room up here, with a stackable washer and dryer, and there was a closet where she thought they would fit quite nicely. Pulling out the Moleskine notebook and the tape measure she never went anywhere without, she opened the closet door.

It looked small, but actually there was a deep space to the left of the opening, not readily visible unless she poked her head in and looked around the corner created by the door-frame. She spied a sheet-swathed object way at the back. Now, what was this doing in here? Phoebe said all the rooms were empty. Christina dragged it out and pulled the sheet aside. It was an oil painting, and from the looks of it, it was both quite old and quite good. She felt the familiar thrumming that she always got when she stumbled on a significant find. The painting showed a young girl, perhaps eight or nine, seated on a patterned sofa. She wore a white dress bisected by a dark sash; beside her slept a silky-eared spaniel whose coppery fur was virtually the same color as her magnificent auburn hair. The brushwork was open and even spontaneous; still, she could see the underlying formal rigor that held it all together. The handling of the paint and the assurance of the palette pointed to a very skilled artist. And the child's expression was the best thing of all; she was alive, almost breathing.

Kneeling, Christina looked for a signature. There might be something there on the bottom left corner, but despite the sheet, the painting was dusty. Taking the linen handkerchief out of her bag, she gently applied it to the canvas. Pressing more than rubbing, she tapped the spot with a light, delicate motion. After a moment, she lifted the handkerchief away. It was gray with dirt, but she didn't even notice. Instead, she was staring at the letters she had exposed: *John S. Sargent 1918.* Sargent!

She knew a bit about him from a course she'd taken in college. born in 1856, a descendant of one of the oldest colonial families; his parents became expats after the death of their firstborn. He'd received little formal schooling, but his mother, an amateur artist herself, encouraged him to draw. He studied art in both Florence and Paris and made several trips to America; he became successful on both sides of the Atlantic. Rich patrons commissioned his portraits and he became known for his indelible images of a moneyed, leisured class in the gardens and parlors, the drawing rooms and orchards, where they conducted their lives. Even though he was often associated with the Impressionists, Christina had always thought there was something stubbornly American about his vision, more solid and corporeal than the evanescent images created by the French.

Was it authentic, though? There were legions of forgers out there, both past and present, who'd learned to simulate every nuance, every last stroke of the brush. Only a professional could decide whether it was real. But first she'd have to tell the Haversticks. Propping the painting carefully against the wall, she hurried downstairs; Phoebe was on the way up and they met midway.

"I want to show you something," Christina said. Phoebe followed her to the little room on the top floor and pointed to the painting. "Have you ever seen this before?"

"Oh my God!" Phoebe dropped down and put her hands on the corners of the canvas. "Where did you find it? She used to have it hanging in her bedroom. It was the only thing that didn't fit in with her crazy color scheme. But I had no idea it was still here. I thought it was sold a long time ago."

"Evidently not," said Christina, gazing at the image. "Do you have any idea about who the sitter might have been?"

"It's a portrait of her," Phoebe said. "She had beautiful red hair as a child and as a young woman; she always talked about it. When it turned gray, she had it dyed, but she said she could never find anyone to duplicate the color."

Ian poked his head into the room. "Where'd you go?" he asked his wife. It sounded like an accusation. "You just disappeared. The girls don't want to see a movie, so I'm letting them play on the computer."

"Ian, look at what Christina just found." Ignoring his tone, she led him over to the painting. "It's a portrait of Aunt Victoria." She peered at the signature and added, "By John S. Sargent."

"Singer," said Ian with a hint of contempt.

"Excuse me?" said Phoebe.

"John Singer Sargent. He's a very well-known painter." He turned to Christina. "What's it worth?"

Christina had been so taken with the painting—the plump cushions lining the sofa, the patterned shawl artlessly draped over its side, the steady gaze of the little girl at its center—that she was jarred by the blunt way he phrased the question. Of course the painting, once authenticated, would be worth a great deal of money. But it also had an artistic worth that seemed lost on Ian Haverstick.

"I don't know," she answered. "You'll need to have it appraised."

"And to think it was just sitting up here, covered by a sheet," said Ian. He turned to Phoebe. "Do you remember seeing it ever?"

"Yes, ages ago," Phoebe said.

"She never talked to you about it, though? Or mentioned it in the will?"

"Not specifically, no. But *the house and all its contents—* that's what the will said—went to me. To us." She patted her belly fondly.

"If it *is* real, it will pay for the work we're doing, college for all the kids, and the hell knows what else," said Ian.

"I would never sell this painting," said Phoebe. "It's been in my family for almost a hundred years."

"Only an idiot would forgo all that money just for some useless heirloom."

Christina hoped her disgust was not apparent. Imagine talking to your wife that way in front of someone else. No— imagine talking to your wife that way at all. "Whatever you decide, it would be a good idea to get it authenticated first," she said.

"I know it's real," said Phoebe. "She said it was valuable."

"Can you trust her, though?" Ian said. "Christina's right— we have to find out for sure."

Christina was silent; she did not want to get in the middle of their argument.

"Well, that wouldn't be a bad idea," Phoebe said. "How do we go about doing that?"

"I'd start with Christie's or Sotheby's," said Christina.

"I've heard a lot of bad things about those places," Ian said. "Wasn't there some big scandal—the head of one of those auction houses was convicted of some kind of fraud and placed under house arrest?"

"I've got a friend who's an independent appraiser; he's considered one of the best in his field. I could give you his name. He's scrupulously honest. If he's handling it, you won't have to worry."

"Would you?" Phoebe said. "That would be wonderful."

"Of course. It's Derrick Blascoe. His loft is on Union Street, down by the Gowanus Canal. He'll come and pick the painting up. In the meantime, you'll want to store it somewhere else, away from all the plaster dust and mess. And you should insure it too. Right away."

Ian was nodding vigorously as Phoebe turned to Christina. "We still have some other things to discuss, right?"

"Right," Christina said. "I've had some new ideas about the space up here. And I wanted to show you some samples of the finishes the furniture restorer gave me."

"Furniture restorer?" said Ian. "I didn't know we were hiring a furniture restorer."

"I wanted to keep a couple of the pieces Aunt Victoria left," said Phoebe. "Christina says we can have them stripped and refinished."

"Are you crazy?" he said to her. "It's a total waste of money to invest in any of that crap."

"I don't know about that," Christina said, trying to keep her tone neutral. "Some of those pieces are very solid and well made; once they're stripped, you won't recognize them."

"Are you getting a kickback or something? Is that why you're pushing this?"

Christina could not reply; if she did, she might have spit. What an awful man.

"Ian." Phoebe's tone was conciliatory and gentle. "I'm the one who told Christina I wanted to keep some of those pieces."

Ian shook his head. "Still seems like a waste," he said, but more to himself than to Phoebe or Christina. "Anyway, I'm going down to check on the girls."

"I'll be right there," Phoebe said. They waited for him to leave before Christina reached into her bag for the samples. She could not even look at Phoebe; she wanted to spare her client the embarrassment of having to acknowledge her husband's boorishness. "For the sideboard, I'd go with something on the light side," she said. "It's a big piece and if you go too dark, it's going to overpower the room—you don't want it to hulk."

Phoebe considered the options while Christina measured the closet. The painted image of Victoria, still propped against the wall, seemed to be giving them her silent approval. Phoebe chose a honey-colored stain for the sideboard and a slightly darker stain for the dining table and the chairs, which she had also decided to keep.

"I'll get the restorer to come pick everything up," said Christina as she tucked the samples and the tape measure away. "How is Tuesday?"

"Tuesday's fine." Phoebe seemed distracted; she was looking at the portrait again. "Don't mind Ian," she said abruptly. "He's not always such a grouch. He's just going through a terrible time at the office."

"I'm sure that's stressful," Christina said. Though how it explained his constantly aggrieved and belittling tone remained a mystery to her.

"So that's it, then? You'll let me know what time on Tuesday?"

Christina nodded and the two women went downstairs. Ian was nowhere to be seen, and after another of Phoebe's bone-crushing handshakes, she was out the door and down the steps.

Christina was not surprised when Derrick phoned the following day. They had always liked each other and had even had coffee a couple of times over the years. "Thanks for sending me the Haversticks," he said. "The painting is an astonishing find."

"I know," she said. "I just about squealed when I saw it."

"I haven't had anything this good for ages," Derrick said.

"So you think it's authentic?" Christina asked.

"My hunch is yes. But I don't want you to say anything to them until I'm one hundred and ten percent sure."

"Of course not," she agreed. "You should be the one to tell them anyway."

"I would like to take you to dinner, though. That's the least I can do."

"Dinner would be great," Christina said. "How's next week?"

"I was hoping you'd say tomorrow," Derrick said. "Why wait?"

Christina laughed. "I'll have to check my book." And when she saw she was in fact free, she said, "All right, then—tomorrow."

The next night, she met Derrick at the Smith Street restaurant he'd chosen. Smith Street and the surrounding area had, in her youth, been even more derelict than Park Slope. She recalled a cheerless thoroughfare lined with liquor stores, check-cashing establishments, and a place that advertised bail bonds; there had been a large correctional facility nearby. But now the street was filled with hip boutiques and destination restaurants; she and Derrick dined on leg of lamb, sweet potato soufflé, and haricots verts. He ordered an expensive bottle of red, and when they had polished it off—he had considerably more than she did—he ordered a second.

"No more for me," she protested.

"Come on, it's a celebration," he urged. "How often does a rogue Sargent turn up in a closet?"

Reluctantly, Christina accepted another glass though she barely touched it. The candles in their votive glasses were beginning to blur before her eyes. Dessert was a complicated, multilayered cake with mocha frosting *and* crème fraîche that he insisted she try even though she was quite full from both the lamb and the wine. When it came time to leave, Derrick offered her a lift home. "Where are you parked?" she asked, weaving a little unsteadily alongside him.

"Right here." He pointed to a lipstick red Miata. "If you like, I can put the top down."

"That would be nice," she said, thinking the night air would feel good. He took down the top and they climbed in. The breeze ruffled her hair, but it did clear her head too; she felt better, less cloudy. Derrick veered left on Union Street, past the dark, oily expanse of the Gowanus Canal; when he got to the other side, he stopped. "Is something wrong?" she asked.

"Not a thing," said Derrick. "I was just hoping you'd come in. I wanted you to see what I'd done with the painting."

"Ah, the painting," she said. "It's late, but I really would like to have a peek. . . ."

"Good," he said, and came around the car to open her door. Had he always been such a gentleman? Derrick's shop was on the ground floor of the building. But he bypassed the metal security gate and instead led her upstairs to his loft above. "Why is the painting up here?" she asked.

"I wanted to have it near me," he explained.

Christina nodded as he went around turning on lights and the radio—tuned to a classical station—too. She realized she had never been to his apartment before. The far wall was covered with books; a rolling wooden ladder made those on the top shelves accessible. There was a low-slung sectional sofa punctuated by several pillows in a folkloric, tribal print, a glass-topped coffee table, and, by the oversized windows, several potted plants. She thought she recognized the pillows; hadn't she gotten those for him?

"How about a nightcap?" he said. "I've got some cognac—"

"None for me," she said. "I'm already past my limit." She continued to look around. "Where's the painting?"

"Follow me." He'd poured himself a drink and was sipping from the glass as he took her hand and led her along. Christina was surprised by the gesture; years ago, she'd felt a mild attraction to Derrick, but it had been too soon after Will's death and nothing had ever come of it. Had he felt it too? She couldn't remember. "There," he said. He led her behind a Japanese shoji screen; there was the painting, propped up on the bed that dominated the back wall of the loft.

"You've done some cleaning, then?" she said as she got closer.

"A little. It didn't need much."

"So you think it's the real deal," she said.

"I do." He sounded excited. "Here, look." He knelt to retrieve an oversized volume that was sitting on the floor and flipped open the pages. "See how the signatures match?"

Christina peered at the book, whose pages showed several enlarged signatures. "It certainly does look like it."

"There's something else too—Sargent pretty much gave up commissioned portraiture around 1907. So if this is his work, it was not a commission and may be even more valuable for that reason."

"The Haversticks will be happy," Christina said.

"He's an idiot," Derrick said. "And she's the wife of an idiot. They don't deserve this painting." He turned to face her.

"I knew you'd appreciate it," she said nervously. Although she agreed with him about Ian Haverstick, his whole tone seemed unprofessional. "And that you'd—" She stopped, because Derrick had put an arm around her and kissed her. She was so surprised that she did not immediately protest, but the glass of cognac he'd been holding in the other hand sloshed slightly and a few drops landed on her neck. She stepped back.

"Derrick, I don't know what to say—"

"You don't have to say anything." He set down the glass and reached out for her. "We've always liked each other, Christina. The timing wasn't right for us before, but maybe it is now."

"No, I'm sorry, it isn't. I just don't feel that way about you."

"Then why did you come back here with me?" His voice suddenly acquired an edge.

"To see the painting," she said. "Isn't that why you invited me?"

"Oh, come *on*." It was practically a taunt. "You can't have been that naive."

"Yes," she said. "I can." She tried to suppress the ribbon of fear that snaked through her. Derrick wasn't a tall man, but with his broad shoulders and well-muscled arms he seemed a little, well, threatening. And just then, he moved closer and put his arms around her again. Tightly.

"Come on," he said again, but this time it was in a gentler tone, as if he was trying to persuade her.

"I told you no," she said firmly, and when he did not release her, she added, "I think we've both had too much to drink; I should go now."

"You're right," he said abruptly, and released her.

Christina exhaled; she had not let herself truly taste the panic until it was no longer so imminent. She started moving toward the door when she realized Derrick was crying; he was bent over and his body heaved. "Are you all right?" she asked tentatively. She did not want to get any closer, but she was concerned.

"Just go," he said, voice muffled by his hands. When she did not move, he raised his head. "Please, Christina, I'm asking you to leave." She did not wait to be asked again.

SEVENTEEN

*C*hristina rushed into the house; she was running late and she still had to shower before Stephen came down to style her for the gala. Dumping her bag and sample books in her office, she went into the bathroom, turned on the water, and stripped. Minutes later, she was scurrying toward her room, head wrapped in a towel, dripping water as she went. Stephen appeared just as she was tying her bathrobe, and the doorbell rang. "That must be Magda," he said.

"Magda?"

"She's the hair and makeup person I told you about."

"Oh, Stephen, I'm sure she's great, but how am I going to pay for her?" said Christina.

"Relax," he said. "She'll barter her services. You must have something in that showroom of yours she'll want. I'll get the door; you just go in, sit down, and let her do her thing."

Christina did as she was told as Magda—an imposing creature with a white-blond crew cut and eyes dramatically rimmed in kohl—got to work. She was actually glad to be absolved of making any decisions for the moment. Using her fingers, Q-tips, triangular foam wedges, and an impressive assortment of brushes, Magda dabbed, dusted, rubbed, shaded, contoured, and covered.

Christina had not told anyone, not even Stephen, what had happened with Derrick. Though she knew it was ridiculous, she did feel a little embarrassed by having gone up to the loft with him; maybe she *had* been leading him on. She had tried calling a couple of times but got no answer and her calls went unreturned. Then all of a sudden it was September. Jordan started her new school. A couple of old clients had returned from vacation with redecorating on their minds, which made up for some of the work Christina had lost the previous winter and spring. She made a trip up to the vast and dizzying flea market in Brimfield, Massachusetts—the issue with her car back in June had turned out to be minor after all—and came back with several major new acquisitions, including a couple of patchwork quilts for Andy Stern's apartment. The evening with Derrick receded in her mind. But Andy didn't. And now that the night of the gala was here, Christina was not sure what to expect.

After about forty minutes, Magda pulled out a hand mirror and gave it to Christina. Her own voluminous lashes blinked several times while she waited for the response.

"It's . . . quite a transformation," Christina said. "I don't recognize myself." And she didn't. It was her face yet not her face.

"My God, you are stunning!" said Stephen when he surveyed her. "Wait until Misha sees you!"

"I held off on the lipstick," Magda said, clearly pleased by Stephen's reaction. "I wanted to wait and see what dress you finally choose." Cosmetic wedge in hand, she indulged in a last bit of blending near Christina's chin. "But do you like it?"

"Yes," Christina said. "I do."

Stephen turned to Magda. "Girl, I knew you were good, but until today, I didn't know how good."

Christina swatted him gently on the arm. "You're making it sound like I was a train wreck before."

"*Au contraire,* darling. Your light was under a bushel, that's all. Now we've just got to settle on what you're going to wear."

Christina went upstairs to try on the blue dress. It had been made in the 1960s, and the color, she conceded, was very pretty. Hanging beads adorned the bodice and the skirt was covered in iridescent sequins. The shape was simple enough—sleeveless, scoop necked, with a zipper down the back. But something was wrong; the dress felt constricting. She took it off and reached for the other. The black lace dress was from the 1950s, and the sequins—also black, like moonlight on the water—and tiny rhinestones gave it a festive but elegant look. And when she slipped into it, she could appreciate the boned silk underlay and the meticulous satin hemline embroidered in a filigree pattern. The Empire waist gave her a long, lean line and the strapless bodice left her neck and shoulders bare. The full skirt allowed her to move freely, unimpeded. This was the one. She buckled the sandals and carefully descended the stairs; these heels were *not* made for walking. There was a brief silence when she appeared in the kitchen.

"Oh. My. God." Stephen stared at her. "I have to say it, Christina. You outstyled the stylist. You know I was campaigning for the blue, but this, *this*—" He paused. "Well, there are no words."

"It's a fantastic dress," added Magda. "And I know just

what lipstick will be perfect." She began looking through the
many tubes she'd laid out on the table.

"I'll be right back," said Stephen.

"Where are you going?" Christina asked.

"You'll see; I've got the perfect accessory." He darted up
the stairs while Magda painted her lips an alarming shade
of crimson.

"I've never worn red lipstick in my life," Christina said.

"Well, this is the time to start. It looks amazing on you."

"What about her hair?" Magda said. "Can we take it down
and brush it out?"

"I always wear it up," Christina said.

"You can wear it up tonight," Stephen said, "*if* you wear
this." From behind his back, he pulled out the rhinestone tiara.

"Oh no!" Christina said. "Not the tiara!"

"Just try it," he begged. "For me."

Christina looked at his eager expression. How hard would
it be to humor him? She'd put it on and then take it off in the
car uptown. But when Stephen slipped the glittering tiara on
her head, she had to admit it felt wonderful, like she'd returned to some more pure, innocent version of herself, the girl
who had fallen in love with Will, not the woman who had
buried him.

"Shades of Audrey Hepburn," breathed Stephen. He
handed her one of the scarves he'd bought—a long, pink chiffon rectangle—to wear as a shawl, he explained, and Magda
put the red lipstick in Christina's black evening bag, in case
she needed a touch-up later.

"I'll get it back to you," Christina said, but Magda told her
to keep it.

Then they went upstairs to pose for pictures. Stephen had

opened a bottle of wine and they were getting pretty silly, like kids on prom night, when Jordan walked into the house.

"Mom?" She dropped her bag and walked over for a closer look. "Do you have a big date or something?"

"It's the New York City Ballet gala," Christina said. "Remember I told you I was going?"

"I forgot. Anyway, where did you come up with this outfit?" She circled around Christina, examining her from all angles.

"It was a joint effort," Stephen said, linking arms with Misha and Magda.

"What do you think?" Christina asked.

Jordan reached up to touch the tiara. "I think you'll be the most beautiful mom there," she said finally.

"Thank you, sweetheart," Christina said, reaching for her evening bag. Andy had insisted on sending a car for her and she had to admit it was a good idea; she did not want to be traveling to Lincoln Center by herself like this.

Jordan stood by the stairs. "Who's your date, anyway?"

"Andy Stern," Christina said. "Didn't I tell you?"

"You're going with *him*? Why?" Disbelief and distaste mingled in Jordan's expression.

"Well, because he asked me," said Christina. "And because I like him."

"I can't see anything to like," she said, and left the room. Watching her go, Christina felt the heady little balloon of her excitement deflating slightly.

"It's not about him. It's about you—she's not used to sharing," said Stephen. Christina nodded. But she would never be able to be serious about a man her daughter did not like. Magda was packing her things up when, outside, two sharp beeps sounded. Stephen looked out the window and then over in her direction. "Christina," he said, opening the shutter wide to reveal the black Lincoln Town Car sitting in front of the house. "Your chariot awaits."

The fountain in front of Lincoln Center spurted upward, spraying tiny droplets of water on the shoulders and back of Andy's tuxedo. Not wanting to get wet, he stepped back and checked his watch. He'd told the car service he wanted Christina here by five thirty and it was now five thirty-two. All around him, people were clustered near the fountain, waiting to go into the theater; he could see the red carpet, along with the attendant paparazzi. The galas had become star vehicles of late, attracting all sorts of socialites and celebrities.

Andy checked his watch again. Five thirty-four. The cocktail reception had just started. It would be followed by the evening's performance, and then a two-thousand-dollar-a-plate black-tie dinner afterward. Rachel had been the balletomane in the family; Andy had always simply been along for the ride. But he found he'd been unable to forgo these tickets, even though they were expensive. Supporting the ballet was one more way of keeping his connection to his dead wife alive. And he remembered she had admired this new choreographer—Russian, and touted as the next Balanchine—and would have been so pleased that his was the featured work on the program tonight. Of course now that he knew Christina's daughter was so involved in the ballet, he had another reason to learn more about it.

Where *was* Christina? He could call her on his cell phone but decided to wait until five forty-five. And at five forty-three, he saw her emerge from the black Town Car, cross the plaza— endearingly wobbly on a pair of killer heels—and walk toward him. As she got closer, he could feel his jaw opening, almost without his volition, in surprise. Look at her, just *look* at her. Incredible black dress, the scarlet lips, the glittery thing on top of her head—was it a *crown*? Even in this celebrity-studded atmosphere—he'd already seen Meryl Streep, Sarah Jessica Parker, Ronald Lauder, and Ralph and Ricky Lauren—heads were turning in her direction. Bill Cunningham, a fixture of the New York social scene, was there with his camera and he snapped several shots of her as she passed; she looked that good.

"Well hell-o," he said, extending a hand. Close up, he could better appreciate the superb fit of the dress, which was strapless, revealing her pale arms and throat. He had a sudden image of her nipples under the wet T-shirt and tried to imagine her breasts beneath the black lace and sequins. The thought drove him a little crazy. "Don't you look terrific," he said, a bit too loudly. "That's some dress."

"Thank you," she said. "I hope you haven't been waiting long. The car came early, but there was traffic."

"No worries," he said. "You're here now. Shall we?" He took her elbow and guided her toward the entrance to the David H. Koch Theater at the southern end of the plaza. Just ahead of them was Barbara Walters talking to Candice Bergen. Stargazing was fun, but Andy was more interested in the woman by his side. There was something tantalizing about how she was at the same time both familiar and different. The dress and the thing on her head were certainly out there; the red lipstick was hot, but she still seemed like Christina, held together by a kind of reserve and poise that transcended what she wore. He bet she'd have that quality even when naked—*if* he was lucky enough to see her naked.

All through the cocktail hour, he was aware that other

people were watching her; it made him feel good. And when he ran into a former patient—there were at least three here he was aware of—he could tell she was very interested in his escort. During the performance, he kept stealing glances at her, though her eyes never strayed from the stage. Was she a true balletomane, or was she imagining her daughter up there one day?

"Did you like that?" he asked during the intermission.

"I thought it was brilliant," she said. "I see why he's being compared to Balanchine. There's a similar precision and clarity to his vision, don't you think? Also a wonderful economy that I think of as quintessential Balanchine."

Andy just nodded. He could not comment on the precision, clarity, or economy of what he'd just seen. Christina did not seem to notice that he had not replied and looked down at her program. The curtain went back up and again, when he attempted to seek her gaze, he saw only her profile, serene and silent.

It was better at the dinner, which was held on the promenade. The waiters had to squeeze between the tightly packed tables to bring the food—salad, beef stew, baskets of rolls—to the guests. The silver-haired man on Andy's right was very highly placed in finance and though he was too discreet to name names, he nonetheless regaled them with stories of fortunes lost and won. Christina laughed, tipping back her head and exposing her smooth white throat. Andy wanted to take a bite out of it. The wine was flowing freely, though he made sure to alternate with water; he did not want to be drunk tonight.

After the assorted *macarons* and Tahitian vanilla ice cream were served, there was dancing. Some of the members of the ballet company got out onto the floor and dazzled the guests with their prowess, but Andy was happy just to have the chance to take Christina into his arms. They swayed gently to the music, and at one point she rested her forehead against his chest. He didn't want to move or even breathe, but yet another of his former patients—this one drunk and sloppy—interrupted, to give him a big, public hug. Then Peter Martins got up and gave a little speech thanking the committee for all their hard work and telling everyone how much money had been raised. The mood was definitely broken.

They left the theater a little after midnight. Although it was September, the air felt as mild as July. People streamed through the plaza. The fountain, lit from below, still gushed and foamed. Andy took a deep, appreciative breath. He did not want the evening to end.

"That," Christina said, "was wonderful. Thank you *so* much for inviting me." In one hand, she held her purse; in the other, the two gifts bags given to each parting guest.

"Thank you for joining me," he said, sounding more serious than he'd meant. "You really made it special."

She said nothing, but began to look around. "I wonder if I can get a taxi up here; so many other people will be trying. Maybe I should walk downtown a bit. . . ."

"That's a good idea," he said. *It was a terrible idea.* "We can head toward Columbus Circle, and I'll make sure you're in safely." They began to walk down the stretch of Broadway that led from Lincoln Center to Fifty-ninth Street and Columbus Circle. Andy was frantically trying to think of a way to move into the next phase of the evening, the one he'd had planned for weeks. Should he suggest a nightcap? A carriage ride around Central Park—not that rides were even offered this late. She seemed unaware of his anxiety, her hair still tightly wound, the thing in her hair sparkling as she turned or inclined her head. Her lips, no longer so vividly red, still held a vestige of color and were formed into a half smile. Around her shoulders, she wore some sheer pink thing or other; it was pretty, but it prevented him from seeing her skin and he wished she would take it off.

Now they were just a block away from Columbus Circle. If he didn't think of something soon, now, he'd be putting her in a taxi back to Brooklyn and the magic of this night would be wasted. Without another word, he stopped and, in the fluorescent glare of a Duane Reade window, took her face in his hands and kissed her. "Can we go somewhere? To talk?" he said, still holding on to her arms.

"Is that what you want to do? Talk?" She raised her eyebrows in amusement.

"Among other things . . ." He was still holding her closely, but he wanted to get off this corner, and out of the light. Taking her by the hand, he stepped closer to the corner, raised his arm, and amazingly a taxi pulled up right in front of them.

"The Carlyle Hotel," he told the driver.

"Andy, what—"

"You'll see," he said, still holding her hand. "Just wait."

"Can you tell me what this is about?" she whispered.

He shook his head. "Let me surprise you." When they arrived, he walked up to the reception desk. "I'm Dr. Stein," he said. "I reserved a room for my wife and myself earlier and left the luggage here."

"Good evening, Dr. Stein," said the concierge. He nodded at Christina. "Mrs. Stein." Christina, playing along, was silent. "Your things are upstairs and the bed has been turned down already. Will you be needing anything else?"

"I don't think so," Andy said. He accepted the key and touched Christina's elbow. Since there was no luggage, they were able to go up to the room by themselves. Still, Christina said nothing until they were in the room, the door locked and bolted.

"Dr. and Mrs. Stein! Luggage sent up! Andy, what *is* all this?"

"A lot of people know me in this neighborhood, so I didn't want to use my real name."

"That's not what I meant! Why did you reserve this room?"

Taking her by both hands, he pulled her gently to the king sized bed. It was lavishly appointed with a down comforter and several pillows; the comforter had indeed been turned down and a small, beribboned box of chocolates sat on the swath of exposed sheet. "Because I was hoping you would be sharing it with me."

She was quiet for a moment, but let her hands remain entwined with his. "What if I'd said no?"

"Then I would have paid for it and that would have been that."

"Are you always this extravagant?" she asked.

"When it's important, yes."

She did not reply, but looked around, eyes lighting on a small overnight case. "Dr. Stein's luggage?"

"Dr. and *Mrs.* Stein," he said.

"What's inside for Mrs. Stein?"

"Why don't you find out?"

Christina got up and went over to the case. Inside was a change of clothes for Andy as well as a wrap dress in a navy and white print with the price tags from Bloomingdale's still intact.

"In the event that you stayed, I didn't think you'd want to wear that"—Andy indicated her black lace dress—"tomorrow morning."

"Very thoughtful," she said.

"There's something else," he said. "Keep going." From a nest of tissue Christina extracted a blush-colored lace bra and matching panties. "I hope they'll fit," he added. "I had to guess at the size, but the saleswoman at La Perla was extremely helpful."

"I guess I'll have to try them on to find out, won't I?"

"So you'll stay?"

"Yes," she said softly. "I'll stay."

He got up and was across the room in seconds. "And your daughter . . . ?" he said, face nuzzling her hair where the glittering ornament still sat.

"Conveniently spending the night with her best friend." She reached up and took it from her head. "How about Oliver?"

"Senior-class community service mission," he replied. "Gone through Saturday."

"So then there's no one expecting us. . . ."

"No one," he said, kissing her again.

"But why here?" she asked. "Why couldn't we just go to your apartment if no one's home?"

"I wanted this night to be special," he said. "Some place new—for both of us." They remained in each other's arms for a few minutes and then Andy slipped off his jacket and began to undo his tie. "Do you need help?" he asked, indicating the dress. She nodded and turned her back to him.

As he slowly unzipped Christina's long black dress, he had the image of her rising naked, like Venus from the sea, from a jumble of lace and sparkles. But when she turned, what

he saw was equally arousing. She wore a simple white strapless bra through which her nipples—he was finally, *finally*, going to get to see them, touch them—were visible, and a white
slip that grazed her calves. There was something both innocent and erotic about this attire; she looked like she'd stepped
from the pages of a long-ago pinup calendar. He reached for
her again, fingers on the bra's hook, which was conveniently
right between her breasts. "May I?" he said softly.

"Please," she said, and in an instant, the bra was on the
floor.

The next morning, Andy was up before six. Even though
he'd hardly had any sleep, his routines were so ingrained it
was impossible for him to stay in bed longer. Anyway, he had
to be at the office later this morning, though he had had the
foresight to cancel his session with Cassie. Christina lay sleeping, back toward him, face nestled into her bent arm. Her
hair—fine, straight, light brown—was spread out over her
shoulders; it was the first time he'd seen it down. God, what a
surprise she'd turned out to be in bed.

Andy grinned just thinking about it, and he continued to
think about it as he first lathered, and then rinsed, in the
shower.

She was up by the time he emerged wrapped in one of the
hotel's thick terry cloth towels. "Good morning," she said, her
hands busy arranging her hair in its customary twist.

"Morning." He sat down on the bed. "That was some
night," he ventured.

She looked down and then at his torso, where beads of
water still clung. "You had a shower?" He nodded. "Can you
wait for me to take one? And then we could have some coffee
or breakfast?"

"You go ahead. I'll call up for room service."

"That would be nice." She let the sheet fall away and got up from the bed.

"Christina," he murmured, running his hands along her body. He wanted to push her down and start all over again. But he had patients to see, several of them, and anyway, he was a little afraid of just how much he wanted her. He forced himself to step away.

While the water ran in her shower, he called downstairs for breakfast: coffee, poached eggs, fresh fruit, a croissant for her. She emerged before the food arrived, wearing the new dress. "Perfect fit," she said, twirling so he could see. "And this too—" She reached into the dress and exposed the strap of the bra. "I'm impressed."

"So am I," he said, pulling her close for a quick, ferocious kiss. "So am I."

EIGHTEEN

tanding in front of her bathroom mirror, Christina applied the red lipstick Magda had given her. She hadn't gotten used to it, but Andy had liked it so much that she decided she would wear it again. She liked how excited it made him; she liked how excited *she* made him. He was coming over today. Soon. Since they both agreed not to tell the kids about the change in their relationship, spending the night together was not easily accomplished and so far they had not managed it. Once they'd met at his office, and ended up making love in one of the examining rooms. Another time, she'd met him for lunch at his apartment while Oliver was at school; they'd hastily eaten the sandwiches she'd brought and then repaired to the bedroom for a heated half hour. But today they would have more time. Andy was not on call and Jordan had two classes; she would be gone for hours. Christina could hardly wait.

After she'd finished her makeup, Christina put the last touches on the meal. Squash and apple soup, arugula salad, quiche with goat cheese and minced red pepper, cranberry walnut muffins. She'd set the dining room table with some of the linens she'd bought when they'd gone to that estate sale together and the flowered Spode dishes that had belonged to her mother; she'd made a centerpiece of bittersweet and mums from her garden. When Andy rang the bell—exactly on the dot of eleven, as they'd agreed—she was ready. "Hello, you," he said. He carried an enormous bouquet of white roses and handed them to her with a flourish.

"You'll never let me forget that conversation, will you?" she said.

"You were so cold I practically got frostbite."

"I didn't stay that way, did I?"

"No," he said, leaning over to kiss her, "you didn't."

Inside the house, Andy was effusive in his praise. He loved her paintings—an offbeat collection of sea- and landscapes, still lifes and portraits—her hand-hooked rugs, her show- and workrooms, her kitchen with its yellowware bowls and Spanish tiles, and her garden. "But what about the bedroom?" he said when she ended the tour in the dining room. "Don't I get to see that?"

"Later," she said. "First we eat." She began serving the food and as soon as he took a bite, he began to praise that too.

"I had no idea you were such a good cook," he said, taking a bite of the quiche. "This is fantastic."

"I'm glad you like it." She reached for another muffin.

"There's just one more thing I'd like," he said.

"Oh, what's that?" she said, looking to see what she might have forgotten. Salt and pepper were there, along with napkins, two kinds of preserves, milk and sugar for the coffee—what was missing?

"I'd like you to take your sweater off," he said.

"My sweater? Off?"

"Your bra too."

"Why?" she said, though the answer was obvious.

"So I can see you while we eat, and imagine all the things I'm going to do to you when we're done."

"Andy . . . ," she said. She did want to, she truly did. But even though she had fallen away from the strict faith of her girlhood—she had started attending the Dutch Reformed church on the corner of Carroll Street years ago, with Will— Sister Bernadette's counsel about the beauty of modesty was deeply ingrained.

"Will you, please? For me?"

Instead of answering him, she began to unbutton her ribbed gray cardigan, one tiny, pearlized button at a time. When she was through, she took it off and hung it over the back of her chair. Then she reached around to unhook the bra—it was the lace one he'd bought her from La Perla—and took that off too.

"There," she said. "Would you like some more coffee?" It was chilly, sitting there topless; gooseflesh was rising on her skin.

"I think I would," he said, eyes fixed on her. "Thanks a lot."

If Christina had thought Andy would rush through the meal so that they could go to bed, she was wrong. He ate slowly, even deliberately so, to prolong the game. She matched him, bite for leisurely bite, all the while feeling the excitement building so that when they finally did leave the table, she was ready to explode. They left a trail of clothes behind them, and had just sunk onto the bed together when Christina heard the unmistakable sound of the key turning in the lock downstairs.

"What's that?" Andy said; clearly he had heard it too.

"It must be Jordan. I have no idea what she's doing home." She got up and grabbed her robe. "Quick!" she said. "There's no time to get dressed. You have to hide!"

"Where?"

For a second she was paralyzed. Here was her lover in her bed, and her daughter on the way up any minute. "In the closet!" she hissed. "Now!" Still naked, Andy scrambled into the closet while Christina ran around gathering all the clothes they had dropped. Pants, boxers, shirt, belt, skirt, shoes . . . She took the whole wad and stuffed it under the bed, straightening up just as Jordan came into the room. "Hi, sweetheart; I thought you would be in class all day."

"That's where I should be!" Jordan looked furious.

"So what happened?"

"There was some kind of accident—an electrical malfunction or some *stupid* thing like that. All the power in the building went out and they had to send everyone home. Isn't that the worst?"

"Oh, that's too bad," Christina said. She was keenly aware of Andy, trapped just behind the closet door.

"Hey, why are you in your bathrobe? Is something wrong?" Jordan touched her sleeve.

"Yes, I had brunch with Misha and Stephen"—she wanted to explain the dishes still on the table—"and afterward I wasn't feeling well, so I came in here to lie down." Stephen and Misha were actually in Sag Harbor this weekend; did Jordan know that? She hoped not.

"Poor you," Jordan said. "Is it because you're worried about money? I thought you had some more jobs now."

"Yes, I do. But this isn't about money anyway, sweetheart. It's just a headache; I don't want you to worry."

"Okay . . . ," Jordan said uncertainly. "I just don't want you to be sick or anything."

"It's nothing serious," Christina said. "In fact, I'm feeling better now. Much better. I'm even going to take care of all the dishes." How she hated lying, the backtracking to cover herself, the fumbling for excuses.

"I can help," Jordan said. "You go back to bed. I'll do the dishes."

"That's very sweet of you, darling," Christina said. "But it's not necessary." Her bra and sweater were hanging off the back of a dining room chair and she did *not* want Jordan to find them. Yet she also wanted Jordan to leave so she could get Andy out of there. Before she could resolve this dilemma, there was suddenly a very audible sneeze.

"Was that you, Mom? Maybe you are coming down—"

There was another, even louder sneeze. Jordan looked horrified. It was clear that her mother was not the one who had sneezed. "Who *was* that?" she said in a tight, terrified voice. "It sounded like it was coming from the closet."

No, Christina thought wretchedly, *no, no, no.*

"Mom." Jordan's voice had dropped to a whisper. "There's someone *in* there; we have to call the police!"

Christina looked at her quaking child. "Yes," she said, "there is someone in there." She walked over to the closet. "You can come out now." The door opened. Andy stood wrapped in a sheet he'd found on a shelf above his head. Under the circumstances, he looked quite dignified.

"Him!" Jordan said. Her face visibly paled. "Why is he . . . I mean, did you really . . . Is he—" She turned to Christina. "How *could* you?"

"Jordan, I'm sorry you had to find out about my

relationship with Andy like this. But you have to believe I never meant to hurt you—"

"Hurt me! You haven't *hurt* me—you just *disgusted* me!" And with that, she fled.

"I'm so, so sorry," Andy said as he stepped from the closet. "There was something in there that made me sneeze, some scent. . . ."

"Lavender," Christina said. "I have all these sachets; they keep the linens smelling nice."

"Well, I guess I'd better be going," he said. "That is, if I can find my clothes."

Christina knelt and retrieved the bundle from under the bed. As she disentangled his pants from her skirt, her sweater from his boxers, she began to giggle. What an inappropriate response; Jordan was so upset, and she was giggling? But when she looked up at Andy, in his self-styled toga, she couldn't help it—she burst out laughing, and then he started laughing too. She laughed so hard that tears really did start to trickle from the corners of her eyes down her cheeks and she could not catch her breath. "Okay," she said at last. "Okay. I've got to stop." She handed him his clothes and he hurriedly started to dress.

"I'll call you," he said, as he tucked his shirt into his pants. "Now go talk to your daughter. That look on her face when she saw me . . ." He shook his head. She saw him to the door and then went back upstairs, where she dressed, fixed her hair, and made sure there was not a trace of red left on her lips before knocking on Jordan's door.

"What?" Jordan said.

"I'd like to speak to you," Christina said. She would ignore the rude reply.

"About what?" Again that sullen tone.

"You know perfectly well about what." She waited.

"Come in."

The room, with its curly maple dresser, rag oval rug, walnut rocker, and framed Degas reproductions on the walls, was, as ever, immaculate. Jordan lay stretched out on her neatly made bed with her laptop open and the rabbit nestled beside her. Jordan was smitten with the creature; for all Christina knew, she slept with it.

"I was going to tell you," she said.

"Uh-huh." Jordan's eyes never left the laptop.

"I know you don't like him—"

"No, you're wrong about that; I hate him!" She looked at her mother then. "And I hate his pothead son too!" She snapped the laptop shut with a vengeance.

"Pothead son? What are you talking about? How would you know something like that?"

"I ran into him near Dance West over the summer. We walked through Central Park and he pulled out a *joint*. It was broad daylight with, like, a million people around. And it didn't seem like the first time either."

"Oh," Christina said. "Oh." She remembered Stephen had said the same thing about Oliver; it seemed apparent to everyone but her. And Andy. She looked at the rabbit, which was positioned on Jordan's stomach like a sphinx. There was something unsettling about its stillness, and its preternaturally bright, unblinking eye. "But what does that have to do with Andy?" Whatever she was going to say to Jordan had grown obscured now, misted over by this information about Oliver.

"I don't know!" Jordan said. "I just don't like him, Mom. I

don't like him and I don't want him in our lives. He's like . . . a bulldozer, mowing people down."

"He's forceful; that's true."

"I can't talk to you! It's like you've gone crazy or something."

"No, sweetheart," Christina said. "Not crazy." Her face broke into a smile. "I think I'm just in love." And to her amazement, she was.

Jordan could not hide her disgust. "Whatever," she said, and opened her laptop again.

Christina waited and when it was clear the conversation was over, she went downstairs, where she began to gather the plates that were still on the dining room table. Her attraction to Andy really *was* unexpected; even though Jordan did not remember much about her father, he had been so very different. Will had had a gentle soul; everything with him had been in soft focus and pastels. This had not been a failing, though. No, it was a respite from the ever-simmering tension of her childhood, the tiptoeing around her father lest she set off one of his explosive, alcohol-fueled outbursts—sometimes the smallest thing, like an unwashed glass left on a table, could set him off. Aunt Barb tried to shield her from him as best she could. And her life at school, with her adored nuns, helped too. But she knew, even back then, that she wanted something else, and Will, soft-spoken and mild-mannered, had given it to her.

Christina opened the back door and shook out the tablecloth; a host of sparrows instantly appeared. Will's ideal Sunday would have been spent lazing over the paper, reading a book, and going out for a late-afternoon stroll; Andy's would involve a run, a swim, and a game of tennis—all before lunch.

In bed, the differences were even more marked. He made noise—*lots* of noise. He wanted the lights on—*So I can see every inch of you*, he had said. He was demanding, critical, quick to ignite. But unlike her father, he got over his huffs quickly. He was willing to say he was sorry. She thought of how he'd stripped off his shirt and handed it to her that day they were caught in the rain—he was a gentleman.

Christina stood watching as the birds made short work of the crumbs and then flew off to their nests. She thought about what it might be like to be married to Andy.

Life would be less serene than it had been with Will. But it would be vivid, intense, and possibly quite wonderful. And when she thought about what it felt like to be in bed with him, she knew it would. She believed she could accept most of Andy's faults and forgive the ones she couldn't.

But even in her romantic reverie, Jordan was a sticking point. Because no matter how compelling Andy Stern might have been, Jordan's antipathy was a deal breaker.

Folding the cloth into a neat rectangle, Christina went back inside. Could Jordan be won over? Would Andy have the patience and tact to accomplish it? Because if he didn't, there was no way it was going to work between them, no way at all.

NINETEEN

*J*ordan arrived at the Cromley-Blandon School before the morning bell rang and checked the schedule she had posted on the inside of the locker door. She saw several girls from her grade congregated at the end of the corridor. One of them was wearing a pair of Christian Louboutin pumps—the red soles were the giveaway—and had a Prada backpack casually hanging off her shoulder. The kids here had way more money than the kids back at Saint James, and they were not shy about letting everyone know it.

Jordan had quickly figured out the pecking order. She knew who the queen bees were, and what she had to do to appease them. She also knew that she would no more feel at home here than she had at Saint James.

First up today was physics. They were doing a lab that involved throwing an egg against a sheet. No matter how many times or how hard the egg was thrown, it did not break. Some kids could not contain themselves during this experiment. Eggs were dropped or pitched against walls, resulting in vivid, gooey splatters. There were giggles, and a few high-pitched shrieks. The teacher had to raise his voice a couple of times. "*Some* people think they're still in kindergarten," Jordan muttered to her lab partner, Ella Kim. Ella did not answer; an almost pathologically shy girl, she was routinely tormented by the cool girls—Monika Banks, Amalia Dart, Brittany Godwin. Ella was, however, a good partner, focused and reliable. "Do you want to work on the lab report together?" she asked. Again, there was no answer.

But as they were cleaning up, Ella said, "Yeah, sure." For a second Jordan did not know what she was talking about; then it clicked.

"Okay, I'll text you," said Jordan. Not that she needed the help. Science, like math, had definite rules, an orderly progression you could depend on. But Cromley-Blandon was big on *cooperative learning* and *collaborative efforts*, so she would score points by teaming up with Ella.

Next was World History, taught in a room plastered with brightly colored travel posters and maps; a globe the size of a beach ball stood in a corner. Hungry, Jordan felt her attention wandering. She tried to focus on the teacher, who was droning on about the conflict between the Catholics and the Protestants in sixteenth-century Germany. Or was it seventeenth-century England? She was just going to have to eat half of the protein bar she had stowed in her bag. Though maybe she could get away with a third. When the teacher called on a girl over on the left side of the room, Jordan discreetly popped a bit of the bar into her mouth. She sucked on it quietly, so it would soften. Even that small bit of food made the difference; suddenly her brain bloomed. The girl on the left didn't know the answer; Jordan's hand shot up.

"Yes, Jordan?" the teacher said. "Did you want to add something?"

"Martin Luther was reacting to what he saw as the corruption of the Catholic Church," she said. "He thought the bishops and popes and all those people had strayed too far from Christ's message."

"Precisely!" beamed the teacher. Jordan looked down modestly. At Cromley-Blandon it was cool to be smart, but not cool to show that you cared.

After history she had a free, and then there was lunch. The lunchroom was already crowded when she walked in. The hot meal today was pasta with tomato sauce. Fortunately, Jordan was not even tempted; in fact, the smell killed her appetite instantly. She loaded her plate at the salad bar: greens, carrots, beets, and cucumbers. Today she was sitting with the queenies because they had asked her to join them. That sauce really did smell gross; she began on her salad. "I like your T-shirt," Monika said. "Where did you get it?"

Jordan looked down at the image of a dancer, on point in an arabesque, stretched across the white fabric. "The gift shop at Lincoln Center. I could get you one."

"Could you? Sweet!" said Monika. She ran a piece of bread across her plate; the sauce-soaked bread turned a lurid, radioactive orange.

"Sure," said Jordan, popping a cucumber into her mouth. It was important that Monika like her; otherwise, she could make Jordan's life hell.

"Thanks, Bun-girl!" Monika said, patting Jordan playfully on the head. Jordan tensed; she did not like her hair to be touched by anyone and certainly not by Monika, who seemed to have no interests apart from new shoes, new clothes, and new boys.

Bits of conversation bobbed and bounced around her: who'd been at which party, whose parents were going to be away next weekend, who was hooking up with whom. Jordan nodded and smiled but did not actively participate. Monika was a dope; she bragged that her parents could afford to endow any college she wanted to get into with "a new library or dorm or whatever" so that she didn't have to worry about grades. Jordan herself was not interested in college, but only because she wanted to dance professionally instead.

After finishing her salad, she brought her tray up to the front of the cafeteria. There was Ella Kim sitting by herself. That was not unusual; Ella always sat by herself. Monika posted all these incredibly hateful things on Facebook about her. Jordan thought Facebook was a colossal waste of time, but also knew reading stuff like that about yourself must hurt. So Monika was not just a dope; she was mean too.

"Can I sit here?" Jordan stopped in front of her table.

"Sure." Ella stared at her plate and Jordan sat down anyway. She understood Ella's reaction; she would have seen Jordan sitting with Monika and the others and probably thought Jordan had come to torment her. This thought made Jordan's heart constrict unexpectedly with pity.

"Let's figure out a time to get together."

"Get together?" The expression on Ella's face was one of pure panic.

"To work on the lab report—remember?"

"Oh—right." Poor Ella; she couldn't seem to trust the invitation. But at least she had looked up from her plate. She was part Asian, with pin-straight black hair, a round face, and slanted brown eyes; Jordan thought that if she didn't look so nervous all the time, she would actually be pretty.

"I don't get home until pretty late on weekdays; Saturday would be better. In the afternoon."

"Saturday afternoon would be okay," said Ella. "In the morning, I take a pottery class at the School of Visual Arts."

"Must be fun." Jordan shuddered at the thought of handling wet clay, but whatever.

"You take classes outside too, right? Dance classes?" asked Ella.

"At the School of American Ballet," she said.

"I know. Everyone says you're great."

Jordan smiled. "So Saturday afternoon. Do you want to come over?"

"Sure," Ella said. "I could do that." The bell rang. Ella hurried upstairs to the gym at the rear of the building. Jordan followed slowly. Because of her dance classes, she was excused from gym. But she stood at the door, watching as Ella, now smiling, raced across the varnished floor.

Jordan's commute to SAB was so easy now; she walked the few blocks and was able to change and get ready in plenty of time. Today's point class was hard, though; under the pink satin shoes, her toes oozed and bled. By the end of the class, she was dying to get the satin shoes off her feet and she headed straight to the dressing room. She did not notice that Ms. Bonner had been waiting for her until her teacher touched her arm.

"I'd like to talk to you," she said. Immediately, Jordan tensed. Maybe she'd been sloppy in class. But Ms. Bonner did not want to talk about her point work. "Normally, only girls on the C level are asked to participate in the Winter Ball. Still, I want to try you out in a small role this year, even though you're still in B2." Jordan stared at her, unable to reply. "This year's theme is celebrating ballet's Russian roots, and there's a folk dance duet that I think you'd be perfect for; you've really got the exuberance the part demands. Do you think you can handle it?"

"I know I can," said Jordan, ecstatic, stunned, and terrified all at once. The Winter Ball was SAB's most important annual benefit. It was held at Lincoln Center, on the same stage where the company performed, and five hundred people attended. Every year, the most advanced students from the school were asked to perform, and Ms. Bonner was asking her to be one of them. It didn't feel real, but here she was, talking about rehearsal schedules and saying she'd need to get permission from her mom. It was real, all right.

During the subway ride home to Brooklyn Jordan felt like she was in a trance. The magical words, *Winter Ball, Winter Ball,* kept running through her mind; the tenth time she thought them was no less exciting than the first. She couldn't wait to tell her mom the news and was so excited that she called as soon as she got out of the subway. But Christina did not pick up and when she got to the house, it was dark. Weird. Her mom had not said anything about going out tonight.

"Hello?" she called out as she let herself in. Silence. She flipped on the lights to reveal the clean, quiet kitchen. No pots, no pans, no evidence of cooking at all, just two tens on the table, placed neatly underneath the sugar bowl. She checked her phone again and saw that she had missed the text.

I'll be at Andy's apartment tonight. Home around 10. Left you money for takeout. xoxoxo Mom

Jordan scowled as she stared at the screen. That stupid Andy Stern again. It was like he had her mother under some kind of *spell*. What if she really got serious and even married him? Jordan did not think she could stand it. She had to figure out some way to get rid of him—she just *had* to.

TWENTY

*O*liver stood in the middle of Riverside Park, waiting. He was supposed to be in English class, but Dread Guy— aka Keith—had called, and Oliver was not about to pass up a chance to score.

It was a windy day in October, and Oliver stuck his hands deep into the pockets of his nylon jacket. He had bought the jacket in a vintage store on Avenue A and it sported a cool, retro logo from some long-ago bowling team. There were major holes in the lining; his fists went straight down, touching the jacket's inner hem. He knew it pained his dad to see him wearing stuff like this; Andy was always trying to get him into Lacoste or Ralph Lauren, but Oliver wasn't buying into all that statusy stuff his dad lived for.

He looked around. Two old ladies inched by slowly, arms entwined, deep in some old-lady-type conversation. A group of dogs romped in a grassy area, owners ringed around them. Where was Keith? Late as usual. Oliver was willing to wait, though. He had Oceanography next period, another class he liked. But if he had to, he'd cut that too. A few leaves blew past his head, spinning and turning in the wind. One caught in his hair, which he had not had cut in quite some time. He gently pulled it out to examine it. It was a maple leaf—his mom was into tree identification, an interest she passed on to him— and red as a lollipop. He put the leaf in the back pocket of his jeans.

"Hey," a voice called. Oliver turned and there was Keith. His trademark dreads bobbed in the breeze. "S'up?" he asked.

"Same old shit." Oliver scanned the park, looking for the best place to conduct the transaction. "How about there?" He indicated a cluster of shrubs they could step behind.

Keith nodded and Oliver led the way. There, behind the bushes, he handed the crisp new hundred, only recently re- trieved from the ATM, to Keith in exchange for three small bags stuffed with weed. He'd never bought this much at one time before, but he was tired of arranging these meetings and wanted to have enough to hold him for a while. "This is a new shipment," Keith said. "The shit is, like, *killer.*"

Oliver nodded, slipping the bags into the pocket of his jacket. "I'll let you know." He gave Keith a fist bump before he turned and left the park. He didn't want to go back to school. Everything was worse this year. Like seeing Jake and Delphine together, especially that first time. Jake had slowed and dropped Delphine's hand as he came toward Oliver. "Dude," he said, but Oliver had just, like, sailed on by. As far as he was concerned, Jake was now officially invisible. He re- membered the thrill of hoisting the laptop over the ledge of the balcony; he only wished he'd been able to hear the crash. When he went down to inspect the next day, there was noth- ing, not a fucking trace. He told his dad his laptop died—not a lie, for a change, though he omitted mentioning that he'd been the executioner—and was given permission to order another. His dad was only too happy to throw money his way; it was much easier than having an actual relationship.

And it was senior year and everyone was getting all bent out of shape about college. Oliver wanted to go to college—sort of—but he couldn't seem to summon the energy to do anything about it. He considered cutting the rest of the day. He'd say he felt sick and go home. He'd sit out on the terrace and take long, soothing hits while he watched the sky get dark. But then he thought of Oceanography, where they were going to watch a documentary about all these really amazing creatures—the anglerfish, which was able to produce a bright light that glowed at the end of this weird appendage just above its mouth; the barreleye fish, with its transparent head; the wrinkled fangtooth; the lionfish; the blobfish, which was nothing but a mass of gray, quivering jelly. Class would have started a couple of minutes ago, but he could slip in quietly, take a seat in the back, and no one would really care.

He entered the building through a seldom-used basement door and went up the stairs. But just as he was reaching for the doorknob to the science room, he was stopped by the huge, meaty paw of the headmaster, Mr. Cunningham. "You're a little late today, aren't you, young man?" said Cunningham.

"Yeah, sorry. But if I go in now, I won't miss very much."

"And I heard you were not in English either." Cunningham had bushy eyebrows that sprouted from his forehead.

"No, I wasn't feeling well and—"

"But you didn't go to see the nurse, did you? I checked and she said she hadn't seen you all day."

"I was in the student lounge." Oliver was getting a little

nervous. So he cut class. Why was Cunningham making a federal case out of it?

"The student lounge is being renovated and not open this month. Remember?" His eyebrows—thick pelts of gray and black—wiggled ominously.

"Oh yeah. I meant the—"

"Oliver," said Cunningham. "Let's stop this little charade right now, shall we? I think we need to continue this talk in my office."

Resigned, he followed the headmaster and, when they reached his office, took a seat across from Cunningham's big, battered desk.

"Now, when we spoke last June, I thought we had an understanding, Oliver. An understanding. I trusted you. I *believed* in you." Cunningham folded his big hands together and let his massive head sink to his fists. "But you've let me down, Oliver. You let me down, you let your father down, you let Mr. Pollock down, and you let Ms. Warren down. But mostly you've let yourself down."

"I'm sorry, sir," Oliver said. The *sir* had worked before; maybe it would work again.

"I'm afraid *sorry* isn't going to do. Sorry isn't sufficient."

Oliver chafed miserably. This office was so *hot*; why did they keep the thermostat turned way up like that? It was, like, such an energy drain. He unzipped the bowling jacket and was about to put it on the chair, when suddenly one of the bags he'd just bought from Keith slid through the bottom of the jacket. The hem must have been ripped through and he didn't even know it. Oliver looked in horror at the bag of weed as Cunningham rose from behind the desk and looked down on the floor.

"Oliver," he intoned, as he stepped from behind the desk to pick up the bag. "Oliver, Oliver, Oliver . . ." He reached over and in that second, Oliver had the mad impulse to dash from the room and the school. But he remained in his seat as Cunningham patted the pockets of his jacket and pulled out the other two bags. "I am sincerely hoping that these bags do not contain what I think they contain," he said. Oliver was mute as Cunningham laid two of the bags on his desk and opened the third. He thrust his nose into the bag, and inhaled deeply. Maybe he'd end up with a nice little contact high and he and Oliver could smoke a joint together before a very chill Cunningham sent him on his way with just a slap on the wrist. Then the deep, sonorous voice of the headmaster snapped him back to reality, like, in a hurry.

"I think you know what this means, Oliver," he said. "I think you know as well as I do."

"Please, Mr. Cunningham, sir. It's not what you think. I mean I—"

"And what is it that I think, young man? Can you read my mind?"

"You think I'm using that stuff. Selling it even."

"I had not even *thought* about your being a pusher, Oliver," Cunningham said. "Though now that you bring it up, I won't rule it out. And as for using—well, yes, that certainly seems to be the case."

"It's just a little now and then, sir. Totally recreational, no worse than a beer. Really, it should be legal and in some states it already is—"

"Enough," said Cunningham. "I'm afraid I'll have to ask you to come with me." So Oliver followed him down the hall and to his locker, where Cunningham watched while he emptied its contents into a cardboard box. "You can take what you can carry now," said Cunningham. "The rest will be in my office; you can arrange to have it picked up. I'll telephone your father." Oliver said not one word while all this was going down; he just filled his backpack with what seemed most essential—which was, like, nothing—and waited. Then he walked behind Cunningham to the doors. "Oliver, I don't know if you will believe this, but I am truly, deeply sorry." To which Oliver wanted to reply, *Fuck you and your hairy-ass eyebrows.* Was it cowardice or self-preservation that kept him from saying it? Anyway, it didn't matter anymore. He was out of there. He was gone.

An hour later, Oliver was on the number one train, headed to the Bronx to see his Grandma Ida. How she would react to his news, he didn't know. But he figured she'd find out soon enough anyway; he might as well be the one to tell her. Besides, since Cunningham expelled him, he really didn't know what the hell to do with himself. He'd taken the weed, of course—*We're not going to press charges, but you do understand I'll have to confiscate this*—so now Oliver didn't even have that as a consolation prize. It didn't seem like a good idea to try to contact Keith about getting some more. The shit had already hit the fan; no need to turn it on full blast.

At the 231st Street station, he got out and boarded a bus that dropped him practically in front of the yellow brick apartment building where Ida lived. She might not even be home. No big deal. He'd just wait, that's all. But when the doorman buzzed, he heard her words clearly, even through the static. "Send him up right now, José!"

"Have you had lunch?" was the first thing she asked. He shook his head. "Come in and sit down, then. I'll make you a sandwich."

Oliver sat at the Formica table in the kitchen. The television was on and Judge Judy was yelling at someone. She yelled at everyone. What would Judge Judy say to him if he ever appeared in front of her? Oliver watched, mesmerized, as the tiny woman—she was, like, no taller than a thirteen-year-old—made all these people look so meek and ashamed. Meanwhile, Grandma Ida was bustling around her kitchen, clearly happy to have this task to perform. He noticed she was all dressed up—black-and-white checked pants, black turtleneck sweater, gold bracelets, necklace of gold, black, and bright blue; the beads were as big as gumballs. In a few minutes, she presented him with a grilled cheese and tomato sandwich, handful of chips, and glass of apple cider. When he bit into the sandwich, he could tell it was made with those slices of American cheese his dad wouldn't even permit in their home; it was delicious, all melted and gooey. "Thanks, Grandma." He took another bite, and then another. "Thanks a lot."

She turned off the television, pulled up a chair, and faced him. "So what's going on?" Her eyes, alert and focused, sought out his. "I don't usually get a surprise visit, and on a weekday no less."

"I'm in trouble," he said simply. "Big trouble."

"Then you came to the right place."

Oliver told her the whole story then, mentioning the head shop on St. Marks, Jojo and Keith (though he did leave out the bit about Raven; he thought it might scare her), the weeks of pot smoking, culminating in today's big-ass purchase in Riverside Park and the subsequent expulsion by Cunningham. She listened intently and did not say one word until he was done. Much better than Judge Judy, he thought.

"So that's it," he said. He took a big gulp of the cider. "They kicked me out."

"Does your father know?"

"Not yet." In fact, it was kind of weird. Shouldn't his father have spoken to Cunningham by now? Maybe there was some crisis at the hospital, some woman delivering, like, quintuplets.

"Tell me something, Oliver. Do you want to go back to school?"

"I don't know."

"Well, before anything else gets said or done, you need to figure that out first. Because if you don't want to go back, that's one path. And if you do, that's another. But only you can decide. And once you do, you can figure out what you need to do next."

"Do I have to decide, like, now? This minute?"

"No, you don't. Think about it for a while. But don't take too long." She eyed his empty plate and glass. "How about another sandwich?"

He nodded gratefully. "I'm so hungry," he said.

"Like your father," she said, rising from her seat and patting him affectionately on the head. Oliver leaned over to turn on the television again. Maybe Judge Judy would be done for the day. He hoped so. Clicking the remote, he found a nature program called *Mysteries of the Deep*. He wondered whether it was anything like the movie he had missed in Oceanography today.

His grandmother served him the second sandwich and another glass of cider. She did not ask any more questions about school and she did not rag on him about getting expelled either. They watched the documentary and then she brought out her ancient Scrabble set whose box had been repaired, like, a hundred times with pieces of now yellowing and brittle tape, and set up the board on the table. Grandma Ida had a perfectly fine living room, with a fat, burgundy velvet sofa and matching armchairs, a coffee table, and a forty-five-inch flat-screen TV. But she seemed to spend most of her time in the kitchen. With its yellow-and-white-checked curtains and souvenir plates from all the places she'd visited plastered all over the wall, it was a comforting place. They spent the rest of the afternoon playing Scrabble; first he beat her by making *zodiac* on a double word score and *oxen* on a triple. But in the second game, she trounced him with the seven-letter *advisor*. The sky outside the kitchen window grew dark.

"Well, I guess I should be going," he said. Now it was, like, positively spooky that he had not heard from his dad and he began to dread the encounter more for its having been delayed. Andy was so into status markers; this would, like, kill him. And although Andy had gone to City College, Oliver knew that he was expected to go to a much more prestigious place. *Too bad about that one, Dad. Guess that plan's been effectively fucked.*

"How about a cup of hot cocoa before you go? It's almost hot cocoa weather."

"Yeah, sure," he said. He remembered how she used to serve it with animal crackers.

When the cocoa was ready, she put a handful of mini-marshmallows in each mug, and sat down with him again. "Let me ask you something else," she said. "I want to know about this woman, this Christina person, your father mentioned."

"What about her? Dad hired her to redecorate the apartment."

"Is there something wrong with the way the apartment is

decorated? I happen to think it looks very nice the way it is."
She blew delicately on the surface of the cocoa.

"Yeah, that's what I thought at first too. But you know, I
think Dad thought it would be a way to move on . . . after
Mom and all. And you know what? He's right. Christina is
making the place a little different, but not, like, too different,
you know? And she's got this really cool plan for what used to
be Mom's office; it's going to be a guest room for when you
stay over."

"It's hardly like I *need* a guest room." Ida looked down into
the mug as if she were deeply interested in the swirled pattern
created by the melting marshmallows.

"Whatever. Anyway, I like her. I didn't at first. But now
I do."

"Why didn't you?" Grandma Ida pounced on those words.

"I thought she was going to, like, erase Mom from the
apartment. But she doesn't want to do that at all. She said
she wanted to honor her."

Grandma Ida made a face that said, *Oh really? I don't believe
it for a second.*

Oliver finished his hot chocolate, brought the mug to the
sink, and ran the water to rinse it.

"Go away! I'll do it myself." She shooed him off. Grandma
Ida was an obsessive cleaner. No one, but no one, did a good
enough job for her and when she came to visit, she was always
puttering around the apartment, not only pointing out all the
things she thought Lucy had missed, but fixing them herself.
Standing at the sink, she scoured the cocoa mugs and placed
them in the dishwasher—not that they needed it now. But she
said it was a way to sterilize them. Then she walked Oliver to
the door. "You'll think about what I said, won't you?"

"I will." Oliver felt sad about leaving. The afternoon had been a respite from his real life. But now he had to go back home and, like, deal.

"Here, take this," she said, pressing a small brown paper bag with a neatly folded edge into his hands.

"What is it?"

"Just a little nosh for the ride," she said.

Oliver opened the bag. There, inside, was the familiar red and yellow box. Animal crackers. He bent down to kiss her cheek, inhaling the scent of her face powder, and the supersweet cologne—it was like air freshener or something—that she always wore. "Thanks a lot," he said.

"For nothing," she replied, and her thin arms enfolded him in a surprisingly powerful hug.

TWENTY-ONE

When the call from Cunningham came in, Andy's latex-gloved fingers were thrust deep in Xiomara's vaginal canal, delicately testing her cervix. Of course he didn't know the call was from Cunningham; though he'd given the headmaster his private number, the phone was on vibrate, and buzzed almost imperceptibly in his pocket. "You can get dressed now," he said to Xiomara when the examination was completed. "I'll see you in my office."

He left, closing the door quietly behind him. Back in medical school, Andy endured the ribbing—some of it playful, some less so—from his male classmates about his choice to go into gynecology and obstetrics. He'd heard his share of crude jokes, tolerated the nickname of Pussy King; none of it fazed him. Though he was appreciative of women's bodies in his personal life, the women he saw professionally did not elicit the same response. He viewed the female body as a miraculous ecosystem, both powerful and fragile, and it was his job to see that this system functioned at optimal levels at all times.

Andy was not so much detached as he was awed by the ability of his patients to conceive, gestate, and give birth to new life; by comparison, the male contribution seemed random and puny.

Sitting at his desk, he waited for his heart rate to slow. Xiomara upended his carefully honed sense of professionalism. She was almost six feet tall, with a full, well-proportioned body that pregnancy had only enhanced. Her belly was a ripe melon; her breasts were magnificent. Once, while palpating them in a routine exam, he'd actually gotten a hard-on; this had never happened to him in all the years he'd been examining women, and he was shaken afterward, like some sacred trust had been broken.

There was a light tap on the door. "Come in," he said. She wore leather pants, and a shawl with long, lush fringe. Her husband, a professional basketball player with the LA Lakers, was not with her today, which ought to have meant the paparazzi threat was slightly reduced.

"Everything's all right, then?" she asked. "You didn't see any problem."

"Not a thing," he said firmly. "The sonogram shows the baby is developing normally; your cervix is nice and tight. How are you feeling?"

"All right . . . Some days, good. Lots of energy. Other days, like I want to fall asleep while standing up. And I'm so hungry! I bought cheese at Dean & Deluca and I couldn't even wait to get home to eat it; I tore the package open with my teeth, right there on Prince Street! Thank God there was no photographer around to catch that!" She laughed, a rippling, melodious sound.

Andy smiled too. "All perfectly natural, everything on

course. Eat when you're hungry, though I want you to make every calorie count. And take naps. Lots of them." He stood and extended his hand.

"I'll see you, then, Dr. Stern." She took his hand, then covered it with her other one, so that for a moment, his fingers were cradled by the warmth of hers. "I'm *so* grateful for everything you've done."

"You're the one doing all the work," he said, flustered by her touch. "I'm just your shepherd here. Your guide dog."

"Woof," she said softly and her white teeth—a small, sexy gap separating the front two—gleamed in a smile. "Woof, woof." Then, gathering her shawl and her bag, she left. Andy stood there a moment, trying to collect himself. Fortunately he had another month before he saw her again; maybe by then he would have figured out how to deal with this maelstrom she set off in him.

Walking into the waiting room, he was distracted by shouts from the street. He moved to the window, which faced Park Avenue and was open; his office was on the ground floor, so that the drama was literally unfolding before his eyes. There was Xiomara, clutching the shawl around her as she attempted to fend off the greedy swarm of paparazzi that had descended. How did these people manage to track her? Had someone implanted a GPS chip under her glorious brown skin?

Cameras clicked, and a crowd began to gather. Putting a protective arm around her shoulders, her bodyguard started to get rough—pushing the reporters back, guiding her toward the waiting car. A camera was shoved into her face; the bodyguard knocked it out of the photographer's hand. It went shooting into the street and bounced off the windshield of an oncoming taxi. The taxi swerved, people shrieked, the body-guard used the distraction to push Xiomara into the car, and the driver sped off. Andy watched in a state of mild shock. When the car was gone, he turned and there was Joanne. "Did you see that?" he said. "Jesus."

"Unbelievable," she said. But then it was time for the next patient. After that, Andy hurried off to the hospital to meet the patient who'd gone into labor. By the time he remembered to call Cunningham back, it was after six. The guy was probably gone for the day. But to his surprise, Cunningham picked up the phone on the second ring. "I had to expel Oliver today, Dr. Stern," he said. And then he proceeded to explain what had happened to bring about this definitive act.

"And there's no way you would reconsider?" Andy said. "Maybe we're not going about this in the right way—" A siren blared, as if underscoring his sense of alarm.

"I've tried every way I could think of," said Cunningham.

"But he's a good student. Or can be, when he puts his mind to it." The siren was gone, replaced by the loud exhalations of a bus huffing down Second Avenue.

"He shows flashes of real brilliance," Cunningham agreed. "His English teacher shared his last paper with me; it was on Emily Dickinson and Robert Frost. She said it was publishable."

"Really?" Andy's heart couldn't help but leap when he heard that.

"Yes, really. But then he fails to show up for three out of the next five classes and flunks a silly little pop quiz. He needs help, Dr. Stern. More help than we can give him, I'm afraid."

"But you've said yourself that he's got the makings of an exceptional student—"

"Which is why I am only expelling him, and not bringing in the police."

"The police!" Whatever fragile place his heart had attained only moments ago was lost as it went thudding down, down, down. "Why the police?"

"He was in possession of *quite* a lot of marijuana; it's possible that he was intending to sell it." Andy was silent as he absorbed this new information. *Was* Oliver selling drugs? That would be the final irony; he gave the boy all the money he asked for, never questioned where it went. Why would Ollie want to do that, unless he had some serious self-destructive urge? Or wanted to *zetz* his father, as his mother might have said?

Andy said good-bye and put the phone away. He had to find Oliver. But he thought he'd better calm down first, so he walked over to Second Avenue, where he ducked into a bar and ordered a Scotch. When it arrived, he called Christina. Maybe she would know what to do. "Oh, I'm so sorry," she said. "I was worried that something like this might happen."

"What do you mean?"

"Well, only that I suspected that he was smoking—"

"You suspected and you didn't *tell* me? Why the hell not?" There was a long silence on the other end of the line. "Are you there?" he asked.

"I don't like being sworn at," she said finally.

You think that's swearing? he wanted to say. *Give me a fucking break.* But instead he said, "I'm sorry. I'm just upset, that's all." He paused. "How long had you suspected?"

"For a while. And then Jordan confirmed it."

"Jordan? How does Jordan know anything about this?"

He had been about to say, *How the hell does Jordan . . .* , but he censored himself. Barely.

"She ran into him one day over the summer and he pulled out a joint in Central Park."

"And you've known that since the summer and kept it from me all this time?" Andy said.

"No. She only mentioned it recently. I wanted to tell you. But I wasn't sure it was the right thing to do. I was building something with Oliver; I didn't want to lose his trust."

"So you let him get expelled from school instead." Betrayal washed over him like a tide.

"Andy, I'm incredibly sorry. I was wrong. I should have told you right away."

He sipped his Scotch, not sure how to respond. They were still new as a couple; he didn't want to ruin things between them, but he was hurt. Angry too. "You shouldn't have kept it from me," he said finally.

"I know. I shouldn't have."

"Maybe if I'd known, I could have done something. Now it's too late."

"They really won't take him back?" she asked.

"Take him back? I'm lucky they aren't calling the police." He finished the Scotch and decided against a second glass.

"What if I talk to him?"

"You? Why?"

"Because he likes me," Christina said.

Andy did not dispute this. "Well, I'm not sure. . . ."

"Can it hurt?"

"I guess not." He suddenly did not want to be having this conversation. He wanted to say good-bye, and get the hell out of there, which was exactly what he did.

Oliver was sitting on the sofa in the dark when he came in; Andy didn't see him and when he realized he was there, he jumped slightly. Jesus, but he was nervous. He sat down in the chair facing his son. "I talked to Cunningham," he said.

"So you know," Oliver said. In the dark, his blond curls seemed to glow.

"I know."

"What are you going to do about it? Ground me? Lock me in my room?"

"Ollie—"

"Stop calling me that!" His voice was suddenly sharp. "I hate that name."

"All right," Andy said, surprised. "I'll stop. And you want to know what I'm going to do? Well, I don't have a clue. Clearly that therapist you saw over the summer didn't help."

"Clearly."

"Do you want to see another therapist?" Andy asked.

"What for?"

That seemed to kill the conversation for several minutes. Andy was quiet while he regrouped. "I have to ask you something important," he finally said. His eyes had adjusted to the dark and he could see Oliver looking at him. "Cunningham seems to think you were planning to sell what he found on you today."

"Dad! Do you think I'm an *asshole*? Using, possession— that's one thing. Selling is, like, a whole *other* thing."

For some reason, Andy believed him and there, in the quiet room, he exhaled a powerful sigh of relief. But there was still the *using* part of the equation. He had no reason to believe Oliver was going to stop, unless he stopped him. How? "I'm not going to be so free with money anymore." There had to be some accountability here, goddamn it.

"Whatever," Oliver said.

"And you'll have to do something. You can't just lie around here all day. What do you want to do?"

"Grandma asked me the same question."

"Grandma? When did you talk to Grandma?" Christ, now he'd have to deal with his mother.

"Today. I went to see her. She made me lunch."

Even in the dark, Andy could see Oliver's smile. "Well, what did she say about your predicament? That is, assuming you let her know about it."

"I already told you what she said. She asked me if I wanted to go back to school. Because if I did, I'd have to take one path, and if I didn't, I'd be taking another."

"What did you tell her?"

"I told her I didn't know."

"Is there anything you *do* know? Anything you *do* want to do?"

"I'm not sure. . . . I was thinking maybe I could just, like, hang out with Christina."

"*Christina?*" Of all the possible answers Oliver could have given him, Andy would never have expected this one.

"Yeah, help her and stuff. Maybe she'd need me to paint something, lug something, clean something. I want to go to those—what do you call them?—like, sales she goes to."

"Estate sales?" Now the kid wanted to start rummaging through all the crap people didn't want or left behind when they died?

"Yeah. Estate sales."

"Well, I could talk to her. . . ." Hadn't Christina said Oliver liked her? Well, she was right about that.

"Grandma was asking me about her. Like, a hundred questions: what do I think of her, is she nice? What's *that* all

about? You'd think she was, like, your girlfriend or something."

Andy sat very still. Here was a small moment of truth,
delivered right into his lap. "Actually, she is my girlfriend," he
said. Even though they had just had their first fight.

"No shit?" Oliver said, and when Andy nodded, *no shit*,
Oliver raised his palm to his father's and slapped it in an exuberant high five.

TWENTY-TWO

*C*hristina hurried up the steps of the Haverstick house. She was so excited; Derrick had called Phoebe to tell her that, yes, the Sargent was authentic and that given it was a late—and therefore highly unusual—portrait, it would be worth even more than he had initially estimated. Christina felt hurt that Derrick had not called her first—she supposed he was still angry, humiliated, or both—but she wasn't going to dwell on it. The important thing was the painting was real.

"Have you had it insured?" asked Christina when Phoebe had ushered her inside.

"Yes, but we'll need to change the policy now that we know it's worth more."

"That makes sense. Why don't you and Ian go ahead and start putting that in motion?"

"Derrick said he'd like to do a light cleaning," said Phoebe. "Do you think that's a good idea?"

"I do. You don't know what's on the surface; what if it's something potentially corrosive?"

"All right, then." She seemed to be thinking something over. "How long do you think that will take?"

"I'm guessing a couple of weeks at most."

"Good. I need time to work things out with Ian," she said.

"Because you think he's going to want to sell it?" Christina phrased this as neutrally as she could.

"I *know* he is," Phoebe said. "Especially now." She stood up. "You had some fabric samples to show me, right?"

Christina pulled them from her bag, relieved not to have to discuss Ian anymore. But she fretted about him all into the city, where she was going to meet Oliver. What was the source of his hostility? She couldn't attribute it entirely to the painting; the feeling had been there almost from the start.

Once she reached the showroom on West Twenty-eighth Street, she was able to push Ian out of her mind. She wriggled her way between the bolts of fabric that were everywhere, stacked horizontally in rows on industrial metal shelving, or standing packed together like saplings. But after half an hour of searching, she still did not see what she had come in search of: a crinkly, douppioni silk in a shade somewhere between pale ale and champagne. A sudden thud startled her. "Oliver?" she called. "Are you okay?"

"Uh, I think so," he called back.

"What happened?" she said when she made her way over to the other end of the store. "Are you hurt?"

He shook his head. "I made kind of a mess, though. . . ." He gestured to the bolts of fabric he'd knocked off a high shelf and which now created a barricade in the narrow aisle.

It was a week before Thanksgiving, and Oliver's third week of working for her. Christina had felt so horribly guilty over his expulsion from school that when he had asked if he could *hang out* with her, she immediately said yes. But although he undoubtedly meant well, he'd been more of a hindrance than anything. He cleaned a season's worth of debris from her garden but had also inadvertently dug up several recently planted peonies; he'd thought they were weeds. He had also broken inventory in her showroom, blown a fuse, dripped paint on her dining room rug—and now this.

"Hey, is everything all right up here?" Drawn by the noise, one of the store's clerks had come bounding up the stairs.

"Yeah, I just pulled a little too hard and they all came tumbling down."

The clerk frowned. "I hope nothing got dirty," he said.

"I'll pay for anything that's damaged," Christina quickly offered. Just like she'd paid for Oliver's other mishaps. And she hadn't told Andy either; the poor kid was in enough trouble as it was.

"I'm sorry," Oliver muttered. Together, they picked up the fallen bolts.

"That's okay," she said. "I think we should go now."

"But you didn't find your silk."

"Another time," she said.

Outside, Christina steered Oliver toward a favorite diner on Tenth Avenue. The area had gentrified rapidly, and now the avenue was dotted with expensive little bistros, bars, and cafés. Still, this place—Nell's—had held on and they were able to find a seat right by the window. Whatever there was of sunlight on this intermittently gray day formed a diamond on the tabletop; Christina reached for a menu and handed it to Oliver. She already knew what she was having—the spinach pie with a Greek salad—because that was what she had every time she came here.

"Do you know what you'd like?" she asked when the waitress appeared at their table.

"A tuna melt," he said, snapping the menu shut.

"Fries with that?" asked the waitress.

"Sure," he said, and then, leaning over to Christina, "But don't tell my dad. He'd lecture me for, like, an hour about the fat, the carbs, the bajillion chemicals in the ketchup."

Christina did not say anything. Andy *was* a bit of a proselytizer when it came to eating. When their meal came, she had to admit the fries did look delicious—crispy and golden— and she accepted Oliver's offer first of one, and then another.

"Our secret," she said. "We won't tell your dad."

"Deal." He took a fry from the plate. "What do you like about him anyway?"

Christina had to think. The first thing that sprang to mind—the erotic connection she had with Andy—was *not* something she was going to share with Oliver. "He has a good voice?" she said lightly.

Oliver snorted. "Come on. You can do better."

"He's smart, he's caring, he has so much integrity about his work—"

"He thinks he's God, you mean."

"You may be right about that." Christina smiled. "And we have a lot in common. We both lost our spouses, and we were both lonely—"

"My dad lonely? Not!" Oliver shook the ketchup bottle vigorously.

"Why do you say that?"

"He's been dating from practically the *second* we buried her," he said bitterly. "It's like he couldn't *wait*."

"He loved your mother very much."

"I know. But when she died, he wanted to, like, put it behind him. Immediately."

"Whereas you wanted to stay in that place for a while longer."

"Yeah," he said. "I did. I still do, I guess."

He took a bite of his sandwich. "I'll bet *you* didn't have, like, a dozen guys buzzing around the minute *your* husband died."

"No," she said. "I didn't."

"He was relieved when it finally happened. He never said it, but I could tell." His bright blue eyes probed her expression. "I was too. I mean, she was in *so* much pain."

"I understand," she said. "It must have been horrible."

"It was." He ate another fry before speaking again. "How did your husband die anyway?"

"In a fire," she said. "It happened quickly. Or at least that's what the fire marshal told me and I so badly wanted to believe him."

"I'm sorry," he said. "Maybe I shouldn't have asked."

"It's all right," she told him. "You wanted to know."

"Yeah," he said.

"A wall of flame engulfed him. I had to identify him by the buckle of his belt; the belt was mostly gone, but the buckle hadn't melted completely. It was fused to the little bit of leather that was left." She looked down at her salad. "I still have it."

"You do?"

She nodded, picturing the charred rectangle covered by the charred buckle; both resided in the blue Tiffany box that had once housed the silver bracelet she always wore.

"Was he, like, the only person who got killed?"

"The only one. He went back in to save a girl; it was an

insane thing to do. But the fire department hadn't gotten there yet. And I know he couldn't have lived with himself if anything had happened to her while she was on his watch."

"And did he? Save her?" Oliver said.

"Yes," said Christina. "She came to see me when she got out of the hospital. Her parents came too. Their relief was so enormous it was like some force field, almost a *glow* that emanated from them. I'll never forget it."

"Wow," Oliver said. "Your husband—he was a hero."

"He was." Christina looked at him. His struggle to understand what had happened—to Will, to his mother—was so visible on his open, undefended face. She wanted to take him in her arms, but she didn't know him well enough for that. Maybe she never would. Yet here she was telling him things she had not shared with his father. Death, it turned out, was even more intimate than sex.

The waitress returned to clear the table and asked whether they wanted dessert. Christina ordered a black coffee, but Oliver opted for rice pudding piled high with whipped cream. "I wish you were having Thanksgiving with us," he said.

"Me too." Given Jordan's open hostility, Christina and Andy thought it best not to celebrate together. He and Oliver were going to Andy's mother's; Christina was planning to spend the morning helping prepare and serve a meal at her church, and for the afternoon she had invited Mimi Farnsworth over with her sons. But now she realized that maybe there was a way that Oliver and Andy could spend at least part of the day with her. "What time do you go to your grandmother's?"

"Around five."

"So you're free in the morning." She sipped her coffee.

"Yeah."

"Why not come to church with me? Not for a service," she quickly added. "A bunch of us volunteer to make Thanksgiving dinner for the residents of a local shelter."

"You make food for, like, homeless people?"

"Yes," Christina said. "That's exactly what we do."

"I am *so* down with that."

It took Christina a moment to realize he was saying yes. "Your father can come too," she added. "That is, if he wants to."

"Yeah, he'll want to," Oliver said. The rice pudding was gone. "He likes pretending he cares about other people."

"Do you really think he's so bad?" she asked, and when he didn't answer, she gave in to the urge to reach across the table and tousle his blond hair. Then she tensed, waiting for the push back. There was none.

Emerging from the subway station, Christina turned the corner and began walking up Carroll Street. There they were again—the Indian couple. Only this time they had two other people with them; one had a camera and was taking pictures of her house. She accelerated her pace, wanting to catch them in the act. What right did they have to take photographs? But before she reached them, her phone buzzed. It was Phoebe Haverstick. Christina hesitated; she did not want to miss Phoebe's call, but she wanted to talk to these people as well. In her moment of hesitation, the Indian man saw her coming and tapped the photographer on the shoulder. He turned in her direction and then they all scurried into the waiting car. They were gone by the time Christina reached the house.

"—and I hope I'm not disturbing you," Phoebe was saying. "But I really needed to talk to you."

"Is everything all right?"

"It's the painting," Phoebe said.

"The portrait." Christina thought again of the clear-eyed girl and her wondrous hair. The Indian couple began to recede.

"Ian thinks we can get a lot of money for it. More than a million dollars, in fact."

"That *is* a lot of money."

"The problem is I don't want to sell it," said Phoebe. "I'd like my girls to be able to live with it. Grow up with it, even."

"If money is not a pressing issue—," said Christina.

"It's not," Phoebe said. "We'll have enough money to pay for college. Ian earns a good salary, plus we have investments, savings. My aunt left us money too; she was always very generous."

"Well, if you don't have to sell it, you shouldn't. It seems to mean a lot to you." Christina wondered about the reason for this call; Phoebe had already made her decision.

"That's what I think. Ian doesn't see it that way, though. He thinks of it the same way he thinks of my great-aunt's furniture—another piece of junk."

"Very valuable junk," Christina murmured. "In more ways than one."

"He says he sees no reason to live with *a useless artifact from an outmoded time.* Those were his words, or close enough."

"That's really too bad," Christina said. "But I'm still not seeing how I can help you." She had not yet let herself into the house.

"You know the appraiser. Maybe he could help. He could explain that the painting would appreciate in value and that the children would be able to sell it at some point if they wanted to."

"Couldn't you tell him that?"

"I know Ian. He thinks I'm being sentimental. But if he hears it from an expert, he might see it differently."

"That's true." She took out her key and opened the door. Just as she was going inside, she caught a glimpse of Charlotte Bickford opening *her* door—and then shutting it again very quickly.

"Please, would you do this for me? I'd be so grateful."

Christina thought it over. It would be a smart move to help Phoebe, who was after all paying her for an extensive job. But even more than the self-interest involved, she felt some empathy for this woman, some sense of kinship born of their mutual regard for that painting. Christina understood the deep tug that objects exerted. "All right," she said. "I'll call Derrick."

"Thank you, thank you!" Phoebe effused.

Christina walked into her office in search of Derrick's number. She had not heard from him since that awkward encounter at his loft. Maybe if she made it clear she was calling in a purely professional manner, he'd pick up or respond. But when she called the number on Derrick's card, she was surprised to hear a recorded voice telling her that the number was no longer in service and no further information was available.

Christina stared at the phone. Maybe she had called the wrong number. She tried again, punching in the numbers very carefully. The message was the same. On the bottom of the card was Derrick's cell phone number written in pencil. Fighting the rapidly rising tide of panic, she tried that number as well. There was a ringing and then someone picked up!

"Derrick, it's Christina," she said in a rush. "I hope you're not angry at me, but I was worried—"

"Derrick?" said an unfamiliar voice. "Derrick no here."

"But this was Derrick's number," she said. "Derrick Blascoe."

"No Derrick," said the voice, which had a thick accent of some kind. "Derrick no."

"Maybe you know something about where he is—," she began, but the person on the other end clicked off. She stared at the phone for a few seconds. Then she went in search of her coat.

It wasn't cold outside and Christina walked so quickly that by the time she reached Derrick's place on Union Street, she was sweating. The workshop occupied the ground floor; there was a metal gate that covered the window. Well, that didn't mean anything one way or the other. It was the night before a holiday weekend; of course it was closed. She stepped back and crossed the street so she could look up. The windows on the second floor were dark, but again, that signified nothing. Maybe Derrick was out of town. She crossed back over and moved to the doorway. There was an intercom with the names of all the tenants. Christina looked for his name amid the others, and that was when she saw it: the freshly exposed space where his name had been—and now was no longer.

TWENTY-THREE

*A*t ten minutes to eight the next morning, Oliver stood in front of the Old First Reformed Church on the corner of Seventh Avenue and Carroll Street in Brooklyn. His fists were jammed into his pockets and the hood of his sweatshirt covered his blond curls, but he was still cold. It was early; he had left himself plenty of time to get here from the Upper East Side. He wasn't sorry Andy couldn't make it. He'd had an emergency—his kick-ass celeb patient, Xiomara, had cramping or something and he'd rushed off to the hospital to deal. Oliver imagined his dad really got off on his power—not only could he bring babies into the world; he could also keep them from getting here ahead of schedule. Whatever. He was just glad the universe had cut him a break.

The door opened. A giant of a guy with a frizzy red beard and a perfectly weathered Elvis Costello T-shirt looked him over. "Are you waiting for dinner? Because it won't be ready for a while. But you can come in and get warm if you want."

"Actually, I'm waiting for Christina Connelly. I'm going to

be, like, helping out." This guy thought Oliver was one of the *homeless* people they were going to serve later on? How hilarious was *that*?

"You're with Chrissy?" Red Beard cracked a big smile. "Well, come on in. No point in freezing your buns off out there." So Oliver followed him inside. Red Beard lumbered along ahead, past wooden pews, stained-glass windows, and a wooden cross hanging up on the wall. When they got to the kitchen, Red Beard stopped. "This is where all the action is today. Chrissy will be here any minute. You might as well put on an apron and I can introduce you to everyone." He indicated a stack of aprons piled haphazardly on a counter.

Oliver nodded, looking around. The kitchen was twice the size of the living room in his apartment, with worn linoleum floors and banged-up-looking cabinets. A guy at one of the two deep sinks was washing what looked like a mountain of cranberries, two other guys were hauling in a ginormous basket of sweet potatoes, and by the windows, two women and a girl were spooning globs of pumpkin mush into pie tins lined with dough.

Something about the girl made Oliver look again. She was around his age, and everything about her seemed round: big, brown eyes, full face, boobs that strained against her apron, round, plump ass that poked out from the other side of it. Even her glossy brown hair, braided and wound around her head, made a circular shape. When she smiled, which seemed to be about every five seconds, dimples appeared in her cheeks. She must have sensed him staring, because she looked up from what she was doing and smiled again, this time right at him. Before he could walk over to her, Christina came rushing in.

"Sorry, sorry, sorry!" she said, shaking some drops from her hair. It must have started raining. "I didn't mean to be so late. But I see Robbie found you and brought you inside." Oliver looked over at Red Beard; so that was his name. The girl had gone back to the pies.

"Hey, Chrissy!" Robbie said, and engulfed her in a giant hug. Oliver watched as Christina deftly extricated herself from the guy's massive embrace.

"Come with me," she said, linking arms with Oliver while simultaneously undoing the buttons on her soft gray coat. She looked kind of wrung out, like she hadn't slept, and he wondered whether she was sick or something. "This is Josh," she said, indicating the shorter of the men. "And this is Lee." Lee gave Oliver a slow wave, and Josh gave him a smile.

Oliver watched as Christina moved off to the other end of the kitchen, plucking an apron from the pile as she went. He wanted to ask her whether she was okay, but Josh was showing him where the knives were and Lee was telling him what he had to do. And maybe this wasn't the best place to talk anyway. He'd catch her later. He soon became so engrossed in the chore of preparing the sweet potatoes—snip off the ends, prick with a fork, and wrap groups of three or four in foil—that he didn't notice Jordan until she was right next to him.

"Hey," she said, smoothing back her hair in its tight bun. She wore jeans and a black turtleneck sweater; her hair was perfectly smooth already.

"What's up?" He hadn't seen her since the day they had run into each other over the summer, but he'd friended her on Facebook. Instead of a profile picture, she'd posted a shot of ballet shoes. They were made of pink satin, but they were in lousy shape, toes frayed, stained, and crushed.

"Nothing really," she said. "You're helping out here today?"

"Your mom asked me to."

"That sounds like my mom," she said. "She wants every-body in the *circle*."

Then Christina called Jordan's name and she went off to another part of the kitchen. He finished with the potatoes and moved on to stirring the cranberry sauce, whipping cream for the pies, and basting the turkeys—there were four of them—that Robbie had hoisted into the ovens. The girl with the braids came over to say hi; she said her name was Summer.

"That's a cool name," he said. "It fits you." Up close she was even prettier.

"You think?"

"Yeah, I do." He wanted to say that she reminded him of all kinds of summery things—waxy, pink blossoms on a branch, dark cherries dangling from their stems, plums burst-ing their skin—but thought she'd think he was weird.

"Thanks," she said. "What's your name?"

"Oliver." He hoped he could hang out with her some more today. The rain outside had stopped and the sun shone in the windows above the stove, weakly at first, but then brighter. The kitchen grew warm; the various smells—turkey, pie, potatoes—from the oven were amazing. Someone put on music; it was nothing he recognized, but he liked the jazzy sound. Soon people started singing along—Robbie, those guys Josh and Lee, Summer, a woman named Miriam, and another one named Louise. Christina came over to where he stood by the sink, scrubbing a pan. Her cheeks were flushed and her apron was speckled with grease. "How are you doing?" she asked.

"Great," he said. "This is fun. I'm glad you asked me."

"We host a dinner here once a month," she said. "We al-ways need help."

"You mean you do all this"—he gestured around him—"every month?"

"Not turkey; turkey's just for Thanksgiving and Christmas. Easter we do lamb. The rest of the time we rotate. Chili or stew—something like that."

Around one o'clock everything was winding down. Summer said she had to go but told him to text her. The food was pretty much cooked. Oliver helped Jordan and Louise set the tables in the meeting room upstairs. The table coverings and napkins were paper; everything else was plastic. But Christina had brought bags of pinecones, acorns, and gourds, and she was busy arranging them into centerpieces. "They look nice," he said. "Really nice."

People were standing at the doors now. People in really shabby clothes, holding steaming plates with both hands. They had been served their food down in the kitchen and were now coming up here to eat it. "Is it okay to sit down?" asked a tiny, wrinkled woman whose hair looked like Brillo.

"Of course it is," Christina said, stepping away from the table.

Oliver stepped back too, and stood alongside Christina as the guests began to file in. Some of them had crammed bags looped around their wrists; others wheeled suitcases behind them. One guy had a shopping cart with a wood board across the top; he used the board like a tray. The faces Oliver saw were old and young, black, Hispanic, Asian, and white. A few scowled and a few seemed to have no expression at all. One guy was talking to himself. He sounded angry. Also loud. "I told them not to ask me again," he said. "I *told* them."

Oliver noticed that people began to move away from him. His wispy beard was matted and he was pulling anxiously on the ends. "Why are they asking me this again?" he pleaded. "Why?" He walked over to the woman with the Brillo hair. "Is it because of *you*?" he said menacingly. "Did you tell them to do it?" The woman shrank back. "I know you did it!" He was shouting. "It was you, it was!" He spun around, arms flailing. A hand glanced off Brillo lady's shoulder and she uttered a little shriek.

"Now, Matt, you know Claudia wouldn't do anything to hurt you." Robbie appeared at the man's side and took him gently by the elbow. "No one here would hurt you. We're your friends, remember?" Matt looked like he wanted to carve a piece out of Robbie, but then Lee materialized at his other side and the two men led Matt off, talking to him softly. Oliver noticed that Christina was standing next to him.

"Is that guy okay?" he asked.

"Not exactly. But Robbie and Lee know how to handle him."

Oliver watched as Robbie sat down with Matt, leaning over the table and talking earnestly to him. Lee had brought over two plates of food and was putting them down.

The sun, brighter now, shone in through the big windows.

The sight of these people patiently filing in cracked something open in Oliver, something he had not known was shut so tightly until this second. These past few weeks, he'd gotten up, gotten dressed, and aimlessly bounced through the hours like a pinball. But today was different. He looked down at his hands, which were raw from scrubbing all those pans. There was a cut on his left index finger from where a knife had slipped; Louise had given him a Buzz Lightyear Band-Aid she had in her purse and Buzz's face was wrapped around his finger.

Everyone was eating now. Lee moved between tables,

pouring cider from a gallon jug. Louise had a basket of hot rolls and was distributing those. People were spearing their turkey, biting into their Brussels sprouts, getting cranberry sauce on their chins or the fronts of their shirts. They were eating, drinking, taking in the food that he'd helped provide. Even the crazy dude had a place at the table. Was there anything more important? Anything, like, more real? Christina said that the church members made a meal once a month. He could come back again. Come back and help. Looking around at the guests in the room, he felt as full as if he'd been at the table with them. His father had said, over and over, that he couldn't just sit around; he had to apply himself to something. Well, he'd just figured out what that something was. *This is it,* he wanted to tell his father. *This is what I'm going to do.*

TWENTY-FOUR

*C*hristina waited in the Riverside Drive lobby while Andy gave their names to the doorman. Although she had hoped for a more intimate way to celebrate her birthday, Andy felt obliged to put in an appearance at the annual Hanukkah party thrown by one of his colleagues at the hospital. "We'll have our own private party later," he said. "I've booked a room at the Carlyle." She had to admit that sounded nice.

Riding up in the elevator, he gave her hand a little squeeze. "You'll like the Gottliebs," he said. "They're terrific people." Christina said nothing. Most everyone there would know one another and many of them were successful doctors at Andy's hospital. *Jewish* doctors. It seemed natural that such a crew would be Andy's friends as well as colleagues; it wasn't like he had time to be cultivating indie filmmakers or aspiring opera singers. How they would respond to a decidedly non-Jewish interior designer from Brooklyn remained to be seen. At least she was confident about her dress, a secondhand Chanel made of plum-colored velvet and piped with black grosgrain ribbon.

"Andy!" Bill Gottlieb, their host, was at the door of the sprawling apartment clapping Andy on the back. "Come on and have a drink!"

"Bill, this is Christina Connelly," Andy said. Christina extended her hand as Bill looked her up and down. There was a brief, loaded silence and then Bill turned to Andy. "Where have you been keeping her?" he said. Christina smiled in relief and allowed Andy to lead her into the room.

Bill gave her coat to a maid, made noises about her dress, and then was distracted by the arrival of another couple. Andy snagged them each a glass of wine from the waiter who was circling the room with a tray. Christina sipped her drink as Andy led her around the living room, introducing her to one colleague after another. Most of the names blended into one another—Hershkowitz, Meyerson, Schaffer, Shengold, Kornblatt, Klotz, Shapiro, and the noticeable outcasts, Ko and Sullivan. The women mostly wore short cocktail dresses and lots of jewelry, though she did notice a gaunt woman with a pixie cut in a pair of flowing silk palazzo pants.

Christina shook hands and smiled but did not attempt to join the noisy group gathered around their host. One of the guests was telling a joke that had something to do with a young woman's breasts; the punch line was, "Of course they're mine; I paid for them!" Although Andy laughed, Christina backed away and turned her focus to the room, which was less the product of intentional decoration than one of organic evolution. One wall was covered, floor to ceiling, with bookshelves. An upright piano dominated another. An oil portrait of two little girls hung next to a series of framed black-and-white photographs; the portrait made her think of the Sargent painting and of Derrick, who had mysteriously disappeared.

But she would not let her worry about him ruin her evening, and she forced herself to focus on the wall's other painting, which was all stick figures and primary colors—the work, no doubt, of a beloved child. The furniture was an eclectic mix— a chesterfield sofa, assorted club and wing chairs, a marble-topped coffee table. The rugs too were a hodgepodge—kilims, Persians, and one that might have been an Aubusson. Even with its imperfections, there was something so pleasing about a room like this; it had a soul. She walked over to the windows in the living room. Though it was dark outside, she could make out a view of the Hudson River, and beyond that, the Palisades.

Another burst of laughter erupted behind her, but she had no desire to be in on the joke. This seemed like a raucous crowd, not her sort of people at all. But as Andy had promised, they would have their own private celebration later on. Ida was spending the night at Andy's apartment with Oliver, and Jordan was with Alexis, so they had the whole evening—and next morning—together. She planned to wear the peach satin nightgown Andy had given her for her birthday—just thinking about it excited her.

Christina turned away from the window and wandered into the dining room. A long table in the middle of the room offered a staggering assortment of food and the sideboard held platters of sweets. Directly above were shelves crammed with decorative porcelain and china. Christina went straight over to see them better. A stunning collection of yellowware bowls far surpassed her own. There were also pieces of Bennington, with its distinctive splatter glaze, as well as Rockingham, with the drippy brown glaze that resembled maple syrup. Her gaze traveled over sleek and surprisingly modern-

looking white ironstone pitchers, iridescent lusterware cream-
ers, and cookie jars shaped, respectively, like an owl, a pelican,
and the face of a clown. What an assortment; whoever had
assembled them had a great eye.

"So you like the tchotchkes too?"

Christina turned to see an elegant woman with a gray
pageboy and a cluster of amber beads gleaming on the front
of her black dress.

"Excuse me?" Christina did not know what she was talking about.

"Tchotchkes? Bric-a-brac?"

"I certainly do," Christina said, enlightened now. "This is
your collection?"

"It's more of a work in progress. I'm always looking for the
next big find. Whenever I bring home a new piece, Bill says,
'Jane, not again.' In the end, he always indulges me, though."

"It's like an addiction, isn't it? The collecting, I mean."

"Or an obsession."

"A magnificent obsession," Christina said.

"Exactly! For some of us, it's not about stuff. It's about the
hunt. And the hunt is just a portal to the past."

"I know what you mean," Christina said, warming to her.
It would be fun to go "hunting" with this woman.

The woman smiled. "I'm sorry—I didn't even introduce
myself. I'm Jane Gottlieb."

"I assumed," said Christina. Jane must have been elsewhere when she and Andy came in.

"And you are . . . ?"

"Christina Connelly; I came with Andy Stern."

"Oh, you're Andy's new lady friend!" Jane seemed delighted. "I can't tell you how glad we are to meet you. We've

known Andy for years and when Rachel died . . ." She paused. "Well, let's just say it was a bad patch. So we were thrilled when he told us he was bringing you tonight."

"Are you a doctor too?" asked Christina.

"Lord, no! I couldn't stomach the sight of blood; even getting an injection makes me woozy. The thought of administering one . . . No, I'm in public relations and marketing. I have my own firm. And you?"

When Christina told her, Jane said, "Didn't you do Angelica Silverstein's apartment?"

"I did," said Christina.

"I adore her place; you did a fabulous job!" Jane reached out to touch the arm of the woman in the palazzo pants. "Flora, *this* is the decorator who did Angelica Silverstein's place." For the next twenty minutes, Christina felt quite the star; it seemed that her work had been noticed—and admired—more widely than she knew. One of the more flashily dressed women in the group—strapless red satin, triple strand of pearls, four-inch red patent leather heels—asked for her card. The woman studied it and then extended her hand. "Ginny Valentine. Pleased to meet you."

"Are you *that* Ginny Valentine? The ballerina?"

"Former ballerina, but yes, that's me."

"I can't tell you how thrilled I am to meet you! I've seen you in so many things—*The Four Temperaments, Concerto Barocco*—"

"You do know your Balanchine, don't you?" said Ginny.

"I'm a balletomane from way back," Christina said. "And my daughter's studying at SAB now; she's fifteen. Wait until she hears I've met you!"

"Fifteen!" breathed Ginny. "Oh, to be fifteen again, and have it all ahead of you—instead of behind."

"What's your connection to the host?" Christina asked. Obviously she wasn't a doctor.

"My husband works at the hospital. I'm the token 'artist' in the room. Or retired artist anyway." She tipped her head back to finish the wine in her glass. "How about you? You're not one of them either."

"I'm with Andy Stern," said Christina. She couldn't decide whether Ginny sounded wistful, bitter, or both. But dancers had short careers and Ginny Valentine's had been longer and more illustrious than most. Was this the best Jordan could hope for?

"Ah, Andy," said Ginny. She signaled to a waiter for a refill. "He treated me, you know."

"I didn't, actually."

"Oh yes. I had a couple of miscarriages and everyone said, *If you want a baby, he's the one who can help you.*"

"I see." Andy had never mentioned that a former ballerina from the NYCB had been his patient. But then, he was very discreet, even protective of the women he saw.

"He was . . . magnificent," said Ginny. The waiter had poured her a refill and she began to make her way through it quickly. "But it was no use. I was just too old and I kept losing them, one after the other. I decided to stop trying." She drained the glass.

"I'm sorry," murmured Christina. How sad. She could imagine Andy as having been . . . magnificent . . . even if Ginny had not ended up with a baby.

"Don't be! I would have made a terrible mother anyway. I had my career and it was a damned good one. You don't get to have everything, do you? No one does." She looked steadily at Christina. "Didn't you say you had a daughter at SAB? What if I give you an autograph for her? Do you think she'd like that? What's her name?" Without waiting for a reply, Ginny set down her glass and rummaged through her red satin evening purse for a pen; she wrote her name with a bold flourish on a paper cocktail napkin and handed it to Christina just as the other guests began filing into the room.

Christina spotted Jane as she made her way toward the brass menorah on the sideboard; Christina had been so busy first admiring her collections and then talking to Ginny that she hadn't noticed it before. It was a beautiful, singular-looking object, ornately worked with a pair of lions flanking either end. Christina guessed it was from the early nineteenth or even late eighteenth century. Jane Gottlieb knew her—what was the word?—*tchotchkes*. Right now, she was saying a prayer as she lit each candle and when all eight were ablaze, the effect was dazzling.

Then covers came off the chafing dishes and people began lining up to fill their plates. Christina saw carved meat and a noodle dish—brisket and kugel according to Andy. A group of waiters began filing in, each with a silver tray held aloft. They carried platters of something that looked fried and golden. "Latkes—potato pancakes," said Andy.

"Oh—right," she said. She had never actually tasted one. When she did, it was delicious—the contrast of the salty pancake and the sweet applesauce was just perfect.

"We'll have dinner here but dessert back at the hotel," Andy said. "How does that sound?"

"Lovely," she said, thinking of the peach nightgown. "But I'm going to have one more pancake. They are *so* good." She signaled to the waiter, who approached with the tray. Someone must have bumped him from behind, though, because suddenly, the tray was upended and Christina was covered in a cascade of latkes.

"Oh no!" she cried. She could feel the warmth of the oily latkes through her dress and she prayed the velvet would not stain.

"Jesus, that's the second time your dress gets ruined when you're with me," Andy said, brushing the latkes to the floor, where the mortified waiter, babbling apologies, knelt to clean them up.

"What happened?" Jane Gottlieb hurried over. "Are you all right?"

"Perfectly fine," Christina said with a smile. "I hope this doesn't deplete your latke supply, though."

"Aren't you a dear!" Jane exclaimed. "Of course I'll pay for the cleaning of your dress; I'll even replace it!"

"I'm sure that won't be necessary," Christina said. She did not want to tell Jane—or anyone else—that one of the latkes had actually slipped down the scoop neck of the Chanel and was now lodged somewhere between the bottom of her bra and the top of her slip. "But I'd love to wash up; can you point me toward the bathroom?"

Once safely behind the closed door, Christina fished out the offending latke. Now what? There was a painted tin wastebasket—empty of course—in one corner; it seemed somehow wrong to deposit the latke there. So she broke it into tiny pieces and flushed it down the toilet. When she emerged, Andy and Jane were waiting.

"Everything all right?" said Jane anxiously.

"Just fine—you can't even see a mark on the dress." She hoped this was true; velvet spotted *so* easily.

"Well, there's still the smell. You'll have it cleaned and send the bill to me."

"Don't worry about it," Christina said. "No harm done."

Jane turned to Andy. "This one is a keeper!"

After dinner, the guests meandered back into the living room, where Bill sat down at the piano. Christina was not familiar with most of the music—folk songs, some in Yiddish—but she had to love Bill, pounding the keys with abandon as the guests sang along.

It wasn't until they had said their good-byes and were out on the street that Christina told Andy about the latke in her dress. He started to laugh and then she laughed too—it really was funny. "Thanks for being such a good sport," he said. "It means a lot to me that the Gottliebs like you."

"I like them," Christina said. "Maybe we'll all have dinner together sometime." She did not mention Ginny Valentine but experienced a private rush of, what—pleasure? Pride even?—when she remembered her praise. Could this night, and others like it, become familiar parts of her life's pattern? She reached for Andy's hand and held it tightly; at this moment, she ardently hoped so.

TWENTY-FIVE

*A*ndy had no trouble hailing a taxi to take them across town and to the Carlyle Hotel. There was very little traffic and the cab sped through the darkened park and downtown, but when they reached Fifth Avenue and Seventy-eighth Street, they were suddenly stalled by a tangle of cars. Horns blared and honked; the driver stuck his head out the window to see what was going on. "Accident," he said when he pulled his head back in. "Who knows how long we'll be stuck here?"

"We can just get out and walk," Andy said as he paid the driver. "It's only a few blocks." They continued east on Seventy-second Street to Madison Avenue and then turned south. The shop windows were filled with bright, holiday displays. "Look at that," Christina said. Eager as she was to get to the hotel, she couldn't help but notice the large cameo in the simple gold oval and she had to stop. "Isn't it lovely?" What had she said to Jane? Addiction? Obsession? The cameo was suspended from a braided gold chain and showed a woman in profile. Tiny grapes were carved into her flowing curls; her lips were parted in a smile.

"You like that?" Andy asked.

"You seem surprised."

"It seems kind of plain to me. Don't most women prefer something with more bling?"

"Do I strike you as being like most women?"

"Hardly," he said, and when he pulled her close for a kiss in the nearly empty street, she surrendered to it completely.

They were at the hotel in minutes. Like the first time they had come here, Andy had dropped off their luggage in advance, but this time he used his real name to register. "I *want* people to know about us," he said. "I want *everyone* to know." When they got upstairs, she was ready to slip into the bathroom to change into the new nightgown, but he stopped her. "Didn't you want to have dessert?" he asked.

"Well, yes, but I don't see any reason—" She stopped when she heard a knock at the door. "Who could that be?" she asked.

"Room service," he said. He opened the door and a busboy rolled in a cart and then began to arrange things, including a covered pot with a Bunsen burner, on the table. Christina was silent until Andy had tipped him and locked the door behind him. Then he motioned for her to come over. "Chocolate fondue," he said, lifting the cover.

"That looks delicious," she said as the aroma of the heated chocolate wafted toward her. She was glad she had avoided the jelly doughnuts at the Gottliebs'.

"Oh, it will be," he said. "We can put it on any of this—" He uncovered a platter of sliced fruit and pound cake. "Or we can put it other places. . . ." He slid a finger in the chocolate and held it up to her lips. "Happy birthday, darling." Christina leaned closer and was just about to take his finger in her mouth when the sound of his phone fractured the mood.

"Damn," he said. He licked the chocolate from his own finger and answered. For a few seconds he listened quietly. Then he said, "How much blood?" Another silence. "Okay," he said. "Try to stay calm. I'll be there as soon as I can." He clicked off.

"Who was that?" she said, but she didn't have to ask; she *knew*. Andy had given his cell phone number to that famous singer; she had called him before when they were together. The first or second time it happened, Christina teased him about having a crush on her; he got so red-faced and flustered that she realized she had struck a nerve. She stopped teasing him—and started resenting the singer instead.

"Xiomara," he said, and went into the bathroom to rinse his finger. "She's staining and she's a wreck. I'm just going to meet her at the hospital and get her settled. Then I'll be right back—back to you." He came over and leaned down for a kiss, but she turned her face away. "Christina, don't be like that. I don't want to leave you, but this is an emergency."

"You're not on call tonight," she said. "You told me that."

"Well, no, but—"

"And it's my birthday! Doesn't she understand that you have a life? That you're not at her beck and call twenty-four/seven?"

"Who said anything about being at her beck and call? She's very anxious; you can understand that, can't you?"

"What I understand is that you're choosing her over me. Again."

"That's ridiculous. I don't even know what you're talking about." He crossed his arms defensively over his chest.

"This isn't the first time she's called and this isn't the first time you've dropped everything for her."

"I take my work—and my patients—very seriously."

"Yes. And some patients more seriously than others. Xiomara is the *only* one who has your private cell phone number. The only one!"

"She's a special case for all kinds of reasons." When Christina didn't reply, he added, "Rachel never complained."

"Maybe Rachel was a doormat."

"That's low. Really low." He picked up his coat. "I wouldn't have expected that from you, Christina."

This was a cue to apologize, but she wasn't taking it; she was too angry. "So you're really going?"

"I told you I'd be back as soon as I can."

"Don't count on my being here," she said.

He shook his head. "You are blowing this totally out of proportion. But I don't have time to fight with you now." And then he was gone.

Christina stared at the door after he'd closed it. Should she make good on her threat and leave? She was certainly angry enough. But when she started gathering up her things, she saw the peach nightgown and sank down on the bed. More than angry, she was disappointed. Was *this* what it would be like with him? There would always be a Xiomara—or her equivalent. Just a little while ago, she could see them as a unit, their two lives woven seamlessly together. Now she wasn't so sure.

The digital clock by the bed read 11:59. It was late, she was exhausted, and she did not want to take the long taxi ride back to Brooklyn. She would stay the night but leave first thing in the morning; who knew when—or if—Andy would be back?

Padding into the plushly appointed bathroom, she filled a glass from the tap and took a couple of Advil; her head was killing her. Then she stripped off her dress, blew out the flame under the Bunsen burner, and climbed into bed. The night-gown remained where it was; she slept in one of the terry robes provided by the hotel.

A slim line of light showed between the drapes when the door opened; she had not thought to bolt it. She felt a surge of fear until she heard Andy's voice.

"Christina?" he said softly. "Are you still here?" She did not answer. Her head was pounding again and her mouth felt all cottony; she hadn't even brushed her teeth last night. He sat down on the foot of the bed. "You *are* here. I'm glad. I thought you left."

"I wanted to," she said. "I *should* have."

"I told you it was an emergency but that I'd be back. And look—here I am."

She sat up straighter. He was a mess—his clothes wrinkled and his collar smeared with what she realized must have been blood. He had not been to bed at all. "You must be tired," she said, her voice more gentle now.

"I am. And I could use a shower."

"So could I," she said. Last night's makeup was still caked on her face.

"Maybe you'd like to join me . . . ?"

Christina hesitated. He was a good man. He cared about what he did, and did it with such passion and integrity. How could she stay angry with him? "I think I would." She got up from the bed and loosened the belt of the robe; he slid it easily from her shoulders.

Afterward, they lay entwined in each other's arms. "Is she

as beautiful in person as she is in the photos?" Christina asked. She ran a finger across Andy's chest where a few drops of water still clung to his skin.

"She's very beautiful," he said. Christina was grateful he did not pretend not to know what she meant. "But I don't love her. I love you." He tightened his grip around her.

Before she could answer, there was a knock at the door. "Did you call room service again?" she asked.

He shook his head and reached for the robe that was heaped on the floor. "You stay there." He got up and went to the door. When he returned, he was holding a glossy black shopping bag tied with a red ribbon.

"Room service of a different kind," he said, offering her the bag.

"What is it?"

"Open it and find out." Inside the bag was a box, and inside the box was the cameo she had admired the night before.

Christina was stunned. "What did you do?" she asked. "Rob the place?"

Andy laughed. "Nope. But I know the owner of the store— I delivered his twins a couple of months ago. One of them is colicky and the only thing that calms her down is a ride in the stroller; I ran into the dad pushing her along Madison and told him about the cameo; he offered to have it sent over to the hotel."

"What a romantic, thoughtful thing to do," she said. "Thank you." Any lingering resentment over the night before was gone now, dispersed like smoke.

"You're welcome," he said. He slid into the bed beside her and they kissed for a long time. Then, all of a sudden, he jumped up.

"What's wrong?" She hoped it wasn't *another* call from that singer; she hadn't even heard the phone.

"I'm starved," he said. "Ravenous, in fact."

"Well, all right, we can order up some breakfast if you like—"

But Andy was busy lighting the burner under the pot of chocolate and uncovering the platter of fruit and cake from the night before. "I know it's decadent," he said with a sly smile. "But I was thinking we could have some chocolate for breakfast. Warm chocolate—if you get my drift."

"How did you guess?" she said with an answering smile. "Warm chocolate was *exactly* what I wanted."

TWENTY-SIX

On the Saturday before Christmas, Andy found himself lugging a tightly bound and mesh-wrapped Christmas tree up the front stoop of Christina's house in Park Slope. This was about the last thing he ever expected to be doing, but he was having a surprisingly good time. The tree, nearly nine feet tall, had a fresh, piney scent, and the exertion of carrying it from the car and up the steps gave him the kind of mild endorphin high he associated with working out. Then there was the fun of Christina herself, pink cheeked and exuberant. She was wearing a loden coat with bright buttons and her hair had slipped a bit from its usual twist; the soft tendrils fell appealingly around her pretty face. Andy liked how well she kept up her end of the load.

"Careful," she said as she maneuvered the pointed tip through the double doors. "You don't want to catch it on anything."

"I'm good back here," he said as he gently eased the fragrant mass inside.

Once they had it safely in the parlor, she shucked off her coat and went in search of the tree stand. Andy sat down to wait. In addition to the tree-buying expedition, she had invited him to both the party she threw on Christmas Day and to church the night before. He'd said yes to the former and declined the latter, though he had not wanted to tell her why. A long time ago, when he was a little boy, his class had gone to the Cloisters in Fort Tryon Park on a field trip. He'd been so petrified of the large, wooden crucifixes on practically every wall—Jesus in all his carved, static agony, spikes pounded through his wrists and ankles—that he'd gone into the bathroom and locked himself in a stall. One of the guards had to climb up and over the partition in order to get him to come out, and he'd cried all the way home. Ever since, he'd avoided churches.

"Here it is," she said when she returned.

Andy had to admit he was fairly useless when it came to positioning the tree, but that didn't matter; she knew exactly what she was doing, and all that was required of him was to hold it steady while she tightened this and loosened that. After about fifteen minutes, the tree was securely in the stand and she used her kitchen shears to cut through the netting and twine that had held it. Immediately, the deep green branches sprang open like wings; they filled the room with their scent.

"Nice," he said as he stood back to admire it.

"Very nice." She switched on the radio to a station that was playing Christmas songs, mostly old ones, sung by the likes of Patsy Cline, Frank Sinatra, and Bing Crosby. "Music to decorate by," she said, and walked over to the boxes of ornaments and coils of lights lined up by the windows. They began with the lights—"always clear, never colored," she explained—

which she wound around the tree and then tucked deep into the recesses of the branches. When that was done, Andy looked more closely at the boxes of ornaments. There must have been more than a hundred; he wondered whether she planned to use them all.

"I like to start by clustering certain ones together. See these?" She held up a tiny pair of pink satin point shoes and hung it on the tree. "I bought them at the Lincoln Center gift shop, the first time I took Jordan to see *Nutcracker*; now I add a new ballet ornament every year." Andy lifted a miniature ballerina from the box and placed it next to the point shoes. "That's good," she said. "You can put the other ones nearby."

After he hung the rest of the ballet ornaments—wooden nutcracker, a tutu, another pair of point shoes made from ceramic—he watched Christina climb onto the stepladder to reach some of the higher branches. "Can I help you?" he asked.

"That would be great. Could you give me that one down there?"

Andy held it up. "A carrot?" he asked.

"It was my aunt Barb's," she said. "Vegetable ornaments were kind of a thing with her." In the same box, he found another carrot, a shiny red pepper, two ears of corn, and a pumpkin. He gave them to her one by one, and waited while she carefully positioned each glass bauble. Then she said, "Now for the fruit."

"Aunt Barb?"

"Aunt Barb."

Andy passed her shining strawberries, plums, limes, and several apples made of crimson velvet. Then she moved on to a group of ornaments in another box; they were all made of the same murky silver. "They seem kind of tarnished," he said. "Are you sure you want to use them?"

"Mercury glass," she said. "They're really old and I've been collecting them for years. I don't group these together; I put them up all over, as a kind of unifying theme."

"I guess there's a science to this," he said.

"More like an art." She smiled.

When they were finally done, she went down to the kitchen and returned with mugs of thick, dark hot chocolate that was nothing like the sweet, packaged crap dispensed by the hospital vending machines. Andy was charmed by the whole experience, it was so nostalgic and wholesome, like he'd wandered onto the set of *It's a Wonderful Life*. This was the first time he could remember not feeling the old sense of exclusion around the holiday, and he found he liked it. He let his mind skip ahead, to the next Christmas and the one after that. He could see waking up with her in the morning and sitting down to dinner with her every night, the hours in between governed by her graciousness, her seemingly innate sense of harmony and order.

"There's one last thing," she said. "The star."

"Okay, where is it?"

"Check that last box; it should be in there."

Andy looked and found the star. It was made of silver glass and set on a hollow glass cone that would sit easily on top of the tree. "Here," he said, but even on the stepladder, she couldn't reach. "Do you want me to do it?"

"Would you?" She climbed down. Andy replaced her on the stepladder and put the star in place. Jesus, he was glad his mother wasn't here to see this.

"Thank you—that's perfect," Christina said. "Putting the star on top can be your official job now."

"You mean I'm invited back next year?" His tone was playful, but he was probing; did *she* see a future for them?

"Why wouldn't you be?" she said, smiling.

He waited a beat. "Do you think we'll be together next year?"

"Do you?" She turned it back to him.

"I'd like that," he said, looking at her steadily. "I'd like that very much."

Before she could answer, Jordan walked into the room. She was bundled in a puffy down coat from which her long, alarmingly thin neck emerged. Clearly she was not happy to see him.

"Hi," Andy said, trying to sound friendly. He'd be damned if he knew why she didn't like him. "Your mom and I just finished putting on the decorations."

"I can see that," she said. "I'm not blind, you know."

"Where are your manners?" Christina said. Jordan just glowered, so Christina continued. "Andy worked on the ballet section; I think he did a very good job with the ballet section, don't you?"

"No," Jordan said flatly. "I don't."

"Jordan!"

"Why ask if you don't want to hear my opinion? You can't even *see* the ballet ornaments; he stuck them way in the back. And they're too close together besides. And did he do the star too? Because it's crooked. But if you don't care, I guess I don't either." She turned and left the room.

"I'm sorry," Christina said as soon as she was gone. "Maybe I should have done the ballet ornaments myself. She's just finding all this very difficult."

"All what?" he said with more edge than he'd intended. "The fact that her mother has a boyfriend who's bending over backward to ingratiate himself with her?" The music, which had seemed delightful just a little while ago, was now as annoying as hell and he wished she would turn it off.

"She just needs a little more time," Christina said.

"What she needs is a firm hand," he said. "You shouldn't let her get away with that." There was a long, uncomfortable silence.

"And you shouldn't tell me how to raise my daughter," said Christina when she finally spoke again.

Andy was ready to snap right back, but he looked at her first, spine perfectly straight, hands folded in her lap. Her cheeks, so pink before, had gone pale. She seemed so vulnerable. Then he thought of how she'd raised Jordan on her own, created this lovely home, a successful business, a life. She *was* vulnerable, but she was also brave, resolute, and proud. A wave of something rose and crested in him——was it love? Did he love this woman sitting across from him? Love her enough to put up with her bratty daughter and a possible lifetime of cloying holiday music? He got up from where he sat and put his hands over hers, as if warming or protecting them. She didn't say anything, but he saw her soften and incline toward him just the slightest bit. He didn't need any more encouragement to take her in his arms.

Despite Jordan's evident hostility, Christina had invited Andy to stay the night. After dinner, Jordan had gone to her room and not emerged; Christina could feel her daughter's resentment emanating through the closed door. Andy had not seemed to notice. In bed, he kissed her shoulders and neck, but when he cupped her breasts with his hands, she murmured, "I can't . . ."

"I'll be quiet," he said. "I promise."

For a moment, she wavered. She loved the feel of him, all muscled arms and sculpted chest. And his caress was very arousing. But Jordan's room was too close for comfort and she moved out of the embrace. "I'm sorry," she said. "I just won't be able to relax." He did not press and they fell asleep entwined.

In the morning, Jordan's door remained shut while Christina made coffee and banana bran muffins. Andy liked the muffins so much that she packed him several to take home with him. As they were saying good-bye, she realized she didn't want him to leave; she wished she could spend the whole day with him.

"Do you have to get right back?" she asked. "I thought maybe we could take a quick walk through Prospect Park first and then you could get a car service from there."

"I've never seen Prospect Park," he said. He looked at his watch. "I don't have all that much time. But yeah, let's do it."

She grabbed her loden coat from its hook and they walked arm in arm up the hill, toward the park. The day was cold but bright; the winter sun felt good on her face.

"I read there was a new skating rink in that park," Andy was saying. "Do you like to skate?"

"I love skating," she said. "We should go sometime."

"Oliver's a terrific skater," Andy said. "I'll bet he'd want to come too. What about Jordan?"

"No," said Christina. "She never really liked it and now she'd never go; she's afraid of falling and getting hurt."

They were both silent; even the mention of Jordan created an awkward barrier between them. Christina was trying to think of something to say when her attention was diverted by a plaintive meowing. A cat, in some kind of distress. But where? They were almost at the top of the hill, very close to

the park now, and the trees here were older and more estab-
lished than in the blocks below. She looked around. "Look,"
she said to Andy, pointing. "Do you see?"

There, in a tree across the street, was a large white cat.
Christina quickly crossed over and Andy followed. "Maddie!"
called a woman who was standing below the tree. "Maddie, come down!"

"Is that your cat?" Andy asked.

The woman, who was quite young, more of a girl really,
nodded. Her braided hair was disheveled, like she hadn't
combed it yet, and she wore a parka and muffler over a pair of
sweatpants. "She got out and when the garbage truck came up
the street, she panicked and went up the tree." From an earth-
enware mug, the girl produced a colossal shrimp. "I was hoping to coax her down with this; shrimp is her favorite." She
waved the tidbit in the air. "Maddie!" Turning to Christina,
she added, "Her name is Madonna because she is *such* a diva.
But mostly I just call her Maddie."

Christina looked up at the cat. She was perfectly white,
with long, luxurious fur and very blue eyes. The expression on
her face was one of pure terror.

"I think she wants to come down, but she's stuck," said
Andy. "See how her back paw is caught in that crevice? I don't
think she can free herself."

"Oh no!" cried the girl. "How can I rescue her?"

"Did you call the fire department or the police?" Christina
asked.

The girl nodded. "The firemen in the local firehouse are
dealing with a four-alarm fire; who knows when they'll be
back? And the police said they would try to send a squad car,
but that was over twenty minutes ago."

"I'll bet I could get her down," said Andy.

"Are you serious?" Christina said. *"You're* going to climb that tree?"

"It's not all that high," he said, and then turned to the girl. "Do you have a ladder?"

"I do!" said the girl.

"Good," Andy said. "Why don't you go get it?"

Christina watched while the ladder was brought out and Andy climbed it as easily as he'd ascended her stepladder the night before. The cat, however, was still out of reach, so he grabbed on to a branch and hoisted himself up.

"Be careful!" cried Christina. He was high enough to get hurt if he fell.

Andy ignored her and focused on the cat. Christina saw how he extended his hand, giving her the opportunity to sniff him. But her front paw shot out and she raked her claws across his wrist. "Andy, are you all right? You'd better come down!" Even from where she stood on the sidewalk, Christina could see the streaks of blood. But Andy remained unfazed.

"She never does that!" said the girl. "She's just so freaked-out!"

"What about that shrimp?" Andy called down. "Can you hand one up to me?"

The girl climbed the ladder while Christina steadied it; Andy reached down to take the shrimp. This time when he approached the cat, he dangled the shrimp where she would be able to smell it. She leaned forward and her pink tongue emerged, giving the shrimp an experimental lick. Andy waited until she had started chewing on it to reach over and free her paw. Then she allowed herself to be picked up as Andy shimmied down the trunk one-handed; the other gripped the cat.

How calm he was, thought Christina. How steady. This was what he must be like in his role as a physician; no wonder his patients worshipped him. When he reached the ladder, the girl scrambled up again and took the cat from his arms. Then Andy climbed the rest of the way down.

"Thank you so much!" the girl cried. "You saved her!" She kissed the cat on the top of her snow-white head; the cat, now freed and sated from the shrimp, just blinked, seemingly no worse from her exploit.

"Let me see that scratch," Christina said, reaching for his wrist.

"God, I feel terrible about that," said the girl. "I'll go inside and get something to put on it." When she returned—without the cat—she handed Christina a bottle of rubbing alcohol, cotton balls, Band-Aids, and antiseptic ointment. "You're, like, totally my hero," she said to Andy. Andy just smiled. Christina opened the bottle as she stepped closer to him. "Mine too," she said softly. "You're my hero too."

TWENTY-SEVEN

*C*hristmas Eve was cold and sparkly; tiny ice crystals glit-tered on the sidewalk under Jordan's feet and she stepped carefully so she wouldn't slip. An injury at any time would be bad; right now, with rehearsals under way for the Winter Ball, an injury would be a catastrophe. She and her mom had just come from a service at the Old First Church and then a party at the house of Tabitha Baylor. Jordan liked the Baylors, though Tabitha did go overboard in the cookie de-partment. She made about a dozen different varieties and set them out in platters all over the house; it took major willpower to avoid them.

"Are you warm enough?" Christina asked as they walked along Eighth Avenue.

"Yes, Mom, I'm warm enough." Jordan was familiar with this routine.

"But you're not wearing a hat."

"I never wear a hat," said Jordan.

"I just don't want you to get sick."

"I won't get sick," Jordan said, slipping her arm into the crook of her mother's elbow. "Don't *worry* so much."

The snow was falling again, in wet, lacy flakes. Snow landed on Jordan's hair and shoulders, and on the tip of her nose. She didn't mind; it made her think of the snow scene in *The Nutcracker*, when the fake snowflakes—iridescent bits of plastic that shimmered when they were caught in the lights and which would be found, for months afterward, everywhere backstage—came whirling down around the dancers as the music lifted and swelled. Jordan had danced in *The Nutcracker* six years running, first as one of Mother Ginger's children, then as a candy cane, and one memorable season as Clara. The long, fluttering nightgown, the hot white lights, the eyes of everyone in the theater fixed on her, and her alone—she remembered it all, and she wanted it all again.

"You're getting wet!" her mother said, anxious voice breaking into her reverie. "Why didn't you wear a hat?"

"We went through this already," Jordan said. "I'm *fine*." Christina did not look convinced, so she added, "Besides, we're almost home." She noticed the large, foil-wrapped package Christina carried. "What's that?"

"Cookies," her mother said. "Come on, let's hurry."

"Do we, like, need to have cookies around?" Jordan said.

"They're not for us. I'm bringing them to Miss Kinney next door."

"Is Miss Kinney even alive?" Jordan asked. "I haven't seen her in ages."

"I haven't either," Christina said. "Though I think I would have heard if she'd died. You know she's been living here since before I was born?"

"That long?" Jordan asked. "Is she, like, a hundred?"

"Not that old." Christina smiled. "But I'll bet she's in her nineties—I hope I'm in such good shape when I'm her age." She went up the stoop of Miss Kinney's house and left the cookies by the door. "She always comes out to get a *breath of night air*," said Christina. "She'll find them when she does."

The next morning, Jordan woke early but remained in bed. She no longer tore down the stairs eager to see what "Santa" had brought. A slight scuffling from Quin's cage caught her attention, and she went over to investigate. The rabbit was way in the back, partially obscured by hay and cedar shavings. His eye, bright and steady, peered out at her. She reached for the outsized carrot she had been saving for Christmas morning and opened the cage to slip it in. But Quin did not seem interested in the offering, and remained huddled where he was. Maybe he just wasn't hungry. Jordan pulled on a pair of old jeans and a sweatshirt—she'd change later—and slid her feet into her shearling slippers. Downstairs, she found her mother curled up in her favorite, paisley-covered armchair with a cup of coffee and the newspaper on her lap. "I was waiting for you," she said. "Merry Christmas, sweetheart."

"Merry Christmas, Mom." She leaned over to give her mother a hug. Jordan could not remember Christmas with her father; she had tried and tried, but nothing came to her. So it had always been just the two of them. But that had not been bad. Sitting in front of the tree—she and her mom had reposi-tioned the ballet ornaments—Jordan felt happy. The room had what she called the Christmas look: soft throws her mom took out during the winter, the bowls she filled with ornaments, the vases filled with tall, piney things.

Christina urged her to open her presents. There was a lavishly illustrated book about Karinska, the famous costume maker who had worked with George Balanchine; a hand-tinted print of the nineteenth-century Italian ballerina Maria Taglioni in a thin gold frame; and a gift certificate to Capezio. Jordan leafed through the book. "Look at this." She pointed to an elaborate scarlet tutu worn by the Firebird; the bodice was encrusted with red crystals.

Christina came over to see. "Maybe you'll dance that role someday," she said.

"I will," Jordan said. She put the book aside and picked up the print. Taglioni looked so dainty and demure, with one hand touching her elbow and the other a spot just under her chin. She had so little in common with today's breed of dancer: fierce, lean, and fast. She looked up at her mother. "These are great presents, Mom. The best. Here." She pushed a wrapped box in Christina's direction. "Open yours."

Christina carefully undid the paper—Jordan knew she would save and reuse it—and pulled out a nubby, oatmeal-colored sweater and matching scarf. "You made these?" Christina said, immediately wrapping the scarf around her throat. Jordan nodded happily; she had taken up knitting, and been working on these gifts for the last two months. "Gorgeous!" Christina proclaimed. "Just my color. And so soft too."

After the ritual of the gifts, they had a quick breakfast before Christina started preparing for the Christmas buffet she held every year. Stephen and Misha would be there—of course—along with Mimi Farnsworth and her boys. There would be friends from church, a few of Christina's distant cousins, a neighbor or two—the regulars, as Jordan thought of them. And then there were the newcomers: the detestable Andy Stern and his son, Oliver.

"I didn't even ask what you were making this year," Jordan said as her mother bustled around the kitchen.

"The menu's on the fridge," Christina said. Jordan walked over to see. Maple-glazed ham, leeks au gratin, carrot ginger salad, green beans amandine, buttermilk biscuits . . . So far, the only thing she would eat would be the green beans, provided they were not slathered in butter, and the carrots. "While you're right there, would you take out the ham, the eggs, and the buttermilk? I'll get the ham into the oven and then start the biscuits while it's roasting."

Jordan did as her mother asked, averting her eyes from the sight of the ham, a gross, pinkish blob. Better to focus on the buttermilk, whose nutritional information revealed that it was surprisingly low in calories and contained very little fat. Maybe she would permit herself one of the biscuits—maybe. She put everything on the counter and then turned, abruptly, when she heard the crash.

"Damn!" Christina was on her knees, gathering the larger of the shattered pieces of the big yellow mixing bowl.

"I'll get the broom and clean it up," Jordan said. "You can start the biscuits."

"Thanks, sweetheart," Christina said gratefully. "I guess I'm in too much of a hurry."

Jordan began to sweep. She didn't mind Oliver; she even kind of liked him. Andy was another story. Ever since that day she'd caught him hiding in her mother's bedroom—the mere thought of what he and her mom might have been doing a hundred, no, a *thousand* times more gross than the sight of the naked, pink ham—her dislike of him had morphed into full-blown hatred. Christina had had boyfriends before. Why couldn't she have stuck with one of them instead? Andy's appeal was totally lost on her. Even his own son thought he was a jerk. Jordan took the dustpan filled with broken crockery outside, to dump in the trash can. The foil-wrapped cookies her mom had left last night were still sitting there by Miss Kinney's door. She went back inside; she should tell her.

"I hope you don't mind too much about Andy's joining us today." Christina was kneading the dough for the biscuits and her arms were dusty with flour.

Jordan stared. She had great respect for her mom's powers of intuition, but this was really weird—like she was a mind reader or something. "Actually, I *do* mind." She put the dustpan back under the sink; Miss Kinney's cookies were forgotten.

"You're not being very supportive," said her mother. "There hasn't been anyone in my life that way for a long time and I really care for Andy. I hope you'll be grown-up enough to set aside your feelings and be cordial." Jordan didn't say anything. "Jordan," Christina said. "Do I have your word?"

"No!" Jordan exploded. "I *won't* promise. I hate him and I want him to know!"

"Are you really that selfish?" Christina burst out. "I work *so* hard to make the holiday festive and nice and you don't care at all; you're just ruining everything." Abandoning the dough, she began to cry. Jordan was shocked. Her mother *never* cried. But it was her own fault for inviting that Andy Stern; he was the one ruining the holiday, not Jordan. Why couldn't Christina see that?

Before Jordan could say this, her mother's phone, which was on the counter, sounded. She made no move to pick it up. "Aren't you going to answer that?" Christina just buried her face in her flour-covered hands and continued to cry. Jordan was scared; what had she done? She reached for the phone and was relieved to hear Stephen's voice.

"My mom's a little busy," said Jordan.

"I have those pecan pies she wanted; do you want to come and get them?"

"Sure, I'll be right there." Jordan was relieved to escape.

"How's my princess?" Stephen said when they met in the hallway that separated the two apartments.

"Okay. I guess." She took the pies, encased in two white boxes, from his outstretched arms. Even through the cardboard, she could smell them.

"Why just okay? Santa wasn't good to you?"

"Santa's always good to me," she said. "It's just that Mom's gone and invited Andy Stern to have Christmas with us." She didn't mention the fight.

"Well, he's her—what shall I call it?—*beau*, isn't he?"

Jordan snorted. "I guess. Did she tell you I surprised them one day? She made him hide in the *closet*. It would have been funny if it wasn't so . . . gross."

"What's gross?" Stephen said gently. "The fact that your mother has a boyfriend?"

"Why does it have to be *him*?"

"I didn't like him at first either," said Stephen.

"Really?" Jordan asked. If Stephen was on her side, maybe he could get her mom to dump this guy.

"I invited your mother to a cocktail party one of my clients was hosting at her showroom. It was in the Meatpacking District, near Tenth Avenue. Andy came along. He complained about the cobblestones in the street—dangerous—and the cheese puffs—unhealthy. My client had hired a few models to wear her clothes while they circulated. Andy said—loud enough for everyone to hear—that one of the dresses looked like it was inside out. Your poor mother."

"I'll bet she wanted to gag him," Jordan muttered.

"Then the crowd began to thin out. Andy and your mom stayed. He started talking to Evangeline—that's my client. When your mom and Andy finally left, Evangeline hugged him and he gave her a card."

"So?" Jordan said.

"She'd been telling him about her miscarriages, and how desperate she was to have a baby. I'd had no idea; she'd never talked about it to me before. She knew of him—he has this incredible reputation— but she couldn't afford to see him. He agreed to see her pro bono—for free."

"I don't get it," Jordan said.

"He said he was doing it as a courtesy to me," Stephen explained. "And ultimately to your mother."

Jordan said nothing. She still didn't like Andy and nothing was going to change her mind. She took the pies and went back to the kitchen. Christina, who had washed her hands and flour-streaked face, seemed to have pulled herself together. "I'm sorry," she said. "It's not like me to lose my temper like that."

"No, it isn't." Jordan set the pies down and stepped back, away from the enticing aroma.

"Anyway, I hope you'll forgive me and we can have a nice holiday." She came over to hug Jordan; up close, Jordan could see that there were still tears in her eyes, but Christina quickly wiped them away.

"I don't want to ruin Christmas," Jordan said in a small voice.

"Then don't." Christina went back to the dough.

Up in her room, Jordan checked on Quin. He was still huddled at the far end of the cage. His food and the big carrot were untouched, though the water feeder was almost empty. He must have been thirsty, because when she refilled the feeder, he hopped over and began drinking greedily. Watching him reassured her; he seemed all right now. Then she changed into a navy blue jersey dress with a draped front and swirl-worthy skirt. Looking in the mirror, she thought she looked very grown-up—*even* if her mom had just implied that she wasn't.

Downstairs, the kitchen was sending forth the most fantastic smells; Jordan's stomach rumbled in anticipation. The house had been decorated with swags of pine draped over the tops of the windows, bowls of pinecones, and an army of tall white tapers. As the winter light faded, the twinkling bulbs and gleaming ornaments of the Christmas tree pushed back the encroaching dark. Christina had changed into a long black taffeta skirt with a single ruffle at the hem and a black sweater whose neckline was lined by tiny black sequins. Her silver bracelet slid up and down her arm as she set out the food, straightened a slightly crooked picture frame or grouping of glasses. Her hair was in its usual twist, though she'd secured a small silk flower on one side. Her mom's Christmas was always special.

Jordan felt a sharp twist of guilt. How hard her mother tried—not just at Christmas, but *all* the time. She had so much on her mind too—she'd been confiding in Jordan more lately, and not just about money. There was something about a guy she knew named Darren or Derrick; he had gone and disappeared with some really valuable painting that belonged to her clients and she was worried sick. Jordan felt a rush of feel-

ing bubbling up—love, gratitude, remorse—and she was just
about to find the words for them when the bell rang and the
guests started arriving and there was no time to tell her
mother she was sorry for being such a brat; there was no time
to tell her anything at all.

For the next hour, the house filled up. Jordan hung coats
on the rack her mother set up every year, and made sure the
buffet table had fresh napkins and enough plates, but Christina owned so many dishes and linens that they had never, in
all the years she had been hosting this party, run out. When
she was satisfied that everything was in order, she finally allowed herself to eat.

The plate she selected was white with a gold border and a
pattern of pink rosebuds around the rim; at the center was a
cluster of those same pink roses. Since Christina didn't con-
fine her collecting to sets, there was only a single plate like this
in the stack. It had always been Jordan's favorite. She filled it
with a large serving of carrots, and a slightly smaller one of
green beans. Mimi Farnsworth had brought a platter of crudi-
tés and Jordan took cauliflower, cherry tomatoes, and broccoli.
She did not really understand the point of raw vegetables;
without the creamy, calorie-laden dip, they had no taste at
all. But they would keep her mouth occupied for a while.

"You need some protein in that meal."

Jordan looked up. There was Andy Stern in a navy suit,
white shirt, and red tie. Looking closer, Jordan saw that the tie
had tiny elves all over it. How could her mother go out with a
man who had elves on his tie? "Vegetables are not enough.
Every meal you eat needs to have some protein," he was saying. Jordan studied her plate—green, red, and pale yellow. So
what if there was no protein? It was healthy stuff, every last,

crunch-filled, tasteless bit of it. And since when did Andy Stern have the right to comment on what she ate? She was just about to say this when her mother materialized.

"Mimi's boys asked if they could see the rabbit," she said to Jordan. And then to Andy, "Are you having a good time? Can I get you anything?"

"I'll take them upstairs," Jordan said, relieved to have an escape. She popped a cherry tomato into her mouth. Unlike the cauliflower, it actually had flavor. "Where are they?"

"With Mimi—see her over there? Sequined sweater and black hair band?"

The boys were tugging on each of Mimi's hands. Jordan made her way across the room. "How is Quin?" asked Max, the older of the two boys.

"Does he miss us?" asked Charlie. He was five, two years younger than Max.

"He's doing great, and yes, he does miss you," Jordan said. The boys bumped and jostled her on the stairway; some of Jordan's carrot salad ended up on the floor. Quin hadn't been interested in the carrot she'd given him this morning; maybe he'd like the cauliflower.

"He does? How do you know? What did he say?" asked Charlie.

Jordan smiled. "Well, he didn't actually *say* anything," she said. "But something about the way he twitches his whiskers and wiggles his ears makes me think he misses you—"

"I want to see, I want to see!" squealed Charlie, and he ran up the last of the stairs and into Jordan's room. Max was right behind and Jordan followed last. But before she could enter the room, she collided with Charlie, who had turned around and was running out as quickly as he'd gone in. "He's dying!" he cried.

"What are you talking about?" said Jordan. Tears dotted Charlie's smooth pink cheeks.

"The bunny! He's shaking and everything. He's sick. He's going to die!"

"No, he's not," Jordan said, straightening up and taking Charlie by the hand. Remembering Quin's odd behavior earlier today, she felt a cold wash of fear. Maybe he really *was* sick. "Let's go take a look together, okay?"

Quin was shaking slightly and his eyes looked wild. Also, he seemed to be breathing with difficulty. Jordan set down her plate, opened the cage, and put her hand inside. Immediately, he began to thump his hind legs so furiously that she took her hand out again.

"Is he okay?" asked Max. "Is he really going to die?"

"No, he isn't," she said, though she wasn't sure of anything. None of the Web sites she'd consulted had described behavior like this—poor Quin looked miserable. She watched him as Charlie clung to her hand, crying noisily. "Come on," she said to the boys. "Let's go get help."

"Help," repeated Max.

"My bunny," whimpered Charlie.

She ushered both boys downstairs again and went looking for her mother. There she was—talking to Andy. "Mom," she said. "I need you *right* now."

"Is everything okay?" She seemed reluctant to pull away from her conversation.

"No," she said. "It isn't." The boys were looking up at Christina anxiously. "Something's wrong with Quin. He's shaking. I've never seen him like this and I don't know what to do."

"Do you think we should take him to the vet? There's an emergency clinic down on Fourth Avenue."

"Can I take him there?" Jordan said. "Now?"

Before Christina could answer, Andy Stern said, "Maybe I can help." Jordan wanted to say, *Are you crazy? You're not a vet!* but Christina was already saying, "Yes, yes, that's a good idea; *would* you take a look at him? You have a way with animals—Jordan, you should have seen him with that cat!" Charlie, whose tears had tapered off since they'd come downstairs, was crying again and this time he was joined by his brother. Mimi came over and the boys repeated the story. Jordan had to choke back her anger as they all trooped upstairs and watched while Andy opened the cage. So what if he had climbed a tree and calmed some random cat? To hear her mother tell it, you'd think it was a tiger.

Andy slipped a hand into the cage. "He's not going to like that," warned Jordan. The thumping started again, but that didn't seem to concern Andy; he gently palpated Quin's sides. The rabbit shuddered. "What are you doing?" Jordan said. "I *told* you he wouldn't like it. You're hurting him; can't you see? Stop it!"

"Jordan, you're being rude," Christina said. "Andy's only trying to help—"

"But he's not!"

"What did you say this rabbit's name was?" said Andy.

"Quin. It's short for Harlequin."

"Well, you might want to consider changing the name."

"What does his name have to do with it?" Jordan said. "Is he all right? What did you do to him?"

"Not him," Andy said. "Her. Quin is a female and I just helped her give birth."

Astonished, Jordan looked in the cage. There, inside, were several raw-looking lumps; their ears were the naked pink of the uncooked ham.

"Baby bunnies!" crooned Charlie.

"He's a mommy," added Max.

"Not he—she," said Mimi. She turned to Jordan. "I didn't know when I gave her to you; I thought she was a male."

"But how did *that* happen?" Christina asked.

"Ella Kim," said Jordan. She began counting the babies.

"Ella Kim?" asked her mother.

"I've been hanging out with her in school and I found out she had a rabbit too—a male. I told her she could bring him here over Thanksgiving—her family was going away—and I'd take care of him for her."

"Oh, I remember now," Christina said.

"The gestation period in rabbits is around thirty days," said Andy. "So that sounds about right."

"Did you learn *that* in med school?" Mimi asked.

Andy grinned. "No. Years ago Oliver had a rabbit. I did a quick immersion course and it seems to have stayed with me." He looked at the babies. "You'll need to remove the mother from the cage and place her back in once or twice a day, to nurse them. And you'll have to check on the kits and make sure they're all getting fed; you can weigh them to be sure. Have you counted them?"

"There are ten," said Jordan.

"Bunnies! Baby bunnies!" chanted Max. He took his brother's hands and began to dance. "Ten bunnies, twenty bunnies, a hundred bunnies!" Mimi used her phone to snap pictures.

"Hey, what are you guys doing up here?"

Jordan looked over at the doorway and there was Oliver.

"Your father was assisting in a birth," Christina said. "Ten brand-new baby rabbits, born on Christmas Day."

"Way to go, Dad," said Oliver as he approached the cage.

But instead of answering Oliver, Andy looked right at Jordan, as if to say, *Am I okay in your book now?* And although she didn't want it to happen, Jordan found the brittle shell of her dislike starting to crack, just the slightest but still perceptible bit. She answered the mute question with a slow, deliberate nod.

"Andy, you said the mother needs to be separated from the babies; should I find a box?" asked Christina.

"That's a good idea," said Andy. "At least temporarily."

Oliver edged closer to the cage. "I guess having a doctor in the family is kind of handy," he said in a low voice.

Jordan turned around to stare at him. Who said anything about their being a *family*? Still, it was comforting to have everyone up here, trying to help. What would have happened if Andy hadn't been around? Oliver was making little sounds at the rabbits; he didn't seem to expect a reply. But Jordan had to admit—if only to herself—that maybe, just *maybe*, he had a point.

TWENTY-EIGHT

ndy opened the cupboard in the kitchen, hoping to find a box of pods for the espresso maker. A morning without espresso was a dismal prospect, but he supposed he could get an infusion somewhere if it turned out Lucy had forgotten to buy them.

"What time did you get in?"

He turned and there was his mother.

"Oh, it must have been about four o'clock," he said. Still no pods. Damn.

"And you're up so early?"

"This is late for me," he said. It was almost eight; he was always up before six, even on the weekends, but he'd been on call last night and there had been an emergency delivery. The mother had been diagnosed with preeclampsia and had only just hit twenty-six weeks; Andy hated to deliver a baby that early. He'd had her on complete bed rest, hoping to delay the birth for at least a week, but last night she'd called complaining of a headache and impaired vision. When he examined her, he also found the rapid heart rate and abdominal pain: bad signs, all of them. There was no choice; he had to deliver her. The baby, a boy, was born after several difficult hours of labor. He was tiny—not even three pounds—but alive, and when Andy had left the hospital in the wee hours of the morning, mother and child were both doing reasonably well. He'd check in on them later today, but right now he needed caffeine. Urgently. "I seem to be all out of coffee and I was going to run out for a cup. Do you want me to bring you something back?"

"I'll wait. We can have breakfast together."

Despite the early hour, her gray hair was neatly styled and she wore very pink lipstick. Andy noted that it matched her bathrobe; did she do that intentionally? Did he need to ask? "Maybe Oliver will be up and he can join us," he said. As if he knew he was being discussed, Oliver appeared in the kitchen. He was all dressed—or least what passed for dressed with him—in shredded jeans, a peacoat that looked two sizes too big, and a lumpy-looking wool hat. "Hey, Grandma," Oliver said. He crossed the room to deposit a kiss on Ida's cheek. "How did you sleep? Isn't the room great? I helped Christina with it, you know."

"It's very nice," Ida said. "Though that quilt looks fragile. I thought I could see some tears in the fabric."

"That's 'cause it's, like, a hundred years *old*," Oliver said. "Maybe even more. Mom would have loved it."

"Yes, she would have." Ida looked at Andy; Andy looked away. "Anyway, why are you wearing your jacket? Are you going somewhere?"

"I'm meeting Christina; I'm going to do some stuff at Old First and when the service is over, she said she'd take me to breakfast."

"What's Old First?" Ida asked.

"Christina's church. They do a lot of really cool stuff. I've been helping out."

"And going to the service? Is that considered part of helping out?"

Andy saw Oliver's eyes—blue, and so like his mother's—widen. "No," Oliver said. "But I like going. The pastor is way into social justice and politics and everything." His gaze shifted from his grandmother back to Andy. "Is there a problem with that?"

"Ask your father," said Ida tightly.

Jesus, Andy thought. *Now I'm in for it. And I haven't even had my damn coffee.*

It was only after Oliver had given them both a cheery good-bye that Ida spoke again. "She's taking him to church?" she said. "And you're *letting* her?"

"It's not such a big deal, Ma," he said. But actually, it was. He had no idea Oliver was going to church with Christina. He knew about the volunteering—not from Oliver as much as from Christina—and he thought it was a good thing. Get the kid out of the apartment, away from the computer. Christina had praised Oliver: his good spirits, his willingness to extend himself, his generosity. Oliver decided the church needed better cookware and ordered an impressive, enamel-covered cast-iron set from Williams-Sonoma. He showed up with other kitchen utensils—apple corer, colander, whisk, measuring cups—and had kept the community pantry well stocked. Andy was fine with all that; he was pleased that Oliver was helping a worthy cause. But helping and worshipping were two different things. He'd have to talk to Christina about it. Only first he needed coffee. "I think you're wrong," Ida said.

"It is a big deal. A very big deal. And you'd be a fool not to see it."

"Oh, so now I'm a fool?" he said.

"If you let this continue without taking a stand—yes. You are."

"I'll talk to Oliver about it."

"It's not Oliver you have to talk to. It's *her*."

"She has a name, Ma," he said quietly.

"Jewish, not Jewish—you asked me what difference it made," she said as if he had not spoken. "Well, *this* is the difference, you see? She wants to take him from you."

"That's not true," he said reflexively. But he had to ask himself whether in fact it was.

"And I know where that leads," she said. She extended her arm, and rolled up the sleeve of her robe. There were the familiar blue numbers, faded and blurred by now.

Andy was shocked—not by the numbers themselves; he was used to them. But by her gesture—he'd never known her to make such a pointed reference before.

"You know, you can have that removed," he said. "There are ways to do it now."

"I don't want to," she said. "I've had this since I was a girl. It's part of me now. It reminds me. And I wish it would remind you too."

There was a tense, charged silence. Andy was the one to finally break it. "I need to call the hospital and check on a patient I delivered last night. After I do that, let's go out and get something to eat. Then we'll go to the Met. That's what you wanted, right?"

"No, you're too tired," she said.

"That's all right; I could still—"

"You don't have to pretend," she said. "We'll do it another time."

Andy was relieved; he truly didn't want to go to the Met today. They went to brunch, and afterward, she would not accept a lift home, but insisted on going by car service. When she had gone, Andy felt an unfamiliar lull in the usual treadmill of his life. He had earmarked the day for his mother and now she was gone. In her absence, he had nowhere he had to be right now, nothing to do, no one to see.

He opened the door to Oliver's room. It was surprisingly, even shockingly, neat. No papers or dirtied plates scattered around, clothes were in the hamper or the closet and dresser drawers. On the floor was a recently acquired Navajo rug, the blues, red, purples, and black all woven in a bold, arrowlike design. The rug had come through Christina and was not cheap—it had cost several thousand dollars—but she assured him it was a good investment and Oliver loved it. He seemed to love anything connected with Christina. Too bad Jordan didn't display a similar enthusiasm for him. Oh, it had gotten a bit better since Christmas and the birth of the rabbits, especially since he'd shown up the next day with a new cage for the dam and enough rabbit supplies to stock a small store. And he'd even found homes for half of them—his receptionist, Joanne, had taken rabbits for each of her five nephews and nieces. So there had been a thaw, but by no means a full-on melt; he could still feel the chill.

Andy sat down on the bed. Maybe he could rest here for a few minutes. There was something comforting about being in Oliver's room, even without Oliver in it. He let his head sink down onto the pillow and closed his eyes. When he opened them, it was dark. Disoriented, he checked the glowing dial on his watch. Almost five. Lucy had left some dinner for him to microwave, but he did not want to sit there and eat alone. On impulse, he took his jacket and scarf and headed out into the January evening. It was just a few days after New Year's Eve, when he and Christina had gone to the theater and then supper at the Firebird, a Russian restaurant on Forty-sixth Street that she had loved. Everything had seemed so promising then; where was that promise now?

He began walking east, toward the hospital. Maybe Oliver would be getting home by now. He texted him and waited for the reply. There was none. The wind had picked up and Andy adjusted the scarf around his neck. He thought about how devastated he was when Oliver was kicked out of school. He'd considered trying to persuade Cunningham to take Oliver back; in his forceful mode he was pretty damn effective. Some instinct, however, told him this was not the way. Oliver needed to prove that he deserved another chance. Which Oliver seemed disinclined to do. He was not particularly upset about getting kicked out; he said he wasn't even sure he wanted to return to school at all. *And what kind of life do you think you're going to have without a goddamn high school diploma?* Andy wanted to shout. *Do you think you're going to live off my money for the rest of your life without any effort on your part?* He'd managed to refrain from saying this—largely through Christina's intervention—but he still certainly felt it. What the hell *was* the kid going to do with himself? They had managed to come to a quasi-compromise: Oliver agreed to meet with a tutor twice a week, just to keep up with the schoolwork he should have been doing had he been enrolled at Morningside. In exchange, he could spend the rest of the time hanging out in Brooklyn, doling out chili and corn bread to the homeless, a noble calling to be sure, but, without a degree in hand, one that wasn't going to get the boy very far.

Andy arrived at the hospital and stepped into the perpetually overheated lobby. Bright lights shone down from the fixtures above; the security guard nodded in his direction. Andy knew about going far; he was the living, breathing example. No dad around, mom working two and sometimes three jobs to keep them afloat. He busted his ass studying in college only to find out that his undergraduate days were *nothing*, a picnic, a day at the *beach*, compared with med school. The cramming he'd done, the all-nighters, the ball-breaking, mind-numbing grind of it, all in the service of leaving that life he'd led above the butcher shop far behind.

Oliver had none of his urgency, none of his desperation. Everything had been easy for him—everything except watching his mother die of cancer. The elevator came and the doors slid open. Yeah, Oliver would have plenty of money and the ease that went with it. But the jagged place hacked out by Rachel's premature and agonizing death would always be there.

Andy stopped at the desk on the maternity floor to say hello to the nurses; he knew them all up here and they of course knew him. "Back so soon?" said one. "I thought you'd be home sleeping."

"Can't stay away," Andy said. "How's Mrs. Petrinovic?"

"She's fine," said the nurse.

"Good," said Andy. "How's the baby?"

The nurse looked over at one of her coworkers. "The baby's not doing so well, Dr. Stern. He had a fever; it was pretty high. They've got him in the neonatal ICU for testing."

"He's a preemie," Andy said. "That could explain it." He

knew there was something wrong last night, damn it. He just *knew.*

"It could be," said the nurse. "But neonatal doesn't think so."

Andy debated whether he should go over to neonatal now, or see his patient first. He decided on the latter, smoothing back his windblown hair before knocking. "Hello, Olga," he said after being told to come in. She'd been staring out the window but turned when he greeted her. Her hospital gown was limp and there were dark smudges under her eyes.

"Did he tell you?" she asked. "About the baby?"

"Only that he had a fever."

"They think he might have some . . . syndrome."

"But they don't know for sure."

"No," said Olga. "But today I had a visit from Dr. Perry." Dr. Perry was the head of the neonatal unit.

"Olga," he said, crossing the room in two swift strides. "Olga, I'm so sorry." He took her hands in his. "There was no evidence during the pregnancy, nothing that could have predicted this—"

"I know, Dr. Stern. It's not your fault."

But he felt like it was anyway. She told him they had decided to call the baby Artyom. "Valentin says he always liked that name." Valentin Petrinovic was a newly minted Russian billionaire; he'd just bought a Fifth Avenue triplex that was rumored to have cost twenty million dollars. So at least there would be doctors and specialists; every option for treatment would be explored.

The walk home was cold and dispiriting. He'd left his scarf somewhere in the hospital and did not have the energy

to go back to get it. A buzz from his phone let him know there
was a text message from Oliver. Finally.

```
Staying over @ Christina's 2-nite.
Home tomorrow.
```

Staying over at Christina's? What the *hell* was that all
about? He wanted to call Christina, who had in fact texted him
as well, but he didn't trust himself not to blow up at her. So
instead, he let himself into the dark, silent apartment—maybe
he needed one of those damn rabbits himself, just to have
some warm-blooded creature to come home to—and poured
himself a brandy from the little bar Christina had created in
the living room. He'd sip the drink slowly, unwind, and then
call her. There—that showed some self-restraint, didn't it?

She *had* been pretty rattled lately—some restorer she'd recommended to her clients had gone AWOL and she was getting
more and more freaked-out about it. Not that she had any legal liability as far as he could see. The couple had agreed to
give the painting to this Blascoe guy, signed whatever papers
he gave them to sign, and let him cart the thing away. It wasn't
Christina's fault that he had now disappeared. Try telling her
that, though. He'd actually suggested that she hire a private
detective and offered to pay for it too, but she flat-out refused.

He swirled the brandy in its snifter—that was one of those
things he'd bought at the estate sale with Christina, months
and months ago, before they'd become lovers and she'd begun
brainwashing his son. Brainwashing? Whoa. He must be
pretty angry to be thinking like that. Hadn't he decorated her
tree and enjoyed it? But this was something else. Although
he'd never admit it to her, maybe his mother was on to some-

thing about Christina—maybe the religious difference counted for more than he knew, and signaled other essential differences: in language, and a way of communicating and being in the world.

He sank slowly into the couch, and directed his gaze outward, toward the river. He couldn't actually see the water, but he knew it was there, black and cold as the sky it reflected. The brandy was good going down—rich, like he was drinking the liquefied wood of a rare violin, with an ever-so-slight afterburn—and the snifter was empty sooner than he realized. *Just a little more,* he told himself. He poured the refill, resumed his seat on the sofa, and pulled out his phone, ready to make that call. But then he was overcome with a wave—and it really felt like a wave, washing over him with a brandy-fueled heat—of fatigue. He closed his eyes and then the next thing he knew, it was morning, the sky above the river glowing like an apricot, and the sound of the intercom letting him know that Cassie was on her way up.

Jesus. This had never happened to him before. He raced to open the door before she buzzed and then apologized profusely for his unprepared state. "That's okay, Dr. Stern," she said. "We can skip today and pick up again tomorrow."

"No, no. Give me ten minutes—no, five. I'll be ready in five. And I'll pay you overtime."

Despite the rush, he was surprisingly on track during the workout and plowed through the rest of the day. Joanne got Perry on the phone; Perry promised him a few minutes later that afternoon. Otherwise it was a typical Monday morning—a new patient who was single, forty, and a DES daughter besides, another patient who had begun spotting, still another who'd just found out she was carrying twins.

The meeting with Perry was discouraging—he was talking possible blindness and even mild brain damage—and Andy's subsequent visit to the Petrinovics was predictably wrenching. Valentin, a stocky man with a fringe of thinning black hair and a cleft chin that must have driven the ladies wild, wept openly when Andy told him what Perry had said; well, who the hell could blame him? Olga seemed to have shrunk in a mere twenty-four hours; she twisted the diamond ring on her finger round and round in a futile, repetitive gesture.

Andy was wrung out when he left. On his way back to his office, he learned that his last patient of the day had canceled, so he told Joanne he was just going to go home instead. He checked his phone; there were two texts, both from Christina. But he didn't want to respond standing there in the street, not with people hurrying by in both directions and taxis blaring gleefully along the avenue.

Quickly, he walked, shivering, to his apartment —the scarf he was sure he'd find at the hospital never having materialized —and after saying a quick hello to Lucy and ascertaining that, no, Oliver was *still* not home, he shut himself in his study.

"Darling," she said when she answered. "I've been wondering where you were. I was even a bit worried."

"Worried?" he said. "You were worried? What about me?"

"Excuse me?" she said. "I'm not following."

"I was worried about what the hell you're doing to my son," he burst out. He meant to rein it in, but he couldn't. "I mean helping out at your church is one thing, but when he starts going to the service there . . . I don't like it, Christina. I don't like it at all. Did you think I'd raise my arms and cry hallelujah or whatever the hell it is you say in church? Did you?" He was nearly shouting now; he hated for Lucy to hear.

Christina didn't reply to this, nor did she respond when he finally stopped and was listening to the sounds of his own breathing. It was only then that he realized she was no longer on the line; Christina had hung up on him.

TWENTY-NINE

hristina sat looking at the cell phone as if she expected it to detonate at any second. Carefully, she set the thing down on the sofa beside her. Andy was wrong. She wasn't trying to convert his son. And she certainly wasn't going to be spoken to that way. When the phone sounded again, she started. If it was Andy, she would not answer. But it was Stephen. "Hey, girlfriend," he said. "I was calling to see if I could borrow your iron."

"Of course," she said. "Though I would have guessed you already own one."

"As a matter of fact I own two. But one just shorted out and I left the other one in the city. And now I have to iron an organdy dress for a shoot first thing tomorrow morning. Do you have any idea what wrinkled organdy looks like? *Not* a pretty sight."

"You can have my iron if I can have your ear. Or maybe your shoulder."

"Bring the iron up; I'll make you a cup of tea. We can talk while I beat this dress into submission."

Ten minutes later, Christina was delicately blowing on the steaming surface of the cup. "He thinks he can just say anything to me."

"He's got a temper—that's for sure." Stephen touched his finger to the tip of the iron and then immediately pulled it away.

"That's an understatement." She took a sip of the tea.

"So you have to tell him that it upsets you."

"Shouldn't he understand without my having to spell it out?"

Stephen shook his head. "Honey, it's been a long time since you've been with someone, hasn't it? A *very* long time. You can't just expect him to read your mind. You have to set the limits. Otherwise he won't know what they are."

"Maybe we're just not right for each other."

"That's not the tune you were singing as recently as last week. I recall certain words being bandied around like 'incredible,' and 'life-changing.'"

"Oh—that," Christina said, looking down at her tea.

"*That,*" said Stephen, "is what most people live and breathe for."

"But it's not everything, is it?"

"No. It's just the thing that makes everything else worthwhile." He bent his head over the dress, a frilly, foamy thing the color of milk.

"I'm not discounting it—"

"Good. Now, when he calls you—"

"What makes you think he's going to call? Maybe he doesn't want to see me anymore either."

"*When* he calls you," Stephen continued as if she had not interrupted, "you'll read him the riot act."

"No, I'm serious. Maybe there *are* too many differences between us."

"Come on. Didn't you and Will fight?"

"Not like this. I don't think he ever raised his voice to me."

"Really?" He clearly did not believe her.

"My father *had a temper*, as you so quaintly put it. He'd have too much to drink and start yelling." Christina felt the familiar dread, just remembering.

"Did he ever hit you?" Stephen asked.

"It always seemed like he might. He once bashed his fist into a wall so hard he needed stitches. My aunt Barb always tried to downplay his 'moods'—that's what she called them: *your father's moods*—but they terrified me. I used to hide behind the washing machine in the basement when he got started. Once I got wedged in and then couldn't get out. It took more than an hour for them to find me."

"Poor little Christina!" Stephen said. "You must have been so scared."

"I was. And I think I fell in love with Will because he was so utterly unlike my father—intellectual, Protestant, gentle. . . ."

"So where does Andy fit in?" asked Stephen.

"Maybe he doesn't."

Stephen adjusted the dress on the ironing board and began to work on the back. "I see this as a difference in style, not substance. And style is mutable—it can change."

"I wonder." She finished her tea and stood up. "Good luck with the organdy. And thanks."

"Oh, I almost forgot to tell you." Stephen looked up. "I've noticed this Indian couple hanging around in front of the house—they were here twice."

"Really?" Christina felt a sudden rush of guilt. She had not told Stephen about the offer on the house; she had not told anyone. "Were they doing anything that seemed suspicious?"

"He was taking pictures with his phone," Stephen said. "I didn't like it."

"I don't like it either." At least *that* much was true. "If I see them, I'll talk to them." What she did not say was that she planned to call Pratyush Singh and have him tell his clients to stop hanging around her property or she would call the police—she was beginning to feel stalked.

The next morning, Christina called Pratyush before she even had her coffee. She was planning to leave a message, but to her surprise, he picked up right away. "I'd like you to ask your clients to stop coming by my house," she began. "They're making me nervous."

"I'm sure they don't intend to do anything of the kind," he said smoothly. "Maybe it's hard for them to curb their enthusiasm."

"Whether they intend to or not, that's what they're doing." She had rethought the threat about the police. The Sharmas had never trespassed; the street was a public space. And according to the zoning regulations, she wasn't even supposed to be running a decorating business from her house. Best not to invite any scrutiny.

"I'll speak to them," he said. "But as long as we're talking, I'd like to put something else on the table. If the deal is concluded in the next sixty days, my clients are prepared to add an additional ten percent to the price they've offered."

Christina paused; that was so much money. "Why," she asked, "are they willing to pay so much?"

"I told you already—," he said.

"We both know that what you told me was a fairy tale,"

she cut in. *"Mrs. Sharma loves this house; she wants to raise her children here.* I want you to tell me the real story."

"Ms. Connelly, you're a businesswoman, aren't you?"

"Yes but—"

"What kind of businesswoman tells a prospective buyer that his price is too high? My clients are offering you the deal of a lifetime and you're questioning their motives? I'd say that wasn't very strategic . . . from a *business* vantage point." Underneath the unctuous tone was something else, hard and unpleasant.

"Just tell them to stop ogling the merchandise," she said. "I don't like being pressured."

"Of course, of course," he said. Whatever edge she had detected a moment ago was totally and completely gone. "You just think about it. The deal of a lifetime."

Christina did think about it while she sent out a batch of invoices, answered her e-mails, and checked the Web site—now live and very spiffy in her view—that Oliver had created for her. She was still thinking about it when the bell rang two hours later; she half expected it to be the Sharmas, asking whether they could take a look inside.

Instead, it was an enormous bouquet, every last petal and blossom a snowy or creamy white, delivered by a messenger in a deep green van. Christina lifted the flowers from their nest of deep purple tissue and inhaled. The white lilacs were intoxicating. A small envelope fluttered to the floor. She knelt down to retrieve it and then slid her finger under the flap.

> I'm a jerk and a loudmouth. Can you forgive
> me? Please tell me that you can. I won't have a
> minute's peace until you do.
>
> Love, Andy

She smiled, a tiny smile. But she did not pick up the phone. Not then, and not for the rest of the day. She was glad that Andy had apologized. Still, she was not ready to make up. Maybe it was unrealistic to think she could replicate the harmony of her life with Will ever again. But that didn't mean she was ready to capitulate so easily.

Later that afternoon, Andy sent her a text message. She did not reply. After a simple dinner—Jordan was in the city, rehearsing—she scanned the television listings for something to watch. The bell rang and she muted the sound. Christina was not expecting anyone; maybe Stephen and Misha had ordered out. But on the stoop stood no polite young deliveryman bearing dumplings. There, collar turned up against the chill, was Andy.

"Can I come in?" he said.

"I was going to call you tomorrow." She stepped aside to let him enter.

"Really?" He did not sound convinced.

"Really." After a moment she added, "Let me take your coat."

He handed it to her and followed her inside, where he sat down and looked around the room, glance settling on the elaborate spray of flowers she had arranged in a large blue and white pitcher. "Did you like them?" he said.

"Very much," she said.

"Then why—" He shifted around, as if trying to get comfortable.

"Didn't I call to thank you?"

"Or reply to my texts. I've been trying to reach you. It drives me crazy when I can't penetrate that Waspy reserve of yours."

"It wasn't my Waspy reserve, as you put it." She did not

look at him. "I'm not even a WASP. I'm a Catholic. Or a lapsed one. Will was the WASP. Anyway, I didn't call back because I was upset."

"I know."

"And hurt. Your temper . . ."

"I admit it. I explode sometimes. But I didn't think it was such a big deal."

"It is," she said. "At least to me."

"Christina." He leaned over and grabbed both her hands. "I said I was sorry. I *am* sorry. But if we're going to keep on seeing each other, we'll have to be able to weather worse than this."

"That's true." She did not withdraw her hands. "About Oliver, though. I am *not* trying to convert him. How could you even think such a thing?"

"Well, I admit I flew off the handle. But you can understand how I felt—what's he doing in a church? If he's suddenly overcome with spiritual yearnings, why can't he go to a synagogue?"

"Why should he, when you're not there?"

"What?"

"Oliver is going to church because I'm there. Also Robbie, Josh, Lee, Miriam, and Louise. And oh—Summer. Has he told you about her?"

"Who the *hell*—" He stopped himself. "Sorry. Who *are* all those people?"

"People he's met through volunteering. And they are all church members. Can't you see? He's not looking for Jesus. He's looking for a community. A family even."

He stared at her. "I guess I haven't been so terrific at giving him that."

"No," she said. "You haven't." When she saw how stricken

he looked, she added, "Maybe you didn't know how. Maybe it was too hard. Throwing yourself into your work, your patients, was easier."

"My patients." It was almost a moan.

"Did something bad happen today?"

"It's happening right now."

"Tell me," she said.

"I will. I want to. But Oliver . . . He's so angry with me all the time. And the thing is, I can't tell what the hell for. I give him plenty of money, and lots of latitude. What else does he want?"

"Maybe he's just angry that you're still alive. And his mother isn't."

"He was *always* closer to her. She did everything. The trips to the playground, the park, the zoo. Helping him with his schoolwork, birthday parties. She knew the names of every kid in his class, all his teachers, what flavor Popsicle, cupcake, *everything* that was his favorite. . . . She"—and his voice cracked a little—"was the *one*. I was always second fiddle."

"You're angry about that," she said gently.

"You're right—I am. He's my only son. I'd like to count with him. To matter." He withdrew one hand—he was still clinging to her—and smoothed back a lock of her hair. His expression softened. "I know what he loves about you," he said. "Because I love it too."

"Are you telling me that you love me?"

"Yes," he said, and leaned over for a long, deep kiss. "I am."

"I love you too," she said softly.

THIRTY

*E*arly the next morning Christina set out again for Union Street. The day was bright but frigid, and she hurried along, down past Third Avenue and the Gowanus Canal until she reached Derrick's building. She had called everyone they knew in common, checked out his Facebook page and Twitter account—all of it led nowhere. At Andy's suggestion she'd even phoned a private investigator, though once she'd heard the price, she decided not to meet with him after all; she simply wouldn't let Andy spend that kind of money.

She was greeted by the now-familiar metal gate and the darkened windows above. Derrick truly seemed to have vanished. In the relentless light of day, the empty space where his name had been shone unnaturally bright. She squinted upward, trying to see the windows, so she didn't notice the man—elderly, walking an obese dachshund—until she'd bumped into him. "Hey, watch where you're going," he said irately.

"So sorry," said Christina, stepping back. He must have

come out of the building; maybe he could tell her something. "I don't mean to trouble you, but are you a neighbor of Mr. Blascoe?" she asked. The man stared blankly as the dog tugged at the leash. "Derrick Blascoe?" she tried again.

"Why do you want to know?" he asked finally.

"Well, I'm a friend of his and I've been trying to get in touch with him. He's not answering his phone and I'm beginning to get worried."

"You his friend? How come I never seen you before?"

Christina did not know what to say. She dug her hands into her pockets—she'd forgotten her gloves and they were cold—and to her dawning delight, her fingers closed around a dog biscuit. One of her clients had recently acquired a puppy and she'd taken to bringing treats when she made her visits. "Is it okay if I give him this?" she asked the man, producing the biscuit. The dog, attention riveted by the possibility of food, poked its long, thin snout in her direction. The man looked at it too, and then down at the dog. His whole demeanor changed. "Yeah, sure. Is it liver flavored? He loves liver."

"I believe it is," she said, though she had not the faintest idea.

"So ya lookin' for Derrick?"

"I am," she said.

"He hasn't been around much."

"Yes, I know." Christina looked down at the dog; he had devoured the biscuit and was looking up at her with wet, hopeful eyes.

"Other people been looking for him too," he offered. "Not just you."

"Really?" She wished she had another biscuit.

"Yeah, some guys come in the middle of the night, pound-ing on the door, cursing, you name it. I gotta get up early in the morning"—he gestured to the dog—"and I did *not* appre-ciate it."

"Do you know who they were? Did they say anything?"

"They kept threatening to break the door down if he didn't open up, but they didn't. If they come back, I'm calling the cops."

"That's a good idea," she said. She extricated her hand from her pocket and reached into her bag. She was looking for her card and found instead another biscuit. She fed it to the dog and then gave her card to the man. "If you see him or find out anything, anything at all, will you call me?" she asked.

He took the card. "*Christina's World*," he read. "You Chris-tina?" She nodded. "Same as my wife, may she rest in peace. Yeah, I'll call you if he turns up. But don't hold your breath."

Discouraged, Christina turned and went home. She had to find Derrick and, with him, the Sargent portrait that had been entrusted to his care. Phoebe had told her that Ian would be in London on business for a few weeks, which had given her a small reprieve. What she would do when it was over, she had not a clue.

Then she remembered—there *was* someone else she and Derrick knew in common. Someone she had not called yet. Her name was Helen something or other; Christina had done a small job for her and she had dated Derrick a while back. Helen Southgate. That was it. Maybe Helen knew something. But the number Christina had for her was not in service and it took her a full hour online to track her down. Helen was now living in New Mexico. Christina could not find a phone number, but she did find an e-mail address and she quickly typed a message. When she checked her own messages a little while later, Helen's name appeared in her box; she had written back right away.

> No, I haven't seen Derrick in a
> long time. He and I parted ways and
> haven't been in touch. I heard he'd
> been having . . . issues of some
> kind. Something personal. I think I
> must have sensed that because I
> knew I didn't want things to con-
> tinue with him. To be honest, he
> kind of scared me.

Christina read these words over three times. She was both amazed that Helen had opened up to her so readily and alarmed by the information she had divulged. Derrick had scared her too. She thanked Helen for her response and got up from her desk. This was futile. She had better turn her attention to something else or the entire day would have been wasted.

Around five, the doorbell rang and she hurried to answer it. She was expecting a package of samples from a factory in North Carolina and hoped this was the UPS man with her delivery. Instead, it was Ian Haverstick. "May I come in?" Ian said. But it was not really a question.

"Of course," she said. Her heart began an unpleasant stuttering in her chest. "Would you like something? A cup of coffee or tea?"

"Not necessary," he said. "But I would like to talk to you for a few minutes."

Christina led him into her office; it felt more professional than either the kitchen or the parlor. And she desperately wanted to feel professional: she had been catching up on some paperwork, wearing her oldest, softest jeans and an oversized cashmere sweater that had belonged to Will. Despite the frayed collar and the large holes at either elbow, she had not been able to part with it. Sitting across from Ian, she felt like she was in her pajamas.

"I want that painting back," he said flatly. "I think you've deliberately been stalling about returning it."

"Why would I do that?" she asked. It took a supreme effort to keep her voice steady.

"Because you know Phoebe and I don't agree about it." He was a tall, slightly doughy man with pale, thinning hair and surprisingly dark eyes. Those eyes were at odds with the rest of his mild appearance and gave him a look of quiet menace. "And you're both hoping that she'll be able to wear me down."

"It's true, Phoebe doesn't want to sell it. But you can understand that. It represents a connection to her aunt."

"I know Phoebe has a soft spot for her; she's just a big softy all around. She lets the girls get away with murder, if you ask me—but that's another story. Anyway, as for the aunt—" He raised his hand to the side of his head and made a circling motion with his index finger. "Nuts."

"Why do you say that?"

"Why else would she keep a painting worth that much money stuck away in a closet?"

"You don't know why it was there," Christina said desperately. She could not keep up this charade. Sooner rather than later she'd have to tell him. *The truth always feels better when it's out there on the table*, Aunt Barb had been fond of saying. Sister

Bernadette had been more succinct: *A lie burdens your soul.*
"Maybe she was planning on having it cleaned herself."

"Or selling it and leaving us the money," he countered.

"But she didn't sell it and now it belongs to Phoebe," said
Christina.

"And to me." How smug and proprietary he sounded.
"Anyway, this so-called cleaning has taken long enough. I
want the painting—*today.*"

"Today?" Christina's voice squeaked up, like a cartoon
mouse. "That's not possible."

"Why not?"

"Well, I don't even know if the restorer is there."

"So call him and find out. Or we could walk over there.
You said he's on Union Street."

"It's so cold out," she said, wretchedly aware of how pathetic her excuse sounded. "Can't we wait for a warmer day?"

"Look, I'm sick of this." He stood up, looming over her. "If
you won't help me get it, I'll go over there myself."

"I'm afraid that won't do any good." Christina stood
up too.

"What are you talking about?" His dark eyes glowered.

"He's gone. Vanished somewhere. I've been trying to find
him for weeks."

"What?" His voice was low and furious. "What are you
saying? Does he have the painting?"

"I don't know," she said.

"You don't know! But you recommended him. You said
you'd known him for years, that he could be trusted."

"And everything I said was true. I'm as astonished as you
are. I would never, ever have guessed—"

"*You* would never have guessed!" he sneered. "And who

are *you* anyway? Some two-bit, second-rate decorator I didn't even want to hire. I don't believe you! You're probably in cahoots with him—the two of you think you can steal this painting and actually get away with it."

"Just leave," she said. She was shaking—with rage, with shame. "Leave right now."

"I'll leave, all right," said Ian. "But as of this minute, you can consider yourself fired. And you'll be hearing from my lawyer. I'm slapping you with a lawsuit so big and so fast it'll make your head spin." Christina recoiled as he marched past her. She beat him to the door, though, and deftly managed to stop it before it was slammed shut in her face.

THIRTY-ONE

lthough it was long past midnight, Christina could not sleep. Outside her window, the March wind whistled and blew. Even though Andy assured her that it was the Haversticks' responsibility to contact the police about tracking down the missing painting, she was still sick about it. And though she may not have had a legal responsibility, she did have a moral one, and so she had called Phoebe. But Phoebe did not return the call. She also failed to return the two subsequent calls Christina made. And she did not answer Christina's e-mail. There was really nothing else she could do. Still, the whole thing left her shaken and upset. That ugly scene with Ian kept replaying over and over in her mind. And even when she managed to banish it, briefly, it was supplanted by the worry over money—she'd gone and lost the biggest and most lucrative job she'd had in a while and right now there was nothing on her immediate horizon that would replace it.

But there was no point to lying here fretting; she would

get up and make herself some hot milk. On the way to the kitchen, she heard the sound of coughing. Jordan. Standing outside her daughter's room, she listened to the ragged, nasty sound for a moment before tapping on the door. "Are you all right?" she said, switching on the light.

Jordan was sitting up in bed, fine light brown hair that was so much like Christina's hanging down over her thin neck and bony shoulders. Christina realized she had not seen her hair down in months and was actually relieved to know that Jordan did not go to bed wearing that tightly bound bun.

"I'm okay. It's just a little cough."

"Hardly little. You sound terrible." She looked over at the rabbits—Jordan had kept one of the babies—and they were both awake as well.

"I'll be fine, Mom. But since you're here, could you get me some water? Please?"

In the morning, Christina wanted Jordan to stay home from school. The Winter Ball was the next day and the girl had been pushing herself relentlessly. But Jordan breezed into the kitchen, hair pulled tight into its customary bun, digging through the cabinets for one of those atrocious bars she insisted on calling food.

"At least let me make you a cup of tea," Christina said.

"No time for tea, Mom. But thanks."

"I'll put it in this—" She held out a stainless-steel thermos. "You can have it on the subway." Jordan looked exasperated—*I told you I'm fine*—but she waited while Christina made the tea, and deigned to accept it before walking out the door. That evening, she had a rehearsal, and refused all offers of dinner when she got home, saying she'd had something to eat with her friends in the city. All she wanted to do was go to bed.

Christina watched her slender young back, straight and resolute, as she ascended the stairs. Then she returned to her laptop, where she had been researching some difficult-to-find silk fringed tassels for a bunch of pillows she was having sewn for a client. Jordan's self-discipline was formidable, and at times even just the littlest bit scary. This past month especially she had given herself no slack at all. She rose early, went to school, ballet classes and rehearsals, brought home superlative grades, and never once complained about her punishing schedule. And if Jordan had not come to love Andy, she was at least polite.

Here was some fringe that looked like it would work— thick and seemingly lush, the tassels were a full three inches long. But it was imported from Belgium and cost forty-two dollars a yard, which meant her estimate was too low; she wasn't sure the client would swallow the added cost. It was a small job, but she was in no position to jeopardize it. She sent an e-mail to feel her out on the price, bookmarked the page, and switched off the computer.

That night, she lay awake for a long time, once more plagued by sleeplessness. Finally she got up and went to Jordan's door. No coughing. Relieved, she went back to bed. She was more nervous about this performance than Jordan seemed to be. Andy had kindly arranged for Lucy to make everyone a light supper and then Jordan could head over to the theater from there. But that afternoon Christina received a call from the school nurse. "Jordan's running a fever and I think she should go home," she said.

"Did she ask to come home?"

"No. She said she had a terrible headache and wanted some Tylenol. She actually was pretty insistent on staying in school. I'm the one who thinks she should leave."

"She has a performance tonight," Christina explained. "It's only a very small part, but she's been under a lot of pressure."

"Maybe if she sleeps for a couple of hours, she'll feel better," said the nurse. "But keep an eye on her temperature. It was a hundred and one when I took it."

While she waited for Jordan, Christina called Andy to say that they would not be joining him for dinner after all. "How sick is she?" he wanted to know.

"One hundred and one," she said.

"Any other symptoms?"

"Headache and a stiff neck."

"Stiff neck? That could be serious. She should see a doctor."

"I don't think she'll agree. And she says she strained her neck in ballet class."

"Are *you* a doctor?" His tone sounded a bit condescending. Bullying even. "Also, she's not eating enough," he said. "Have you noticed how thin she is? What does she weigh?"

"I don't ask her questions like that."

"Well, you should." Again that tone. "Are you really going to let her perform tonight if she's not well?"

"Let me see how she seems when she gets here. I'll pump her full of Tylenol and then take her to the doctor tomorrow."

"You're her mother. If you insist she has to see the doctor today—"

Christina heard the key in the lock. "That's her now," she said. "I'll call you back." Honestly, he could be so pushy at times.

Jordan looked awful. There were two hectic spots on her otherwise pale cheeks, and her eyes looked glassy. "Oh, you poor darling!" said Christina. "Why don't you go right upstairs and lie down?"

"I'm not missing the performance tonight," Jordan said defiantly. "I'm *not*." She let her backpack tumble to the floor; a couple of pens and a highlighter rolled out and scattered, coming to rest at the edge of the rug.

"No one said anything about not performing tonight. I just want you to rest now so you'll feel well enough to dance later."

"All right, but you *have* to promise to wake me up in time. Otherwise I'll *never* forgive you."

"I promise," Christina said. "Now please—go upstairs!"

Once Jordan was safely in her room, Christina began to make plans. Jordan needed to arrive early, so she would call a cab for her. She would go a little later to the theater herself; she wanted to be nearby in case Jordan needed her.

When Jordan woke, Christina took her temperature—now down to ninety-nine—and made her drink a cup of hot tea laced with honey. "And you should eat something," she urged. "Even something light. You need the protein."

"I'm too nervous to eat," Jordan said, expression darkening.

So Christina packed her one of those vile protein bars and a bottle of Tylenol. She noticed that Jordan kept pressing her fingers to the back of her neck. "Why are you doing that?" she asked. "Does it still hurt?"

"I strained it doing a *port de bras*," Jordan said. "I told you."

"Stay in touch, sweetheart," she said as she watched Jordan get into the cab. Then she went back into the house, where a heavy blanket of unease settled over her. She found she couldn't concentrate on anything and decided to start getting ready for the ball.

She put on the blue dress she and Stephen had bought together back in September; why did it suddenly look so dowdy? If only she could have worn the black dress again, but she had loaned it to Stephen for a shoot. Christina's anxiety seemed to get louder, an irritating buzz in her ears. Maybe Andy had a point, and she *should* have insisted Jordan see a doctor. Was it too late now? Probably, but suddenly she wanted to get there as soon as possible, limp blue dress and all. What did it matter what she wore?

She shoved her feet into a pair of black pumps and on her way to the mirror to gauge the effect, the heel on one snapped. Oh no! Leaving the ruined shoe by the bed, she slipped out of the other one and went into the bathroom. Even though it was March, she could wear those black sandals she'd bought back in the fall; she wouldn't be outside all that much. She reached for her compact and, in her haste, sent it careening to the floor. The tiny, round mirror cracked and shards of glass mingled with the mess of pressed powder that remained. She threw the whole thing into the garbage, wishing desperately Stephen were here to help her. But he was on that shoot; he would be at the theater, along with Misha, later.

She put on the sandals, grabbed the faux-fur jacket Stephen had left for her, and stuffed her cosmetics into her evening purse. Then she hurried up the street to where her car was parked. Her feet, in the sandals, were freezing, but she wasn't going back. She turned the heat on high, pulled out of the spot, and drove as fast as she dared toward the bridge. But once she got there, she was forced to wait; the traffic was horrendous. Christina stared at an SUV ahead of her, willing it to move. The SUV, along with the long line of cars in front of it, remained impervious to her wishes. No one was going anywhere.

● ● ●

Jordan felt horrible when she arrived at the theater. Her head was throbbing, her mouth felt dry, and her neck was aching. But there was no way she wasn't going to perform tonight. A ramp led down to the stage door at the southern end of the Lincoln Center complex; she had just started down it when a voice behind her caused her to turn. It was that stupid Andy Stern, the absolute worst boyfriend her mother had ever dredged up.

"Jordan!" he said, striding over. "I'm so glad I caught you."

"What are you doing here?" she said, not caring whether she sounded rude.

"I was worried," he said. "I wanted to make sure you were all right."

"I'm fine," she said. She reached up to massage her neck, which was killing her; she was so, *so* tense.

"I'm not so sure of that. Why are you rubbing your neck?"

"It's nothing," she said. "Now could you please move? You're blocking my way." He'd planted himself right in front of her.

"Your neck." He acted as if he hadn't even heard her. "That's a bad sign. You need to see a doctor. I tell you what— let's go inside. I can give you a quick exam and if I think you need to see someone else, I can—"

"You!" She took a big step back. "I don't want you to touch me—ever!"

"Fine, then we'll find someone else, but you have got to see someone right away."

Jordan felt the minutes rushing by. She needed to get inside, and get into her costume, put on her makeup. Also to sit down; she felt herself starting to sway. "If you don't let me by, I'm going to start shouting."

"Jordan, you're being stubborn. I'm here to help you—"

He took her arm. He had a strong grip and though she tried, she couldn't pull away.

"Help!" Jordan cried. "This man is bothering me!"

A security guard opened the stage door and poked his head out. Then he started up the ramp. "What's going on here?" he said when he reached the spot where Jordan stood wriggling in Andy's grasp.

"He won't let me go!"

"This girl is sick and needs medical attention!"

The guard looked at the two of them; recognition settled on his face. "Jordan," he said. "Is this man someone you know?"

"Yes, but he won't let me go and I need to get inside!"

"Excuse me, sir, but you're going to have to release her."

"I told you: she needs to see a doctor." He held tight and Jordan thrashed like a fish on the line.

"Sir," the guard said. "Don't make me call the police."

Andy looked at Jordan and she glared right back at him. He finally released her arm and she clutched it to her chest. "Thank you, Willie," she said to the guard. "Thank you for saving me," she said, and hurried down the ramp without looking back.

Christina was still on the bridge—had it *ever* taken so long?—when the call from Jordan came in. "Mommy!" she cried. "Mommy, I hate him *so* much! I never want him in our house again. Never!"

Mommy? Jordan had not called her *Mommy* in almost a decade. "Slow down," Christina said, trying to rein in the wild horse of her own anxiety. "Tell me what happened."

"It's Andy! He came to the theater, Mommy! He tried to keep me from going inside. He said he thought I shouldn't be dancing tonight. Then he grabbed my arm and wouldn't let go. I tried to pull away, but I couldn't. He *hurt* me! I started to yell and Willie, the security guard, came over and made him go away. I loathe and despise him!"

Christina felt herself go hot with rage. How *dare* he! Accosting her child, upsetting her, inserting himself into something that was none of his business—she snapped back to the immediate situation when she heard Jordan weeping softly into the phone. "Sweetheart," she said. "Sweetheart, I want you to get a grip. I'm on my way and I'll be there as soon as I can. In the meantime, I want you to go in the bathroom and wash up. Have a drink of water. Can you do that?" There was a strange noise, almost like a mew. "Can you?"

"Yes, Mommy," Jordan said meekly. "I can. I'll see you soon." She clicked off.

Poor darling, thought Christina. *She's just at the end of her tether.* But she would pull herself together; Christina was sure of it. The traffic started moving again and soon she was over the bridge and across Chambers Street. She was cruising along the West Side Highway when the phone buzzed again; she pounced on it, ready to dispense comfort to her daughter. But it wasn't Jordan. It was Andy. "You!" she said. "I cannot believe what you did! Can. Not. Believe. It. What were you thinking? You are so pushy sometimes!"

"Pushy *Jew,* isn't that what you mean?"

"I never said that—you did! But how dare you make such a scene? Who asked you to intervene—"

"Where are you anyway?" he interrupted.

"In my car, on my way to the theater. A place *you* had no business being, I might add."

"Forget the theater. Come to St. Luke's Hospital."

"St. Luke's? What for?"

"Your daughter has just been admitted. After I wasn't able to talk any sense into her, she went into the theater, where she promptly collapsed in the dressing room. She was rushed to the ER; fortunately, I was still hanging around, so I saw the ambulance pull up and I waited. Damn good thing I did, too." His voice was grim.

"Maybe it's nerves, or she's feeling light-headed from not having eaten. I couldn't persuade her to have any dinner; she said her stomach was unsettled and—"

"You and your fucking denial!" he shouted. "It's not *nerves* and she's *not* feeling *light-headed*. She's got *meningitis*, for God's sake! And not only that, it's been exacerbated by how god-damn thin she is; she's got a pretty serious eating disorder that you haven't wanted to deal with." He paused, as if gathering steam for the finale. "Now get your ass up here as quickly as you can. Call when you're outside and I'll tell you exactly where we are. They're still doing some tests." And before Christina could utter another word, he abruptly ended the call.

The time between the end of the phone call and Christina's arrival at the hospital were the longest and most agonizing minutes in her life as a mother. *Jordan has meningitis,* she kept repeating to herself as she headed toward the hospital. Her daughter had meningitis and she hadn't even *known*. She was a terrible mother, terrible person. If Jordan were to *die*— but she would not let herself go there. If she did, she would crumple right here, right now, and never make it to the hospital where Jordan lay waiting. Ignoring the tears that seemed to have materialized on her face, she drove to St. Luke's, mouthing prayers she had not uttered in two decades—*Hail*

Mary, full of grace. When she arrived, she left the car in a spot that had a clear No Parking sign posted. Let the city give her a ticket or tow it. She didn't care.

She called Andy as soon as she was inside the doors. Jordan was in the ICU; she saw Andy conferring with a white-coated doctor in the corridor. When he saw her, he introduced her to the attending physician and then took her hand. She was so grateful he was there.

"It's bacterial," said the doctor, whose name tag read ZACHERY MARVIN. "We usually give penicillin and cefotaxime, but we're seeing a lot of resistance to penicillin these days. So I've got her on a drip of vancomycin and cefotaxime; let's see how she does. On the whole I'm optimistic, though."

Christina just nodded stupidly; she was too numb to process what was being said. "Can her mother see her?" Andy asked Dr. Marvin, and when he said yes, Christina donned a mask and gown to enter the ICU. "I'll wait for you here," Andy told her.

Jordan lay in the bed, looking pale and positively emaciated. How had Christina not seen how thin she was before? What else had she missed? Guilt gripped her throat, cutting off her air, and she had to take deep breaths or she thought she would pass out.

There were tubes in Jordan's arms but nothing in her mouth; her breathing was rapid and shallow. Her eyes were closed, and against her pallid cheeks, her lashes looked dark and spidery.

"Sweetheart, can you hear me?" said Christina through the mask. Jordan's eyelids fluttered open and then closed again. But when Christina put her hand in Jordan's, Jordan pressed back. She remained at Jordan's bedside, tears trickling silently down her face, wetting the mask. Her nose grew clogged, but she would not budge; in that moment, Christina believed that her hand in Jordan's was the sole current that kept her child alive. It was only when Dr. Marvin returned that she allowed herself to be led away.

"She's stable for now," he said. "And you look spent. Why not have a cup of coffee in the cafeteria and then come back up? I've got your cell number now; your husband gave it to me." *Husband?* thought Christina. Suddenly she wished he were her husband; she needed him in a way she had not realized until now. She did not correct the doctor but took the elevator with Andy down to the cafeteria.

"Thank God you were there," she kept saying as he got coffee, milk, and sugar and directed her to a table. "Thank God you saved her." Andy said nothing. It was only when they had sat down together that she was able to focus on how serious he looked. "Dr. Marvin says she's all right," she told him. "She's going to pull through." She ignored the coffee he placed in front of her and grasped his hand, bringing the knuckles to her lips to kiss.

But Andy gently extricated himself. "I'm as grateful and relieved as you are that she's going to be all right," he began. "She's going to need some help, though. Help and clear direction. And you're the one who's going to have to give it to her—alone."

"What are you talking about?" This was how she had felt when she first encountered Dr. Marvin—she heard the words, but they made no sense.

"I'm talking about us, Christina. Or rather—the end of us."

"Why?" she cried, not even caring whether anyone around might hear her. "Why now?"

"We're too different. You called me pushy—"

"I'm sorry! I was frantic; can't you see that?"

"But on some level, that is how you feel about me: too pushy, too loud, too *Jewish*. There's always something I'll do or say wrong, some way in which I'll transgress. I don't want to live walking on eggshells around you. That's why I think we should end it—before either of us gets even more hurt."

"No." She shook her head. "Please no." She was *whimpering* for God's sake.

"I'm sorry, Christina. It all became clear to me when I was waiting for you to get here. I can see the pattern and I can see it repeating itself. I piss you off and I'm going to keep pissing you off. I'll never make you happy." He placed his hand on her cheek for a moment; then he stood and left her staring at the now stone-cold coffee.

THIRTY-TWO

Jordan's hospital room was filled with brightly colored balloons; they had gravitated toward a corner of the ceiling and were set quivering by the warm air blasting from the heating ducts on the wall. Jordan closed her eyes so she wouldn't have to see them.

She'd missed performing in the Winter Ball. Missed it entirely, all because she'd gotten some stupid infection. And as if that weren't bad enough, the doctor had said that her body needed to be stronger—a code word for *fatter*—to fight it successfully. Another girl wore the Russian peasant costume and got to perform the lively, folk-dance-inspired steps. Another girl took the bow and the applause—her applause.

There would be other dances, other costumes, said her mother, Alexis, and all the girls from SAB who'd come to visit her, and even Ms. Bonner, who had shown up with a plush teddy bear wearing a pink tutu and pink ballet slippers on its chubby teddy feet. "You're still the same dancer you were before you got sick," Ms. Bonner said. "Now you get better and come back to class as soon as you can." The teddy bear sat across from Jordan on the windowsill, the bitterest of consolation prizes.

"Good morning, sweetheart." Jordan opened her eyes. There was her mother, standing at the doorway.

"Hi," said Jordan. She closed her eyes again. When she opened them, Christina had sat down in the chair next to the bed.

"How are you feeling today?" her mother asked.

"Better. I guess."

"The doctor says you can come home soon—maybe as soon as tomorrow. You won't be able to go back to school or class right away; you'll have to build up your strength first."

"You mean gain weight," said Jordan, glaring at her mother as if she held her personally responsible for this.

"Well, a little, yes—," said her mother.

"I'm not anorexic. I'm not!" Jordan said.

"No one said you were anorexic, Jordan," Christina began. "You're just very thin, and—"

"And I'm not bulimic either! I hate throwing up."

"You're getting all upset," her mother said. "Try to calm down."

"I am calm." But of course she wasn't. And she didn't want to talk about this anymore. To change the subject she said, "You can take some of these flowers home if you want. How about those—aren't they nice? Andy sent them." The lavish floral arrangement dominated one corner of the room. Christina turned but said nothing. "I'm sorry for getting so mad at him, Mom. I guess he kind of saved my life. At least that's what they told me."

"It's true," said Christina. Her voice sounded strangled.

"He did. If it hadn't been for him, you really might have died. I didn't know you were so sick; you hid it from me."

"I know." Not only had Jordan experienced that blinding headache, but her neck was stiff and she'd felt nauseated too— all classic signs of the disease.

"And when I think I could have lost you— " Christina put her face in her hands and began to cry.

"Mom! I'm all right! I didn't die." Jordan sat up straighter against the pillows. "What's the matter, anyway?" Christina didn't answer. "Is it something else?"

"It is."

"Tell me," she said. She already knew, though.

"It's Andy. He decided we should break up."

"Oh," said Jordan. "I'm sorry." Was she?

"So am I," said Christina. Even though there was a big box of tissues sitting nearby, she rooted around in her purse until she found a handkerchief; Jordan could not remember ever seeing her mother use a tissue. "I'm sorry. I didn't mean to burden you." Jordan didn't know what to think. She should be happy now, right? She hated him. Or at least she used to, and now she had her wish—he and her mom had broken up. So why did she feel so bad?

Two days later, Jordan was still in bed but this time at home. The balloons and flowers had trickled off a bit, but she had plenty of visitors, including Alexis, Ella, and Oliver. Jordan was surprised when her mom showed him into her room. She knew he'd been hanging around her mother a lot these past few months, and she'd seen him at church too. But now that Andy was not going to be a part of their lives, she'd assumed he'd just kind of disappear. Wrong. He came in carrying a glossy shopping bag that said *Dylan's Candy Bar* across its brightly striped front and handed it to her. "Just some stuff to make you feel better," he said, settling himself into a chair.

"Also to make me fatter."

"Well, yeah."

"I don't know why everyone is still harping on that," said Jordan. But she peeked inside the bag. There was a necklace made of candy, candy dots stuck to a long strip of paper, licorice twists, jawbreakers wrapped in cellophane. Kid stuff. Silly stuff. "Thanks," she said.

"Glad you like it." He smiled. "So, when are you going back to school?"

"Next week," she said. "Ballet class the week after. But I have to gain at least three pounds first. Preferably five."

"It won't even show," he said.

"Not to you, maybe. I'll see every ounce."

"Must be rough having to worry about all that shit."

"It's my life," she said simply. "I'm used to it." He seemed to be studying her. "How's your dad, anyway? He sent me these really nice flowers in the hospital."

Oliver shrugged. "Same as ever, I guess."

"That night at the theater? When I fainted?" Oliver nodded. "I *hated* him. I yelled at him when he tried to get me to leave with him; the security guard came over and made him leave. And even after all the horrible things I said, he stuck around, and went with me to the hospital in the ambulance." She leaned back, exhausted from the recollection. "I never got to thank him for that. Not really. Not the way I should have. And now he's gone and broken up with my mom, and she's so sad all the time. I don't get it."

"Neither do I," Oliver said. "But I wish he'd change his mind."

"Do you think he might?" asked Jordan. She couldn't believe she was even asking this question.

"I can't tell. He can be really stubborn sometimes."

Jordan closed her eyes. "I think I need to take a nap," she said. "I get really tired all of a sudden."

"Sure," Oliver said, standing up. "I'll be back." He ambled over to the rabbit cage and inserted a finger through the wire mesh.

"Careful," Jordan said. "She might think you're a carrot and take a bite."

"Would you do that?" Oliver said to the bunny as he stroked her head. She remained where she was and her baby—practically as big as she was now— was huddled right behind her.

The days in bed, away from school and ballet class, almost didn't count—she was so weak that she slept most of the time. It was when she was allowed back to school, but not to ballet class, that she really suffered. The doctor had told her she couldn't return until she gained three pounds. But even though she'd agreed, she found she couldn't do it; her throat felt like it was closing up and she wanted to gag whenever she ate something rich or fattening, like the gross milk shakes her mother was always waving in her face. Brenda, the therapist her mom was forcing her to see, told her she was having this reaction because she had a distorted body image.

"You still think you're going to get fat, obese even, if you allow yourself to gain any weight at all," she said, sitting across from Jordan in her Upper East Side office with its soft couch, overstuffed armchair, and thick rug.

"No, I don't," Jordan said, but it was a lie. That was exactly what she thought. And coming to the office only confirmed her fear; even the *furniture* in here was fat. But she would not be allowed back in ballet class unless she saw Brenda, so she nodded her head and pretended to consider the therapist's words seriously.

The second week out of bed, she went to SAB, not to take class, but to watch. Francesca was at the head of the barre and in the front row during the center work. It seemed to Jordan that she had gotten even better during the last few weeks. The line of her arabesque was like an arrow, pointing up toward the sky; her turns—she routinely did three pirouettes—were easy and graceful, like the revolving of a top. And she was so thin! How come no one was pestering *her* to gain weight? Jordan was so upset she had to leave before the allegro.

When she finally did return to ballet class, she was shaky. The barre was okay. But when she got to the center, she was a mess. And forget about jumping. "Don't push yourself," Ms. Bonner told her after class. *What are you talking about?* Jordan wanted to scream. *Of course I have to push myself. If I don't push myself, I'm nothing—don't you get it?* When class was over, Alexis and a couple of the other girls wanted to hang out, but she couldn't leave fast enough.

On Broadway, it was cool but the sky had a springlike brightness to it; now that it was April, the dark didn't come so suddenly and so hard. She came to the subway station and on impulse kept walking. She'd get on at the next station. Jordan thought about how much she had lost in such a short time, and how hard she would have to work to get it back. She came to the next subway station, at Fifty-third Street and Seventh Avenue. But she did not descend the steps and she walked on, until she'd reached the crazy, pulsating hub of Times Square. The gigantic billboards, flashing lights, and frenetic pace made her feel dizzy for a minute, dizzy and weak, like she'd felt that night at the theater when Andy had tried to stop her from performing.

She continued south, past Times Square, until she came to the big box on Thirty-fourth Street that was Macy's Department Store. When she was little, she and her mom used to come here at Christmas, to visit Santa, and then to see the tree at Rockefeller Center. "It's even bigger than the tree in *The Nutcracker*," she'd said. As she continued to walk in the fading spring light, Jordan thought about that first night in the hospital. Sick as she'd been, she had stared at the digital clock by her bed, thinking, "Now I'd be doing the *pas de chat*, and now comes the little waltzy thing." But if Andy hadn't shown up, she might have gone into a coma; she might have *died*. Then there would be no more *pas de chat*, no more waltzes, no more anything. She owed Andy Stern an apology; she really did. How to tell him, though? Call or text? Give him a message through Oliver? She thought about it pretty much nonstop for two days. Then the answer just hit her, and after her next therapy session, she walked over to the office whose address she'd found on Google; it turned out to be only a few blocks away.

"Do you have an appointment?" said the receptionist when she walked in.

Jordan shook her head vigorously. She had, with revulsion, gained a whole pound and a half; did this woman think she was actually pregnant or that she wanted to be? Eww. "Just tell him Jordan is here to see him." She waited a beat and added, "Please."

"Well, he's with a patient now," the receptionist said. "You'll have to wait."

Jordan sat down and began to flip through a magazine

entitled *Modern Prenatal Medicine*. Gross. But not as gross as the hugely pregnant woman sitting across from her; her belly, big as a beach ball, strained against the front of her dress. Jordan put the magazine down and unzipped her backpack. She had to have some work in here she could do. She had just finished her math when Andy, dressed in a white doctor's coat, stepped into the waiting room.

"Jordan," he said. "What a surprise. Won't you come in?"

She followed him into a small room with a big, dark desk and three chairs; one large padded one was on his side and two smaller ones were on the other. Taking the one nearest to the door, she sat down.

"So you're better," he said.

"All better." How awkward was *this*?

"And you came to tell me that?"

"Uh, no. I came to tell you I was sorry. And to thank you. For everything you did that night. I know I wasn't very nice."

"You were a brat," he said. Affronted, Jordan sucked in her breath, but he just continued. "I understood, though. It was a clear case of *kill the messenger*. I'm just glad that things turned out the way they did."

How about my mom? she wanted to ask. *Are you glad about that too?* But the intercom buzzed and he picked up. She watched while he listened intently and then he put the phone down and stood.

"I'm sorry," he said. "Emergency."

"Oh, yeah, sure," she said. Maybe he had to deliver a baby—or two—right away. She stood too and headed for the door. Even though she didn't look back, she could tell he wasn't paying attention to her anymore. As far as Andy Stern was concerned, she was already gone. What did she expect anyway? When he was dating her mom, he had a reason to be nice. Now there was none. Deflated, she left the office and walked toward the subway. She would have never guessed that being snubbed by Andy Stern would have hurt quite so much.

THIRTY-THREE

*I*da Stern placed the crystal goblet on the table, peered at it, and frowned. There was a spot on the glass, right near the rim. She brought it to the sink, where she washed and dried it once again before replacing it exactly three inches from the Wedgwood plate and just above the folded napkin. Ida was a stickler about her Passover table; everything had to be perfect. She surveyed the other elements—dishes, silver, linens, and flowers—leaning over to straighten this or adjust that. When she decided that all met her exacting standard, she went into her bedroom to get dressed. The girls—Betty, Sylvia, and Naomi—would be here soon. Andy and Oliver would arrive soon too. But not the *shiksa* girlfriend and her daughter; Andy had told Ida that, no, they weren't coming after all. "Maybe another time, then?" Ida ventured. She had not been sure what this change in plans signified.

"I don't think so," Andy said curtly. "I'm not seeing her anymore."

"Oh." Ida was silent. Her first thought was *Thank God.*

Andy might not think it mattered if he got serious with a non-Jewish girl, but Ida knew better. There would always be a line, a clear demarcation, between Jews and Gentiles. It was foolish, and even dangerous, to think otherwise. Those blue numbers on her arm, faded and softened now by time, were proof of that. "What about that nice Jennifer Baum you used to go around with? You could invite her. And didn't you say she had a little girl? She could come too."

"Jennifer Baum is *not* coming to the seder, Ma," Andy said. The annoyance in his voice was apparent. "And while I appreciate your efforts to ramp up my social life, I think I can handle it on my own, okay?"

"All right," she had said. "You don't have to bite my head off."

Then Andy apologized—he was, at heart, a good boy, a good *man*—and she apologized too because sometimes she did butt in; she couldn't help it, it was just her way. Ida had last seen *her* mother when she was a girl, barely fourteen and with a baby of her own. She remembered how her mother had tried not to cry as she packed things for the baby—an extra cap, socks she had crocheted, a felt ball to keep him quiet on the ride. None of it had done any good; the guard took the wailing baby from Ida's arms before she even got on the train. She had never seen him, or her parents, again. So she didn't know what it was like to be a grown woman and yet a daughter too; she had never had the chance.

In the bedroom, her dress was laid out and waiting. It was black and gold with puffy sleeves and a full skirt. The dress had come from Loehmann's but not the Loehmann's of years ago, when she could find real French, designer clothes—labels cut out—for a fraction of their original price. Today,

Loehmann's was a pale shadow of itself, never mind the big flashy store on 236th Street in Riverdale, where Ida nonetheless went with her friends, largely out of habit. "You can go to a nicer store," Andy had said many times. "Go to Saks or Bloomingdale's and send me the bill." But Ida saw no point in wasting money, even money that was not her own. Her son, thank God, was a good provider. Let him keep his money; maybe one day he'd have a wife again—a nice, Jewish wife— on whom to spend it.

The bell sounded and Ida hurried to get the door. Betty and Naomi stood outside, each clutching tissue-wrapped parcels. "Sylvia will be down in five minutes," Naomi said. She came inside, followed by Betty, and handed Ida her package. "She said not to get started without her."

"I wouldn't dream of it," Ida said, tearing the tissue. "Chocolate-covered matzah!" she said. "My favorite."

"I brought the same thing." Betty turned to Naomi accusingly. "You didn't tell me that's what you were getting."

"Yes, I did," Naomi said. "You just don't remember."

"You did not!"

"It doesn't matter," Ida said soothingly. "In my house, there's never enough chocolate-covered matzah." When the bell buzzed again, she opened the door to Sylvia, who had a tissue-wrapped package of her own.

"Did you bring Ida chocolate-covered matzah?" Betty demanded.

"No," Sylvia said, looking perplexed. "I brought mixed nuts; is that all right?"

"Mixed nuts are wonderful," Ida said, ushering her friends into the living room, where the table had been set up. "I love mixed nuts."

"Ida, everything looks perfect. Including you," said Sylvia.

"Thank you." Ida went into the kitchen and returned with a dish for the nuts.

"So now we're waiting for the doctor son," Naomi said, settling on the sofa and popping a nut in her mouth.

"And the *shiksa* girlfriend," Betty added.

"No *shiksa* girlfriend," Ida said.

"A Jewish girlfriend?" Sylvia asked. Her hand hovered above the nuts but did not alight.

Ida shook her head. "Just Andy and Oliver."

"Do you think he wants to be fixed up? My niece is divorced and she's a *prize*."

"I don't know," Ida said. "I'd have to ask him first."

"Feh!" said Sylvia, taking a sizable handful of nuts. "These kids. If you ask, they always say no. Better to arrange the meeting without telling them." She punctuated this with an audible crunch.

"Sylvia's right," Betty said. "Kids can't tell what's good for them. They're all holding out for some Hollywood idea of romance. And that's nice in the beginning. But after ten, twenty, thirty years, who cares about any of that? You want someone you can get along with, someone compatible."

"Two of a kind," Sylvia mused. "That's what Myron and I were. . . ." Myron had died only last year and it was true: he and Sylvia had seemed especially well suited to each other.

"My Andrew is not a kid," Ida said. "And he's stubborn. Always was. He knows his own mind, goes his own way." She was proud of him too, even though he could be exasperating.

"You have to be stubborn to get ahead," Naomi said. "Look at how successful he is."

"So where *is* he, anyway?" Sylvia asked. "Mr. Big-Shot-Successful-Doctor?"

"He's very busy," Ida said. "And I'm sure there's a lot of traffic."

"Well, I hope he gets here soon," said Sylvia, taking another handful of nuts. "Otherwise we're going to polish these off and we'll have to break out the chocolate matzah before we even sit down to dinner."

"That won't be a problem." Ida smiled at both Betty and Naomi. "We've got plenty."

$\mathcal{T}\!here$ was a ton of traffic on the Henry Hudson Parkway. Oliver didn't care, but he could tell it was making his father crazy. Andy drummed the wheel with his fingers and craned his neck out the window—as if any of that were going to help. He also consulted his watch, like, twenty times and let the occasional *shit* or *fuck* slip from his lips when it was clear that they were going nowhere. But Oliver had his iPad with him and was able to tune his dad, and all his tapping, drumming, cursing impatience, out. Eventually the traffic began to move and pretty soon, they were at his grandmother's building.

"Boychick!" Ida said, and kissed him twice, once on each cheek. She wore a red checked apron over a gold and black dress and her hair had a three-inch pouf. "We were waiting for you."

"The traffic," Andy said. "Horrendous."

"That's what I told the girls," Ida said, nodding at the three older women who sat around the table. "But now you're here and we can start." She ushered Andy into a seat at the head of the table and put Oliver right next to her. "You remember my friends? Oliver shook his head. "This is Betty, that's Naomi, and that's Sylvia." Each of the women smiled at Oliver and Andy; Andy, the doctor-god son, smiled back like a king waving to his subjects. Oliver wanted to put his face right down in his matzah ball soup; he didn't know how he was going to sit through a whole night of this shit. Christina and Jordan were supposed to be here tonight, but that was before his dad had made the colossally stupid move of dumping her.

The seder itself was abbreviated and apart from the reading of the Four Questions, Oliver kept his mouth shut. This was more than okay with him; Grandma Ida was a good cook and he happily scarfed the meal she made. No one really bothered him as long as he was stuffing his face. Andy kept the three ladies entertained with stories from his practice, stories in which he came across as a superhero, a magician, or both. Oliver had heard them *all* before.

There was an awkward moment over the brisket when Sylvia asked what grade he was in, but before Oliver could answer, Andy swooped down with the phrase *gap year.* Sylvia did not seem entirely sure what that was, but she didn't pursue it and Oliver could feel the relief that passed between his father and grandmother. Not that he was dying to talk about being expelled from school, but still, the question had been, like, addressed to him and he should have been given the opportunity to answer it.

"Andy, can't you tell the girls about the celebrity who's your patient now? I'm sure they would love to hear." She put seconds of the brisket, carrots, and roasted potatoes on each of the plates without waiting to be asked.

"Ma, I told you I can't discuss that, not with you, not with anyone."

"Can't you at least tell them who it is?" Ida said.

"Well, since that's already common knowledge . . . It's the singer Xiomara."

"Xiomara!" said Sylvia.

"That voice!" added Betty.

"And a beauty besides," Naomi said.

"Andy says that she's very nice too," Ida said. "Not stuck-up or snobby in the least."

"Imagine," said Sylvia. "Beautiful, talented, rich . . . *and* nice. Some people have it all." She looked at Andy. "Speaking of having it all, I want to tell you about my niece. Divorced, an attorney with a very fine firm, two boys. Also a real looker."

Oliver, who'd been counting the minutes until this would be over, was suddenly alert. Was there a plan to, like, fix his dad up? But there was already someone in his dad's life. Or someone who should have been. Someone who was absolutely perfect.

"Ta-da!" Ida said. Ignoring Sylvia's last remark, she set out a huge dish of chocolate-covered matzah and a round, multi-tiered Jell-O mold.

"You better move fast," Sylvia said, playfully wagging her finger in Andy's direction. "I promise you she won't be single for long."

"That's very thoughtful of you, but you see, I, that is—"

Oliver listened to this exchange with interest. Well, if his dad could answer for him, why not return the favor? "Oh, you don't know?" he said to Sylvia. Everyone turned to look at him. "My dad's dating this terrific woman named Christina. Christina Connelly. They're, like, practically *engaged*." There was a brief silence in which all heads swiveled to stare at Andy. Then everyone started talking at once.

"But you said—," began Ida.

"Well, that's very nice—," added Sylvia.

"We'd love to meet her," Naomi said.

"Connelly?" asked Betty. "So she's Irish. Don't they say the Irish are one of the lost tribes of Israel?"

Oliver sat quietly and observed the little flurry he'd set in motion. Now, why had he said that about Christina? To bug his dad? Maybe. Wishful thinking? Maybe that too. He'd like it if Christina married his father and came to live with them.

"Christina and I are hardly engaged, Oliver," said Andy. Again, there was silence and this time it was broken only by Ida.

"That's enough about Andy's lady friends," she said as she cut into the mold; the translucent layers quivered a bit from the assault of the knife but otherwise remained intact. "Now, who's having Jell-O?"

The Sunday after the seder was bright and clear, perfect for raking and bagging dead leaves, and picking up the random soda bottles, candy wrappers, and all the other crap that had blown into the garden in back of Old First Church. Oliver hauled a big black bag over to the far end and took another bag to fill. He had not stopped coming out here; even though his dad was being such a dickhead about Christina, there was no reason *he* had to give up seeing her. And to his relief, Andy had not suggested it.

And hey, there was Christina now, dressed in jeans, a gray sweater, and those cool white Keds she liked to wear. Oliver stopped his raking and went over to say hello. She gave him a hug; if she was thinking about his father, she never let on. Then she picked up a pair of clippers and went over to the hedge along the church wall where a couple of people were clipping back dead branches. Summer was one of them.

Oliver stood with the empty bag in his hand, watching

Summer twist and stretch. Her boobs strained against her sweatshirt; he could stand here all day looking at them. For the past couple of months they had been hanging out. They hadn't actually, like, *done it*; Oliver had not *done it* with anyone. But Summer would be the one, so he could take things slowly, get to know her first. It felt kind of good.

"Louise said I'm your partner for today."

Oliver turned around to see Liam, a pudgy sophomore whose dad occasionally dropped in for the monthly church meals.

"Sure, whatever," Oliver said. "Want to grab a bag?"

Liam got the bag and joined Oliver in the cleanup. He didn't talk much, but that was okay; he worked hard.

"They let dogs back here?" Oliver scrutinized the turds he'd just uncovered.

Liam looked over. "Cat shit," he said succinctly, and went back to bagging.

It was getting hot. Oliver unzipped his hoodie and peeled it off, leaving it in a heap on the ground. When it got in his way, he nudged it aside with his foot.

"Hey, careful. You might step on that." Liam knelt down to pick up the black iPod Touch that had slid out of the hoodie's pocket and was now gleaming in the sun.

"Thanks. I, like, totally forgot I had it in there."

"You *forgot*?"

"Yeah, well, I never use it anymore. I listen to music on my iPhone. . . ." His dad had upgraded him to the latest model just recently.

Liam was still looking down at the black rectangle. "Whatever," he said.

Oliver stood there awkwardly. It was so obvious what

Liam thought: rich kid who not only didn't appreciate having an iPod, but rich kid who didn't even *remember* having one. Liam did not live in a shelter; Oliver knew that much. But if his dad was bringing him to meals at the church, they couldn't have a lot of money. Liam handed the iPod to Oliver, who was about to put it in the pocket of his jeans but abruptly pushed it back. "Here, you take it."

"What?" asked Liam.

"Keep it," Oliver said.

"You're kidding, right?"

"I never use the thing. Like I said, I forgot I even had it."

"Well, thanks, then. Thanks a bunch." He ran his fingers reverently over the iPod and then carefully tucked it away before picking up his rake.

Oliver was about to do the same when he thought of something else. He checked the hoodie, and there in the other pocket were the earbuds. He handed them to Liam, who took them without a word. But when they broke for lunch— sandwiches brought by Miriam and Lee—Liam brought Oliver a sandwich, a bag of chips, and two cookies before taking his own food. Then he plunked down beside him. "So, like, what bands are you into?" he asked.

Going back on the subway that night, Oliver was tired but happy. The day outside, working, had been satisfying, and the unexpected incident of the iPod had made him feel like he'd done something, like, useful in the world. He and Summer were going to hang out tomorrow. And to his surprise, his dad was home and asked if he'd like to have dinner together.

"You mean one of those no-fat, no-taste meals Lucy makes?"

"I thought we could order in . . . Japanese, Thai . . . ?"

"Okay," said Oliver, warming to the idea. "Where's the menu?"

But when the food came, Andy's phone buzzed and off he sprinted to the hospital, leaving Oliver to eat his spring rolls and pad Thai alone. When he finished, he felt restless. He didn't have any weed—he'd been too scared to score after his expulsion from school—and his dad's liquor cabinet did not hold much appeal. Neither did the zillion and two offerings on television, which he clicked through furiously before abandoning the remote in disgust. He tried the porn on his computer, but even his favorite sites felt all wrong. These girls were getting *paid* to do this shit. That had never mattered before, but tonight, it just turned him off.

The computer was still on, though, and on impulse, he navigated away from the picture of the naked girl on her knees, blowing some guy with a shaved head. He wanted to write something, but he wasn't sure what. It had to do with the day he'd spent, at least the part of it before he had gotten home and it had taken a nosedive. No, he was thinking about the first part, with that, like, hard, enamel blue of the sky above him, the smell of the soil, the bright burst of flowers—he didn't know their names—the way his back and shoulders ached, but in a good way, from all that raking and bagging. The thing with the iPod would be part of it. Summer too. Also a poem about gathering leaves by Robert Frost he'd read when he was still in school. He remembered the first few lines and easily found the rest online. Sweet. He'd call his essay or whatever it was "A Day in the Garden," and it would be, like, a little of everything: memoir, journalism, even poetry. He started tapping, furiously, impatiently, on his laptop. Seven pages later he looked up. It was almost eleven o'clock. He went into the kitchen for a glass of water, returned to the laptop, and tapped out another five pages. Then he read it once, twice, a third time, making little changes as he did. And then, for no reason that, like, made any sense, he sent the whole thing off to his former English teacher at Morningside. She loved the paper he'd done on Robert Frost; maybe she'd like this too.

It was after midnight when he got into bed. Lying in the dark, he heard his dad's key in the lock, and a minute later, his dad's voice outside his door. "Oliver?" Andy called softly. "Are you still up?" But he didn't answer, and his father went away. The words he'd written seemed to carry him up and over some crest, and he fell asleep with their rhythm still tapping softly in his brain.

THIRTY-FOUR

The sidewalk in front of the hospital was so jammed Andy had to fight his way to the entrance. Not only was there the usual crowd of paparazzi associated with any move Xiomara made, but there was also a construction crew; now that her delivery was imminent, she had paid the hospital some exorbitant sum of money for the privilege of redoing the VIP suite where she would give birth. The workmen were supposed to use the service entrance, but clearly some of them had not gotten the memo.

Andy was fed up with the media circus. It just made his job so much harder. But he knew he'd do the same thing next time he was asked. Once these women sat across from him, poured out their stories—miscarriages, stillborns, ectopics, moms who'd taken DES—he listed toward them like plants in the sun. "Excuse me," he said, trying to get past a camera-wielding guy blocking his path. "Coming through." The guy was planted like a redwood in the middle of the sidewalk. "I'm a *doctor*; I *work* here and I need to get in." Still no response. "Could you please move?" Finally, acting like he was doing Andy a major favor, the guy stepped aside. *Je-sus.*

The VIP suite, down at one end of the maternity ward, was sectioned off by double doors that could be locked. It was as spacious as some Manhattan apartments, with a kitchenette, a large private bath that had both Jacuzzi and sauna, ample closets, and three good-sized windows that the construction workers were now covering with plywood—Xiomara was taking precautions against an intrepid photographer scaling the walls of the hospital and finding a way to snap pictures of the birth itself. Wouldn't those fetch a nice price? Though he'd heard that she had agreed to sell the first shots of the baby to *People* or *Us* for some ungodly sum—this to appease the media gods no doubt—and then planned to donate the money to a women's hospital in Africa. There were also painters and a carpet installer at work; someone was overseeing the arrangement of various pieces of rented furniture as well as a fifty-odd-inch plasma TV. What a production.

Andy watched for a few minutes before heading out the door and back down the hall. It was excessive, to be sure, but if rich people wanted to pay for the right to redecorate, why not let them? The hospital could certainly use the additional revenue. He'd have to tell Christina about this—then he remembered he wasn't seeing Christina anymore. God, he missed her. Missed her more than he'd expected given they had only been seeing each other for a few months. She didn't have a big presence, but damn, she had an enduring one. He wondered whether she had started seeing anyone else; he hadn't, though one of his old college buddies, Joey Colabella, was trying to fix him up with someone. Andy agreed to meet the woman but then kept putting it off; he just didn't seem to have the heart. He was going to be seeing Joey and the rest of his college crew soon and he hoped Joey wouldn't harp on it.

He stopped in to the see the patient he'd delivered the day before; both she and her twins were doing well. Then he thought of Artyom Petrinovic and he decided to stop in at the neonatal ICU to see how he was doing; maybe Perry could update him. Perry wasn't around, but Andy managed to find a nurse he knew on this unit. "How's the Petrinovic baby?" he asked. "Last time I checked, he'd gained a couple of ounces."

"You haven't heard?"

"Heard what?" It wasn't looking good.

"We lost him. Not even an hour ago. Dr. Perry was going to call you."

"Jesus." He shook his head. "Where are the parents?"

"They're here, filling out some paperwork. Come on, I'll take you." She brought him to a small office where Valentin and Olga Petrinovic sat, a mountain of forms in front of them on the table.

"I just heard," he said. "And I can't say how sorry I am."

They swiveled, as if in unison, toward him. "Thank you, Dr. Stern," Valentin said. His normally ruddy cheeks were pale and his eyes were red. Olga did not speak at all, but pressed her face into her husband's chest. There was something so intimate about the gesture that Andy felt he had trespassed simply by witnessing it. "I haven't spoken to Dr. Perry yet, but from all accounts, this was some horrible twist of fate, some fluke—"

"God's will," Olga said bitterly. "If you believe in God. Which I do not."

"What I mean to say," Andy began again, "is that no one could have predicted this. No one. And if you ever consider trying again, I hope you'll let me be the one to help you through."

Valentin put his arm around his wife. "If we try again . . ." He let the sentence trail off.

Andy was glad to get out of there. He was through seeing patients for the day and ready to head back home, but he continued west and stopped in at the florist's on Lexington Avenue. "Hello, Andy," Gus said. "What can I do for you?"

"I need a bouquet of flowers, very simple, very elegant," said Andy. "And all white. You can call Joanne in the morning; she'll give you the address."

"Your friend in Brooklyn? Don't worry; I've got her on file—"

"No, not her," said Andy. "This is a condolence bouquet. A patient's baby died."

"Oh, I'm sorry," Gus said. "I'll take care of it first thing. And when you need to send flowers to Brooklyn again—"

"I don't know when I'll be doing that," said Andy. "Or if."

"You look like you had a tough day. Rotten day, in fact."

"That I did," Andy said.

"I'm just about to close up here; what do you say we go and knock one down together? My wife's got her book club tonight, so I'm on my own."

Andy waited while Gus closed up and then they sat together over a couple of beers. Gus ordered chicken potpie and Andy, broiled halibut. He didn't talk about the Petrinovics' baby or the split with Christina. Instead, they moved from the Yankees to the Jets, to soccer and then golf. It was only after they'd finished and Andy had handed his credit card to the waiter, waving off Gus's attempts to chip in, that the conversation turned somber again. "Your Brooklyn friend?" Gus said. "I thought she seemed . . . special. Like she might be the one."

"You met her?" Andy said.

"She came into the shop, don't you remember? You sent her."

"Oh that's right." Christina had had a job helping stage an apartment for a Realtor; she'd needed some flowers and Andy had recommended Gus.

"I liked her a lot," Gus continued. "I thought she was a real lady."

"Maybe *too* much of a lady." Andy looked down at the crumpled napkin in his hand. "We were just too different."

Back in his apartment, everything was quiet and dark. He thought Oliver was out but decided to peek into his room just the same. He was almost startled to see his son, body curled like a comma, asleep on his side. His face was not visible, only the mass of blond curls; this was the way he used to sleep when he was a toddler. Andy was about to close the door quietly and leave, but some impulse sent him into the room, where he stood, hovering. He had an urge to kiss him on the top of his fair, curly head, and he gave in to it—lightly, stealthily— hoping he would not get caught.

The next day, he had to slog through his session with Cassie; he'd been chased out of a lousy night's sleep by a series of nightmares that involved tunnels, swamps, and an earth- quake thrown in for good measure. But he got through the workout and, as always, felt better as a result. Oliver was up early and ate a bowl of cereal while Andy had his coffee; their conversation wasn't stellar, but it wasn't barbed either. He then walked briskly to his office feeling like he'd been restored, at least partially. Yeah, he was still dejected over the breakup with Christina and deeply saddened by the death of the Petrinovic baby. But today offered a fresh start.

His first patient of the day was Beth Klein. She was pregnant, just over three months, which meant she had passed safely through the most vulnerable stage. He wasn't taking any chances, though; he would continue to monitor her very closely. He sent her into the ultrasound room and waited a few minutes before following.

When he stepped inside, the lights were turned down and the screen and monitor all ready. Pam, the technician, had everything set up just the way he liked; the lubricating jelly had even been warmed, so he did not have to deliver the cold, rude squirt onto his patient's bare skin. "How are you feeling?" he asked, applying a smooth coat of the jelly.

"Fine," she said. "But I'm being super careful, just like you told me."

"Good," he said. "Careful is good." He passed the wand over her abdomen. The fetus was about three inches in length by now. The neck was developed even though its head was still disproportionately large; he could see it clearly on the screen. He could see the tiny arms and legs too. Everything looked just as it should. He moved the wand up and down, back and forth. He might even have been able to tell the sex if the legs had been splayed, but he didn't bring that up; some patients wanted to be surprised.

He put down the wand and reached for the Doppler. Last time Beth had been here, she'd heard the heartbeat for the first time—fast, like a horse galloping down the track—and she had wept with joy. He wanted her to hear it again today and he pressed the Doppler against her skin, trying to pick up the heartbeat. But in the contained space of Beth's uterus, there was only silence. Andy felt the first prick of anxiety.

"Is anything wrong, Dr. Stern?" asked Beth.

Andy said nothing. Though he tried to be so careful, she quickly picked up on his apprehension. They all did. And of course this was the one time the husband wasn't here. *Shit.* Even in the dim light he was aware of Pam watching intently; he did not want to catch her eye. He kept moving the Doppler. Nothing. He put it down and took a slow and exacting breath. "All right," he said, touching her on the elbow. "You can get dressed now. I'll see you in my office. We can talk there." Pam shot him a look; it was filled with dread and pity. He took a quick look at Beth's face; it was a mask of wordless panic.

Andy waited in the examining room, trying to compose himself. There had been a heartbeat two weeks ago, loud, clear, and steady. Those early fetal heart tones were much faster than those in an adult; they made a very distinct sound. So why couldn't he hear them now? He knew the answer but could not admit it to himself. There was no heartbeat because the fetus was dead.

"Dr. Stern?" Pam poked her head in the room. "She's waiting for you; I think she's crying."

He sighed, a massive, resigned sigh. "I'll be out in a second," he said.

"You couldn't find the heartbeat. . . ."

"Because there *was* no heartbeat." Goddamn it to hell. Why couldn't this woman get a break? *Why?* She was doing everything right; he was doing everything right. There had been no bleeding, no spotting, no warning of any kind. But the little heart, no bigger than a pea, had stopped. Just like that. Nothing to do with her previous history. A *vanilla miscarriage* was the term. No particular reason. Statistically, a certain number of pregnancies ended that way. Though statistics would be of no consolation to Beth Klein.

When Andy finished delivering the crushing news, he was in serious need of a drink. He'd sat there while she got her husband—in Chicago on business—on speakerphone, and offered his support and sympathy during the tearful conversation that ensued. Then he'd had Joanne schedule Beth for a D & C. He did not want to discuss the next step yet. But he was not sure this woman could endure another pregnancy, and if he continued to feel that way, it would be his professional, to say nothing of ethical, obligation to tell her.

It was after five when he left the office, a mild and balmy evening. He was just deciding whether he wanted to stop in for that drink on his way home or wait until he got to the apartment when his phone buzzed. It was Xiomara. "I hate to bother you," she began. "But I was wondering if I could see you? Like now?"

"Is there a medical emergency?" he asked. She'd been in fine shape the last time he'd examined her. But look at Beth—things could change quickly.

"It *is* an emergency," she said. "Though I'm not sure it's medical."

"Well, I was just leaving my office. I could go back and meet you there. Are you nearby?"

"Yes," she said. "I am."

Andy walked to the office. It was not the first time he'd been "summoned" by a celeb patient. And it was not the first time he'd said yes. These women were used to getting what they wanted, when they wanted it. He'd had one who treated him like a glorified errand boy, another who berated him for the strict rules he'd imposed, never mind that they were for the safety of her baby. Xiomara wasn't like that, though. She'd always behaved respectfully and seemed to value his expertise. He thought of the VIP suite he'd seen at the hospital the day before and supposed that a woman who thought it necessary to install wall-to-wall carpeting—and then pay to have it taken out again—in a room she'd be inhabiting for three days max would not think it excessive to tell her doctor she needed to see him right away.

Joanne and Pam were gone; the office was quiet and the waning light filtered through the windows in the waiting room. He went and sat down at his desk. When the doorbell buzzed, he went to answer it. And even though he knew who would be standing there, he was unprepared for the effect she had. To accommodate the girth of her very pregnant belly, she wore a long, loose dress of some crinkly, golden material; above the low-cut neckline, the column of her firm, brown neck rose splendidly. Her hair had been piled high on her head, and her lips gleamed. She looked at the burly bodyguard who stood by her side. "Wait in the car, Felix," she said. "I'll text if I need you." Felix grunted in assent and turned to go. He was so muscle-bound that walking seemed like an effort.

"Come into my office," Andy said. Jesus H. Christ, was he actually feeling the stirrings of a hard-on? She followed him inside and he took a seat across from her. The desk was a comforting buffer—wide, professional, and distancing.

"I appreciate your willingness to see me on such short notice, Dr. Stern. Especially when it's not *exactly* medical."

"The mind and the body work in concert," he said. God,

why did he have to sound like someone had shoved a pole up his ass? Because he was nervous, that was why. He was nervous sitting here alone with this goddess, only the desk between them. He had a sudden image of pulling her onto that desk and plunging his hand down the front of that golden, goddess dress of hers—

"They do, they do," breathed Xiomara. "And though the body is fine"—she patted her belly lovingly—"the mind is not doing so well."

"Are you feeling anxious about the birth?"

"A little. But more anxious about Badu." Badu was her basketball star husband. Apart from their initial visit, he'd never been back to the office with her again.

"What's been going on?" Andy asked, leaning a little closer.

"Nothing!" she said. "Just about a big, old nothing. He won't touch me, Dr. Stern. Won't even get near me. You'd think I had the plague. The last time he saw me stepping out of the shower, he said, *Would you please cover yourself.*"

"Some men are made uncomfortable by pregnancy, particularly in the latter stages. It's not admirable, but I hear it from a lot of my patients." He tried not to think about her stepping out of that shower—now he really did have a hard-on, damn it.

"What about you, Dr. Stern?" she demanded. "Is that how you did *your* woman after you'd gone and knocked her up?" She gestured to the photo of Rachel that was still on his desk.

"My wife is dead," he said stiffly. "It's been almost three years since I lost her."

"Oh!" Xiomara's lovely, ring-bedecked fingers flew to her lips. "I am so, so sorry."

"You were talking about your husband—"

"So after months of acting like I'm this, this freak, this monster, I begin to get annoyed, you know? I began to rag on him. Pick fights." Andy nodded sympathetically. "And after one fight, he didn't come home all night. I made Felix track him down; he found Badu with some other girl, Dr. Stern. Some tramp he'd picked up. And when I called him on it, and broke down crying and told him how much he'd hurt me, he turned around and told me it was my fault. *My* fault! Can you believe it? For pushing him into someone else's arms."

"You must have been very upset," he said.

"I was," she said. "I am. I just want a little affection, Dr. Stern. A little tenderness. You understand, don't you? I *know* you do. I can *feel* it." She leaned forward so that the desk was a bridge, not a barrier. And then she kissed him.

Andy reacted to that kiss as if a gun had gone off in the room. He was astonished, aroused, intoxicated—but mostly he was horrified that the fantasy had stepped out of his head and into his office. Yes, she was the most gorgeous woman God ever made—but she was his patient; to give in to her would be to violate everything he'd ever believed in, worked for, achieved. "Xiomara," he began, waiting for his heart to stop its insane throbbing. "You are a beautiful and desirable woman—"

"Even like this?" She waved a hand over her belly.

"*Especially* like this," he said. "But I'm your doctor. And as your doctor, I have a professional obligation to you and to your baby. You don't want me—"

"You're wrong—I do. I do!" She tried reaching for him again, but he moved away.

"No, you want to hurt Badu the way he's hurt you. But

you'll regret it. You'll regret it and you'll blame me for not stopping you. So I'm going to save you all that regret and blame." He stood up. "I want you to go home and talk to your husband. Tell him you're going to forgive him—but once and only once. And tell him he's on notice. As for you—you're going to stop picking fights to get his attention. You have something to say to him, you say it—right out in the open."

"I just wanted . . . I mean, I just thought —" She fluttered her lashes, which, though obviously false, still made for a highly effective gesture.

"I know what you wanted and I know what you thought." He came around the desk to see her out. "And it's all right. It really is. We never have to mention this again. It will be our secret." Amazingly, he was even able to smile. "You text Felix and tell him to come in here and get you now."

She placed her finger on his mouth and gently touched his lips. "Dr. Stern?" she said. "You're a good man. A *good* man. And good men are hard to find."

"Thank you," he said. "I try." He didn't feel like a good man. He felt like he'd dodged a bullet. One minute more alone with her and who knows what he would have done?

"There's a woman in your life now?"

"There was," he said, suddenly scorched by the image of Christina, hair spread out across the pillow and reaching her arms up to him. "But not now."

"Well, you deserve a woman," she said firmly. "You deserve the *best*."

Andy opened the door and there was massive Felix, impervious as a tank. "I'll see you next week," he said, determined to sound professional and in command. God knew what Felix thought; he'd seen it all—and more—before.

"Thank you again, Dr. Stern," Xiomara said. She had one hand on Felix's arm; the gold cloth shimmered as she went. But in one swift, fluid movement, she turned and deposited a last, lingering kiss on Andy's mouth. Felix didn't even blink.

THIRTY-FIVE

Although it was a mild late April morning, Christina woke shivering and almost too weak to make it out of bed. She got to the bathroom just in time; another minute and she would have thrown up all over the floor. She rinsed her mouth thoroughly and shakily reached for the thermometer. No fever. Well, that was a relief. And once she had showered and vigorously brushed her teeth, she was fine—at least physically.

She didn't feel the same sense of shock and outrage she'd felt when Will died; that grief had been vicious, attacking her with claws and talons. No, breaking up with Andy had just anesthetized her. Despite the relentless advent of spring— tulips, daffodils, and hyacinths bursting from window boxes and planters all over the neighborhood, ordinary city trees made briefly glorious by their clouds of pink or white lacy blossoms, the madly twittering sparrows and cooing doves in her own garden—she herself was a figure carved from ice.

Over and over she replayed the scene in the hospital cafeteria. Could she have done anything differently to change the
outcome? But what? Pointed out that his failure to tell her
about Jordan's eating disorder was no different from her not
telling him about Oliver and the pot? In the end, it would have
done no good. His mind was made up.

She had thought of calling him, writing to him, even
showing up at his door. She did none of the above. She wasn't
going to beg; she had her pride, even though Sister Bernadette
had railed against pride as one of the worst of the seven deadly
sins. Since then, she'd gone through her days like a sleep-
walker, even though she was busier than she'd been in months.
The Web site had brought in a couple of new jobs; those jobs
in turn had spawned others. Her reach was beginning to extend beyond Brooklyn: she was working on a loft in Tribeca, a
pied-à-terre on the Upper East Side, and a little cottage in Sag
Harbor that belonged to friends of Stephen. Good jobs all,
and she was grateful to have them.

The next morning she awoke again with that horrible,
nauseated feeling, but it wasn't until the third day that its true
meaning finally hit her. On her way back from the loft in
Tribeca, she stopped in a Duane Reade to pick up the pregnancy test and used it as soon as she got home. The stick
turned instantly and emphatically blue.

Pregnant. Holy Mary, Mother of God. She was *pregnant*.
There was a loud and vigorous thumping, which could
have been the sound of her own, frantic heart. But it was
only Jordan's rabbits, steadily beating their hind legs against
the bottom of their cage. As if in a trance, she went to the
refrigerator, pulled out some lettuce leaves from the crisper,
and placed them in the cage. The rabbits fell upon their

treat with rabbitlike delight, which is to say, they methodi-
cally and steadily consumed the leaves until they were
gone. Then they both remained close to the front of the cage,
nostrils flaring delicately, as if waiting to see what she would
do next.

She left the room. It was almost six, time to start dinner.
Since her illness, Jordan was eating a bit more, and Christina
made every effort to entice her at mealtime. It was like having
a picky toddler all over again, but at least her daughter no
longer looked so painfully gaunt. The doctor who had treated
her at the hospital had suggested a therapist who specialized
in eating disorders and stipulated that she not be allowed back
to ballet class unless she agreed to see her.

Tonight Christina was preparing chicken, brown rice, and
asparagus she'd purchased on Saturday at the local farmers'
market. With any luck Jordan would eat small portions of everything. The asparagus stalks were a bit thick; she decided
she would shave and then steam them. The chicken would be
roasted and she'd perk up the rice with the skillful deploy-
ment of herbs and spices rather than butter or oil. She performed these tasks on autopilot, her hands moving efficiently
despite the chaos in her head.

How could she be pregnant? She had thought they were
being careful; evidently they had not been careful enough.
Thinking back, she tried to calculate how far along she might
be. Eight weeks? Ten? That meant she could still have a first-
trimester abortion, though the idea filled her with sorrow.
Even though she'd left the Catholicism of her girlhood behind
and believed in a woman's right to choose, that did not mean
she would choose an abortion. But how would she manage
with a baby at this point in her life? She wouldn't be able to

work; who would support them? And how would a new half sibling affect Jordan?

She looked down. She had been so diligent in peeling the asparagus stems that there was virtually nothing left of them; on the counter was a pile of the clustered buds. She scraped the shavings into the covered enamelware pot she kept for compost; her hands were shaking. Abandoning the asparagus, she sat down at the table. She would have poured herself a glass of wine, but under the circumstances that did not seem like the most prudent idea. *Under the circumstances.* What was she thinking? That she was going through with the pregnancy? If she did, she would have to tell Andy. But wouldn't she tell Andy in any case?

When Jordan called to say that she would not be home for dinner after all, Christina was relieved. She finished preparing the meal and then, overcome by a sudden ravenous urge, ate it all. She had to force herself to take a plate and sit at the table; otherwise, she would have stood at the stove, shoveling the rice, chicken, and what remained of the asparagus right from the pots and into her mouth. After she finished, she went prowling through the cabinets in search of something sweet; an open box of amaretto cookies was tucked in the far reaches of a top shelf. Stale as they were, she finished them, along with the ice-crystal-encrusted remnants of a pint of dark chocolate gelato. Afterward, she had to lie down. She remembered those surges of hunger from her first pregnancy; they were like a feeding frenzy.

But she couldn't remain still for long. She had to do something, talk to someone. Andy? No, not yet. Stephen. Of course. She did not bother to phone, but trotted up the stairs to knock on his door. "Hi, doll," he said. "Misha and I were all set to watch a movie. Want to join us?" Mutely, Christina shook her head. She had not yet said the word *pregnant* out loud; she almost couldn't bear it. "Are you all right?" he added.

"No," she said. "I'm not."

"One sec." He disappeared for a moment and then returned. "Misha's going to start without me; you and I can go to your place to talk." He followed her downstairs and as soon as they had reached Christina's parlor, she turned, put her head on his chest, and started to sob. He must have been startled; in all the years they had known each other, she had never done such a thing. But he did not ask any questions and instead patted her back until she was calmer. It was only when they were seated on her love seat that she began to talk.

"So you're sure he doesn't know?" Stephen asked when he'd heard the story.

"Positive."

"And what are you planning to do about it?"

"I don't know. But whatever I decide, I think I have to tell him. Don't you?"

"Yes. Only . . ." He looked down.

"Only what?"

He lifted his gaze again. "There's something you should know before you do. Something I was going to tell you about; Misha and I were just trying to figure out the best—that is, the *kindest*—way to do it."

"Tell me now," she said. "I need to know."

"I'll be right back." He got up and Christina waited in uneasy suspense. What could Stephen and Misha know about Andy that she did not? Their worlds were totally separate. When he returned, he handed her a folded newspaper. "Read it and weep."

Puzzled, Christina opened it up. She found herself holding a cheap tabloid with the headline *Xiomara's Baby Doc Gets
Up Close and Personal.* Underneath was a large photograph of
Andy kissing the very pregnant singer. Her body was pressed
close to his; even in the photograph, Christina could see how
her ample breasts grazed his chest. Quickly, she scanned the
article—if you could call it that. It was really just a bit of sala-
cious reportage, hinting at a rift between Xiomara and her
basketball player husband amid rumors of infidelity on his
part, and the speculation that she might now be linked roman-
tically to her ob-gyn, the handsome, eligible widower Andrew
Stern. The piece concluded with a mention of Xiomara's recent
redecoration of the VIP suite at the hospital where she planned
to give birth; the estimated cost of the work was more than ten
thousand dollars.

Christina put the paper down on the love seat. So it was
true. There *had* been something between them. And it looked
like there still was. "This thing is a rag; I wouldn't believe
anything I read in here. But the picture . . ." The picture was
like an ice pick to her heart.

"I still think you should tell him," Stephen was saying.
"But I just wanted you to have all the information first."

She reached for the folded paper and then stopped. She
didn't want to see it again.

"Whatever you decide, you know I'm there for you," said
Stephen.

"I know that," she replied. "And I'm grateful." She stood.
Stephen stood too, and kissed her lightly on the forehead before he left. When he had gone, she opened the newspaper
again and looked at the picture for a long time.

She felt like she was thawing, coming to life after being

frozen by grief. She was lucky he'd broken up with her—she really was. She didn't want him, and she didn't want the life she would have led with him—turbulent, erratic, governed by his moods and his outbursts. Whether she would keep this baby was a different matter. But if she did, she would raise it without him.

The next day, Christina was able to schedule an appointment with her gynecologist, Amy Wenders. Amy said she was about eight or nine weeks pregnant—still time for a first-trimester abortion. "And I can perform it for you," Amy said.

"I want to schedule it now, and give myself a week to live with the idea."

Amy nodded. "We can do that." She reached for an appointment book. "I don't want to pry, but I'm assuming that the male part of this equation has not been informed."

"Not yet," Christina said. "I'm going to tell him, though." *But when?*

She spent the next few days veering between bouts of nausea and surges of appetite. The eating she tried to do in secret, not wanting to arouse any curiosity—or suspicion—in Jordan. It wasn't that hard; Jordan was home even less than usual. And all the while she thought of Andy: how to tell him, what words to use. Nothing she came up with ever seemed right. She told Stephen about the abortion she'd scheduled; he arranged to take the day off to accompany her. But two days before, she called Amy again. "I can't do it yet," she said. "I'm not ready."

"How about if I give you another four days?" Amy said. "I don't want to pressure you, but I don't want you to wait too long either. Once you go past twelve weeks, the procedure is . . . quite different."

"I understand," Christina said. "And Amy—thank you."

After she'd said good-bye, Christina knew she could not wait another day to tell Andy. And she would do it now, before she lost her nerve. But before she could make the call, her phone buzzed. For a second, she thought it might be him, and even though she had told herself she was done with him, hope lifted inside her. Then she saw the unfamiliar number—it was not Andy after all. When she answered, the low, snarling voice had such menace that she thought it might be an obscene call and was about to hang up when the word *painting* caught her attention. "—and I don't know what kind of scheme you've cooked up with that so-called restorer, but I'm on to you, do you understand?"

"Who *is* this?" she said. But then she knew: Ian Haverstick.

"You think I believe that story about his conveniently disappearing? Do you think I'm an idiot?"

No, I think you're a crude, insensitive bully, she wanted to say. Instead, she said, "I expect you to believe the truth. And the truth is that I'm as shocked by Derrick's disappearance as you are."

"Save it for the judge," he spit. "Because you're going to need to tell it to him."

"What are you talking about? You know I was not a party to the contract you signed."

"I'm bringing charges against you for theft. Because I think you're hiding him and I aim to prove it."

"You're bluffing," she said, though she was not at all sure this was true. "You haven't got a shred of evidence against me because there isn't any evidence to have."

"Wait and see. When I'm done with you, you won't have a

client left. And I hope you'll like the correctional facility upstate I've got picked out for you—maybe if you're a model pris-
oner, they'll let you redecorate the cells!"

"How dare you call me up and browbeat me like this?"
The words came tumbling out. "You're a brute, a philistine,
and you're . . . delusional! I pity your wife. I really do!" And
then she ended the call.

Christina was shocked at herself. She had never once
yelled back at a client, even one who had abused and fired her.
It would be bad for business. Word always got out in the
neighborhood. She pressed her open palms to her cheeks; they
were so hot they felt feverish. Would he involve the police? Let
him! She had nothing to hide. But her plan to tell Andy about
the pregnancy evaporated. She couldn't face another confron-
tation right now; she just couldn't.

The next day, Christina had a visit from a detective, a
lanky man with a large beaky nose and a bald spot he tried,
ineffectually, to cover with the thinning wisps of his remaining
hair. He showed her his badge and said he was with the local
precinct; so Ian Haverstick had not been bluffing. She invited
him in and answered all his questions—there were many—as
best she could.

"You had no warning or clue that he would disappear?"
he asked.

"None at all." They were seated in her office and she could
see him looking around.

"When was the last time you saw him?"

"He invited me to dinner shortly after the Haversticks
hired him." Christina did not want to answer that question.
But Sister Bernadette's lessons were too deeply etched inside
her to lie.

"Dinner? When?" He perked up.

She reached for her date book and found the entry, showing the page to the detective.

"Okay, so he takes you to dinner; was it a date?"

"I didn't think so," she said. "But he did."

"Meaning . . . ?"

Christina told him the whole story then—the wine, the visit to the loft, the kiss followed by the weeping. "I don't really think that had anything to do with his disappearance," she said. "Do you?"

"It's my job to explore *all* the possibilities," said the detective. "This is just one more to add to the mix."

"Apart from that night, we've always gotten along well. He sent business my way and I did the same for him."

"Like the Haversticks."

"Exactly. I thought he would be able to appraise the painting for them and do any light cleaning that it needed." *Was* she in some obscure way responsible for what had happened? She didn't think so, but she couldn't be sure.

"Ian Haverstick claims that you were trying to influence his wife against selling."

"If that's true, is it a crime?"

"No, it isn't. But let me rephrase that. Mr. Haverstick believes that you tried to influence his wife for your own gain— you would steer the painting to Blascoe, who would then disappear with it."

"Mrs. Haverstick didn't want to sell it," Christina said. "I had nothing to do with that. The argument was between those two—not with me. I was just doing what I was asked."

"Which was?"

"Getting the painting authenticated and appraised.

That was the first step no matter what they decided. They needed to know if it was authentic, and if so, what it was worth."

"You thought it was authentic, didn't you?"

"I did." She was surprised by the question.

"Why?"

"I can't really say," she said. "Just a hunch. But I'm not a pro, the way Derrick is. He's got a good track record."

"Or he did," said the detective drily.

Christina had to concede that point. Then she let him look around. He found nothing incriminating—naturally. There was nothing to find. "I'm going to want phone records, e-mails, things like that," he said as he was leaving.

"Fine," she told him. "You can have anything you need."

When he left, she realized she had been shaking. But he was not the one who had made her feel so afraid. It was Ian Haverstick; the memory of their last conversation was still lacerating. She thought of her father then, lurching around the house, his voice thunderous, his breath heavy with whiskey, his hands careless and potentially hurtful.

When the letter came two days later, Christina assumed it was from the detective. She opened it and at first, the words did not make any sense:

It has come to our attention that you have been operating a prohibited business out of your residence, which is in direct violation of code . . .

The letter was not from the detective; it was from the local zoning board. She felt the alarm bleeding outward, like a stain, as she continued reading:

You are required to attend a zoning board hearing on . . . and if found in violation of this code, you will be required to shut down above-referenced business immediately or face a maximum penalty of . . .

Christina clutched the letter tightly. She knew that operating a decorating business out of her home was illegal. But she had always been discreet, never putting a sign up on her door or window. Why, after all this time, were they coming after her? The answer was obvious: Ian Haverstick. It must have been him. And a call to Mimi Farnsworth confirmed it. "Oh yes, he's been tight with all those zoning people in the Slope for years," Mimi said. "But I had no idea he'd do anything like this. I feel terrible—I recommended you for the job to do you a good turn and now look."

"It's not your fault," Christina said. No. It was Ian's.

"Do you want me to talk to him?" asked Mimi. "I would be glad to do it if you think it will help."

Christina thought of Ian's dark eyes, two hot coals in the pale expanse of his fleshy face, and of the insinuating snarl of his voice on the phone. "No," she said. "It wouldn't. But thank you for offering."

She said good-bye to Mimi and reread the letter. The hearing was not for another three weeks. Depending on the findings, she'd have to either move her business or close it up entirely. But she knew what they would find—she had been operating out of her home and even if she'd wanted to, there was no way to pretend otherwise. And then there were the fines—she had no idea how much they would be.

Christina sank down into her zebra-striped chair. She didn't have the money to pay rent on another space and continue to live here. If she had to assume the cost of an office, she'd have to move out and rent the garden apartment. Just the thought of someone else sitting amid the rosebushes or inhaling the lilac that was so lush in May made her heart constrict; she didn't think she could stand it. The only thing worse was the thought of actually selling the place. But right now, it looked like she didn't have a choice.

THIRTY-SIX

*T*he first thing Jordan did when she got home from ballet class was to peer into the kitchen garbage pail. Way down, underneath the crumpled paper towels and some other yucky stuff, she found two empty cookie boxes, the wrapper from a chocolate bar, and an empty container of Ben & Jerry's Heath Bar Crunch. Her mom was really powering through the sweets. And she was trying to hide it too—Jordan had never actually caught her in the act. Still, Jordan was an expert in eating espionage. She knew all about hiding what you'd eaten—and what you hadn't.

But it wasn't just the secret gorging that was bothering Jordan; it was her mom's *other* secret—her pregnancy. Even though she'd overheard her talking about it, she was having a hard time believing it. How could her *mom* be *pregnant*? The more evidence of her mother's bingeing she found, though, the more real it became.

She *so* did not want to deal with this and she went around and around in her mind, trying to figure out what to do. To-

day, while she was at the barre in ballet class, the answer came
to her. Oliver. She waited until she got home and then texted
him; she was in the kitchen now, waiting for his reply. And
when her phone made its anticipatory noise letting her know
a text had come in, she raced up the stairs to her room and
closed the door so she could read it in private.

R u kidding? Good 1. LOL. Jordan stared at the screen and
started typing furiously. *NOT kidding. This is 4 real. Do u think
he knows?* She waited and there was the reply. *NO!* While she
was figuring out what to say next, her phone buzzed.

"I don't believe it," Oliver said.

"Believe it."

"How can you be sure?"

"She was talking to a *doctor.*"

"A baby!" Oliver said after a pause. "Cool!"

"It's not a baby yet." She resisted adding, *you jerk.* "She
never said she's actually going to have it."

"You mean, you, like, *talked* to her about it?"

"No, but they were talking about an abortion."

"Oh."

"You sound disappointed."

"Well, not disappointed exactly, even though a baby might
be, like, fun."

"It's a *baby*, Oliver. Not a puppy. Anyway, if she's not telling your dad, someone has to."

"He's away."

"Where'd he go?"

"On a vacation. It's this male bonding sort of thing he does
with his best buds from college. He asked if I wanted to come
along. Yeah, right. He's going to be gone for another two days.
Maybe three. I forget."

"Can you call him and tell him?"

"Me? Are you crazy? I would *never* talk to my dad about something like this." He was quiet for a moment, but Jordan could hear him breathing. "But I know who would."

"Who's that?"

"My grandmother."

"You think so?"

"I *know* so."

"Oliver, you *have* to tell her."

"I will."

"Promise?" Why was this so important to her anyway?

"Promise."

"Okay, then. I'm *depending* on you."

They got off the phone. What if her mom went ahead and had this baby? What *if*? Jordan couldn't even begin to imagine it.

Oliver had not been anywhere near Morningside Grammar and Prep since his expulsion last fall. So when he rounded the corner and saw the familiar structure looming in front of him, he felt the dread rising like noxious little bubbles that seemed to swirl and burst above his head. A few days ago, for no reason that he could pinpoint, he'd decided to "borrow" his dad's Ray-Bans. And now he was so anxious about running into someone he knew—which was, like, practically the entire junior and senior class—that he'd worn them in an admittedly pathetic attempt at a disguise. But fortunately he didn't see anyone in front of the school. Ms. Konkel had said she would meet him at the side entrance, and look, there she was, waiting for him just like she'd promised. She was okay, she really was. The dread subsided just slightly.

"Oliver, it's good to see you," she said. "Let's go some-where we can talk privately."

"Fine by me," he said, falling into step beside her. They walked to a café on Columbus Avenue, sat down, and ordered an extra-large iced latte—for her—and a vanilla chai for him.

"So these pieces that you've been sending me, Oliver," she said, tearing open a package of sugar and pouring it into her froth-topped glass. "How many have there been?"

"Maybe, like, ten? Twelve? I haven't been keeping track."

"Seventeen. You sent me seventeen essays about what you've been doing since you left school. The volunteer work at the church. Preparing food, cleaning the church kitchen, working in the garden. The 'crazy dude' who shows up and how the community deals with him. Your new friendship with Liam. Summer." She stirred in the sugar, took a sip of her coffee, and tore open another packet. "I have to tell you I was impressed by what I read. Very impressed. Not just with the writing—which is excellent by the way—but with the think-ing behind the writing. Some of your observations—about people, and about yourself—are so sophisticated. I kept for-getting you were just a kid."

"Thanks. I, like, figured you'd understand." He looked down into his chai, not wanting her to see just how much her praise mattered.

"And I always did like *you*," she said, sucking the latte in through a straw. "I was so sorry when you were expelled. I even felt a little guilty."

"Guilty?" He looked up at her. *"Why?"*

"I just wished I had been more . . . attentive. Maybe if I had, I'd have seen that you were heading down a bad path. And I would have tried to do something to stop you."

"Hey, it wasn't your fault," he said. He sipped his chai, which was so hot it scalded his tongue. "I can't blame you—or anyone—for the stupid shit I did. And I can see now it was stupid."

"In the essay about Liam, you went into all that," she said eagerly. "I thought you handled it quite well."

"He told me that his school is so crowded that he has to carry his coat with him everywhere he goes because he doesn't have a locker. Lunch is at nine thirty in the morning. His Spanish teacher didn't remember his name; his trig teacher didn't even know he was in her class. And here I went to this school where, like, so much was done for me. But I blew it off. I just blew it off."

"Are you sorry?"

"Not exactly . . . Well, maybe, like, a little." He tried the chai again. Better now. "Yeah. I guess I am."

She grinned as if he'd given her the answer she'd been waiting for. "That's what I thought. So that's why I took the liberty of showing your essays to Mr. Cunningham."

"You did?" Oliver was surprised. "What did he say?"

"He was . . . impressed. So when I urged him to give you another chance, he said yes. With certain conditions, of course."

"Another chance? What do you mean?"

She leaned across the table. "A chance to come back to school in September," she said gently. "But no more cutting classes, failing tests, or even *thinking* about getting high. It wasn't easy to persuade Mr. Cunningham; don't blow it again."

"I don't know what to say."

"Say yes, Oliver," she told him. "Just say yes."

He leaned back in his chair. Had this been what he was

angling for when he'd sent her his writing? Secretly and deep down? He wasn't sure. But he was flooded with an incredible sense of accomplishment. Andy hadn't pulled any strings or used his position to impress, cajole, or intimidate anyone. He'd done this, for himself and by himself. His big-shot dad had nothing to do with it. "All right," he said. "I'm saying yes." He grinned at her, but really, in his mind, he saw his father's astonished, delighted expression when he told him the news.

Oliver just about floated up the street to the subway. Never mind that he'd hated Morningside when he had been a student there before. And never mind about what Konkel had said about basically being put on probation; he knew Cunningham would be, like, watching him, but he didn't care. He'd changed in these past months. Changed for the better. He wished he could tell his mom about it; he was sure that, like Ms. Konkel, she would understand. Well, he couldn't tell her; he didn't believe she was up in heaven or anywhere else watching him. That was a stupid-ass story for little kids. And morons.

Right now, he had no time to tell anyone, though. He had to head uptown to see his grandmother. When he got there, she wasn't home, so he parked himself on a bench near her apartment building and waited. It was a nice day—blue sky, hardly any clouds, plenty of sun. He saw three people walk by with dogs and thought, hey, he'd like to have dog too—a big dog he could take to Central Park and let run off the leash. He didn't know how his dad would feel about this but sensed that when he told him about Cunningham's offer, he'd have a bit of leverage. He'd go to, like, an animal shelter and—

"Oliver!"

He looked up. There was his grandmother in this wacky

straw hat and big black sunglasses. He realized he was still wearing his dad's Ray-Bans and wondered whether Andy had missed them by now. "Hey, Grandma."

"I wish I'd known you were coming. Have you been waiting long? At least it's a nice day; I'd hate to think of you sitting out here in the rain. Did you have lunch? Let's go upstairs and I'll make you lunch." She delivered all this without waiting for him to reply. But he followed her up to her apartment, where she parked him at the kitchen table while she busied herself with making the grilled cheese. Then she set his sandwich—a celery stalk and pickle slices arranged neatly on the side—on the place mat. Oliver picked up one of the triangular halves. "Like last time," he said. He hadn't realized just how hungry he'd been until he took a bite.

"Last time?" She bit into a celery stick with a crunch.

"The last time I came up here by myself. Remember?"

"Oh yes," she said. "I remember." She chewed her celery thoughtfully. "You were in trouble back then. Are you in trouble now?"

"No," he said, thinking of Ms. Konkel, of Cunningham, and how the news would go down with his father. "I'm actually not. But my dad is. Only he doesn't know it yet."

"What," she said, putting down the celery stick, "are you talking about?"

THIRTY-SEVEN

*A*ndy gazed out over the azure water, squinting against the glare. Before he'd left, he'd searched all over the apartment for his favorite Ray-Bans. They failed to turn up and even though he'd been to three stores since arriving here in Miami, he hadn't found a pair he liked as much. Well, he'd just have to settle for some other style; he didn't want to spend a day on the boat without sunglasses.

"Hey, buddy." Andy turned, and there was Joey holding an outsized mug. "How did you sleep?"

"Like the dead," Andy answered. "Any more of that coffee?"

"Plenty," Joey said. "Come inside and I'll fix you a cup."

Andy followed Joey inside the condo. There were no signs of their other two college pals, Mark and Gavin; they must have still been asleep. The four of them had been getting together annually—just the guys, no girlfriends or wives—since their graduation, and though Andy had missed a couple of years during Rachel's illness and after, he was glad to be back in the fold again. He loved these guys, he really did; they went *way* back.

Joey handed him the steaming mug. "Any milk or sugar in that?" He still had the thick, dark hair Andy remembered, only now he kept it more closely cropped and little strands of gray had begun to show at the temples.

"Black's just fine." Andy sipped. Not as strong as he liked.

"So it's fishing out on the boat today?"

"Fishing sounds great," Andy said. "As long as there's no cell phone or Internet reception."

Joey shot him a look. "Got it." He pulled a banana from a bunch on the counter. "You must have been . . . deluged."

"One hundred and twelve e-mails, almost as many texts, phone messages . . . It was *insane.*" *It* was that god-awful tabloid cover showing Xiomara pressed up against him in a kiss. How the hell had the photographer even gotten into the building? Distracted or bribed the doorman? Posed as a UPS delivery guy? Whatever the method, the resulting avalanche of attention had been immediate. He'd spent a crazy day attempting triage, and then gave up. Instead, he concocted a formal statement, instructed Joanne to disseminate it, and packed his bag for Miami.

In years past, the guys had met in a lodge in upstate New York, a cabin on a lake in Michigan, rented houses in Montauk, Cape May, and Vermont. They'd been so tight in college that even though they'd veered off in wholly different directions— Joey in real estate, Mark a patents lawyer, Gavin a wine importer—he still felt they were like family.

"So was she as hot as she looks?" Joey asked, sipping his coffee.

Andy wanted to tell Joey that it wasn't like that, not at all.

That the moment she'd stopped being a fantasy, everything had felt off-kilter, and wrong. But just then Mark walked into the room, followed by Gavin, and Joey, the self-designated chef, decided to make banana pancakes and the conversation moved on. Mark, who had definitely put on weight, ate three helpings of the pancakes; Gavin and Joey ribbed him about that. Mark wadded up a napkin and would have pitched it at Joey, but Andy caught it before it reached its destination and said, "Hey guys, we're not in college anymore."

After breakfast, they slathered on sunscreen and added hats. Then they piled into the rental car and drove over the causeway to the marina, where they had rented a fishing boat—and its captain, John Barker—for the day. Boarding the boat, Andy turned off his phone's ringer. He wouldn't get reception out here anyway, but it felt good to actively disengage; disengaging did not come easily to him. He'd left ample backup—and backup for that backup—for his patients, and he knew of no imminent crises on the horizon. They'd be okay for a couple of days without him. And he figured he'd even be okay without them. He had not had a vacation since Rachel died and he was seriously overdue.

If the glare had been bright from the condo's balcony, it was all the more intense out on the glittering expanse of open water, but fortunately Gavin had come up with an extra pair of sunglasses. Gavin had always been like that: the caretaker, Mr. Fix-It; he just knew what you needed and managed to get it for you.

There was a breeze out here, brisk and bracing, and the wavelets that lapped at the prow of the boat seemed jittery in their motion. Mark had told him that down below there was an air-conditioned stateroom with a color television, a stereo, and couches. But Andy had no interest in any of that. He wanted to be here, in the open air and overlooking the wide stretch of water.

Joey came up beside him as he leaned over the boat's railing. He was a big guy, but solid. In college he'd lifted weights and it looked like he still did. "She'd still like to meet you," he said. When Andy looked blank, he added, "Julia. I told you about her—she works in my office. Super-nice woman—you'd like her."

"I've been busy . . . ," Andy said.

"Busy, my ass," Joey said. "You're just stalling. What gives?"

"I don't know," Andy said. "There was this woman I was seeing for a while. . . ."

"That sexy blonde—Jen?"

"No, that fell apart. This was someone different. And I really thought it was going to work out. But I was wrong."

"That's why you have to get out there again, Andy, man. You can't sit around moping."

"I'm not moping—"

"Hey, I think I've got a bite," called Mark. Andy was grateful for the diversion; they all turned to watch Mark struggle in the fighting chair as he attempted to reel in the fish.

"Looks like a big son of a bitch," Gavin said.

"It sure does," said Joey.

"Easy, now," said the captain. "Easy does it." He walked over to Mark. "You want to tire him out first," John said. "He's not going to give up without a fight." Mark tightened his grip on the rod; Gavin and Joey gathered around. But Andy turned away and walked to the prow.

The breeze had picked up and seemed to be tossing the

clouds around the sky; the water shimmered up at him, a deep, inviting blue. Gulls flew overhead, squawking and flapping their wings. Andy heard the shouts of his friends coming from the stern—*You've got it, you've got it. Don't let go. He's a feisty bastard*—and John's calmer, authoritative voice cutting through it all.

Talking to Joey about Christina brought her back. He thought of that night in East Hampton: the walk down to the shore with the bag of squirming lobsters, the thrill of their release, and then the kiss as the waves eddied around their bare feet. He was filled with a rush of longing. *Had* he made the right choice? He remembered that day in the hospital—how he'd felt perpetually judged and wanted to hit back. And she *had* said she was sorry—

A roar from the stern made him turn around just in time to see Mark reeling it in: a silver, shimmering tuna, flopping in the sun.

"Way to go!" said Joey.

"Not bad," added Gavin. He turned to the captain. "Can we measure him?"

"Photo op," said Mark, standing proudly with his catch. "Can you guys stop talking and take some pictures already?" The fish was measured, photographed, exclaimed over, gutted, cleaned, and packed in the cooler.

"Here's your dinner, guys," said Joey, patting the cooler, "and maybe even your breakfast too."

They ate the lunch they had brought, drank beer, and caught up on one another's lives. Mark's oldest kid was going to be a senior at Princeton; Gavin's wine business was expanding; Joey had just closed a major, multimillion-dollar deal on a commercial property. "Can you believe that it's been twenty-six years since we graduated?" said Joey. "It's gone by in a blink."

"I hate to break it to you guys," said the captain, who looked to be about seventy, "but the next twenty-six are going to go by even faster."

"That calls for a drink," said Gavin, opening another beer. He reached into the cooler and started passing out the bottles. Soon the sun began to sink on the water, and the sky streaked pink, orange, and an intense, slatelike blue. Andy glanced down at his arms, which, despite the sunscreen, had gotten some color. He was still nursing his first and only beer of the day. He hadn't caught anything, but he didn't care. The camaraderie of his old friends had been a balm and he'd felt his equilibrium had been restored. No matter what that headline said, he hadn't succumbed to Xiomara, hadn't compromised himself, or her faith in him. The picture caught a moment taken out of context and the words were all just a pack of lies.

Driving back to the condo, Joey put the radio on, very loud. Mick Jagger's rendition of "Just My Imagination" filled the car and though Andy wasn't really a Rolling Stones fan, he let the music wash over him. Gavin started singing along and then Mark joined in; it was hard to tell who was more off-key. Andy did not sing but thought of Christina, and how they had sung their way through the downpour. Should he call her when he got back? Just to see how she was doing? Or should he move ahead and agree to meet this Julia that Joey was campaigning for?

Back in his room at the condo, Andy switched on his phone. There were sixteen messages. Sixteen. Jesus Christ. *More* fallout from that damn picture? His mood soured. But then he saw that they were all from a single caller: his mother.

Fear was like a kick in the chest. He called her immediately. "Ma?" he said when she answered. "Ma, are you okay?"

"Oh, Andy! Finally! I've been trying to reach you all day."

"I was out fishing with the guys. No reception." He didn't want to tell her that he'd turned the ringer off.

"Well, I'm so glad I got you. You have to come home now. Immediately. Or else she's going to have the procedure."

"Procedure? What are you talking about?"

"That woman you were dating, Christina."

"Christina! What does this have to do with her?"

"She's pregnant, don't you see? Only she's thinking of having an abortion and if you don't come home immediately, you may be too late and oh, Andy, that would be terrible, wouldn't it? I mean if she had the abortion?"

"Would you please slow down?" His own heart was galloping. "How do you know she's pregnant and considering an abortion? And why didn't she tell me herself?"

"That picture, you know, that nasty picture? She thought you had taken up with that singer and didn't want her anymore."

"She knows me better than that," he said. But then he thought, *Does she?* And if she didn't, whose fault was it? He was the one who had said they were through. His mother was still talking, explaining what Jordan had heard and then told Oliver, who'd told her—

"I've got to think about this," he interrupted. "I'll call you back when I've figured out what I'm going to do." He clicked off and went into the kitchen. Gavin was tearing lettuce for a salad and Joey was outside on the balcony grilling the fish. He felt dazed and disoriented. *Pregnant, she was pregnant.* The formerly neat pieces of his life were now scattered, helter-skelter, all around him. "We're out of beer," said Gavin, looking over at Andy. "Go get a six-pack? And while you're out, you could get some ice cream too."

"Beer and ice cream," said Andy. "Sure."

He left the condo and went in search of a convenience store. The streets of South Beach had a festive, Mardi Gras quality. Hordes of young people, many in couples, swirled past the low, pastel-colored buildings and the palm trees swayed in the mild breeze. He passed cafés, bars, restaurants, but no place to buy beer, so he kept walking. Just a little while ago, on the boat, he'd been thinking about Christina, missing her—and now the news of the pregnancy. Could it be a sign, a marker that would point his life in a new direction? He told his mother he would get in touch with her. But what the hell would he say? And would she even listen? He continued along, no longer paying attention to the people around him. "Watch *out*, dude," said a very tanned young guy with an equally tanned girl on his arm. "You *hit* me."

"Sorry," Andy muttered. Until the breakup, he had fantasized about marrying Christina; he loved her, he wanted her, and he knew she loved and wanted him. Oliver loved her too. Yeah, Jordan was a pain, but he could win her over—look, she'd even shown up at his office to apologize. Andy had actually gone as far as thinking about how they might blend their lives—a new apartment big enough for all of them, maybe even a weekend house in the Hamptons, so Christina could have a real garden. But having a baby had never been a part of that vision. Diapers, sleepless nights—could he do all that again?

"Hey man!" said a tall Latino guy. "You just plowed

right into me." Andy offered an apology and skulked off. Finally he spied a place to buy the beer and he went in. Back outside, he turned and retraced his steps, trying not to slam into anyone. When he walked in, the grilled fish was laid out on a platter. There was a salad in a glass bowl and another bowl of saffron rice. "Finally!" said Mark. "We've been waiting for you."

"Yeah, the food's getting cold," said Joey.

"Here's the beer." Andy began putting the bottles on the table.

"What about the ice cream?" Gavin asked.

"Damn—I forgot."

"No ice cream?" asked Mark. He looked disappointed.

"Sorry," Andy said, sinking into his seat.

"*You* don't need ice cream anyway," Joey said, poking his midsection. "You're getting soft, Mark. Soft and fat."

"All right, all right. Let's eat already." Mark began passing the food around.

"Andy, what's wrong?" Gavin asked quietly. "You look rattled. Off. Did something happen?"

"She's pregnant," Andy blurted out. Damn, he hadn't meant to say it like that.

Gavin, Mark, and Joey exchanged looks, but it was Gavin who spoke. "Who's pregnant?"

"That woman I was dating all winter."

"What woman?" Gavin said. "How come none of us have ever met her?"

"Well, you won't get to either. We broke up."

"I'm not following this," said Mark. "You've split with her, but she's knocked up? How do you even know it's yours?"

"Trust me, it's mine," Andy said.

"What's going to happen?" asked Joey.

"Damned if I know."

"Have you talked to her?" Gavin asked. When Andy shook his head no, Gavin said, "You've *got* to talk to her. Now." Still Mr. Fix-It.

Andy took out his phone and stood. "Go on—start eating," he said. He went into his room and shut the door. There was no answer when he tried Christina, but instead of going back to report to his friends, he made another call. Then he returned to the table. "I'm going to have to cut this trip short," he said. "I just changed my ticket; I'm flying back to New York first thing tomorrow."

"Good move," said Gavin. "I'll drive you to the airport in the morning."

"We'll all go," said Joey. "Won't we, guys?"

Andy's flight was not very crowded and he was able to stretch out a bit; since he'd barely slept the night before, he sank into a deep sleep almost immediately. He dreamed of small, helpless creatures: mice, kittens, a litter of piglets. When he woke, he felt clearer than he had since he'd gotten the news about the pregnancy. It *was* a sign. An unequivocal sign. Christina was pregnant and he did not want her to end the pregnancy. No, he wanted her to have the baby, and he wanted to be there when she did. It would mean a huge change in his well-ordered life, but he—no, *they*—would handle it. They belonged together.

The flight attendant appeared with a small container of juice; how had she known how thirsty he was? Although it was warm, overly sweet, and essentially flavorless, it went down like it was nectar from the gods. *A baby,* he thought. *Our baby.* He just had to hope she would see it the same way. As soon as he touched down at LaGuardia, he tried her again. Still no answer, but this time he left a message. *I need to see you as soon as possible,* he said. *Please.*

THIRTY-EIGHT

Kneeling in the dirt, Christina carefully dug around the roots of her rosebushes and patted the dark, coarse coffee grounds into the soil. The grounds lightened the soil around the bushes, making it easier for the roots to grow. And they attracted worms, which aerated and loosened the soil still more, so that the roses were able to get additional oxygen and water. Although the roses themselves were fairly ordinary—a common shade of pink, rambling, blossoms of no particular rarity or beauty—their smell was unusually strong, dizzying at moments, and she cultivated them tenderly for that and the fact that her mother had planted them; Aunt Barb had told her so.

Finally, she straightened up. It was early—not even seven—but she'd been waking before six these days, unable to stay asleep or in bed once the morning light had broken. She had taken to coming out here to putter in the garden, engaging in the small, satisfying chores that distracted her from the decision that was looming: she'd rescheduled the abortion for this coming Tuesday though she honestly did not know whether she'd be able to go through with it. Believing that a woman had the right to choose whether to abort her fetus was a different matter from undergoing it herself. She and Will had dreamed of having at least two if not three more babies—both had been somewhat isolated only children and wanted their own children to have a very different sort of life. Will's early death had derailed those plans.

Now life was handing her a surprise gift: a baby when she had least expected one. It would be an enormous undertaking, having a child alone. How would it affect her work, her life, and her daughter? She could not predict. But she did have an ace up her sleeve, one that she had not told anyone about—yet. She had fished out Pratyush Singh's card and left it in the center of her desk. The sum he offered—for *Mira's whim*—was life changing. If she took it, her financial troubles would be over. She could find an apartment in the neighborhood and rent a storefront for her business. The beloved house in which she had grown up would be sold, but she would still have her daughter—and her baby.

She went back into the kitchen, where she made herself a cup of herbal tea—her usual latte felt too scouring right now—and then took a quick shower. Andy would be here at nine o'clock; she wanted to be ready when he arrived. She would tell him today, of course. No more procrastinating. Even if she did decide to have the abortion, he deserved to know.

Finding something to wear was not a simple matter. Most of her summer clothes were now too tight, but deep in the recesses of her closet, Christina was able to locate a loose-fitting caftan that she usually wore as a cover-up at the beach. When she added her silver bracelet and a pair of leather sandals, she decided she looked presentable enough. Though presentable enough for *what*, she was not sure. Andy had not said where they were going, only that he would be there with his car and that he wanted to take a short drive. That was another mystery. No one else was home. Why did they need to go somewhere?

Before she went back downstairs, she stopped in Jordan's room. As usual, the bed was neatly made and the room was immaculate. The only place where order did not reign was the rabbit cage; the two animals had strewn straw through the wire mesh and onto the floor, and Christina saw that they had upset the food bowl as well. She peered in to have a closer look. The mother rabbit eyed her suspiciously, though the daughter—the pure soft gray of a chinchilla and the same size as her parent—seemed more receptive. Although she had never told Jordan, she didn't like the rabbits. But she slipped a finger in to touch the gray rabbit's head anyway. Under the fur, the bones of the skull felt alarmingly fragile.

The bell downstairs sounded. Andy was here. Turning from the rabbits, she left the room and took the stairs slowly and carefully; she did not want to trip. There was a moment of hesitation as she stood before the door and then, in a single decisive motion, she pulled it open. He looked good, all tan and even more muscled than she remembered. His eyes scanned her face—anxiously, she thought—and he did not say anything right away.

"So," she said, breaking the silence. "You wanted to see me."

"I did," he said. "And I hope you wanted to see me."

She didn't reply. "I'd invite you in, but you seemed so insistent on taking a drive."

"It's such a nice day," he said. "And I thought the car would be a good place to talk. No distractions."

"All right," she said. Though how many distractions would there have been in her empty house? "Give me a minute." She left him standing there while she went to collect her purse. Everything seemed so stilted and wrong between them; maybe whatever there had been was not meant to last.

"I like your dress," he said when she returned. "It makes you look . . . exotic."

Was this a compliment? She wasn't sure, but followed him to the car and slid in the seat beside him. She had not a clue as to where they were headed, and was puzzled when he got onto the Brooklyn-Queens Expressway.

"How have you been?" she asked. Oh, this was so awkward. The unmentioned pregnancy obliterated every other conversational gambit; she was reduced to the most inane sort of small talk.

"Pretty well. Busy as usual, though I was in Florida for a few days."

"Florida?"

"Every year I spend some time with my old gang from college. This year we picked South Beach."

So he had not been with that singer. She was surprised at how relieved this made her.

"How about you?" He turned to look at her.

"Fine," she lied. She could not meet his gaze.

Another silence settled over them; Christina was so uncomfortable she wanted to leap from the car at the next light. She knew what she needed to tell him; why was it so hard? He seemed like a stranger: impervious and remote. Now they were on the Long Island Expressway. Maybe he was planning

to take her out to the Hamptons for the day. "Andy, aren't you
going to tell me where we're going?" she said finally.

"Does it matter?"

"Well, I guess not, but I was just wondering, that's all."

He said nothing and she stared at his profile as he kept his
gaze on the road ahead. They were in Long Island now and
she began to pay attention to the road signs.

"Are we going to Great Neck?" she asked.

"I thought we would," he said.

"Oh." She was puzzled. "Is there a particular reason why?"

"Because that's where we met," he said. "At Angelica's
wedding. Remember?"

As if she could have forgotten. But all she said was, "I haven't
been in touch with Angelica in a while. I wonder how she is."

"She's doing really well. Terrific, in fact." He waited a beat.
"I just spoke to her last week. She's pregnant."

"So am I," Christina said. There! She had done it. Now it
was Andy's turn to say something. Surely he would stop the
car, turn to look at her, and—what? Take her in his arms? Ask
if it was his? Either scenario seemed possible.

Instead he said simply, "I know."

"What?" she cried. "Since when? Who told you? Why
didn't you *say* anything?"

"I've known for a couple of days. Jordan found out and
told Oliver, who told my mother. And then my mother
told me."

"Did she also tell you that I've scheduled an abortion for
this coming Tuesday?"

Andy glided the car to a stop in front of a sign that read
VILLAGE GREEN AND ROSE GARDEN.

"Yes," he said. "She did. And she told me to get home right

away so I could stop you. Which is exactly what I'm trying to do."

"Your *mother* said this?" She knew how much Ida disapproved of her.

"She did. She wants you to have the baby and for us to get back together. The baby is a sign, don't you see?"

"A sign?" She was wary. "Of what?"

"A sign that we really are meant to be." He took her in his arms, but when he tried to kiss her, she turned away. Even without looking at him, she could imagine the confusion on his face. The hurt too.

"I'm not so sure," she said.

"*You're* not so sure?" he said. "That's not what you said when we broke up."

"*We* didn't break up; you broke up with me."

"I was an idiot. A jerk. Also, impulsive, hasty, and a jackass. As usual."

"I know," she said. "Which is why I decided you were right about us. That we really don't belong together. I don't think I could stand a life with your . . . moods, Andy. I've had enough of that in my life." When he didn't answer, she continued. "And what about you and that . . . singer? I haven't even *mentioned* that."

"You saw that ridiculous picture."

"It looked pretty convincing to me."

"Xiomara is my patient. That's all."

"Is that how you act with all your patients? Especially the ones that can call you any time of the day or night."

"*She* kissed *me*," he said. "It was a bad time for her and she thought that was the answer. But it wasn't."

Christina said nothing. Could she allow herself to believe

that he'd changed his mind about the two of them, and that he actually wanted her to have this baby? "So why did you bring me here?" Looking out the window, she saw cluster upon cluster of roses, some just coming into bloom, others open and at their fragrant, ephemeral peak.

"Because this is where we met and this is where I thought I should propose." From his pocket he withdrew a small, velvet-covered box. "Will you marry me, Christina?" She looked down at the box but didn't answer. "Aren't you going to look inside?"

She opened the box. There was a gold ring with a ruby at its center; the ruby was surrounded by a circle of tiny seed pearls. The ring was clearly an antique; the stone and workmanship were exquisite. She let herself admire it before she closed the box again.

"Don't you like it?" He sounded so miserable. "I knew you wouldn't want a diamond, so she steered me toward this."

"She?"

"Jordan. I asked her to help me pick it out."

"Jordan helped *you* to choose a ring for *me*? In what alternate universe did this happen?"

He smiled. "She said she thought you would love it."

"It's very beautiful."

"Then you're saying—"

"No, Andy. I'm saying no." She handed him the box and, unable to look at him, kept her eyes on the riot of roses outside. Through the scrim of her tears, they began to melt and blur. "I'd like you to drive me home, please," she added. "Unless you'd rather I took the train."

The ride back to Brooklyn was silent and miserable. She did not look at Andy once, and kept her eyes trained on the view out the window, though she did not register one thing that they passed. When they reached her house, she got out without a word. And without a word, Andy started the car and drove away. She did not cry, because she would not let herself. Instead, she went into her office where Singh's card waited patiently on her desk.

"Ms. Connelly," he fairly purred when he answered. "I had a feeling I'd be hearing from you."

THIRTY-NINE

*I*da had not been on the subway in a very long time and marveled at how different everything was. No more tokens—just flimsy blue and yellow things called MetroCards. No token booths either, but plenty of ATM-like machines at which to buy the cards. The train she boarded was new, shiny, and it was so cold she wished she'd brought along a warmer jacket. But it was also very fast and soon she was in Brooklyn, emerging from the station at Grand Army Plaza and consulting the directions she'd gotten from Oliver. She could have taken a car service of course; Andy paid for all her trips by car. But this was a trip Andy did not authorize and she didn't feel right about taking his money for it. No one could ever accuse Ida Stern of being a *schnorrer*.

The streets of this unfamiliar neighborhood in late spring were lovely: brownstone and limestone houses side by side, mature trees, flowers in urns, window boxes, and planters. In another mood, she would have stopped to linger, but today she had a mission. An urgent mission. It was the unborn baby.

The baby that belonged to her son and that this Christina person might actually abort. To Ida, the loss of this baby would be a fresh sorrow heaped upon so many past sorrows. She didn't think her old heart could stand it.

There had been another lost baby, decades ago, fathered by Jurgi, the boy who lived across the road. He'd been her best friend for years, like a brother, until they'd been hurriedly married and practically shoved into a room alone together after the wedding. "Do you know what we're supposed to do?" he had whispered, suspecting, correctly as it turned out, that their parents were listening anxiously at the door.

"Not really," she had answered, knowing she should be more nervous than she was, but this was Jurgi and how could she be nervous with Jurgi? They did not figure out what they were supposed to do that night, or the night after that. But on the third night, he came into the room at Ida's house that they were now told was theirs looking very serious. "I understand now," he said to her. "My father explained it all to me."

"Why do you look so sad?" she said.

"Because you're not going to like it."

"No?" she asked.

"No." He turned out the light and began to unbutton his pajama top. When he saw her sitting there without moving, he said, "You too."

"Do I have to?" She and Jurgi had swum and played naked at the pond just outside their town, but that had been years ago. Her body had changed since then. So had his.

"Yes." The sound of his voice, so sad and grown-up, had made Ida afraid for the first time. But she took off the white, embroidered nightgown she wore and did as he asked. She did not cry out loud because she did not want to hurt his

feelings. He knew anyway, and used his hand to rub at the
tears that leaked from the corners of her eyes. "I'm sorry," he
said into her hair. "So sorry."

Nine months later, she delivered a fat, beautiful baby boy
with butter blond ringlets and blue stars for eyes. They called
him Petras, and they all doted on him. "He'll be the one to
save you," Ida's mother had predicted. "You'll see. He'll save
us all." But she was wrong. Jurgi and his parents were deported first, sent away on a train belching smoke and crammed
with anxious, fearful people. Ida and her family went next.
Handing little Petras over to the guard had been the worst
moment in Ida's life; she would have collapsed had it not been
for her mother's firm grip just under her elbow. "Give him the
cap and the socks," her mother said in an unfamiliar, steely
voice. Ida did as she was told. Petras looked startled; then he
smiled, his chubby little hand reaching for a brass button on
the guard's coat.

For years afterward, Ida allowed herself to think that her
boy had been saved, shielded by his gold hair and blue eyes.
Some barren German woman, longing for a child, would
claim him, and call him her own. She'd rename him—Franz
or Albrecht or even Adolf. Ida didn't care as long as he was
alive, somewhere. Every year on his birthday, she'd open the
grayed, tattered birth certificate she'd folded and tucked in her
shoe and kept against all odds at the camp, even though she'd
been so hungry at times she'd been tempted to eat it. She
would trace the letters of his name, and hers and Jurgi's too.
Jurgi was dead, along with the rest of his family and hers. She
was the only one to survive the war.

Afterward, she'd been sent to a DP camp in Belgium where
she'd met a man who, like her, had lost everyone. They had

married ten days later, and gone first to Cuba and eventually New York. He'd been a bitter, haunted soul, though who in those years was not? Ida thought that a baby would change things. But year after year went by and no baby came. It was because she gave the other one away, she told herself. She was being punished. Then, when she had all but given up, it happened. She was not young anymore; she was almost forty, with gray-threaded hair and little creases pinching her mouth. When the baby came, she felt like she got it all back—her youth, her hope, her belief in a future that did not include the past. Her husband—he didn't see it that way. He resented the baby. Resented the crying, the diapers, the broken sleep, but more than that too. He resented that Ida loved the baby so much. More than she loved him; she could admit it now. Much more. They fought, and then they didn't even care enough to fight. When he left, she was almost glad. Now she would have her boy all to herself.

Ida looked at the slip of paper she carried. Here was the house. It was made of brick, and very handsome, though she could see that the steps leading to the double doors were not in good repair. But the window boxes, like miniature gardens, were the prettiest on the block and the Japanese maple in front was as graceful as a girl. *This is it.* She had to compose herself before she rang the bell; so much depended on this meeting. A door opened and she froze: she did not want to be caught on the street this way. But the lithe young person that skittered down the stairs and up the street did not even notice her. Her hair was pulled into a tight bun and she carried a big, bulging bag over her shoulder. She climbed the hill that Ida had just descended in what seemed like seconds. That must have been the daughter Andy had mentioned. A *shayne maidele* too. But here she was procrastinating when she had important work to do. The house, she saw, had two entrances. One was the pair of doors from which the girl had just emerged. The other was below the steps. *Up or down?* she asked herself. The girl had come from above, so she decided she would try there first. Grasping the black iron railing, Ida mounted the stairs.

Christina was on the parlor floor, in her showroom—though not for much longer—when the bell sounded. She rarely had visitors at this entrance; her clients and friends, along with UPS, FedEx, and the mailmen, knew to ring the downstairs bell. "Excuse me," she said to the two men whose loft in Red Hook she was redoing. "I'll be right back." She left the couple to inspect the pair of Eames chairs they were considering to answer the door.

"Can I help you?" Christina was sure that the small, older woman, dressed in a China blue linen suit, had the wrong house.

"I'm Ida Stern," the woman said. In her hand she clutched a taupe leather handbag made in a style that had been popular at least forty years ago. "Andy's mother."

"Oh!" Christina had not recognized her at first. "Please come in." She stepped back to allow Ida to enter. "I'm with some clients right now, but will you wait for me? I won't be long." Ida followed her down the stairs and allowed herself to be seated at the kitchen table. She refused offers of iced tea, coffee, juice, or lemonade, though she finally did accept the glass of club soda—she called it seltzer—that Christina put in front of her.

"You go back upstairs," she said, taking a small, demure sip. "I'm perfectly fine right here."

Christina was rattled when she returned to her clients.

Rob, the more effusive half of the couple, was enthusiastic about the chairs; his partner, Greg, less so. "It's the color," he said, rubbing the leather as if the pressure of his fingers could somehow change it. Ordinarily, Christina would have done a little pitch for the chairs, explaining their significance in terms of midcentury design, their relatively reasonable price, and their undeniably excellent condition.

Today, she only nodded and said, "Why don't you two talk it over and get back to me in a few days? Maybe I'll have some other options to show you by then."

"That's a good idea," Greg said. Rob looked disappointed, but he followed his partner out. Christina abstained from expelling the huge sigh she had been holding in her lungs until the door closed behind them.

Now she had to deal with Andy's mother. For a change, she wasn't nauseated, but her face felt sticky and she was sure her hair was a mess, so she ducked into the bathroom to freshen up. What she would say to the older woman was an utter mystery to her. After the weeks of pining for Andy in the wake of their breakup, Christina's refusal of his proposal was as surprising to her as it was to Stephen when she'd told him. "But, girl, this is the answer to all your troubles. Marriage, baby, new life with the doctor hubby." He ticked them all off on his fingers. "Looks good from where I sit."

"We'll make each other miserable," she had said. "We'll fight all the time. Or, if not, I'll be walking on eggshells, always anticipating the next explosion. Like my father."

"So that's what's behind this," Stephen said. "Well, I think you're wrong. Andy Stern is not your dad. And you're not your mother. When he gets out of line, you'll tell him. That's what couples—strong couples anyway—do for each other."

"I don't want to have to police him," she said.

"Think of it as being a guide and a partner. You'll be his better half and all that."

"Stephen, who knew you were so old-fashioned?" She had not told him about her secret plan, her safety net; she just couldn't bear to yet and she fervently hoped he would not feel betrayed when she did.

The zoning board had given her a little grace period to wrap up her business in the house and she was taking it. Today's two clients might be the last ones she would see here. The money from the sale would pay the fine, the relocation, the apartment—everything wrapped up in one tidy, neat package. Now all she had to do was tell everyone in her life about it.

While she waited, Ida looked around. With its blue and white plates hung on the walls and sizable collection of yellow mixing bowls, the kitchen was an orderly, welcoming place. Through the window she saw a sliver of the garden; Andy had told her Christina liked to grow things. She would make a good wife for him, this *shiksa* with her bowls and her flowers. A good wife and a good stepmother for Oliver. And as for the baby she carried . . . Ida had to tamp down the elation she felt about that; it would not help her case if she appeared too emotional or desperate. She finished her seltzer and got up to put her glass in the sink. She noticed a collection of tarnished candlesticks sitting alongside it. Next to them sat a pile of rags and various kinds of polish. The candlesticks were mostly brass, but a lone silver example caught her attention and she picked it up to examine it more closely. It was fairly short, and had two rounded sections, so that it looked like the body of a woman. A pattern of incised lines, some like semicircles, covered much of it. Ida's mother had owned a similar pair of candlesticks; Ida remembered them from her girlhood. They had been a wedding gift to her parents, and unlike the brass candlesticks that her mother used every Shabbas, the silver ones were only brought out on the most special occasions. "They'll be for you one day, *tochter*," her mother used to say, one hand gripping the candlestick and the other busily polishing until the surface gleamed, moon-bright. "When you get married." Well, her mother had not given them to her when she married Jurgi, but Ida had understood, even without being told, why. That wedding was not the joyful union of two souls, sanctioned by their community and their faith. Her marriage to Jurgi was a desperate act; survival, not happiness, had been its goal.

Funny how familiar the weight and shape of this candlestick felt in her hands; she could have been back in her parents' house, setting the table for a holiday dinner, her mother's cross-stitched tablecloth starched as crisp as paper laid on the table. Look, here was a little nick at the base. One of her mother's candlesticks had had such a nick; it happened when her mother had dropped it on the stone floor in the kitchen. She'd never forgiven herself for that and always said she was going to take it to a silversmith in the city to have it fixed. Ida turned the candlestick over. There was something engraved on the bottom, but she could not make it out because of the tarnish. Curious, she took one of the rags, soaked it with a bit of the silver polish, and began to rub.

When she'd rubbed the spot clean, she peered down to read the engraving: too small—she would need her glasses. She brought the candlestick back to the table and fished them from her pocketbook. Now she could see. The words were in

Lithuanian, a language she had not read in decades. But that did not matter: she knew them by heart.

For Chana and Yossel on the occasion of their wedding
25 September 1926

The candlestick, her mother's candlestick, dropped with a clatter and rolled across the floor. Christina came hurrying into the room and picked it up. "Is everything all right?" she asked.

"That candlestick," Ida croaked. "Where did you get it?"

Christina looked down at the candlestick in her hand, and then back at Ida's face. Under the two spots of blush on her cheeks, she had gone alarmingly pale. "Let me get you some water," Christina said, setting the candlestick down.

"No, I'm fine," said Ida. "I just had a jolt, that's all."

"From this?" Christina gestured to the candlestick.

Ida nodded. "May I?" she asked.

Christina handed it back to her.

Ida turned it over and pointed to the engraved letters and what appeared to be a date. "You see?"

"I see, but I don't understand," Christina said.

"This candlestick. It's one of a pair that belonged to my mother. I thought it looked familiar, but when I saw the engraving, I was sure."

"That's astonishing." Christina went to the drawer for a magnifying glass so she could see more clearly.

"Where did you get it?" Ida asked again.

"In an auction. With the rest of those." She gestured to the group by the sink. "I think they threw it in because it had lost its mate; that compromises the value, at least for some people."

"Not for me," Ida said, fingers reverently following the curves of the thing.

Christina was silent. She had always understood the secret language of objects—they could be totems, evidence, idols, or talismans. This candlestick was something else, though; it was a witness to the past. "I want you to have it," she said when they were both seated at the table. "It's yours." She nudged the candlestick in Ida's direction.

Ida shook her head. "No. Keep it and marry my son. I would have given it to him anyway." When Christina didn't reply, Ida continued. "He's heartbroken that you turned him down."

"I still love him," said Christina when she finally spoke. "But we wouldn't be happy. And didn't you tell Andy to break up with me? Because I'm not Jewish?"

"I did." Ida folded her hands in front of her on the table. Her nails were lacquered crimson. "But that was before I knew about the baby." She paused. "A baby changed everything for me. And it will for you."

"What are you talking about?" Christina asked.

"Years and years ago, I had a baby, a baby that was supposed to save me. His father was my best friend and playmate; our parents were told that people with children weren't being deported, so they saw to it that we had . . . a child."

"And you did?"

"Yes," said Ida. "We did. But that was a lie. We were deported anyway."

"What about the baby?" Christina asked. She didn't know if she could stand to hear the answer.

"No, not the baby. He was . . . killed. There. I've never said it out loud. For so many years I believed he was somewhere else, somewhere safe. But there *was* nowhere that was safe—at least not for him."

"Andy doesn't know this, does he?"

Ida looked deep into her eyes. "No. Why should he?" When Christina didn't reply, she added, "*He* was my miracle baby, not the other one. God gave him to me when I had abandoned hope; he saved me. Now you have a chance for a miracle too, don't you see? Have this baby; it will give you a new life: a husband, a family."

"I'm going to keep the baby," said Christina. She'd known that all along but hadn't been brave enough to admit it to herself.

"And what about Andy?"

Christina shook her head no. "But he can see the baby if he wants. And you too. I won't shut you out."

"Thank you," Ida said. "Thank you very much." She stood, clutching her pocketbook to her chest.

If Christina had thought Ida would cajole or beg, she was wrong. "Take the candlestick." She stood as well. "Please."

"No," Ida said. "It's for the baby. Something you can give him or her after I'm gone."

After Ida left, Christina polished the remainder of the candlestick. What an extraordinary coincidence that it had come all the way from Lithuania to her kitchen in Brooklyn, only to be recognized by its original owner—an owner who then refused to take it back. She would never sell it, not at auction and not to the client whose mantelpiece she was looking to adorn. No, she would do what Ida said, and keep it for the baby. The *baby*. Her heart clattered. It would be hard raising a child by herself. But she'd have the money from the sale of the house, though her throat burned at the thought of it. Jordan would be here to help. Stephen and Misha too—at least she hoped so.

The rest of the brass candlesticks still stood by the sink. Christina polished every last one of them, wiping away the years of dirt and neglect. But after that, her sense of purpose dissolved. She had no appointments for the rest of the day, though there were plenty of things she had to do: call Amy, check in with the Realtor, call the lawyer who was handling the sale, and begin the monumental task of packing. She did none of them.

Instead, she slipped into her inventory mode, moving around her house as if looking at it from the outside. She had said she did not want the kind of life she'd have with Andy. Then what kind of life *did* she want? She walked around the home that she'd created to see whether it held the answer. Here were the things she loved, the velvet love seat, the small but exquisite Persian rug that lay in front of it. In the dining room, her pine sideboard, her ample table, her assortment of mismatched but, to her eye, perfectly coordinated chairs. Her prints, her plates, her odd bits of silver, of crystal, porcelain, wood, and brass. Totems, idols, talismans, evidence, fossils. What would become of all these things when she had to leave? Some she would take, but others she would have to leave behind. How to choose? The thought was crushing, as if all those things she had accumulated, restored, and loved suddenly began to rise up, and start swirling—crazily, dangerously— around her. She had to lie down. Immediately. Retreating to her bedroom, she stretched out and closed her eyes. Sleep, like a drug, came almost at once.

When she woke, her panic subsided. She had made her decision to sell; wallowing in regret would get her nowhere. She picked up the phone to call the lawyer. The sooner the sale was completed, the better off she would be. Christina then spent the remainder of the afternoon in the basement, bundling back issues of the many shelter magazines to which she'd subscribed; it was still light when she hauled two of the bundles outside to the curb. Her neighbor Charlotte Bickford was on her stoop. Charlotte scowled when she caught sight of Christina and, just like the last time, practically slammed the door in her hurry to get back inside. *There's* one *good thing that will come out of this*, Christina reflected. *When I move, I will never, ever have to see Charlotte Bickford's miserable face again.*

FORTY

*J*ordan noticed the woman first. She wore a beautiful sari in a deep shade of greenish blue; the edges were trimmed in gold. She was so busy looking at her—she moved like a dancer, really she did—that Jordan did not notice the people she was with right away. But as soon as she did, she remembered the guy with the slicked-back hair and the other one with the turban—she had seen them here before. There was another guy with them too. He was short, with nerdy-cool black glasses and sandy hair that spilled over his forehead into his eyes. He was waving his hands as he talked; the other two men were just nodding. Only the woman seemed apart from them all, lost in a strange kind of trance as she stared at the house. Jordan's house. What was she doing here? What were *all* of them doing here? Hitching her bag up more securely on her shoulder, she marched over to find out.

"Hi," she said. "Can I help you?"

"Hello," said the guy with the slicked-back hair. "Do you live here?"

"I do." Did her mom know about these people? They didn't *look* dangerous, but you never could tell.

"Ah, you must be the daughter. Your mother spoke of you." He had an English accent, all snobby and proper sounding.

"You mean you talked to my mom? She knows you're here?" Jordan decided she did not like him.

"Oh yes," said the man. "She knows all of us." He gestured toward the little group.

"Well, anyway, if she knows you're here, I guess it's okay." She shifted her bag again.

"Considering she's in the process of selling the house to my clients—"

"Selling!" The word was a slap. "What do you mean selling?"

The man looked uncomfortable. "Oh, excuse me. I assumed she would have discussed her plans with you; so sorry." He was backing away now; they all were.

Jordan didn't answer. Instead, she ran up the stairs and burst into the house. She had to run up and down before she found her mother sitting in the garden. She was alone, and she did not appear to be doing anything—not weeding, pruning, planting, or any one of the million other things she did when she was out here.

"Are you selling the house?" she demanded. "To those people I met outside? Mr. Turban and Ms. Sari?"

Christina turned slowly. "I am," she said quietly.

"Mom!" Jordan wailed. "Oh, Mom!" She dumped her bag on the ground and then she flopped down beside it. "It's because of the baby, isn't it?"

"Yes." Christina seemed older and more worn-out than Jordan could ever remember.

"Why didn't you tell me? And how can you sell the house?

You promised me you wouldn't!" She flung herself into a chair and began to cry.

Up above, a window opened. Stephen stuck his head out and called down, "Is everything all right?"

Christina turned her face upward. "No, actually it's not," she said. "Maybe you could come down and we could talk?"

Jordan, whose own face was now covered by her hands, did not look up. But she was glad Stephen was coming down to talk to her mom. Maybe he'd help make sense of things. Because right now, nothing made any sense at all.

Telling Jordan that they were selling the house was the hardest thing Christina had to do since telling her daughter that Daddy had died in the fire. But once it was done, she felt a massive sense of relief. Stephen was understanding, it hurt—*I just wish you would have told me sooner*, was what he said—and she prayed her failure to have done so would not cause a permanent rift between them. Now that everything was out in the open, she felt galvanized, and sprang into action. There were spaces, both personal and professional, to be seen. And a call to Amy, to tell her that she was going ahead with the pregnancy. "I'll want to see you in a month," Amy had said.

In two days, Christina saw thirteen apartments and an equal number of professional spaces; on the third, she called Holly Shafrin, the real estate agent, to tell her she had settled on a two-bedroom rental on Plaza Street until she could figure out where—and if—she wanted to buy again. But the question of the business was left up in the air. "I just can't decide on everything so quickly," she said. Holly understood, and even helped her find a local storage place where she could stash all the merchandise from her showroom.

Christina tried to be a booster about the new apartment.

"It's about a three-minute walk to the subway station," she told Jordan. "It will make your commute so easy!" Jordan glared but did not reply. She was still acting like the decision to sell the house was a personal betrayal. Christina just let it go. The subject of the new baby was even more verboten. Whenever Christina tried to bring it up, Jordan left the room. Who knew what she was thinking? But Christina could not speculate for long; she was too busy trying to get everything done. It was on one of those busy mornings that she heard from the detective at the Seventy-eighth Precinct.

"I just thought you'd want to know that we found Derrick Blascoe," he said. "He's been in Florida for the last several weeks, moving from hotel to hotel; we found him in Key West and think he was on his way to Mexico."

"Florida? And then Mexico?" asked Christina.

"It wasn't pretty," said the detective. "He'd been on a very long bender—booze, coke, and girls—a couple of them underage."

"I can't believe it," she said, trying to avoid a pair of women pushing strollers and a small child on a scooter. But then she thought of that last night she'd spent with him, and she could.

"Good thing we caught him when we did. He was trying to sell that Sargent."

"Please tell me that he didn't." She was surprised at how much this mattered, how much she wanted that auburn-haired girl to go back where she belonged. To go home.

"No, the dealer he approached had been alerted and contacted Miami police; they contacted us. He's in custody now and he'll stand trial in New York."

"Well, that's a relief. But the rest of it—what a terrible

story." Christina paused, letting the sadness of it sift through her. Poor Derrick. How had his life come to this sorry pass? She hoped she had not played a part in his unraveling.

"I just want you to know that you've been completely exonerated in all this; he was questioned thoroughly and you were in no way implicated."

"Thank you very much for telling me."

Christina walked back to her house thinking of Derrick. She was still thinking about him later that day when the bell rang and she found an unexpected visitor on her doorstep: Phoebe Haverstick. "I know I treated you very badly and I'm sorry," Phoebe launched right in without even saying hello. "I wouldn't blame you if you didn't invite me in, but I'd be so grateful if you did." Phoebe wasn't pregnant any longer; Mimi Farnsworth had told her she'd had the baby back in the winter. Christina wondered whether the nursery she designed was working out; the pleasure she'd taken in designing it was what made her step aside and let Phoebe in.

"I don't even know where to begin," Phoebe said once she had settled into a chair in Christina's office. "I was just heartsick when the painting went missing and Ian, well, he had me convinced that you had something to do with it."

"I would never have done that," Christina said quietly. "And I wish you had taken even one of my calls to let me tell you that myself."

"I was a coward," Phoebe said, lacing her fingers together tightly.

"The painting is coming back to you; my good name is restored."

"Yes, but now you have to move your business! And that's Ian's fault. He went to the zoning board; he knows people."

"It's not just my business," Christina said. "I'm selling my house too."

"Oh no—does this have anything to do with the findings of the zoning board?"

Christina looked at her in disbelief. Was the woman really so insulated by her wealth as to not know the answer to that question? All she said was, "Yes."

"Oh, I feel even worse now!" Phoebe said.

Can you imagine how I feel? Christina endured some more useless breast-beating on Phoebe's part before she was able to get the woman out of her house—and her life. She never wanted to hear from either of the Haversticks again.

Later that night, the bell sounded. The pregnancy was making her tired and she was already in her bathrobe. She was not happy to find Phoebe standing there; this time she was *not* inviting her in.

"Please, I just had to see you again," she said.

"I was just going to bed," Christina said coldly. "Can't it wait?"

"No, actually, it can't. I'm begging you, Christina."

The good girl in Christina won out. Stepping aside for the second time that day, she let Phoebe come in, but kept her standing in the hallway.

"I want you to know I feel sick about what's happened. Just sick!" Gripping the doorknob tightly, Christina said nothing. "And I want to make it up to you."

"I don't think that's possible," Christina said. "This is the house I grew up in. And because of your husband, I'm forced to sell it." She was gratified to see the stricken look on Phoebe's face. Even worse, she suddenly imagined doing harm, not to Phoebe, but to Ian. He had sabotaged her, taken away what she loved most. She could have responded in kind, looked for something that would wound him. An eye for an eye, as the Bible counseled. Why had she backed off so meekly from the fight? But when she looked at Phoebe, standing there with tears trickling slowly down her face, she knew why. Despite everything, she actually felt sorry for this woman. Instead of revenge, she had turned the other cheek—contradictory wisdom from the same source. Awkwardly, she reached over to pat Phoebe's shoulder. "It's all right," she said. "I'll be all right."

"Oh God, I just feel terrible!" Phoebe was crying in earnest now. But at the same time, she was fumbling in her bag, like she was trying to locate something. "Here!" she said, thrusting a thin, flat package at Christina. "This is for you." Puzzled, Christina opened it. Inside was a small oil sketch, done on paper. The pose was different, but Christina recognized the redheaded girl immediately. "Victoria!" she said, looking from the portrait to Phoebe. "Where did this come from?"

"I found a bunch of pieces like this in a folder," said Phoebe, sniffling but no longer crying. "This one was the best. Or at least that's what I thought. And I wanted you to have it."

"You did?" She was incredulous.

Phoebe nodded. "It seems like the least I could do, after the way Ian treated you."

"Does he know you're doing this?"

"No," she said. "But there's a *lot* that Ian doesn't know."

Christina nodded, looking back down at the sketch. Although the background was a mere blur of color, the face was beautifully rendered.

". . . It's not worth as much as the painting, obviously, but it's worth quite a bit," Phoebe was saying.

"Oh, I don't want to sell it!" Christina said.

Phoebe smiled. "No," she said. "You wouldn't, would you?"

Christina thanked Phoebe and then submitted to a hug, which was as bone crushing as her handshakes had been. When she was gone, Christina took the sketch into her office and propped it on her desk, so she could enjoy it before packing it up. She only wished that Ian Haverstick had been here; how she would have *loved* to witness the expression on his smug, infuriating face when he saw it.

Christina heard the echo of her footsteps as she took her final walk through the Carroll Street house. It was a sultry June morning and banks of gray clouds hovered ominously overhead. Though sticky and uncomfortable, she didn't want to open the windows because she'd be leaving soon, and would only have to close them all again. Jordan had said her mournful good-byes the night before and was staying with Alexis; she couldn't bear to witness the final exodus. Stephen and Misha had also decamped to their new place in Fort Greene. That they were not angry about having to move was just one more small but precious thing for which Christina could feel grateful.

She walked up the stairs, running her hand along the smooth banister down which she once used to slide. The boxes were all on the parlor floor and the rooms above and below were empty. But even empty, they were crammed with memories, recent ones mingling freely with those from the past. The parlor window in front of which she and Will had put their first Christmas tree as a married couple was the same window she'd hung the paper snowflakes she'd cut out with Aunt Barb. The apartment where Stephen and Misha had hosted their soigné dinner parties had once housed her beer-drinking, ever-boisterous aunt.

If there had been a chair left in the house, Christina would have sat down. But there was no chair and so she continued her solitary meandering. The papers were signed, and the money—all 3.3 million astonishing dollars of it—was in her possession. For the first time since Will had died, she would have no more financial worries. She could buy an apartment or even a house—or not. She could run her business, send Jordan to college—if she elected to go—hire a nanny to help with the baby, and, if she was prudent, even start planning for her retirement. So why was she feeling so bereft?

Christina heard the groan and wheeze of a truck out-side—the movers were here. She hurried downstairs and out the door to check. But the red lettering emblazoned across the side said HANDLE WITH CARE; that was not the name of the company she had hired—she was sure of it. Maybe they were using another company's truck? At just that moment, Charlotte Bickford stepped out onto her stoop. "Right on time," she called to the driver of the truck, who had poked his head out of the open window. "Everything's ready; you can start when-ever you want."

"You're moving? *Today?*" Christina was so shocked that she forgot she had not spoken to Charlotte in more than five years.

Charlotte turned just as the driver had stopped in front of her house and a pair of brawny young men got out and hur-ried up the steps. When they passed, she finally said, "Yes, I am."

"So am I," said Christina. "I'd say that's an astonishing coincidence."

"Not really," said Charlotte. "The Sharmas want to start demolition as soon as possible and so the sooner we're out, the sooner they can get going."

"Demolition?" Christina was sure she had misheard her. In all her negotiations with Pratyush and the Sharmas no one had said anything about demolition. "What are you talking about?"

"You mean you really don't know? When the Sharmas bought these three houses, they were planning to tear them down and build a single new structure on the lot." Charlotte seemed supremely gratified to deliver this news.

The words landed like bombs. "Three houses?" she asked. "What do you mean *three houses*?" Mira Sharma had taken both of Christina's hands in hers, doe eyes misting prettily as she thanked her for selling the house to them. She had gestured to her black-haired daughter and said that she wanted her to grow up right *here*, in this house, on this block. What a snake! What a liar!

"Next to you, of course."

"Miss Kinney? She would never sell. Never." Christina heard the desperation in her own voice. But then she was hit with a sickening memory: the foil-wrapped cookies that had remained untouched in front of the older woman's front door. At the time, it had not meant much. Now it meant everything.

"Geraldine Kinney hasn't lived in that house in months; her family put her in a home last November. Hadn't you heard?"

No, Christina had *not* heard. "The Sharmas never said anything about buying three houses," she said, still refusing to believe Charlotte. "Or demolishing any of them."

"Well, no, of course not. That would have driven the price

up even more. As it was, they paid me a bonus for not mentioning the sale to you."

They had done the same thing with Christina! "They tricked us—that's what they did," she said. Her initial shock was swallowed by fury. "They tricked each one of us—you, me, and Miss Kinney."

"Miss Kinney isn't thinking about her house; her daughter told me she has dementia. And *I'm* pleased as punch with the whole deal. The Sharmas paid me a lot of money and I'm going to buy a studio in Manhattan and a place upstate. There's only one person here who seems to think she's been tricked." Charlotte's voice oozed with pity and contempt. "And that person is *you.*"

Christina went back inside and immediately called the lawyer, who said that she had no legal recourse. The houses were not in a landmarked zone, and Geraldine Kinney's family had agreed to the sale, as had Charlotte Bickford. There was nothing preventing the Sharmas from tearing down Christina's house, or the two houses on either side. Christina was the linchpin in the whole deal because her house was at the center—that was why they had offered her so much money. "Mrs. Sharma said she *loved* the house," Christina said to the lawyer, trying not to cry. "She told me that personally."

"She may have loved it," said the lawyer. "But I just got off the phone with her attorney. She loves the idea of the big house she plans to build on the lot even more. She's moving her whole family in—not just her husband and kid, but her sister, brother, and their spouses and kids, her mother, *his* brother— it will be like a village."

"A village built on my childhood house, my *home*," Christina replied.

"The Sharmas paid you a lot of money," the lawyer said. "Well over its market value. You could buy another house in the neighborhood with all that cash."

"It won't be the same," she said miserably, and got off the phone so she could surrender herself to the torrent of tears that had been waiting to fall. Then another truck pulled up, beeping and honking at the one that was already loading up Charlotte's furniture. She wiped her eyes furiously with her hands before stepping outside. There was the moving truck she had hired, and when it pulled up with its own crew of brawny young men, she could do nothing but stand aside and let them complete the sorrowful task of emptying out her home.

FORTY-ONE

"It's bad enough we had to move," Jordan said irritably. "When are we going to start *living* here? It's like a warehouse or something." She was standing by the door, ready to leave for her dance class.

"I know, sweetheart," Christina said. She had only recently gotten up and was still in her robe. "I've just been . . . busy." *Also pregnant, exhausted, and wretched.* "It will get done, though. You'll see."

"I hope so," Jordan said, and while she did not exactly slam the door, she did not take special care not to let it slam either. Christina flinched slightly from the sound; the pregnancy had made her hypersensitive to loud noises. But Jordan was right. It was like a warehouse in here. Ever since they had moved in a month ago, Christina had been overcome by a crippling lassitude. Oh, she could blame it on being pregnant, but she knew that was only part of it. Her anger at the perfidious Sharmas had been displaced onto the apartment—it was as if she blamed this handful of rooms for what had happened and wanted nothing to do with them. She could not bring herself to unpack, let alone decorate, and the place was still piled with unopened boxes and shrouded furniture.

Today would be different, though. Today she was going to try to make a dent in the chaos. Getting dressed was the first step; brushing and fixing her hair was the next.

She made herself a strong cup of tea—at least the kettle was unpacked—and, perched on a big box, sipped it while she called today's clients to reschedule. Then she called Stephen, who immediately offered to come over and help; he was there within the hour. But once he arrived, whatever slight bit of energy she had summoned seemed to scatter, like beads from a broken necklace.

"So where do you want the love seat?" he asked. "In front of the windows or facing them?"

"I don't really care," Christina said. "Put it wherever you think best."

"Christina!" He sounded exasperated. "You have to care."

"Why should I?" she said. "This place isn't a home."

"Not until you make it one. Girl, what is wrong with you?" But when he saw the tears, he moved away from the love seat and crouched down next to her. "I know," he said. "Honey, I do know."

Christina sniffed and looked around the room. "What do you need?" he asked.

"A handkerchief?"

Stephen smiled. "Just this once," he said, digging in his pocket for a packet of tissues, "you're going to have to use this."

She accepted the tissue and blew her nose. "I'm sorry," she said. "It's the hormones."

"You'll feel better if you start unpacking some of this stuff. Trust me." He straightened and walked back to the love seat. "Now, come on, work with me here."

Sweet Stephen. He was trying so hard. She had him try the love seat in both spots, and in the end, she settled on having it face the windows. The living room had a partial view of Prospect Park; she might as well take advantage of it, even if the vista offered her little pleasure. Next, Stephen put the coffee table in front of the love seat. Obvious, but practical. After the coffee table, Stephen unwrapped and moved another chair, the dining table, and a pair of lamps. Then his phone sounded. When he got off, he said, "I've got to get over to the studio. The shoot's been moved up a little. I hope you don't mind."

"Of course not," she said. "I appreciate your coming over at all."

"I want you to get your groove back so you can come over and give us advice about our new place," he said as she walked him to the door.

"I'd love that," she said, and meant it. It was only this place that left her so very cold. She had never cared this little for her surroundings and her apathy was unsettling; without her innate sense of knowing—and caring—what belonged where, she almost didn't know who she was.

When Jordan arrived home later that afternoon, she dropped her bag on the floor, walked straight over to the love seat, and plopped down. "Finally! You did something. It looks *so* much better in here."

"Do you really think so?" asked Christina.

Jordan studied her. "I do," she said finally. "Don't you?"

"I don't know," Christina said. "I can't really bring myself to care."

"Mom!" Jordan jumped up from the love seat. "Stop—you're scaring me."

"I'm sorry," said Christina. "I'm just moody, that's all. It'll pass."

Jordan looked around at the boxes still stacked against the walls. "Let's unpack some of those," she said.

"I've done enough for one day."

"*I'll* do it, then," Jordan said. "You can just sit here and tell me where stuff goes."

"You're very sweet but—"

"No *buts*, Mom!" She led Christina to the love seat. "Now, where should I start?"

Without waiting for a reply, she opened the closest carton. "Okay, here's your rolling pin, your juicer, and a whole bunch of cookie cutters. Kitchen, right?" Christina nodded and Jordan went to put everything away. When she returned, she dug out a Pyrex baking pan, an enamel pot, and a clutch of wooden spoons.

"Here. I can put those away."

"No, I said I would do it. You rest." For the next hour, Jordan continued to unpack while Christina directed; a wastebasket went in Jordan's room and another in Christina's. Books taken out of their boxes were stacked neatly in piles; throw pillows were plumped and placed.

"That's enough for now," Christina said, though she had to admit she felt more cheered by this process than she would have imagined. Maybe that was because Jordan was a part of it.

"No way," Jordan said. "I'm just getting into it." She walked over to two boxes that had been under some of those that were now unpacked. "What's in these?"

Christina got up to inspect. "I don't know," she said. "They were in the basement and I didn't have the chance to look through them before we moved."

"They look *ancient*." Jordan peeled off the strip of dusty tape and began burrowing. "What's this?" she asked, holding up a man's plaid bathrobe. "Was it my dad's?"

"Let me see," Christina said. "No, it belonged to your grandfather." The Pendleton robe, a red and black tartan, was something she had bought for her father's sixtieth birthday. He liked it so much that he wouldn't take it off, and spent the day remarking on how soft and warm it was; that was one of the few times she remembered pleasing him. What else would be in there? A black silk bow tie and cummerbund he'd worn when he'd married her mother, his monogrammed bowling ball bag and a crushed pair of bowling shoes. Also his old *Ellery Queen* magazines and a jacket with a pair of bowling pins appliquéd on the back.

"I've never seen any of this before," Jordan said.

"That's because I haven't opened it in decades." Christina turned to the other box; she already had an idea about what was inside and she wasn't entirely sure she was ready to look. But if not now, when? She stripped the tape and found Will's collection of antique maps—many of them gifts from her—the binoculars he'd used on his bird-watching walks, two cameras, and the snow globe he'd been given one Christmas when he was a little boy. Jordan shook it gently and Christina watched the glittering flecks settle down over the tiny house, barn, and pair of horses.

"Can I have this?" Jordan asked. "I don't have anything of his."

"You have so *much* that was his," Christina said, eyes

filling. "But yes, of course, take it." When Jordan had taken the snow globe to her room, Christina surveyed the jumble before her: artifacts from the two most significant men in her life. What to do with this accumulation? She had a powerful urge to get rid of it all.

"Mom?" Jordan was back in the room, her arms full. "This is some other stuff I found. I wasn't sure what to do with it. I think it may belong to . . . Andy."

Christina reached out to take the small bundle. Here was one of Andy's familiar pima cotton shirts, this one pale blue and now somewhat creased. She could see him buttoning it as he headed to his office or the hospital. And she could see him unbuttoning it, more quickly, when they were alone together. Along with the shirt was a baseball cap—was it the one he had worn the day her car broke down and he surprised her with his sweetness and his tact? The last thing in Jordan's haul was a brown silk tie with a tiny allover green design. It was only when she looked more closely that she saw the design was actually made up of tiny artichokes—Andy had an endearing weakness for whimsically patterned ties.

"Are you okay?" Jordan was still standing there; Christina has almost forgotten. She looked again at the shirt. It had touched his body and she wished she could press it to her face and inhale whatever of his scent it might still hold. But she would not do such a thing in front of Jordan.

"I'm fine," she said. "I'll take care of getting all this back to him." Andy Stern was a significant man in her life too. He had her father's temper and impatience but also his work ethic and his energy. And he had Will's sweetness and ability to love. He *had* loved her, hadn't he? Did he still? Jordan was still there, watching her. "I've been meaning to ask you something," she said. "What made you go with him to buy that ring? I thought you despised him."

"I changed my mind," Jordan said. "I mean, he did save me."

"He did," said Christina. She remembered that day at the hospital and felt the nausea rising up, like the morning sickness had returned.

"I actually kind of miss him," Jordan was saying.

"You what?" Christina was so surprised, her nausea subsided. "You *miss* him?"

Jordan nodded. "I do. I mean, I never thought of him as my dad, but when we were all together with Oliver and everything, we were kind of like a family."

"I never thought I would hear you say *that*," said Christina.

"I know. Weird, huh?" Jordan waited before speaking again. "When the baby is born, you'll let him come visit? I mean, it is his and all."

"He'll get to see the baby," Christina said. *And when he does, it's going to tear me apart.*

The next morning, Christina went to see a potential space for her business. When she returned to the apartment—she still could not call it home—she felt energized enough to begin one of her customary prowls, taking inventory, the way she always had. That view of those treetops—so lush and full at the moment—really was nice; she would want to play that up more. But the flat white walls were dull and could use some help. In the kitchen, she decided the black-and-white back-splash tile and checked linoleum floor were not bad; some bright accents would help, though, and she began to visualize a fire-engine red teakettle sitting on the stove. Yes, red would be good—energizing and bold. But when she reached the room in which she had been sleeping, her spirits began to plummet. The walls were bare and the mattress lay on the floor; the Sargent oil sketch, still covered in Bubble Wrap, was next to it. Most of her clothes were in suitcases or boxes and hardly any of them fit her anyway; the few maternity things she'd bought dangled forlornly on wire hangers in the nearly empty closet. The room right next door—billed as a study by the rental agent—would be for the baby. Right now, it was empty.

Jordan's room was a bit more lived in; her daughter had unpacked all her clothes and either hung them in the closet or stored them in the bureau that she had unwrapped and dragged in here by herself. Will's snow globe sat on top of it. Jordan had even knocked some nails in the wall. (Where had she gotten the hammer? As far as Christina knew, it was still buried.) Several pairs of point shoes hung suspended by their pink satin ribbons. The sight made Christina's heart twist; for all her complaining, Jordan was doing a better job of getting adjusted than she was.

A noise caught her attention and she turned: the rabbits. Today they seemed almost ominous, with their black, staring eyes and perpetually twitching ears. She would have been glad to pass them on to a family with a yard, but Jordan said no. In the Carroll Street house, Misha had built a big play area in the basement; there was no room for anything like that here. Jordan didn't seem to think it was so important, but Christina could not stand to see the two creatures cooped up.

She turned her attention elsewhere. Anyone else would consider this a nice apartment, a fine place to live, at least temporarily. So why did it feel like a cage, a prison? She thought of the house she had loved and lost. But it wasn't just the house; it was the people in it who had mattered. Her mother dead too young, and her angry, alcoholic father with whom she'd never properly made peace. Barb. Stephen and Misha, the surrogate family upstairs.

So what did that leave her with now? Jordan and the baby. Andy's baby. She walked back into the bedroom and looked at the mattress. She missed him, in bed and out. Missed him because she loved and needed him. Just as he loved and needed her. Boisterous, strident, generous, and impulsive, he would break down the bars of any cage she ever tried to erect for herself. She had sent him away, though, told him she did not want him. How could she go back to him now? He was probably so angry he wouldn't even see her. Still, she should try, shouldn't she? She *had* to try. She hurried out of the room in search of her phone. When she found it, she hoped she could reach him; she might not have the courage to try again.

"Christina." His voice was soft with surprise. "Is everything all right?"

"Everything's fine," she said. "I just wanted to know how you were."

"Me? All right, I guess. I've been better."

"So have I," she said. "Been better, that is."

"Everything's all right with the pregnancy? What does the doctor say?"

She told him about her last visit to Amy Wenders and then there was a lull. Even in the shared silence, she felt he was close to her, close enough to reach if only she dared.

"There was something I wanted to ask you."

"Ask away."

"It was about that ring." She paused, trying to assemble

the right sequence of words. "The one you wanted to give me. I never tried it on."

"No," he said. "You didn't."

"Do you suppose I still could—that is, if you still have it—"

"Yes," he said. She could hear the happiness in his voice now, surging like a current, invisible but strong, connecting them. "Yes, I do. Yes, you could. Yes."

FORTY-TWO

After the heavy rain the night before, the July morning dawned clear and bright; it promised to be a glorious day. Christina saw that the place beside her in the bed—no longer on the bedroom floor of her apartment, but properly set up—was empty. Andy was in the shower; she could hear him singing the chorus from "Oh, What a Beautiful Mornin'" loud enough to be heard above the rushing water. Even though he could not hear her, Christina chimed in. She loved the score from *Oklahoma!* too and if there had been more time, she would have slipped into the shower for a duet. But Jordan would be up any minute now and they all had to be out of here early; the wedding at the Brooklyn Botanic Garden was scheduled for nine o'clock.

Two hours later, Christina circulated among the small group assembled right inside the entrance. Andy had first suggested Great Neck—*It's where we met,* he said—but Christina said no. She had not liked him on that initial meeting. And Great Neck was where she had turned him down. No, better to marry in a place that held none of those associations. She was a Brooklyn girl through and through and she could think of no better symbol of the borough than this beloved garden.

Jordan came up to her. "Are you nervous?" she asked. She wore the same dress she'd worn to Angelica's wedding last year and a pair of pearl studs Andy had bought for her. Christina had a new dress—raw silk ivory with a scalloped hem and a forgiving waistline to accommodate the small but noticeable swell in her stomach. Her bouquet was a cluster of gardenias and there were gardenias woven into her upswept hair.

"A little," she admitted. "Getting married is still . . ."

"What?" Jordan prompted, looking genuinely curious.

"A momentous occasion." She leaned over and kissed her daughter on the brow.

Oliver, looking very grown-up in a suit and with newly shorn hair, came over to join them. "My dad finally saw the light," he said.

"I think he saw it before I did," Christina said. She straightened his tie—the first time she'd ever seen him wearing one—because she felt she was permitted to do that now. He patiently submitted to the adjustment and then asked, "Does it look okay?" There was still something of the boy about him, haircut and suit notwithstanding.

"Yes," she said. "Very handsome." Then she turned to look for Andy. The rest of the wedding party—Ida, Stephen and Misha, Mimi, a few friends and colleagues of Andy, the florist, Gus, who had provided all the flowers, and his wife—were here; Andy was the only one missing.

"Should we get into position now?" Misha asked. Along with Stephen and two of the college friends, he would be responsible for the small chuppah.

"That would be a good idea," Christina said. The garden allowed weddings from nine to ten o'clock on weekends; it was already nine fifteen and though the ceremony was not long, she did think they should get started. The rabbi—chosen by Andy—and the pastor from the Old First Church were chatting. There was Ida in a shantung suit topped by an elaborate straw hat, beaming. Everyone else was present and ready. But no Andy. Christina scanned the semicircular area with its Italianate landscaping, vine-covered pergolas, burbling fountain, and limestone benches. Beyond was the emerald lawn, fresh and shimmering from all the rain the night before. It was the perfect place to get married. Only where was the groom? They were all waiting.

She heard him before she saw him. "Tell her not to worry; it's going to be fine," he was saying into his cell phone. "I'll call her later. I'm busy right now."

"Yes," Christina said, walking up to him when he came into view. She plucked the phone from his grasp. "You are." Andy looked splendid in his fine Italian linen suit, only a few shades darker than her dress. One of her gardenias was pinned to his lapel. She gave the phone to Oliver, who silenced it before slipping it into his pocket. Then, stepping under the fragile canopy of the chuppah, Christina and Andy joined hands.

Photo by Keira Price

Yona Zeldis McDonough is the author of four previous novels and the editor of two essay collections. Her fiction, essays, and articles have appeared in *Bride's, Cosmopolitan, Family Circle, Harper's Bazaar, Lilith, Metropolitan Home, More,* the *New York Times, O, the Oprah Magazine,* the *Paris Review,* and *Redbook.* She lives in Brooklyn, New York, with her husband and two children.

TWO
OF A
KIND

Yona Zeldis McDonough

This Conversation Guide is intended to enrich the
individual reading experience, as well as encourage
us to explore these topics together—because books,
and life, are meant for sharing.

A CONVERSATION WITH
YONA ZELDIS McDONOUGH

*Q. More than once you have dealt with the theme of interfaith ro-
mance or love in your work; has this been a conscious decision on
your part?*

A. Perhaps because I myself have made such a marriage, I
am drawn to the subject of how Jews and Christians mix
and mingle. Orthodox Jews keep to themselves and tend to
avoid serious interaction with non-Jews, but many Jews who
are not Orthodox assimilate, and as they do, they come into
contact with the non-Jewish population. How do Jews retain
their identity as Jews when they are part of the larger world?
What are the joys and perils of such relationships? I am attempting to work out the answers to these questions through
the vehicle of my fiction.

*Q. You have chosen to tell this novel from five different points of
view; can you say more about that authorial choice?*

A. I love novels that are told from shifting or multiple points
of view and I often use this device in my fiction. I'm inter-

ested in how each person's perspective informs and enhances the story. Everyone has his or her own truth to champion and the multiple-point-of-view approach allows all these truths—for there are many—to have their say.

Q. Do you have difficulty writing from a male point of view?

A. Not at all! I enjoy trying to imagine "the other" and welcome the chance to slip into a consciousness that is not my own but somehow is not alien to me.

Q. You have written fiction, nonfiction, and books for children; how do you see the relationship among these different aspects of your writing life?

A. Since I usually have more than a single project going at any one time, moving back and forth between them gives me a freedom and flexibility I appreciate. If I'm stuck with a novel, I turn to a children's book or an essay, and if I'm able to make progress in one of those areas, then I find I can return to the novel more easily, as if I've somehow unlocked something in the process of turning my attention elsewhere.

Q. How do you structure your writing day?

A. It varies from project to project. I have no set hours, but I try to write every day. Recently I have begun staying up later and later; I can be quite productive in the quiet, wee hours of the morning. The only trouble is not sleeping late enough in the day to compensate.

Q. Some writers pine for the seclusion of writers' colonies and retreats; others need a designated outside writing space that they pay for or opt for a spot at the local coffee bar. Where do you tend to write?

A. I never want to leave my house to write. I have a tiny but cheery little room overlooking my tiny (though not so cheery!) yard. And I am very attached to my stuff: my pillow, my chair, my favorite mug. I don't want to write anywhere else.

Q. Do you think that the advent of the electronic age will spell the end of novels as we have come to know them?

A. No! I think people have always craved narratives (what is the Bible but a series of narratives that include love, war, incest, adultery, and the like?) and will continue to crave them. The delivery system for those narratives may change and more people will be reading on electronic devices. But I'm convinced that the appetite for narrative is hardwired: narratives or stories are how we make sense out of the randomness that comprises our lives; narratives show us how to find and create meaning from our experience.

Q. What are you working on now?

A. I've got two ideas for novels—one set in the present, the other in 1947. I don't want to say too much about either one of them now except that I'm aching to get back to both of them.

QUESTIONS
FOR DISCUSSION

1. What are your first impressions of the two main characters, Christina Connelly and Andy Stern? Are they positive or negative?

2. Did those initial impressions change over the course of the novel, and if so, how does that happen?

3. How does the old adage "Opposites attract" play out here?

4. Do you feel that the differences in these two characters can be successfully overcome and that their marriage will stand the test of time?

5. What role does Andy's mother play? Do you feel Ida is a sympathetic character?

6. How do Jordan and Oliver affect the relationship of their parents? Do you think they will be able to blend successfully and become a family?

7. Oliver accepts Christina much more easily than Jordan does Andy. Do you think that has more to do with who Andy is or who Jordan is?

8. Both Christina and Andy were happily married prior to the novel's opening. What effect do those prior relationships have on the one they are trying to build?

9. What significance does Christina's house play in the novel? How did you feel about what happens to it?

10. Christina is a believer in the poetry of objects. Are there particular objects that elicit this kind of response in you?